THE DILEMMAS OF HARRIET CAREW

THE DILEMMAS OF HARRIET CAREW

CRISTINA ODONE

Harper
Press

Harper*Press*
An imprint of HarperCollins*Publishers*
77–85 Fulham Palace Road
Hammersmith, London W6 8JB
www.harpercollins.co.uk

First published by Harper*Press* in 2008

1

A catalogue record for this book
is available from the British Library

This novel is entirely a work of fiction. The names, characters
and incidents portrayed in it are the work of the author's
imagination. Any resemblance to actual persons, living
or dead, events or localities is entirely coincidental.

ISBN 978-0-00-726365-3
TPB ISBN 978-0-00-727659-2

Typeset by Thomson Digital, India

Printed and bound in Great Britain by Clays Ltd, St Ives plc

Mixed Sources
Product group from well-managed
forests and other controlled sources
www.fsc.org Cert no. SW-COC-1806
© 1996 Forest Stewardship Council

FSC is a non-profit international organisation established to promote the
responsible management of the world's forests. Products carrying the FSC
label are independently certified to assure consumers that they come
from forests that are managed to meet the social, economic and
ecological needs of present and future generations.

Find out more about HarperCollins and the environment at
www.harpercollins.co.uk/green

To Edward Lucas

1

Driving a Merc is like wearing a push-up bra. Suddenly everyone notices you, and makes comments like 'You look great, Harriet …' As I park the hired S320L outside the dry cleaner's, the Polish woman behind the counter gives me a thumbs-up sign; I only go there a few times a year but I'm suddenly worthy of the smile reserved for bankers who bring in their shirts and boxers every day. At the greengrocer's, the doltish assistant, who usually slouches against the counter, rushes to carry my bags to the car. The rhubarb and pears which I was expected to carry easily when I was on foot are deemed too heavy for the driver of a high-performance sports car.

I turn out of the Tesco car park. Janet Miller, patroness of the charity I work for (HAC – Holidays Association for Children), stops her Range Rover Sport, rolls down the window and for the first time ever chats about children, schools and the holidays. Hers: a month in a villa, with pool, in San

Gimignano; ours: a fortnight at my in-laws' cottage, with coin-operated electricity meter, at Lyme Regis.

I'm in a rush but everything seems bearable as Guy has decided to use our upgrade vouchers, obtained after I complained when our last hired car broke down, to get this Mercedes rather than the usual Renault Scenic.

'Your carriage awaits ...' Guy, with mock ceremony, hands me the keys after lunch. I feel like Cinderella – an impostor stealing away in a swanky set of wheels. But this way, I can run my errands in style:

Mario's to get my hair cut and set up an appointment for my roots, which haven't been seen to since May. Charlotte's to return the drill, Foot Locker to buy Alex's trainers, the greengrocer's and Tesco's for tonight's dinner party.

It still strikes me as pure madness to have people for dinner tonight of all nights, but Guy insists that it's the only date Oliver Mallard can do. Guy is convinced he will be the man to pull us out of penury. So I give in, thinking that at least I can use the car to lug around some heavy carrier bags. There are seven, to be precise, adding up to a whopping £93 – but that includes three bottles of quite decent Merlot.

Normally, I do the shopping on foot: a nightmare where Maisie's pushchair doubles up as a pack-mule; I give my biceps and triceps a thorough work-out (who needs a gym when you can go to Tesco's?); and progress is slow, with me constantly checking and repositioning the more precious items – handbag, wine, eggs, jars – lest they spill on to the pavement.

The Merc, instead, makes everything easy. I smile to myself in the rear-view mirror; as they say, I could get used to this.

I've never thought of myself as materialistic. At home we always had enough, and if Dad's car was no Merc (he drove a Rover which later gave way to a Peugeot), we never felt we were missing out on anything.

Mum had a wish-list of holiday destinations, but 'next summer in the South of France' became a family joke rather than a bitter disappointment. We had a comfortable bungalow in Kent, Dad's dental practice flourished and Mum pottered about the house while Mel and I did our homework: I felt that I had the best possible start in life.

The rest, I would go out and get for myself – and if I really did want a Mercedes, by the time I'd grown up, I'd be able to afford it. Or my husband would.

Now, purchasing an S320L is absolutely unthinkable. As are foreign holidays, a home north of the river, taxi rides, restaurant meals, and regular sessions with Mario. It's been years since I bought an item of clothing that was not second-hand or on sale; years since we decorated a room or bought theatre tickets.

Guy and I consider ourselves middle class. We earn better, travel more, and live longer than our parents and ancestors could ever dream of. And yet, throw into this happy mix two little words, and the result is an avalanche of debts, doubts and despair. 'School fees': the two scariest words in the English language. Our parents took it for granted that they would offer their children a better deal than the one they'd had, but we can't do the same for our brood. Behind those crocodile rows of matching jackets and trousers or skirts lurks a sweaty-palmed, terrifying vision of huge bills and sniffy bursar's letters. For what should be the best years of your life you can talk and breathe nothing but entrance and scholarship exams, gift tax, league tables, advance-fee schemes, instalments, catchment areas, fee-protection insurance in case you die, and a blizzard of acronyms and codewords: GCSE, AEAs, A-levels, the IB. Everything else must take second place.

I check my watch: half past two. I catch Mario and his minions watching me through the window. Mario usually has time only for the regulars who can afford to see him weekly: but, eyes on the silver Mercedes, he smiles. I step into the chrome-and-mirrors salon and immediately am welcomed with offers of *Vogue* and a cappuccino while I wait, Silvia doing my nails while Mario cuts my hair, and a menu card from which to choose any other treatment I might fancy. Given that usually I'm lucky if I get a worn copy of last month's *OK!* and have never been offered so much as a glass of water, I bask in this temporary pampering.

While a young Japanese girl in a mini and platform sandals washes my hair I run my eyes down the glossy card in my hand: facials for £50, reflexology for £45, half-leg waxing for £25, Brazilian for £30 … I can't afford any of them, either in time or money. Who can?

But even as I ask myself the question, I see before me, hair wrapped in tinsel foil, fingers and toes separated by cotton wool, Leo Beaton-Wallace's mum. She is tall, blonde, and her husband runs a hedge fund: the living embodiment of all a Griffin mum should be.

I've been piloted to a chair behind her, but I can see her in the mirror. And vice versa, so I fervently hope Mario hurries over before she sees me with wet wisps of hair and no make-up. At thirty-seven, my natural look could have me banned by Health & Safety.

Peals of electronic children's laughter erupt in the salon. 'That's my phone!'

Leo's mum picks up a slim little mobile that has been sitting on the counter among the combs curlers and brushes. 'Hullo ...' she twitters. 'Oh, darling, what a thrill!! I'll see you Monday at start of term? I'm getting myself ready as we speak – it's practically a catwalk these days, isn't it? ... No, no, the works: colour, manicure, pedicure ... I can't bear not keeping it up. You see some scary visions out there ... That clever boy's mum, have you seen her? Lets her roots grow until she's got black-and-yellow tiger stripes ... That's the one, Alex Carew ...'

Me! I seize up with shame and duck under the counter, pretending to rifle through my bag. It's so unfair. I've been trying my best, ever since Alex started at the Griffin, to put up an appearance of casual elegance. I've scoured the sale racks and those of the hospice shop for bargains that don't scream 'Last Season's Left-Overs'. I've filed my nails before every gathering of Griffin parents (well, almost) and I've stepped up my visits here to Mario's ... but obviously it wasn't enough. I've been spotted as the blackhead in the Griffin mums' otherwise perfect complexion. I've been outed as the fake Yummy Mummy, the outsider who tried to smuggle herself in as 'one of us'.

Oh, for the blissful 'who gives a toss' shrug of state schools, where parents sport pierced belly buttons, tattoos and shabby jeans without worrying about what little Leo's mum will whisper to little Max's mum. It's almost worth putting up with the thirty-five-to-one child-to-teacher ratio, the twelve-year-old boys with knives and the twelve-year-old girls with child, the bullying, the swearing, and the terrible exam results.

I'm still crouched under the counter, determined not to be spotted by Leo's mum. I'm at an awkward angle, hunched over, feeling the strain in my waist, and wonder how long I can hold this position. Sunglasses, that's what I need. I'll look odd – but anonymous. I fumble in my bag, sifting feverishly through keys, purse, loose change, sweet wrappers, a sticky half-eaten lolly and plasters.

'The new car – I like it! *Brava!*' Mario comes to my chair. I turn my head to look up at him, sleek and Latin and twirling a comb in his hand. Mario frowns. 'I need you to come up from down there.'

I smile apologetically and just then, Hurrah!, my fingers make out the sunglasses and I triumphantly slip them on. Only to realize, as I sit up, that these are Maisie's pink plastic star sunglasses, bought at Lyme Regis for a pound last July.

'Hmmm … this pink –' Mario shakes his head in the mirror '– it is not you.'

I leave Mario and the ghastly Griffin mum, marginally soothed by hair that is now more tabby than tiger. It's three thirty. Just enough time to get to Charlotte's and then Foot Locker. I head past the common; it's been a wet summer, and the grass stretches as thick and green as a carefully tended lawn. The sky is a deep blue and the air sparkles.

But I feel the usual September melancholy: summer has ended, school looms. I shall take up once again the routine of chaotic breakfasts, school-gate encounters, office admin, hovering over homework and making supper.

Despite the daily check-up telephone calls from Cecily Carew, the maddening way the electricity meter ran out just as I curled up in bed with my Plum Sykes, and the boys' breaking the springs on their beds, Lyme Regis suddenly seems a little corner of paradise. I miss the constant exposure to the children, the way all three, bronzed and bursting with loud energy, run in and out of the cottage and garden; I miss watching Guy scamper about with them, and take out his work only at sundown. In Lyme Regis, even school fees seem a manageable wave we can easily surf.

I turn into Charlotte's crescent. Leafy and elegantly lined with white Georgian houses, road bumps protecting the stillness, this is a choice bit of Clapham. It's south, and we're north – and that works out at about £200,000 difference. Charlotte wants her drill back: ours burnt out as we tried to rehang the Carew medals in Guy's study. Guy keeps them above the fireplace, in a glass-fronted mahogany box, pinned against blue velvet: a century's worth of Cecils, Claudes, Berties, Reggies and Hectors honoured with enamel and ribbon. There are medals from India and Africa, an early Distinguished Flying Cross and, in pride of place, Great-Uncle Claude's Victoria Cross.

Virtute non verbis: 'Deeds not words', the family motto, is carved into the wooden box, reproaching Guy as, seated at his desk, he wrestles with his prose. His worries about deadlines and narrative flow and realistic pictures seem pedestrian in comparison to his ancestors' gritty valour as they survived malaria, starvation, rationing, and mustard gas. Or so he keeps telling me.

Charlotte lets out a wolf-whistle as I pull up. My best friend stands on the doorstep of her immaculately painted white stucco house. 'Guy must have finally written his bestseller.'

'Only hired for the weekend,' I say, ignoring her put-down. Charlotte has never quite believed in Guy's talent.

When I started going out with him, Guy was twenty-one and *Lonely Hunter*, a comic account of an African safari (featuring a hungry cheetah, a Masai warrior and two repulsive white British hunters) was a bestseller. He was much fêted and, to my eyes, grand and glamorous. I suspect that Charlotte, at Bristol with me, was a bit envious of my new boyfriend – a published author, at Cambridge and even profiled in *Tatler*. In our unspoken rivalry, he gave me the edge.

When we married, I was convinced that *Lonely Hunter* would be the first of a string of great successes. My future would be as Guy's muse, inspiring the genius in his quest for the perfect travel tome. My life would be spent riding side by side with him across the Kalahari and over the Himalayas, the two of us braving perilous, intoxicating adventures.

This has not been the case, quite. Instead of trekking across the desert, a song on our lips and hair blowing in the wind, Guy and I can barely move under the burden of school fees, mortgage repayments, utility bills, taxes and those unforeseen 'extras' private schools lob at you like hand-grenades: uniforms, school trips, music lessons, birthday presents and, God forbid, extra tutoring.

'It's very nice.' Charlotte's eyes are still on our hired car. 'Jack tried out that model before getting the Porsche.'

If we could afford a car at all I'd be happy, I think; but I say instead, 'When we grow up, we'll be fund managers, too.'

'Well, you have all the fun: or at least Guy does, with all that travelling ...'

I hand over the drill. I notice she is in her matching pink DKNY tracksuit and remember that on Saturdays she has her Pilates and tums&bums back to back. As opposed to Fridays, when she has her session with the Ashtanga yoga instructor; or Wednesdays, when it's the personal trainer ... I always hold in my stomach when we're together.

'Last weekend of summer.' Charlotte deadheads a rose by her front steps.

'I know,' I sigh. 'The Griffin starts on Monday already ... Hello, school-fee headaches.'

Charlotte shakes her head. 'If God had meant for your children to go to Eton, Harrow or Wolsingham, he would have married you off to an investment banker.'

Or at least to a man who doesn't believe in the Carew Gospel: that it is a parent's duty to send every male child to a top prep school, and then to Wolsingham, 'their' big school, and in this way ensure that they imbibe the virtues of courage and discipline and hard work, together with an excellent education, that will stand them in good stead in the challenges ahead.

'There are plenty of good schools that cost less than the Griffin and Wolsingham,' I plead with Guy.

'The Griffin feeds into Wolsingham, and Wolsingham is part of the Carew tradition, Harry.'

'So was the army, but you broke with that tradition.'

'I know – and my father has only now started talking to me again.'

Jack is a successful hedge-fund manager, so it makes perfect sense for Marcus and Miles to move from St Christopher's C of E primary school to Hampton House, a prep school that rivals the Griffin in its access to the big three – Eton, Harrow and Wolsingham.

But for us … Guy and I wake up at night worrying about the latest school bill. We lie there at three in the morning and outline different scenarios: Guy will develop a lucrative side-line writing coffee-table books about far-away places; I shall forget about my yearning to be the perfect stay-at-home mum and work full time at HAC; the children will learn to go up chimneys.

'Coffee?'

I'm tempted, as always with Charlotte. I can glimpse the neat and gleaming kitchen, miraculously exempt from the scuff marks and greasy paws of unruly children, not to mention the ever-floating hair of an overly affectionate mutt. I can smell the chocolatey aroma of real coffee as opposed to the instant we keep on hand. And I can hear the soft strains of Classic FM uninterrupted by a screeching toddler or rowing boys. Charlotte has three children, who almost match mine in age, and yet her life shows none of the dents, scratches and handprints that cover my own. Amazing what a difference money makes.

Reluctantly I shake my head. 'Afraid not, I've got to cook for you, remember?'

'I know, I know. It's the man behind those cruises for wealthy OAPs – Drake, isn't it?'

'Mallard. He's launching a monthly glossy magazine called *Travel Wise* in January and he's looking for an editor.' I don't need to say more.

'Fingers crossed.' Charlotte crosses her fingers and raises them.

'And thanks for the drill: the family honour has been saved. Eight for eight thirty.' I wave goodbye and rush back to the car. As I'm about to step into the Merc, a green van pulls up: Charlotte's organic shopping.

Good for you, good for the environment: the motto is printed in bright red-and-yellow letters across a basket of fruit and veg. Bad for my purse, I think as I start the car.

It's four thirty: getting late. I'm making an old favourite, pork belly with juniper berries and fennel seeds, and it needs at least three and a half hours in the oven. Working backwards, if we sit down at eight forty-five … damn, I don't have time to do Foot Locker. I'm about to turn back, then with a pang realise I won't have time to shop tomorrow as Guy has planned an outing to Richmond Park; and I think how Alex will get into trouble at school if he doesn't have his trainers. As it is, Evie, the matron, keeps telling me that Alex doesn't have the full complement of regulation grey flannel shirts:

'Why don't you order another from the school outfitters?'

It doesn't occur to her that this would cost us twice as much as anywhere else.

Argh ... I step on it, and am pleasantly surprised by the instant response of the Merc.

I'm cross with Alex for this needless trip and expense: only last week I got him the pair of black trainers that are part of his school's absurdly elaborate sports kit, but somehow he managed to lose one.

(Me, voice rising in irritation: 'Where could you possibly have lost *one* shoe, Alex?' Him, 'I dunno ...' Me, openly cross: 'I'm going to deduct it from your pocket money.' Him, shrugging with nonchalance: 'You never pay me my pocket money anyway.')

The shop is packed. I try desperately to catch the eye of now one assistant, now the other. Nothing. A host of harassed mums and gum-chewing pre-teens are ahead of me in the queue. Finally, I thrust the lone black trainer at a young assistant called Pawel, and ask for the matching pair at £18.99. Ten to five.

I rush back to the car, calculating: if I'm lucky the guests will arrive at closer to eight thirty than eight, so we won't have too long to sit around trying to make polite conversation while waiting for alcohol or the discovery of a mutual acquaintance to loosen our tongues. If I work quickly without the usual interruptions (can I find Guy's notepad, have I got Tom's book, have I seen Alex's fleece), I should be able to stuff the belly's flap of fat with the herbs and stick everything in the oven by ... say, quarter to six.

I pull up in front of the house and make out three figures in the kitchen. My heart sinks: the children will be demanding tea of Ilona. But our au pair can no more make a toasted cheese sandwich than wear a modestly cut dress. Slowly I start taking the carrier bags out of the Merc. I feel loath to trade this quiet interior, with its polished wood and ivory leather, for the chaotic yellow kitchen, with its peeling linoleum floor and scrambling family scene. I look up at the house. It's never been a beauty, but when we first bought it I had visions of investing in a few well-chosen improvements that would work a magical transformation. We could rebuild the wooden door frame at the entrance, paint the grey brick white, maybe even consider a loft extension. All we needed was to wait until Guy had secured a good contract for his next book. That was twelve years ago, and nothing's been done – and we have only forty years left on the lease.

'Mummy!' Maisie interrupts her drawing to stretch out her arms to me.

'Mummy, can we have pizza?' Tom peers into the carrier bags as I walk in.

'Can't we have spag bol, Mummy?' Alex stands by the open refrigerator.

'Darling,' Guy wanders in, Rufus in his wake, 'I can't find chapter one.' He scratches his head, peering hopelessly around the kitchen: he wears that expression of total absorption that takes over as he nears completion of a book. And God knows, *Rajput*, Guy's on-going magnum opus about the warrior kings of Rajasthan, has been nearing completion for almost a year now. 'I'm sure I left it here somewhere.' Anything is possible: various parts of Guy's books have routinely surfaced next to the toaster, in Maisie's buggy, in my sewing basket.

'Don't keep the door open, the fridge is playing up. Sausages for your supper, but first I need to prepare pork belly for dinner. Check for *Rajput* by the radio, Guy; you had it in your hands when you were listening to *Any Questions?*' I start unpacking the carrier bags, trying not to kick Rufus as he weaves in and out of my legs. 'There's still shopping in the car, please.' A burst of feverish activity follows the chorus of protests.

'Eureka! I *knew* it was here somewhere.' Guy lifts the radio from a wad of typed pages and hugs his manuscript to his chest.

I preheat the oven. 'Did you have a chance to look at the microwave?'

Our microwave door has refused to shut since before Lyme Regis, but Guy fancies his DIY skills and won't let me replace it. Which is also his attitude to the kitchen-unit door (off its hinges) and the shower head (still drip-drip-dripping).

'Not yet, but I *have* fixed the broken tap.' He proudly points out a wodgy lump of brown masking tape around the cold tap, whose cracked plastic knob split in half last week. I know how it felt.

'Mummy, look!' Maisie holds up her drawing for me to admire. Then, as I haven't jumped to her side in record time, she repeats in a reproachful tone: 'Look, Mummy!'

I bend over her notebook. 'Beautiful, darling – is that our house?' I point to the large square with misshapen roof that sits in the centre of the page.

'No, that's Lily's house. This is ours –' Maisie points to the teeny-weeny box beside it. Oh gawd: even my three-year-old suffers from property envy.

'That S320L is really cool!' Alex is staring out of the window. 'Can't we keep it until Monday? You could drop me off.'

'Afraid not: has to be back tomorrow night.' Guy is tapping his fingers on his manuscript.

'Da-ad …' Alex wails, 'you've got to make up for the time you came to the school gates in that Skoda.'

'We've never hired a Skoda!' Guy protests indignantly.

'I was teased for a month. I'm the only boy at school whose parents don't own a car.'

'What the Griffin should be teaching you is that there are more important things in life than a set of wheels.' Guy thumps the table decisively. His sons roll their eyes.

'I'm off.' Guy retreats to the downstairs loo. It's his favourite room in the house, lined with framed photos of him in the Wolsingham boater and jacket; punting on the Cam; and the cover of the first edition of *Lonely Hunter*. These are the bits of the past that Guy seeks when he wants a haven from a hostile world of luxury cars, Poggenpohl kitchens and expensive holidays.

While Guy communes with his past, Ilona arrives. As she discards her tight-fitting leopardskin jacket, our au pair casts an approving smile in my direction.

'Mrs Caroo, you have new car?'

The last time Ilona addressed me by my surname was when I interviewed her for the job. I can see now how to earn her respect. 'Mehrtsedez –' she points at the window with her thumb. 'Booteeful.' Without my having to ask her, she lays the table. Perhaps if I bought myself a pair of Jimmy Choos she might start cleaning Maisie behind the ears, and if I wore a Diane von Furstenberg wrap dress she might finally do the boys' laundry.

'Only a hired car, Ilona.'

'Ah …' Ilona's sighs are always eloquent.

I rub salt into the pork and then put it in the oven. I turn my attention to the children's supper.

'Pete, he have Corvette.' Her boyfriend of the moment, a tattooed butcher's assistant from Essex, has a ten-year-old red Corvette that Guy calls the pimpmobile. They met through Blinddate.com – which has Ilona pinned to the computer for hours on end. 'He coming for me now. We go to Empire Leicester Square.' The charming thing about Ilona is she never asks anything of us but simply informs us of her plans.

Guy surfaces once more.

'Is the Mercedes the most expensive car of all, Daddy?' Tom's face is still glued to the window.

Guy does mental arithmetic: 'A car like this would be … more than two years' school fees.'

The mere prospect is enough to crumple Guy, and he sits down with a sigh. Shirt collar frayed, shoes scuffed, he looks worn out by the effort to live up to his forebears, do the best for his offspring and keep up with his peers.

'If only …' he begins. The boys and I ignore him. We've already heard every possible dream that Guy could unfurl before us, and know that he will finish that sentence with one of the following: they make a film of *Lonely Hunter* (an option on the book did pay for our boiler last year, but we haven't heard anything since); the Carew parents' family home in Somerset is suddenly valued at ten times last year's modest estimate; *Rajput* proves a sensation and sells millions.

There are unspoken hopes too. Aunt Sybil dies: ruthless, I know, but Guy's widowed great aunt is apparently worth a fortune and allegedly considers him her favourite relative. So far, though, she has come to stay on countless occasions but has never so much as hinted at a legacy. Or that Guy's agent, Simon, reverts to treating Guy as a great writer with a great future. He doesn't need to take him out to the Ivy every week, which is how he courted him in the days when *Lonely Hunter* was a bestseller, but he could show more interest than the annual Happy Winter ('Best Eid, Hanukkah, and Christmas wishes to all of you') card.

CRASH! We all jump. The kitchen window rattles as if we've survived an earthquake. Before the boys can run to the kitchen door, Ilona walks in, her tattooed boyfriend and a string of expletives in her wake.

'Some idiot has parked his Mercedes next to your house!' Pete swaggers, vest tight over his chest. 'He'll have a right shock – nasty scratch all down the side. Cost him a pretty penny, that will, cheeky bugger. We'd better be off before he notices, Ilona ...'

2

'It was a disaster.' Guy shakes his head as he lovingly dries one of the crystal tumblers that he inherited from his aunt Amelia. I'm standing at the sink, hands in foamy water, wondering, once again, what is the point of owning a dishwasher when half your crockery is so fragile that it has to be washed by hand?

'It went well.' I rinse the third tumbler. 'Oliver made you an offer.'

'Not the one I wanted,' replies Guy bitterly. 'In fact, it sounds daft.'

'Nothing to be sniffy about.' I remain stubbornly upbeat. 'And despite the shock announcement, it was quite a success.'

'Hmmm ...' Guy examines a tumbler against the light: mercifully, no chips.

'"Hmmm" nothing,' I snap, exasperated. 'A job offer doesn't happen every day. You didn't even try to look interested.'

'I'll ring him, I promise.' Guy sounds despondent. 'And the pork belly was delicious, darling.'

Not just the pork, I think: the Merlot was excellent and for once I didn't have to whisper 'FHB' (Family: Hold Back) to Guy in the kitchen. And the peculiar sea-buckthorn juice which he had brought back from his trip to Lithuania gave my trifle an almighty kick. In fact, Guy should be grateful because, once again, we have managed to pass off our thread-bare household as a proper, middle-class one.

'I don't know …' Guy sets down the tumbler on the tray with the rest. 'Maybe it was the news that Pete's not insured and that ours kicks in only for damage above £600. We don't need another expense.'

'We certainly don't,' I agree.

Five hours earlier, at eight o'clock, I find my one remaining pair of tights without a run hanging in the children's bath-room. I sniff a strong, familiar scent: the Lynx 'Africa' antiper-spirant which Alex insisted on buying during our last shopping expedition.

'Alex?! Why are you putting on antiperspirant at night?'

My eldest pops his head through the door. 'I never remember to put it on in the morning.' He wolf-whistles as I wrench on my tights.

I rush back to our bedroom to get dressed, wondering if my thirteen-year-old is now too old to see his mother only par-tially clothed.

The doorbell goes.

'Whaaaaat?' I ask, disbelieving.

'No … it can't be …' Guy is outraged. 'Who shows up on the dot at eight when dinner is eight for eight thirty?!'

I sneak a peep from our bedroom window: the Mallards are at our front door. 'Your guest of honour, that's who.'

'Harriet!' Guy panics. 'Get dressed!' Still trying to fix his cufflinks, he rushes downstairs, three steps at a time.

Quickly, I zip up my navy-blue Paddy Campbell dress, a £14 find from the Sue Ryder shop on Clapham High Street last summer, and put on some mascara. I'm nervous: by the time the pork belly is crispy, we will have spent almost ninety minutes in one another's company – and how can I be entertaining for that length of time? Guy manages these occasions as if they were a school play and he the enterprising and determined Head of Drama who knows how to get the best out of little Joey as Bugsy Malone. All those Carew clan gatherings, school debating societies and Cambridge sherry parties, all those trips to Uganda, Uruguay and Uzbekistan have prepped him to win over an audience – from the cantankerous old cow to the acid-tongued megalomaniac.

I, on the other hand, feel like the tone-deaf girl in the school choir: caught between faking it and hitting a false note. God, let the pork be ready before anyone finds out I don't know the name of the dictator in Belarus, or what's on at Tate Modern, and before I'm outed as the one who prefers to talk to her children rather than to a well-known entrepreneur.

I draw a deep breath and walk downstairs.

Our dinner parties, Guy always says, are more about trompe-l'œil than truffle oil: a candlestick hides the mend in the linen tablecloth; Guy and I have the sagging chintz-covered chairs; a drape covers the split sofa cushion. But in the candlelight, the drawing room, as Guy grandly calls our living room, looks inviting. The carpet, from a long-ago visit of Guy's to Tehran, has withstood admirably the pitter-patter of tiny feet and paws; and the portrait of Great-Grandfather Hector in his major's uniform smiles protectively upon the room. Even the Carews' mahogany monstrosities, an over-sized dining table, a matching sideboard, and a chaise longue that cannot be sat on without first undergoing a medical check-up, gleam elegantly. Perhaps Guy's vigorous weekly polishing, which he insists on carrying out with beeswax, makes a difference after all.

Once upon a time, I dreamt of a home with sleek and con-temporary furniture, neutral walls and pale wood floors. It would be a mixture of Scandinavian and Conran, and bear witness to the smooth, serene family life unfolding within its neat confines. What I live with today is an inherited jumble of battered antiques and flowery fabrics, a mix of High Victorian pieces and low-cost foreign finds, a home that bears the brunt of three children, one dog, ever-changing au pairs, and a husband caught between copy deadlines and school fees. I sometimes feel there is too little of me in these rooms – a few photos, my silver christening cup, a painting by a friend who went to the Slade and then disappeared from sight. The rest is all Carew. Then the boys burst in, or I find Maisie cuddling Rufus on the chaise longue, and I realize *they* bear my imprint, even if the interiors don't.

'In the Carpathians, I came across a mother wolf looking for food for her cubs …' Guy is entertaining the Mallards. 'She was medium size, with a dark longish pelt. We looked each other in the eye … I tried to explain that I was a parent too.' Oliver, a big bear of a man, chortles appreciatively. He's brought us a bottle of Veuve Clicquot and stands by the fire-place, champagne flute in hand, eyes taking in everything from the push-button television to the overdue bills glaring red on my desk by the window. Everything has confirmed Oliver's image of his Cambridge friend being in need of his largesse, and he beams kindly in our direction.

Oliver's wife Belinda, decked out in enough Dolce & Gabbana to start her own boutique, is something glamorous in PR. Before I can find out what, she has dismissed my fund-raising for HAC with 'You *are* good', which means frumpy and worthy. I can tell that she finds me unsettling: what she sees as my do-gooding, as well as my part-timer status and unfash-ionable clothes, make her as self-conscious as if I'd announced that I would be kicking off the dinner party with a Latin grace.

I nervously check the grandfather clock in the corner: it's only eight thirty. Another hour to go. Belinda's PR skills fail to conceal her dissatisfaction with the situation. Guy has dragged Oliver into the study for a viewing of the ancestral medals and I am scrabbling for a topic of conversation. I remember vaguely Guy warning me not to raise the subject of children with the Mallards – a terrible accident? A bitter cus-tody battle? Belinda doesn't look the gardening sort, or the country type. I can't remember what's on in the West End. What about books? I belong to a book club, after all.

'Have you read …?' I venture.

'Oh, I haven't read a book in ages. Simply don't have the time!' Belinda looks through me. Then, searching for a crumb of praise to cast my way: 'Very nice glasses.' She holds up one of Aunt Amelia's crystal tumblers, half full of her G and T.

'Yes ... from one of Guy's aunts ...' And I find myself babbling about Amelia Carew and life in Delhi during the last days of the Raj.

I realize how little I've engaged Belinda when she suddenly squeals, '*There* you are!' and rushes up to the two men, who've surfaced from the study.

The doorbell goes: Hallelujah! Charlotte and Jack bounce in, looking lively and in a good mood. My friend's haircut, manicure, and Marni jacket reassure Belinda that here at least is someone who understands.

Guy pulled a face when I suggested Jack and Charlotte be included. He is fond of Charlotte, but Jack makes him wince. 'Sorry, HarrietnGuy, I know it's rude,' Jack will mutter as he dives for his ever-throbbing BlackBerry, 'but this is a big one ...' And then, after a few minutes, he'll explode: 'Ben, boy! You've got yourself a deal!' But we have to invite the Collinses because, as I reminded Guy, we owe them. They invited us to *La Traviata* at Glyndebourne last summer, which would have been a truly wonderful treat, had it not been that we had to buy them programmes at £20 each and champagne at £10 per glass. Guy and I had to pretend we were on a mid-summer detox and made do with tap water.

Jack is one of our few friends wealthy enough to impress Oliver: his bonus last year was five times our combined incomes. Despite the personal trainer Charlotte has signed him up with, who takes Jack out on the common twice a week like a well-trained dog, Jack remains stubbornly portly. Although Charlotte tries valiantly to derail his train of boasts tonight, within minutes he manages to work into the conversation the new Porsche and the Tuscan villa they rented for a fortnight last month.

'Back in your box, Jack!' Charlotte wags her finger as her husband is about to launch into the price of villa rentals in the Tuscan-Umbrian region.

'Yes, love.' Jack nods and bites his tongue.

Guy, I can see, breathes easier. Oliver, who had been asking a lot of questions about real estate near Florence, looks disappointed.

'Now, tell me about your company – sounds so high-powered ...' Charlotte turns her large, awe-struck eyes on Belinda. A successful career woman is calculated to fill my best friend simultaneously with fear and fascination. We both left university with only the vaguest idea of what we'd like to do professionally: something in the arts – which translated into both of us waiting on tables at the Chelsea Arts Club for that first summer. The minute Charlotte married Jack and it became clear she wouldn't have to work, she luxuriated in her status of stay-at-home wife as if it were a bath full of Aveda essential oils. But every now and then, when confronted with a tough-talking, high-gloss success story in heels, Charlotte feels a pang of dissatisfaction. These women talk knowledgeably about profit margins and annual returns on investments, but they also have two storybook children, can wear a sleeveless dress without fear, their YSL Rouge Velours is without chips, and they have read the latest bestselling biography of Stalin's chef. Scaaaaareeeee, as Charlotte would say. Happily for her, Jack constantly reminds his wife that, in his book, career women are ball-breakers, and mums who work child-wreckers. He likes her, he assures her, just the way she is. And he shows his appreciation with count-less expensive gifts, weekends away, and 'second honeymoons'. Charlotte basks in these attentions, while I resent them as reminders that the last time Guy organized a weekend away, we ended up camping with the children in a muddy Devon field; and the last gift he gave me was a clumsily mounted and rather smelly wolf's head from Moldova.

The conversation proceeds like a school run: everyone sets off confidently if carefully, certain of where they want to get to and by what route. But little by little we are held up by other people's dithering, or inconvenienced by their selfishness, and all propriety is ditched as we grow irritable, fearful, and aggressive.

The first to grow irritable is me.

'HarrietnGuy, this will come as a bit of a surprise to you two,' Jack practically does a little jig of delight as he tells us, 'but we're moving to Chelsea.'

'Chelsea?!' I gasp.

'Chelsea,' Charlotte confirms. She doesn't meet my eye – she knows this is darkest treachery. We've always lived in Clapham, we've always joked about being a short bicycle ride from one another's kitchen ... and now ... The clock's brassy gong calls me to the pork belly.

'Nothing like a man who wears his wealth lightly,' Guy mutters as he brings a tray of dirty glasses to the kitchen. 'A four-bedroom house in Chelsea!'

'Chelsea is *so* yesterday,' I whisper, trying to cheer him up. But in fact I am just as put out: Charlotte and Jack moving north of the river means they're really out of our league. And to spring it on us – on me – as a surprise!

Guy is doing mental arithmetic: 'That'll be … oh, at least £1.5 million. Like putting five children through ten years of boarding school.'

Back at the table, Jack is beaming. 'Never thought we could afford Chelsea … Pimlico, yes, just about …'

He drones on, and I find myself almost nostalgic for the Carew conversational code: no talk of money, religion, or women.

'This pork is delicious, Harry.' Charlotte is trying to steer Jack's enthusiastic talk away from the move. 'Organic?'

I know Charlotte too well to fall into her trap. 'Of course.' It's an outright lie, but I have no remorse. Charlotte's new-found zeal for the 'natural way' goes to such ridiculous ends that I have to ignore her diktats.

'We've become Freegans –' Guy gives 'Manic Organic', as he calls Charlotte, a wicked look '– we only eat food that's free. Berries, mushrooms, a quick scour of the dustbins at the back of Safeway and Tesco's, and' – he prods the pork with his fork '– road-kill.'

Charlotte shudders in distaste: she never knows how to react to Guy's teasing.

But I'm on Guy's side. Charlotte drives half an hour in her Chelsea tractor to get to the Nature and Nurture Centre that sells wheatgrass at £35 a bundle, and buys faded, dimpled, wrinkly little fruit and veg at three times the price of their non-organic equivalents. This, despite her regular botox injections, eyelash tinting, and enthusiasm for very unnatural slimming powders.

'Isn't your son at Millfield?' I turn to Oliver Mallard – and realize too late that this was out of bounds.

'Don't get me started,' Oliver sighs, and shrinks into himself like a concertina.

'Francis is having a rather mixed time,' chips in Belinda warningly.

But Oliver cannot be stopped. Francis, he explains, is a 'late developer'. Late developer is the ambitious parent's favourite euphemism. Poor marks, insufferable behaviour, detentions, suspensions and expulsions: everything can be blamed on their offspring's late development rather than sheer ineptitude. In Francis's case, development is so late in coming that the school has told the Mallards that there is no point in his applying to Cambridge, even for Land Economy.

'Never gave us a clue until now. Always led us to believe he was on track for Oxbridge ...' Oliver shakes his head, inconsolable. I can see he is still grappling with the shock that none of his brilliance has rubbed off on his only son, and none of his money can shoehorn the boy into Papa's footsteps.

'Shocking, the way the school handled it!' Belinda barks indignantly. 'And now, what are we supposed to do? Look at an ex-poly somewhere?'

You would have thought Francis faced a career as a plumber's mate.

Guy doesn't make matters any better by referring cheerfully to his cousin Bertie, who, having failed Oxbridge, went to a red-brick and is now a dope-smoking carpenter somewhere in Devon.

'Exeter's better than Oxbridge in some subjects, you know,' Jack bursts out at one point, defending his alma mater.

Oliver doesn't listen and goes on grumbling. Why is he paying £24,000-plus a year for a school that can't deliver a place at Oxbridge? Why are the terms so short, and the breaks so frequent? 'We end up seeing our children almost as much as their teachers do. It's outrageous.'

As there is nothing like the failure of someone else's child to reassure a proud but poor parent that their sacrifice is worthwhile, Guy is all sympathy and solicitude, eyes practically tearful as he asks Belinda if they've tried private tutoring.

The sympathy dries up instantly when she lets slip that her suntan, and Oliver's, are due to a month in St Tropez. This turns the debate back into us-against-them. For some parents, school fees, like the St Tropez holiday, are just another expense; others are forced to live on what's left.

But in Guy's eyes there is no other option. Sending the children to private school allows him to hold his head high under the disapproving gaze of those ancestors on his study walls. Military and colonial to their bones, they would otherwise sneer at an heir who scribbles travel books for a living. And so Guy and I divide our lives into school terms: pre-paid, paid in part, paid in full. We earmark our work in terms of what it covers of the children's schooling: Guy's regular editing of manuscripts for his friend Percy's publishing house pays for almost a full year at the Griffin; his article on Marrakesh for an in-flight mag paid for Alex's and Tom's second-hand uniforms;

my three days at HAC cover – well, not even enough to contribute to the school fund, actually.

While Guy repeats the mantra, 'Nothing is more important
than the best possible education', I'm often filled with doubts.
Do I really believe that we should bankrupt ourselves and
worry frantically before every deadline for paying school fees,
in order for our children to study Greek and Latin among a
host of Hugos and Isabellas? Do I really believe that their
intelligence, confidence, health and moral compass will be
compromised unless they attend the same establishment their
Carew forefathers thoroughly loathed so many years ago?

Guy remains immovable: tradition is sacred, and good
schooling a pillar of Carew faith. He really believes that a stint in
a particular red-brick building will make all the difference in life,
and that a dribbling old wreck called Podge Fitch, who taught
Greek and Latin to Guy's youngest uncle and Guy himself, will
prove the 'most important figure in Alex and Tom's lives'.

'They think you've married up,' my mother likes to remind
me. 'They', in our conversations, are always the Carews. 'That
means you have to take Podge Fitch with the Chippendale
sideboard.'

No, I want to report: I'm stuck with Podge Fitch's boring
anecdotes about bygone boys *and* no Chippendale.

'I think Oliver would be easy to work for.' The guests have left,
and we are clearing up.

'A few blurbs on cultural tours.' Guy stacks up the place-
mats. 'I thought I'd make a great editor for his mag, and he
thought I'd make a passable writer of brochures.'

'Never mind.' My voice is resolutely cheerful. 'Oliver said the brochures would be really well paid.'

'Well, we certainly need it. I've only got half the school fees to hand over on Monday.' Guy looks as crumpled as the tea towel in his hand. 'But it means I have to take time away from *Rajput*, which I hate to do, because it pushes publication back again.'

'*Rajput* can wait,' I snap. I'm not letting Guy postpone indefinitely Oliver's generous offer. As it is, I could see that Oliver was surprised that Guy didn't jump at it. Was he in fact hinting at something, when he talked about 'alternative employment' for talented writers? Oliver described at length how some well-known authors wrote brochures for travel agents and tourist authorities, 'humbled themselves and wrote for retail mags and hotel chains … Flexible, that's what you need to be these days.'

Guy had hardly seemed to take this in, but I listened attentively. Since Guy's last (or, more accurately, only) success, we have lived on promises. Or to be specific, we have lived off a modest legacy he had from the sale of an elderly cousin's estate. We decided to invest it in buying time, so that Guy could work un-distracted on delivering another bestseller to a grateful public. Yet when, every two years or so, Guy does publish a new tome, the drum rolls, applause and cheers are conspicuously missing. He sometimes gets a good review, sometimes gets invited to sign copies at a local bookshop, and twice has been asked to speak at a women's book club. But success, thus far, has proved elusive. Guy's freelancing brings in dwindling amounts. The legacy is long gone and I had to go back to work far earlier than I wanted.

Oliver is right, and the time has come for Guy to compromise. To my husband this will sound like blasphemy – but blasphemy is preferable to bankruptcy.

'I'm whacked.' Guy hangs up the tea towel. 'Let's go to bed.'

He looks so worn out and disappointed, my frustration melts and I suddenly feel a twinge of love and compassion. 'Darling,' I begin. But before I can reach out to stroke his head, Guy is walking up the stairs.

On the landing I pick up a fat brown teddy and a sock with a hole (Alex's? No, there's no name tape: must be Tom's). I tiptoe into Maisie's room and place the teddy on her chest of drawers. Rufus lies asleep on her feet. I shoo him off. The children are forever sneaking him into their bedroom, but he knows he's to sleep in his basket in the kitchen. Maisie stirs, stretches her arms out on the pillow above her head. I kiss her hot sweaty forehead.

In the boys' room, chaos reigns. The DVDs of *Lord of the Rings* lie on a pile of dirty clothes and Alex's books for next term teeter, like the tower of Pisa, in a corner. Alex, sleeping without his pyjama top and wrapped in a faint haze of Lynx 'Africa', lies sprawled on the top bunk. Beneath him, Tom lies curled up under his Tintin duvet, his face, uncluttered by spectacles, suddenly perfect.

By the time I have wiped off my make-up and brushed my teeth, Guy is snoring in our bed. I undress in the dark, slip on my nightgown and crawl in next to my husband.

'Side,' I tell him firmly. He rolls over obediently, and the snoring stops. I fit snugly against him – the only way for me to keep warm. And I fall asleep.

Three hours later I wake with a jerk to find Guy alert beside me. 'I've been thinking ...' He stares up at the ceiling, one arm behind his head: what was once his favourite post-coital position is now a sign of money worries. 'We could move to the suburbs. It would solve a lot of problems.'

'And create new ones,' I reply, full of visions of Norwood and Nunhead.

'Cheap housing, great state schools, too, if it comes to the crunch,' Guy continues. 'And it's a good time to sell here: house prices in Central London have gone through the roof. We could get half a million for this.'

'I don't think we could get anything like that,' I resist. 'There are only forty years left on the lease.' Not to mention a series of ominous leaks and cracks.

'There's so little on the market right now, people are desperate.' Guy has sat up.

'They're not blind.'

'The thing is, even if I do accept Oliver's offer, it's going to be difficult to make up the rest of the school fees. I doubt he pays on delivery.' He tugs at his chin pensively. 'I suppose I could approach Dad.'

Guy and I long ago decided that begging money from his parents, who, though generous, are not well off, should be left for those exceptional circumstances when really nothing else was possible. But perhaps this is what we are up against now.

'Is it that bad?' I hardly dare ask.

'Well … we could consider the country. Anywhere with grammar schools: Kent or Buckinghamshire. There's a brilliant one in Devon.'

'Oh, goody: we could live with my mum in Tonbridge.'

'Wellies …' Guy is lying back again, 'cow pats, mud and lots of wife-swapping. That's country life for you. We'd fit right in.' He rolls over and pulls me towards him. 'Except for the last, of course. Wouldn't swap you for anyone.'

He pecks my hair. We are about to have a 'marital moment'. We haven't made love for over three weeks now. It's probably my fault: I've started taking off my make-up in front of him, and my underwear, in Ilona's not-so-tender care, has gone grey. I cast off my nightgown.

'Mummy! Mummy!' A little figure, teddy trailing, pushes open our door.

'That's it!' Guy snaps crossly as I make room for Maisie on my side of the bed.

'Forget suburbia, I want all three at boarding school asa*P*!'

3

'In a cavern, in a canyon, excavating for a mine,' Guy sings as we cycle across the common: first Guy, then Alex, then me. Alex refuses to join in his father's warbling. It's bad enough to arrive at the Griffin on a bicycle as opposed to in a Merc or a BMW, but to be caught singing in chorus with one's parents is social suicide. My son is also, though he'd never admit it, slightly nervous. It's only his second year at the Griffin, and it is more than twice the size of St Christopher's, the C of E state primary school where he went and where Tom still goes. It is also twice as competitive. The competition is over school work, athletic prowess and parents' wealth. Alex excels in the first two, to my deep and bursting pride, but when it comes to the third, Guy and I let the side down. There are Griffin parents who think nothing of taking over a river-boat for their son's thirteenth birthday party, hiring a band and a caterer too. We take Alex and his friends bowling or ice skating and offer them Marmite sandwiches, crisps and Coke in a two-litre bottle.

Most Griffin parents buy two or three brand-new sets of uniform jackets, trousers, shirts and socks, as well as regulation tracksuits and trainers, for their son. We buy the uniforms at the school second-hand shop, and count ourselves lucky if we find jackets that, more or less, reach Alex's wrists, or trousers that more or less cover his ankles. Most Griffin families, the directory shows, live in Belgravia, Notting Hill and Chelsea – while we make do with an address on the unfashionable north side of Clapham.

But I feel for my eldest – especially today, as the Rolls and the Mercs and the BMWs roll slowly past our bikes as they make their way down the tree-lined avenue to the towering wrought-iron gates of the Griffin. We'll arrive red-faced and slightly out of breath, Guy with his corduroys stuffed into his socks, me with my skirt wrinkled and my hair flattened by the bicycle helmet, and all of us mud-splattered because it rained this morning.

'Couldn't we hold on to the Merc, Mummy?' Alex was pleading non-stop yesterday. 'Couldn't I do the first day of term in style?'

But Guy refused to keep the hired car. 'At forty pounds a day? Ludicrous! We'll begin as we intend to go on.'

The Merc was rather poorly repaired, in the end, by Pete's chum Mike, for an astronomical £230 – 'It's Sunday, ain't it?' We had to forego our outing to Richmond Park, and Guy left it at the car-hire place yesterday at seven p.m. 'The lighting in their car park is appalling, they won't notice the paint job,' he muttered hopefully, but every time the phone rings he jumps a mile, terrified that we've been found out.

* * *

The Griffin has occupied, for the past 130 years, ten acres of prime real estate in Wandsworth. The school's three-storey red-brick building is surrounded by a trim green lawn, with tennis courts, rugby pitches, and two cricket fields within a ball's throw. Once you have driven or, in our case, cycled, through the school gates, you find yourself in a pre-war world of calm, blazers, brogues, perfect manners and received pronunciation. There is no doubt, as you step into this quiet, regimented space, that the Griffin will offer its students some enlightenment; aspirations will be nurtured and ambition rewarded. By the time they leave its hallowed corridors, the young Griffin boys will exude the self-confidence of those who know their place in the world – and like it.

For Guy, this is familiar territory, a variation on the theme of public schools. He was at a very similar one in Somerset until he was thirteen and slipped seamlessly, with top marks in his Common Entrance, into Wolsingham – the school that generations of male Carews have attended. He has been brought up with similarly self-confident children, ancient buildings, sentimental school songs and extensive grounds.

For me, this world is as unreal as South Hams, where we holidayed when I was young: you left your front door unlocked, the car keys in the ignition, valuables on the beach as you swam, all in the confidence that you could trust everyone around you. Stepping into real life was a difficult transition.

It was all rather different at Bruton Grammar School, a squat modern building in Kent. We were the clever daughters of respectable doctors, accountants and lawyers – as well as bricklayers, plumbers and greengrocers. We all worked hard and the girls from Lady Chesham, the local private girls' school, called us 'swots'. It was true. They had horses and nannies, 'places' in France or Italy, and, later, their boyfriends had cars. Even their uniform was not the dull grey and navy we were stuck with, but a dashing turquoise. We were very conscious, as we prepared for our A-levels – in my case *Macbeth* and the Romantic poets, the English Civil War, and the art of Renaissance Italy – that we were the ones who got the most places at university, and the most girls into Oxbridge.

Still, the Lady Chesham girls continued to haunt me, even at my first meeting with Guy's parents.

'Where did you go to school? Tonbridge? It must have been Lady Chesham – did you know the Lanchester girls?'

'Actually, I wasn't at Lady Chesham,' I correct her. 'I went to the Grammar School.'

'Ah,' said Cecily, after a pause. 'How clever of you.'

'Drove she ducklings to the water,' yodels Guy.

'Dad, pleeeeeeeeease!' Alex hisses furiously. But what with the pedals pumping and the wheels whirring and other people's cars rolling past us, Guy can't hear his anguished plea.

'Every morning just at nine!'

'Stop it, Dad!' Alex shouts loudly.

Alarmed, Guy jams the brakes on, skids and hits the kerb. He falls. Alex and I stop on our bicycles immediately, and turn to watch as he slowly picks himself up: mud cakes his hands and a rip gapes at his knee.

'Oh, darling,' I moan – the 'darling' is for Alex, who looks devastated at the sight of his dad.

'Nothing to fuss about,' Guy calls out cheerfully, mistaking the object of my concern. He dusts himself off and mounts once again on his steed of steel. A huge silver Jaguar *whooshes* past us.

As we approach the school building, I see the same picture replicated all over the car park: large, imposing cars, perfectly coiffed and groomed women, sleek men in expensive suits, and uniformed boys in all shapes and sizes, standing around or running about.

'We'd better clean off some of that.' I search my handbag, which I've stuffed in the cycle basket, and hand Guy one of those wet-wipes I always keep on hand for Maisie. I remove my helmet and rake my fingers through my hair, trying to fluff it up. I'm about to be inspected, and I doubt I'll pass muster as a Griffin mum.

We lock up our cycles not far from where a chauffeur leans against a Bentley. Guy unrolls his trouser legs, Alex checks his.

'Hey, Alex!' A blond boy waves our son over to his family's Land Rover. Alex runs off without a glance in our direction. Guy and I slowly follow him up the path to the school; on the front steps, we are surrounded by boys sporting glowing tans who dart in and out of the door, talking loudly about their holidays in Panarea or Provence.

'Ben: great hair cut – NOT!'

'Theo, you've shrunk!'

'Whoa! Alex, have you seen Johnny's scar?!'

We pile into the school hall, a cavernous, gloomy, oak-panelled room, for a bracing service of hymns and pep-talk. Alex easily takes his place among his friends, and I see his dark head bob among a large group until he eventually becomes indistinguishable, one among many jostling uniforms.

I swallow hard; the ritual has begun, once again. Five days a week, from eight to four o'clock, our son is learning at the feet of some of the best and brightest in the land; 24/7, we are tightening our belts to provide this opportunity for him.

'Lord, Behold us in Thy presence once again assembled here …' I look around the whitewashed hall, filled with boys, parents and teachers; this is what we have sacrificed so much for.

We file out of the hall, in a crush of expensive scents and clothing. 'I'll see if I can pre-empt the bursar …' Guy says, looking uneasy. He leaves my side and I can see him trying to make his way to Mr Cullen.

I spot a forbidding clutch of Griffin mums. My stomach churns and my ears ring with the contemptuous comment about my roots that I overheard at Mario's. As usual, my efforts to fit in with my new Whistles skirt, bought on sale last month for £25, have come to naught: cycling has wrinkled the skirt, and Rufus's pleading pawing as I walked out of our front door has given my smart white cardigan two black smears, right under my breasts.

Real Griffin mums fall into two categories – and both are always sure of a soft landing. The McKinsey mums run hedge funds or a chain of glamorous florists, and look as if they can crush the life out of any difficulty. The Boden belles married money and look as if life gets no worse than a milk spill on their Cath Kidston tablecloth. Neither group has any experience of the unsettling sensation of sliding further and further down the property and career ladders, irrevocably pinned down by the combined forces of school fees, mortgage payments, taxes, credit-card demands and bills. They worry about whether their children will get into the right school. We worry about their getting there – and our having to pull them out because we can't afford the fees.

Stage fright fills me as I approach the group of mothers. I feel as if I am back at school, a plump swot trying to fit in with the popular girls. But without a boyfriend, C-cup breasts, or expensive clothes, I didn't stand a chance.

Now, some twenty years later, I make a vain effort to smooth out my skirt and shake my hair into place as I approach another terrifying clique.

'Hullo, Alex's mum!' A pretty blonde waves to me. Perhaps I needn't worry, this is one day when every woman is only someone's mummy, after all. Alex's popularity makes up for my unglamorous wardrobe and borderline size-14 figure. 'Julian was so disappointed that Alex didn't come and stay.'

I recognize her now: Julian Foster-Blunt is one of Alex's best friends, and invited him to stay with his family in Sardinia. Only £59 return on Ryanair, but there were also water-skiing lessons: Julian had one every morning, he told Alex, at £80 a time. 'Outrageous!' Guy had exploded. 'A day's safari in Botswana costs less than that!'

'Maybe next summer?' Julian's mum smiles benevolently at me. 'Xan and the children love the villa so much, we're buying it.'

Before I can reply, another mother, in a Chanel suit, has jumped in. 'Thank God it's all over! It's been non-stop sea-sickness, sunburn, hay fever, and even the youngest knows how to text now. You should see the mobile phone bill I've been landed with!' I identify the Chanel wearer as a McKinsey mum, and she immediately proves my hunch was correct. 'That's it, that's all I'm going to get from Goldman's for holidays this year.'

'American banks don't do vacations, do they?' Laura Semley, school governor, steps in. Laura used to run her own PR company, but has given that up to run her sons' school, in the same fashion. 'Well, another year begins.' Laura waves a regal hand to encompass the school, boys and teachers. 'I just hope –' she lowers her voice conspiratorially '– that Merritt is as good at running a prep school as old Jellicoe was.'

'Oh, he seems steely enough.' Julian's mother looks relaxed. 'And the teachers are fab. Worth every penny, really.' I doubt, somehow, she counts her pennies; but there is something so sunny about her, with her golden highlights, carefully screened tan and tasteful chains, that it is difficult to resent her the good fortune she obviously enjoys.

'Hmph!' Laura Semley eyes up McKinsey Mum as a kindred spirit. 'Actually, it's been under-performing for five years now. The results look OK, but they are tweaking it. When you drill down, those scholarship figures include all sorts of bogus "all-rounder" awards at places like *Wellington College*.' She sniffs in disgust. 'We used always to have at least one Queen's scholar at Westminster, plus two at Winchester, and one at the other top-notch schools. But they've got the scholarship set all wrong. They are confusing stocks and flows: the point is not to make the most of what they've got, but to constantly select the cleverest ones and ditch the under-performers. We've got a governing body academic sub-committee open meeting on this. Maybe you should sign up for it?' She is addressing herself exclusively now to McKinsey Mum. She can tell that Julian's mother and I wouldn't know a balance sheet from a duvet, and couldn't drill down through data if you put the apparatus into our trembling hands.

'With boys like these, Common Entrance results should certainly be better too,' chimes in McKinsey Mum. Her mobile interrupts her. 'Yes? No. Of course I will. Absolutely. Just getting petrol now, will be there within the hour.' She switches off and frowns. 'Can't afford to remind them that I've got children, let alone that I sometimes drop them off at school.' She looks suddenly deflated: her shoulders stoop, her chin drops, even the pearl buttons on her blue Chanel suit seem to have lost their sheen. 'I'd better go. Max! Max!' she shouts, and waves at a boy running past us. She sets off after him.

'Oh, look at that – Molly Boyntree!' Julian's mother points, excited, at a tall brunette in a boxy trouser suit. 'She writes for the *Sentinel*, doesn't she? We never get it at home because Ollie says it's too lefty, but I've seen her on the telly.'

'Oh yes, I recognize her.' I turn to take in the well-known journalist. 'She was on *Question Time* last Thursday.'

Laura Semley snorts her derision. 'She earns a hundred grand a year attacking the establishment and then sends her children here; the oldest is at Eton. The hypocrisy!'

'Arabella?!' Julian's mother peers at an Amazonian blonde nearby. I recognize Leo Beaton-Wallace's mum, the one who had me down as a tiger. I roar, silently, at her.

Laura Semley raises an eyebrow. 'What *are* you doing, Harriet?'

'Nothing,' I whisper back.

'Arabella Roslyn! My goodness, I think I've just seen someone I was at Heathfield with!' Julian's mum rushes off, and I watch as the two women hug enthusiastically.

'It's extraordinary, really, how many of us discover connections with this school.' Laura Semley beams benevolently at the reunion. 'Either I was at school with someone's mum, or my husband works with the dad, or we're neighbours in the country, or our families were. It really is a small world.'

I say nothing, but hear a scream of laughter as the Heathfield old girls obviously share some fond memory: caught smoking on the roof? Carpeted for staying out too late with an Etonian boyfriend? I try to imagine what boarding school life was like among girls of this kind.

'Don't you think?' Laura is asking me. I don't know if she's still referring to the cosy little circle of Griffin parents, but I do know I want to escape.

'Ah, Guy has found Mr Cullen. Better go. Bye bye!' I make my way quickly towards Guy. He is standing in one of the building's side entrances, talking under an ivy-covered archway with the bursar.

Unfortunately, the conversation I join is even more awkward than the one I've left behind.

'Well, it's simply that …' Guy looks flustered beneath the bespectacled gaze of Mr Cullen. 'I don't think we … will be able to pay the full amount at this point …' Guy shifts his weight from foot to foot while Mr Cullen fixes him with a glacial stare;

he has spotted the torn trouser leg, and his eyes sweep from my husband's face to his knees and back again. 'I'm expecting to come up with the whole lot by the end of this month.'

'I'm afraid I shall have to apply the penalty charge, Mr Carew.' Cullen shakes his head slowly and I can almost hear the mournful sound of a bell tolling a funeral. 'I can't extend the deadlines at whim, you will appreciate. Some parents make the most extraordinary efforts to pay on time, and it wouldn't be fair on them.'

'Of course, of course … It will be in by the end of the month,' Guy stutters. 'Alex is in the scholarship set; we're very very keen for him to stay on and do well.'

We certainly are; if he passes his scholarship exam this summer, the otherwise unaffordable fees at Wolsingham shrink by a quarter.

I feel torn: my sympathy is with Guy because poker-faced Mr Cullen seems to be enjoying the humiliation of a hard-up parent; yet surely we aren't the only family to find it difficult to pay £15,000 a year for our son's education? I know that on our way home Guy will spend the entire time working out what commission, ghost-writing or speech-writing he can embark on between now and the end of the month. On the other hand, Guy's difficulty is self-inflicted: the Griffin is important to *him;* I don't have a tradition to keep up, only three children to educate as best we can.

'Mum! Dad!' Alex bounds across to us. He recognizes Mr Cullen, and, guessing that money talk is taking place, falters momentarily. Then he quickly bounces back. 'I wanted to show you my new classroom.'

Even Mr Cullen melts a little at the sight of such boyish excitement. 'Well, you'd better go with your son,' he tells Guy. 'I shall have a word with the Head. But the end of the month please – no later.' Mr Cullen disappears through the archway into an inner courtyard, and Guy blows out a huge sigh, as if he'd been holding his breath all this time.

We follow Alex out of the main school building. I marvel as ever at the polished brass, the cupboards packed with silver cups, the shiny black-and-white tiles, the portraits of solemn men who look down on this budding grove of academe: yesterday's life of learning, at today's mad prices.

Alex shows us his classroom. Large, sun-filled, and with twenty battered iron-framed oak desks, their flip-tops etched with the names of past generations of Griffins. Guy scoots around, turning off the radiators and shutting the windows, muttering savagely, 'Talk about burning money!' At home he won't let me turn on the heating until the end of October.

'Well, that's that, then.' Guy squeezes my hand as we descend the stairs. I hug Alex. 'Good luck, my darling.' Guy does the same. After seeing Guy hug and kiss his eldest goodbye, Grandpa Carew once muttered, 'Must you slobber over the boy?' I watch the two of them smile bravely at one another: the son fears the school year ahead, the father, the bills in its wake. I am struck once again by how similar they are, with their dark floppy hair, lanky frame and eyes shiny with curiosity. My heart fills with tenderness. Then, in a flash, Alex is out of his father's embrace and running back to his classroom where the first registration of the school year is already taking place.

Guy and I make our way back to our bicycles through the straggling parents still chatting or waving goodbye on the tarmac. Slowly, I put on my helmet and mount my bicycle. I look back at the gracious façade: is this really what is best for my children?

'I'm going to ring Percy and see if I can edit a couple of extra manuscripts,' Guy says as he tightens the strap of his helmet under his chin. 'If he can pay me up front, then we'll have the money by the end of the month.'

My husband has no doubts: we must do everything we can to ensure our children a place in this world.

'Ye-es,' I say automatically. And then I wonder if I shouldn't be thinking of asking Mary Jane Thompson for five days instead of three at HAC. I'd sworn to myself that I would get the balance right between work and home, that I would hold down a satisfying job but somehow manage to be on hand with a tissue or a plaster, ready to help out with schoolwork or a misunderstanding among friends. How realistic is it now, when soon we'll have two sons at an unaffordably priced school?

'Waltzing Matilda, Waltzing Matilda,' Guy intones as he pedals.

'Who'll come a-waltzing Matilda with me?' I sing along, trying to still my doubts.

4

'This is Harriet, our fund-raiser and fixer, and this is our receptionist, Anjie.' Mary Jane Thompson, Secretary of HAC (South London branch), introduces us to a potential donor. The pin-stripe suit, clean-shaved face and confident expression suggest a City man. Mary Jane's syrupy tone confirms his net worth to be in the six-figure range; she doesn't do nicey-nice unless at the prospect of a big reward.

'Oh, hullo.' City man bestows a benevolent smile at us underlings before following the boss into her office.

Mary Jane calls her tiny office the 'inner sanctum'. We call it Fortress Thompson, as she could barricade herself inside and survive for days, lobbing deadly questions and put-downs all the while in our direction. Inside, she keeps a personal kettle because she complains that the one Anjie and I share constantly needs descaling; a small fridge to keep the Cokes cold for her contacts; and a digital radio tuned to Radio 4 at all times. She has Tippexed 'MJT's chair' to mark her ownership of the only decent chair in the office.

Mary Jane doesn't talk; she dictates memos.

As in, 'Team spirit can only thrive when negativity is replaced by positive feedback.' In other words, any criticism of the way Mary Jane does things is not welcome. And, 'Privacy is key to creating the mood of trust and competence necessary to secure a big donation.' Which means, leave me to deal with the rich, important men over lunch or behind closed doors.

Before she shuts the door behind her latest visitor, we hear her opening gambit – the one we have come to know word-for-word: 'Ah that?' she exclaims, as if surprised that the visitor has spotted the one and only photograph hanging on her wall. 'It's me and Gordon on the steps of Number 11 – back in 1998, when they chose me as one of the ten recipients of the Inner-City Community Workers' Achievement Award. I was really very chuffed, though of course I'd never expected to be honoured in any way … I like to get things done and … well, I think I can honestly say I do get them done …' She issues a self-deprecating chortle. 'Well, as Gordon said to me as he handed over my award …' Here, as always, she shuts the door – so that Anjie and I have never heard the memorable exchange between Gordon Brown and our boss.

Anjie begins to sort the post, I check my emails.

Anjie is a beautiful, voluptuous Jamaican, with two perfect children who smile on her desk, photographed in their St Peter's C of E Secondary School uniform. Anjie's husband, whom she calls 'his nibs', works as a builder. 'His nibs got so much cash out of those sheds he built, he's been showering me and the children with presents.' Anjie rolls her eyes. 'Girl, he's given me a bottle of scent and a hat – have you ever seen me wear a hat?! And Paula got a new dress and Luke got a scooter ... I say to him, "Why don't you save, William Jones, why don't you put some money aside for the rainy days ahead?"' She sighs, takes up a paper knife to slit open an envelope. 'Does he think money grows on trees, I want to know.' And then her usual refrain: 'If I'd known then what I know now ...'

But I know she doesn't mean it. William, a slim, sleek man with a beaming white smile, drives his wife home from the office every evening – and just before five thirty Anjie takes over the teeny bathroom we share, applying another coat of lipstick and mascara.

The South London branch of HAC has its office on the second floor of a shabby Victorian building, above an Indian take-away. By mid-morning, a pungent curry smell fills our two rooms, and we can hear the owner yelling in Bengali at his cooks. We are on Clapham High Street, and from our windows we can see brand-new banks and fast-food chains, old unkempt houses and cafés, shops and a criss-crossing of buses, cars, pushchairs and passers-by.

I sit under the poster Mary Jane brought in last summer: a bespectacled bumble bee at her computer. The caption underneath reads, *Worker bee*. 'Isn't it fun?!' Mary Jane had squealed with delight at her purchase. 'Though, in your case,' she had added archly, 'it should say "part-time worker bee".'

Mary Jane cannot forgive me for being here only three days a week. To her, part time means half-hearted. 'I suppose the brood is baying for its tea?' she'll ask sarcastically when I start clearing my desk and showing signs of an imminent departure. Or, 'Trouble at the homestead?' when I am on the telephone trying surreptitiously to ascertain that Guy and Ilona have tea, schoolwork or Calpol dosage under control. For Mary Jane, a divorcée with no children, my priorities are all wrong. 'Work gives you back what you put into it. Families wring you out like a tea towel,' she likes to warn, 'and then drop you when they realize they've got something they'd rather do.' We gather from this that Mr Thompson left his wife for someone else. But Mary Jane does not confide in us, and Anjie and I have no wish to press her.

'We've got trouble on our hands.' Anjie holds up an official-looking letter. 'Social Services want to know why we refused to take on Jesus Jones again. Wasn't he the thug from Camden?'

'He was …' And I start cataloguing young Jesus's sins on my fingers: 'He spat at the counsellor, he punched one of the boys on the holiday, seduced one of the girls and tried to set fire to the barn at Hadley House. Hardly an HAC success story, I'd say …'

'And they called a demon child like that Jesus – heavens!' Anjie, a born-again Christian, is incensed.

'Yes. Parents with a sense of irony but no notion of discipline. I'll write to Social Services today.'

I check my emails. A City banker I'd approached for a corporate donation asks for yet another meeting. An advertising big shot turns down the chance to sponsor our annual fundraiser: 'Your celebrity-punch is good, but not great: you can't deliver Jeremy Clarkson, Rory Bremner or Ian Hislop. These are the names you need to get people like me on board.'

A local printer refuses to charge 'your excellent charity' for his work on our forthcoming brochure – yikes! I remember that I am supposed to be finalizing said brochure this week with Mary Jane. And a handful of retired professionals, prepared to put up with Child Protection checks and foul-mouthed disadvantaged youngsters giving them lip, volunteer to help us staff the holiday projects, which consist of a week in our homes in Devon and Suffolk.

I steal a look at the big planning diary on my desk, and the red circled dates stand out like chicken pox spots: they warn me when the Griffin school fees are due. The thirtieth, only a week away. Can we make it? Guy's chum Ken Wright needs a speech-writer for his forthcoming presentation to a leisure firm: that should bring in a fair amount, and Ken is usually quick to pay. The bursar was quite clear that, if we missed the deadline, he would need to bring the matter up with Merritt, the headmaster – and, who knows, maybe the Board of Governors? The thought of those Griffin parents, well-off and smugly confident that their children have the best of everything, makes my heart sink. I'd rather spend every weekend stacking shelves at ASDA than face their pity.

Indeed, I wonder whether shelf-stacking might not be better paid than working for a small charity. I had never dreamed of becoming a Lady Bountiful. I had met a few among my mother's friends, and they struck me as middle-class, middle-aged women who liked the sound of their own voice. They welcomed the opportunity to do good, but above all to organize other people's lives – or at least coffee mornings and bingo evenings, raffle sales and the collection of second-hand books.

I was determined to work in an art gallery and maybe one day organize exhibits of contemporary figurative painters.

Before Alex was born, I'd managed to find a job at a small gallery in South Kensington. But Alex's arrival swamped me: I found I had no strength and no wish to leave my home. The gallery owner found someone else to help out, and I get a pang of dissatisfaction every time I find myself in a certain corner of South Kensington.

When I heard about HAC from a mother at St Christopher's two years ago, I was only half interested in the charity that gave disadvantaged children a holiday. The main attraction was the schedule: 'Three days a week with potential to increase to full time.'

But soon I found myself engaging with the work. There is the challenge of ensuring that the professional 'facilitators' and their three supervisors manage a week's break for a dozen children without them running amok or wreaking devastation on our houses; making sure that the GP or social worker is promoting the right child for the experience, rather than fobbing off on us countless Jesus Jones types who turn a holiday into hell; finding generous sponsors who will keep us going. And there is the reward of receiving postcards and letters, in childish scrawl, from the children. Many of them have never had a holiday in their life, and pack their toothbrush, spare pants and T-shirt in a bin liner because they don't have a case. Their gratitude repays every effort we make.

Still, in between the holidays themselves, routine work at HAC can be dull, and Mary Jane Thompson's presence overbearing. All too often, I find her straying into my territory.

'I think when it comes to the bigger sponsors, Harriet,' she repeats to me, as she returns from yet another expensive lunch, 'you should leave it to me: I have a way with rich men who need to be parted from their money.'

Then I find myself looking on this job as purely a way to make ends meet, even though the salary is only £15,000; and I think wistfully of the exhibitions I would have loved to curate, and the art gallery I would have loved to run.

The phone rings. ''Arriet?'

It's Ilona, and I immediately expect the worst: Maisie's hurt, Maisie's got a roaring temperature, Maisie bit another child at nursery. Then Ilona remembers what I taught her about telephone communication and pre-empting maternal fears: 'Maisie is OK.' Ahhhh, I sigh, and then instantly am besieged by another set of images: Ilona wants to leave us for one of her Internet beaux, Ilona is being stalked by one of the same, Pete is offering to make an honest woman of her …

'Someone wants to speak with her mamma,' Ilona says, before handing over the telephone to Maisie.

'Mummy!' My baby is tearful down the phone, and I feel ready to bolt back home, take her in my arms and snuggle up with our worn copy of *We're Going on a Bear Hunt*. 'I want youuuuuuuu,' she wails, and I can tell Ilona is having to pull the receiver from her hand.

For the umpteenth time I decide to postpone asking Mary Jane for a full-time position. I'm pretty sure five days a week would bring in £25,000, but does the difference in salary really make up for the time missed with my children? Motherhood – and this is an admission, like fancying my cousin Will when I was fourteen, or being disappointed about not getting into Oxford, that I will make only to myself – has put an end to my modest professional ambition. It hasn't just poured water on the flames; it has sprayed fire-extinguishing foam on them, then beaten the embers with a spade for good measure.

'Why do we always have to be the ones to compromise?' Charlotte sighs every time I mention working at HAC. I ask myself what kind of compromise my best friend thinks she's been forced into: she has a devoted and wealthy husband who keeps her in a style far grander than anything she and I grew up with; three perfect children and a nanny to keep them in line; and no call on her time between nine thirty and four. That's the kind of 'compromise' I could live with.

'You were brilliant at that gallery – you always had an eye for good paintings ... And here you are, trying to shoe-horn feral children into a holiday environment.' Charlotte snorts.

'They're not feral, they're damaged.' I always jump to my charges' defence. 'They've had the worst possible start in life.'

'And you'll come to the worst possible end, if you don't watch out. Those kids give me the heebie-jeebies.' Charlotte's brown eyes widen in dramatic fear. 'I hope Guy appreciates what you've taken on so that he can try his hand at travel books!'

In Charlotte's eyes, Guy staying at home to write somehow doesn't count as a proper job. 'Be honest, Harry, how many copies does he sell? I bet it's not enough to keep the kids in school uniforms, let alone in school.'

'He has his fans, you know,' I reply defensively. 'And one of them is a telly producer who thinks *Lonely Hunter* would make a fabulous documentary series.'

Strange but true. Last weekend we went to Waterstone's to look for a book that Maisie could take to Theo Wallace's birthday party. As usual, Guy was scouring the Travel section for copies of his books. 'They've got only one copy of *Lonely Hunter* and none of *White Nights*. And a whole row of Crispin Kerr. Preposterous! I'm going to complain ...' He was about to make off in the direction of the bespectacled boy at the till when the pretty redhead leafing through the volumes on the table turned to him. '*Lonely Hunter*? It's great, isn't it!'

'Er ...' Guy puffed up with obvious pride. 'I wrote it.'

'*You* wrote it? You're Guy *Carew*?' Wide eyes and a wider smile turned on Guy with undisguised admiration.

Guy nodded. 'Er ... yes.' He studied his fan with something like suspicion: this had not happened in a long, long time.

'But your books are brilliant! I *loved* the campfire scene in *Desert Flower*!' Guy began to melt in the heat of her admiration. 'I came to that lecture you gave at Essex University last year: fascinating!'

For the next ten minutes, Maisie, the boys and I were ignored as the stuffy library air of the bookshop resounded with 'Kalahari!' 'Masai!' 'Nairobi!' and peals of laughter.

'Her name is Zoë Jenning and she's a producer for Rainbow Productions, some independent TV company.' Guy could hardly contain his excitement as we pushed the buggy and the boys out of the shop. 'She thinks *Lonely Hunter* would make great telly!'

'Daddy's gonna be on telly! Daddy's gonna be on telly!' Alex and Tom chanted down the pavement.

'Don't hold your breath' Charlotte warns me: 'Most of these independent television companies are dodgy cowboy outfits. They milk you for information by promising you a series of your own, and then they drop the show but steal your idea.'

'He's very excited.'

It's an understatement: Guy has been waiting for Zoë's phone call ever since, and will not listen to caution. 'You'll see, Harriet; a whole new career beckons!'

I sigh. The 'old' career was bad enough. It consisted of long sessions at the computer in his study alternating with even longer sessions daydreaming about the future success of the project at hand. Guy believes wholly, and without reservation, that he will write a great bestseller, a *Richard and Judy* selection that will also appeal to the intellectual elite; a magnum opus that will secure his place among literary giants. And despite the obvious scepticism of his agent, Simon, who grows ever more distant, and of friends like Charlotte and Jack; despite the countless times I have voiced our financial worries; and despite the prospect of spiralling school fees for three children, Guy won't be deflected.

He scours the book pages of the *Telegraph* and the *TLS*, studying the reviews, latest publications and bestseller lists, and scoffs at 'the competition'. 'I don't believe it, Harriet! Look here – Francis Bolton has managed to get something published. A biography of Diane de Poitiers ... I mean, who's going to buy that? She's French, for a start; and she didn't do anything, really, apart from having an affair with a man half her age who happened to be King of France.' Such acerbic observations will be followed, a few weeks later, with outrage: 'Can you believe it, Harry – that silly book by Bolton is number two on the bestseller list. I swear to you, that man is incapable of doing proper research – it'll be just a cut-and-paste job. What is the world coming to?'

Guy's most vicious attacks are reserved for the authors who dare stray into the rather far-flung area he considers his patch: 'What?! That idiot Crispin Kerr – the one who looks like a shampoo advert with all that blond hair – he's got a book out on the Gobi Desert. What does that ignoramus know about the Gobi? Nothing, *nada, niente*! How could anyone be fooled by that man!' And, 'Ha! Did you see what's happened to Seb Colley? That pathetic TV series of his on the last maharajahs has bombed. That brilliant TV critic, the one on the *Sunday Tribune*, L.L. Munro, he's really put the boot in. Calls it "Curry kitsch" and a "sorry sari saga".'

I admire my husband's single-minded pursuit of his objective – but I sometimes yearn to remind him that the 'idiot' Crispin Kerr's books and documentaries and Francis Bolton's 'silly' biography must be nice little earners.

It's almost lunch time. 'Does she have a lunch today?' I ask Anjie hopefully. Most days, Mary Jane takes out, or is taken out by, some bigwig, allowing us a breathing space that I usually fill with running errands and Anjie with catching up on the stars in her secret stash of *Grazia* and *Heat*.

'Yup.' Anjie gives me a happy wink.

'Good.' I have been meaning to check out the hospice shop for a winter coat. My old black one from Hobbs, which has stood by me as long as Guy has, is embarrassingly threadbare.

Mary Jane emerges from her office, visitor in her wake. As usual, her expression is impenetrable, and it's impossible to gauge whether HAC has just received a donation of a quarter of a million pounds or a ticking off for a poor performance.

'It was a pleasure, thank you ever so much.' Mary Jane puts on the gracious hostess act. 'Would you like Anjie to order a minicab for you?'

But the moment the City man disappears, shocking Mary Jane by preferring tube to taxi, our boss reverts to type:

'I've got a lunch.' She stands by Anjie's desk and looks down her nose at her. 'I'm expecting a couple of important calls. I hope it's not too much to ask that you put the answering machine on when you go for lunch.'

'Will do,' Anjie answers breezily, looking up from her screen for a nanosecond.

Mary Jane turns to me with an appraising look. 'There's someone I want you to meet. He's a big potential donor. A property developer who's ruffled a few feathers, so he's trying to win brownie points by helping local charities … We'll check dates when I come back.' With that, she's off.

Out comes *Grazia*: 'Oh dear, I think Liz is getting too thin,' Anjie worries over a photo of Liz Hurley looking gaunt.

'I'm off to the hospice shop. See you in about an hour.'

'Don't rush back, girl. I'm meeting my William for a sandwich,' Anjie answers, immersed in Brangelina's latest exploits.

* * *

The hospice shop is on the High Street, a few minutes' walk from HAC. I enter, and find myself surrounded by rows of sagging paperbacks, with *Polo* next to *Crime and Punishment* next to *Forever Amber*; musty fox collars; and chipped, incomplete china sets. A tiny, bent woman, laden with carrier bags, is scouring the shelves. Unkempt grey curls escape her rain hat and mumbled words escape her lips.

I toy with the thought of buying the ancient porcelain doll that sits, staring in blue-eyed surprise, above a dented Lego box and a plastic Christmas tree. Maisie, for Christmas? But then remember my mission and set it down again on its ledge.

I pick my way past the counter that displays gaudy paste jewellery and silver cigarette lighters and christening cups, and make for the rack of second-hand clothes.

Guy calls the hospice shop the 'bankrupts' boutique'. Bankrupt is right. Alex came rushing in after school yesterday with the joyous news that he has been chosen for the First XV. Guy and I delighted in his achievement – until he explained he would now need a First XV blazer that costs £79.99, a tie for £12.99, and rugby shirt at £19.99, not to mention new boots and a proper kitbag with school logo.

'A kitbag?' Guy can't hide our mounting despair. 'Is that strictly necessary?'

'Da-aaaaaad! I don't want to be left out when the others all have one.' Alex throws us a look of such wretchedness I swallow my reservations and hear Guy do the same. 'OK, OK, we'll see what we can find at the second-hand shop.'

Alex smiles and then stuns us with: 'And guess what? Mr Farrell says we're going on tour to South Africa at Christmas!' Alex punches the air. 'Cape Town here we come!'

The trip to Cape Town, coupled with the discovery that the Griffin's second-hand shop doesn't have a blazer that fits our son, means I have no choice but to get myself a coat here. I had hoped to buy the charcoal wool one I had seen in Debenham's pre-season sale, but that would mean condemning Alex to a hopelessly short-armed rugby blazer.

At Bristol as an undergraduate I bought all my clothes at the Oxfam shop. As did Charlotte: we had a spectacular array of flapper dresses for our evening wear, and some very pretty cropped beaded cardigans and flouncy skirts for everyday. My Oxfam bargains amused James, my then boyfriend: 'Ooooooh, a bit unconventional, isn't it, to wear someone's granny's cardigan?' But as I was doing English, with lots of Keats and Coleridge and the Gothic novel, and Charlotte, Art History, our romantic taste in clothing matched our subjects.

'Who wants to be like those dreary Sloanes?' Charlotte would pout prettily as she donned an Oxfam cardy and gypsy skirt. 'All those silly Laura Ashley pastels and bright-coloured cords?'

Never in a million years did I suspect that I would continue shopping at Oxfam. It was fine for a cash-strapped eighteen-year-old, but the sight of shabby elderly women browsing among the bric-a-brac nowadays sends a little shiver of anxiety down my spine. Will I be the same in my sunset years? Badly dressed, hunched under the weight of debts and family burdens, myopically searching for something 'nice' to cheer up the house, or the grandchildren. Penury in my thirties is one thing, but I really don't want to be still hand-to-mouth when I'm in my sixties.

Guy refuses to address the issue of our retirement. I've told him how Charlotte and Jack plan to buy a farmhouse in France when Jack retires, because the living is cheaper and the French state health-care better than the NHS; and how my mother's neighbours have moved to Spain because of the sun and the fact that they can live in a villa by the sea for the price of their little house in Tonbridge.

But Guy infuriates me by refusing to even consider making plans. 'Oh, Harriet, you needn't worry: things are going to get better. Just you wait: I have a very good feeling about *Rajput* – it's like Bollywood meets *Dad's Army*.'

I, however, am not convinced that those bickering maharajahs are going to be our meal ticket.

I resign myself to the prospect of being a regular client of this hospice shop for many years to come. Apparently, this is not as shaming in Guy's circles as it is in mine: Guy's mother was very open about buying her tweed suits at the charity shops in Gosport. I had assumed the Carews would consider buying second-hand clothes as demeaning as buying their own furniture. Instead: 'Spending money on frocks is such a waste.' Cecily Carew eyes me up and down as if I were a clothes-horse. 'School fees and the house: those are our family's priorities.'

For my part, I don't want to be caught scouring the racks of clean if slightly musty clothes that someone better-off has set aside for the 'less fortunate', so I plan each foray to the hospice shop with precision. A) Fold one of my oldest skirts into a carrier bag. B) Step into the shop with said carrier bag. C) Look around: if I see someone I know, I smile, hand in the cast-off, and retreat. D) If the coast is clear, I pick what I want and slip behind the curtain to try it on. Then I buy it and sneak out of the shop.

In this fashion I have bought a Donna Karan skirt (£8) a MaxMara jacket (£18) and a Whistles linen dress (£12).

From the cash register, a middle-aged woman, head nodding out of time with the Classic FM on the radio beside her, smiles at me: she recognizes me from previous visits. Depressing or what?

I stop the self-pity when I spot two coats in sizes 12 and 14. As I step into the makeshift dressing room, I ask myself who else knows about my struggle to keep up with my middle-class friends on half their salary? I look in the mirror. Well, does it matter if I can't keep up the appearance of being self-confident and solvent?

It matters rather less, I decide, than the fact that the size-12 coat, a camel-haired and deliciously cosy number from Ronit Zilkha, is definitely too tight. I'm going to have to start the Modified Atkins that I read about in *Vogue* at the dentist's last spring. Why did my mother have to burden me with her classic English pear shape? The coat fits my top but hugs my hips and bottom too snugly. Regretfully, I slip it off and try on the size 14, a navy-blue Jaeger in plain wool: it's a perfect fit and at £24 it is a steal.

I walk my bargain to the cash register, and as the cashier gives me a complicit smile, I suddenly see, standing ram-rod straight in a boxy designer-looking twill suit, Mary Jane Thompson. She sees me too – and the coat.

'Harriet! Find anything nice?' My boss smiles condescendingly. 'I'm just dropping off two jackets from last winter, a bit worn around the cuffs.'

Shame contracts my throat. Then inspiration strikes: 'It's for Alex. They're doing *Bugsy Malone*.' I beam. 'The drama head at the Griffin couldn't find anything that fit him.' I wave. 'See you in a tick.'

I step outside. Social humiliation avoided – just.

5

'Oh, what do you care?' Charlotte giggles when I tell her of the encounter. 'Maybe if she thinks you're really hard-up, she'll give you a rise!'

We're sitting in my kitchen, a teapot and two mugs on the table between us.

'Ha! Mary Jane's idea of compassion is to perform the Heimlich manoeuvre on you when you sneeze and offer you a hanky when you choke.'

Our eleven o'clock coffee has given way to a pot of organic tea. Manic Organic prefers very expensive organic green tea which she buys for me at Nature and Nurture and assures me will make me live longer.

'I don't want you to think I'm being ungrateful,' I moan, 'but who wants to live longer when you have no money, second-hand clothes, and soon three kids at public school?'

A piercing scream reaches us from upstairs. 'No-no-no-no, Mr Caroo!'

'Omigod!' Charlotte's eyes widen in alarm.

We hear Guy's footsteps running down the stairs.

'She's barking!' He comes into the kitchen. 'Hullo, Charlotte. Our au pair is absolutely barking!'

'What's happened?' I ask. I don't care if she's barking; as long as she doesn't eat children, steal money, or shrink my one and only silk blouse, I want to keep Ilona as long as she'll have us. 'Why did she scream?'

Guy holds up his best white shirt, now a dismal shade of pink. 'I told her if she doesn't check the children's pockets for pens, I'm going to ban the computer from her room.'

'Oh, Guy, that's cruel,' I begin.

'Is she into Internet dating, Facebook, or computer games?' Charlotte asks.

'So far we only have evidence of the former. We've had a cat-walk of Essex men, Cubans, Poles, Russians and one very odd American who claimed to be the reincarnation of James Dean. But I've worked out that what she's really interested in is their cars. Ilona doesn't do public transport.' Guy shakes his head. 'Women are tricky beasts.' He disappears back into his study.

Charlotte laughs. 'He sounds like our Italian count, doesn't he?'

I immediately re-live our trip to Italy when we were nineteen, and our encounter with the Roman count who, seeing us salivate over a menu card outside an expensive restaurant, bought us dinner – at the price of listening to his reminiscences of English girlfriends.

There was also the lifeguard who came to 'save' us when we were bathing in the Med, although we had never cried for help and all he did when he reached us was rub his hands up and down our bodies. By the end of our Italian trip, Charlotte and I had sealed our best-friendship, and were relieved to return to the relative safety of Bristol, and our boyfriends – Jack (Charlotte's) and James (mine).

I study my best friend now, with her glossy dark hair, her carefully assembled casual look and bright eyes. We have different schedules, have married very different men, and see each other no more than once a week. But I cannot imagine life without Charlotte, and her living only a few minutes' bike ride away has been one of the perks of this shabby house in this run-down area. Which is one reason why her proposed move to Chelsea has shocked me so. But as I watch her, at home in my messy kitchen, among half-empty bottles and tins that haven't been put away, giggling about our past as she strokes Rufus at her feet, I know that not even an upmarket move will upset our friendship.

I look out of the rain-washed window. The garden looks bare already and the ground muddy and unkempt.

'Biscuits?' I ask as I take down a tin from the cupboard. Maisie's latest autumnal composition comes unstuck from the cabinet door, leaving four little pebbles of Blu Tack.

'I shouldn't …' Charlotte shakes her head as she stretches out her hand for a biscuit.

I notice a big new gold ring on her third finger. 'Gosh, is that new?'

'Yes.' Charlotte smiles down at it. 'Jack bought it for me. It was for our fourteenth anniversary and …' She stops, blushes prettily and gives me a quick look. 'He is soooo romantic, Harriet. He really is a Romeo at heart.'

I ask myself when was the last time Guy acted like Romeo, and decide it was when he stood under my window, slightly the worse for wear, calling up to me in the middle of the night because he'd locked himself out.

'It's as if we're living through a second honeymoon – he's so considerate and sweet and –' Charlotte gives me a wicked grin '– passionate.'

I sink my teeth into a biscuit.

Charlotte's and Jack's very demonstrative relationship has always been a source of amusement for Guy. 'Flirting with your husband is in bad taste, Charlotte,' he likes to tease her. But it has always secretly irked me. I can't help but wonder if the Collinses really do have vast quantities of great sex. How often do they do it a week? Twice? Three times? More? I feel at once envious and guilty. Half the time, when Guy snuggles up with intent, I stop him with an, 'Oh, darling, I can't.' I'm so exhausted by the endless clucking and feeding, answering of children's questions, office work and shopping that, by the time I make it to bed, the last thing I want is communion with another person.

But surely this is only normal, after fourteen years' marriage. Isn't it?

The doorbell stops my dissection of conjugal sex. It's Lisa, our American neighbour, with her house keys: she sets off for Barbados tonight.

'Barbados: isn't she lucky!' I say to Charlotte as Lisa follows me into the kitchen.

'You're lucky not to have to work.' Lisa never seems to take on board that I do work, even if part-time.

'I do,' I object.

'Oh, I know, I know,' Lisa holds up her hand to stem my protest. 'There's all that picking up after the munchkins and buying enough cotton buds and loo-paper rolls, and checking your husband's got a clean shirt. I know that's important, but I have to worry about how China's exports are doing, and which country has the most solid manufacturing base.'

Yes, Lisa has the luxury of thinking about grown-up issues. But motherhood is like a washing machine that only has one setting – the hottest – and shrinks your interests from reading Italian art critics to getting the Stain Devil on your skirt before the jam from Maisie's toast sets in; from analysing the pre-Raphaelites' technique to checking that the stench emanating from Tom's book-bag is not last week's packed lunch rotting away. Motherhood means the almost total suspension of big thoughts and big books, exhibits, theatre outings, even reading the newspaper from start to finish. You promise yourself every day for fifteen years that, next year, it will be different; you'll finally be free of bedtime schedules, school runs, homework, and Yoga for Twos. But every year you also acknowledge that Maisie wants more attention than you give her; that Tom is shy and needs you to bring him out; that Alex doesn't take his work seriously enough and needs constant monitoring; and that your place is unquestionably with them.

'It's harder than it looks,' Charlotte sulks as Lisa strikes a pose against our refrigerator.

She looks slim even in a baggy white tracksuit. Charlotte sets down the biscuit she was nibbling.

'Such a blessing,' I tell Lisa, 'to be free of the school schedule.'

'You'd better believe it.' Lisa tosses her glossy highlights. 'I wouldn't be caught dead in a hotel with kids around. They make a racket and pee in the pool. Gross.'

'Tea?' I offer, but Lisa shakes her head. Of course: she only does H20 and Dom Pérignon. 'Doesn't your mother live there now?'

'Barbados? No, Bahamas. Down, dog, down!' Lisa pushes Rufus's snout away from her all-white outfit. 'Lives with her analyst. I hope he gives her a discount!' Lisa laughs. 'Anyway, it lets me off the hook!'

'Oh, hullo!' Guy's radar for Lisa's infrequent visits is fool-proof; the hermit who can't be prised from his refuge when Charlotte, Ilona's boyfriends, the gas man or the postman are at the door, pops out the moment our leggy neighbour drops by.

'Hi there!' Lisa automatically shifts into testosterone response: her eyelids flutter, mouth puckers in a pout, and her breasts lift as if suddenly fitted into a balcony bra. No male is exempt from her full blast. I've even caught Lisa fluttering her lids at Alex and Tom.

Guy's eyes are on Lisa. 'Are you off then?'

'Yup. Can't wait. Need my sun.'

'Some people have all the luck.' Guy flicks the switch on the kettle. 'If you're ever in need of a chaperone, I'm willing. I mean, lying in the sun sipping daiquiris next to half-naked women will be burdensome and unpleasant, but someone's got to do it.'

'I thought you were a hard-working writer, tied to his desk?' Lisa teases with a flick of her hair. So did I, I think sourly.

'For that kind of assignment, I think I could put *Rajput* on hold.'

But Lisa is checking her BlackBerry. 'Hey, it's eleven o'clock! I've got to go to my threading. Listen, I really appreciate it. I'll get the kids a T-shirt.'

I see her off, then slump in the kitchen chair.

'Please don't tell me what threading is.' Guy shakes his head as he takes his mug and retreats to his study.

'God, I would NOT like her next door. She's a living reproach, isn't she?' Charlotte shoves the rest of the biscuit in her mouth.

'I know. And all three males in this house hyperventilate in her presence.'

Rain spots the window pane, it's chilly despite my cardy, and before me stretches a decade of noisy kids, peed-in pools, and humdrum holiday destinations. Even Charlotte and Jack, who can afford it, can't go away during term time, and in the holidays they have to bear in mind Charlotte's father, a widower in Staffordshire, who complains of dizzy spells.

'Typical no-com,' Charlotte mutters.

Charlotte's theory is that the world is divided between the no-commitments like Lisa, and the over-committeds like us. No-coms can spend hours on threading, St Tropez tans and Brazilians, without worrying about robbing children or elderly parents of quality time. Over-coms can't. No-coms can spend their holidays without the in-laws and Christmas without some batty aunt, and they can stay late at dinner parties without fearing the au pair's sulk the next day. Over-coms can't. No-coms can be spontaneous about cinema and sex. Over-coms can't see the latest George Clooney or lock the bedroom door without first ensuring that the kids, Ilona and Rufus are safely occupied. In fact, over-coms cannot move for fear of failing someone in our lives.

I pour another cup of tea. Charlotte looks positively depressed.

'Cheer up!' I smile reassuringly. 'Once Lily and Maisie are about … oh, sixteen, I reckon we can be more like no-coms. Only thirteen more years to go.'

'There's something I haven't told you.' Charlotte has turned puce. 'I'm pregnant.'

'But she's the same age as you!' When I ring my mum with Charlotte's news, she sounds genuinely, and rather insultingly, shocked. 'Isn't that dangerous?'

'Well, maybe … But that's not the point!' I cry. Though I am not sure what *is* the point. Is it that it's proof that Jack and Charlotte really do have a very active sex life, as opposed to my dormant one? Or is it that I'm feeling broody but know that there is no way Guy and I could afford to add to our present financial woes? Or am I worried about growing older? My mother's shock at the prospect of Charlotte being pregnant makes me think that I've reached an age already when people think I'd be better off taking up bridge rather than being with child. Charlotte's pregnancy proclaims to the world that she is still fertile, fecund, womanly; while I am just beginning to feel … well, *almost* middle-aged.

'What a thing to do!' my mum continues. 'Though I suppose Jack can afford to have a big family. Have they moved to the house in Chelsea yet?'

'Oh, Mum, it's not always about money,' I remonstrate. But I know it is. When I discovered that I was pregnant with Maisie almost four years ago now, Guy's reaction struck me like a slap:

'My *God*, Harriet, we can't afford another £120,000 in school fees! And that's without counting the rest – food, clothes, bigger house, all those soft toys, train sets, let alone the computers they demand.' While I sat mute on a kitchen stool, stroking my stomach and its gentle swelling, my husband pulled at his hair. 'Where will we put him? There's no room as it is. We'd have to give up on the au pair's room, and then it's just when you were thinking of going back to work and …'

I just listened, frozen with shock, and suddenly Guy must have seen my expression, because he rushed over to me guiltily, and pulled me into his arms.

'Oh, Harry, I'm sorry. I'm sorry, darling, of course we'll find a way, of course we'll make room. And you know how I adore the boys, another one will be fab!'

In the end, it was not a baby boy but a girl, and Guy truly was adoring, walking with Maisie stretched, tummy down, on his forearm, showing her off to anyone who dropped in. 'My little girl, just look at her!'

But his reaction had been a warning: our finances cannot cover surprises. So that even last winter, when I was giving away all the baby paraphernalia we've had about the house since Alex's birth – the high chair, the crib, the pastel Beatrix

Potter mobile, the baby steamer and plasticated bibs – I felt only a little twinge of regret. A fourth child is not an option.

'Harriet? Harriet, are you still there?'

'Yes, yes, I am.' I'm staring at the ominous damp patch on our bedroom ceiling. Only a week ago, it looked like a cricket ball; after five days of wet weather it has swollen to the size of a pumpkin. Please, please don't let this mean we need to have the roof seen to. The most recent estimate would have covered two terms' tuition at the Griffin. Where would we get the money from?

'How's Guy? Has he finished the Indian book?'

'Not yet.'

'Now there's a surprise,' my mother says drily. 'I love Guy dearly, but you both would be a lot happier if he'd settled down in a proper profession a long time ago.' My mother pauses, then, at my silence, changes tack: 'How're the children?'

'Brilliant. Alex got into the First XV, did I tell you?'

'That boy would do well anywhere,' my mother points out. 'He doesn't have to go to a prep school that costs fifteen grand a year.'

'We can't skimp on the children's education. You and Dad were always saying how important good schooling was.' I look at the photo of my dad: small and wiry, he grins at the camera with total confidence. Yet only a few weeks later he was dead of a sudden stroke – leaving Mum broken-hearted and me floundering, in my second year at Bristol. Brief, sleepless nights gave way to interminable days punctuated by weeping fits and long calls home to Mum and Mel. After all this time, my eyes still fill when I look at his photograph, though now my tears are accompanied by the warm realization that Tom resembles him like a son.

'Those were different times. Sending a child to prep school did not mean you had to take out a second mortgage.'

'They were different times,' I say patiently, 'because sending your children to state schools didn't mean they'd end up in gangland, or dealing with teachers who won't tell off a student because they might get beaten up by his parents after school. There are schools in London where half the kids can't speak English. And the other half, you wish they couldn't,' I sigh. 'And house prices near the decent schools are way beyond us.'

'Then the obvious solution is for you to move. We have excellent schools here. And I'll baby-sit every night for free if you move down here.' My mum's words rush out of her, and I feel a wrench. She lives alone, my sister is far away, and she dotes on my children. Would moving out of London be so bad? Guy was talking about it again last night. It's not just the bill for the Griffin's second term looming; we're £1,200 over our overdraft limit.

'It's a lot greener and quieter than London,' my mother continues.

'I know, Mum. I *am* tempted. Even though I'd have to give up HAC.'

'You wouldn't need to give up working, though. We'd find something else for you here.' My mum, who has never done a day's work in her life, is proud of my job, even if it is only part-time. 'Buys your independence,' she always says, 'builds your self-confidence, keeps your wits sharp. I only wish I'd had the courage to do something myself.'

'But it would be hard on Guy. He has his heart set on the boys following in his footsteps, and about a hundred other Carews before him, and going to Wolsingham.'

'Oh, those Carews! They have all the wrong priorities,' my mother sniffs. 'Army families always spend their lives looking backwards and then are surprised when they fall flat on their face.'

'I think if we threatened not to send the boys to Wolsingham, Archie and Cecily would sell their house and the cottage in Lyme Regis to cover the fees.'

'Then they're truly mad. Penury for posh classmates – it's nonsense.' My mother sighs. 'I know I'm wasting my breath. Mel rang …' My older sister, who married an Australian architect, lives in Sydney. 'Did I tell you Kim's firm has been commissioned to do Sydney's new library?'

'Yes, I think you mentioned it last time you rang.' You bet she did. I was the youngest, my father's favourite, and the one who got the better marks. But Mel always had twice the self-confidence and ambition. She ended up moving to Australia and starting up a business in gourmet baby food, which she sold three years ago for a tidy profit. Her husband Kim is a highly sought-after architect, who according to my mum designs half of Sydney these days.

My mother may be saintly, but she cannot resist stirring up a bit of sibling rivalry.

'Mel's done very well for herself.'

'Yes,' I agree meekly. 'Better go, Mum – the kids will be home from school soon.'

I get off the phone and vow that I will not lose sleep over my pregnant BF or my wealthier and more successful sister.

But it is neither Charlotte or Mel who keep me awake that night. Footsteps resound on our stairs, then someone stumbles and cries out '*Kurva!*' I look at the clock on my bedside table: three a.m. What on earth!? I get up, still half-asleep, and tiptoe, so as not to wake Guy, to open the door. It isn't one of the boys, as I had feared, but Ilona who is weaving up the stairs, certainly not stone-cold sober, followed by a thick-set man with a pony-tail. I withdraw into our bedroom, shut the door and slip back into bed beside Guy. That's it. This is worse than her ruining Guy's best shirt, worse than her handing out Rufus's dog biscuits with cheese to the children, worse than her looking me up and down when I wear one of my charity-shop finds, worse even than the day she clogged up the sink with red hair dye.

But how on earth can I get rid of Ilona and still go out to work? It's Ilona who takes Maisie to nursery, then fetches her again at one. On the days when I'm at HAC, it's Ilona who gives Maisie, and sometimes Guy, lunch; she who plays with my three-year-old or takes her to her playgroup. And it's Ilona who picks up Tom from St Christopher's when Guy or I can't, and Ilona who watches over the boys when they have their tea, and stops them from downing entire jars of Nutella, reading at the table and leaving their chocolatey prints on every surface.

I feel depressed at the thought of what the ponytailed visitor dooms me to. Hours on Mumsnet and Gumtree.com, placing ads and answering them; endless chats with the lonely Pakistani newsagent who posts Polish and Latvian girls' ads in his windows; and possibly a long, horrific drive in yet another hired car to Stansted, Heathrow, Gatwick or Luton, hoping against hope that this one, finally, is a good one.

Next morning, I have resolved nothing except that I must have a good night's sleep soon or lose my mind completely. At breakfast Ilona surfaces in one of her more clingy tops, and I snap at her to put something warmer on. Is Ponytail upstairs, under the duvet, waiting for last night's date to sneak him toast and tea? Or did he manage to tiptoe down the stairs and out the front door at the crack of dawn?

Maisie spills cereal on the table and I scold her, setting off a tantrum. Tom has lost his maths notebook, Alex is running late, and Guy can't find some crucial book on some sixteenth-century maharajah of Jodphur. I feel as if I want to crawl back to bed. Ilona gives me a long, cold look which manages to tell me simultaneously that she thinks I'm pre-menopausal, jealous of her pert figure, wearing the wrong clothes, and a nag.

For once, HAC seems a refuge. Mary Jane is locked in Fortress Thompson all morning, and Anjie is surreptitiously reading *Heat* from cover to cover. 'Poor Ulrika, she just can't get it right, can she?' And 'Robbie needs a nice girl to just come and save him, doesn't he?'

By lunch time, when Mary Jane surfaces, I'm up to speed with the love-lives of half of Hollywood and most of the *EastEnders*' cast.

'I've been trying to get a few dates out of you ...' My boss stands in front of my desk. 'Can you check your diary now, please?' She is wearing a pretty cherry-red, light wool suit that I've never seen before and her trademark red-rimmed spectacles are nowhere to be seen. Mary Jane's in a good mood, and tapping her fingers on my desk to hurry me through my diary. 'That property developer – he could be very important. What can you do? Eleventh, twelfth, say? Morning?'

'Yes, whatever suits.' I can tell the donor has impressed my boss.

Mary Jane takes out a small powder compact and dabs at her nose. 'I'm going to soften him up for you: we're having lunch. Well, speak of the devil!' She emits a weird, girly giggle. Anjie and I stare at each other: Mary Jane Thompson is trying to flirt!

I swivel in my chair to see the object of her attentions – and find myself face to face with James Weston.

I can't believe it: James, my first ever boyfriend. James, the man I once thought I would marry.

'Harriet Tenant!' He smiles down at me. 'You – here!'

I sit as if turned to stone – or back to the shy eighteen-year-old who all those years ago felt herself being watched by a handsome student across the crowded cafeteria.

'You know her?' Mary Jane sounds amazed.

'We haven't seen each other in fifteen years.'

I feel myself blush under his gaze: 'Ye-yes, something like that.'

His eyes move up to the wall behind me and I am painfully aware of the Worker Bee poster. Then, seeking my gaze: 'You look exactly the same.'

I smile, unconvinced. 'You too.'

'Do you live around here?'

'Yes. I, we, live on Elton Road. It's Clapham North. The less expensive bit.' I feel I'm babbling, betraying my penury and my husband's failure to keep me in style.

'We should catch up – what about a coffee next week?'

I nod and try to smile.

'James –' Mary Jane is impatient '– we'd better go, they don't hold reservations long.'

'I'll ring you.' James waves me and Anjie goodbye as he follows Mary Jane. At the door he turns back to me: 'I suppose we'll be seeing a lot of each other now.'

Only when the door has shut behind him do I remember that, the last time we met, James told me I had betrayed him and he never wanted to set eyes on me again.

6

'You're better off without these people.' Igor, Ilona's new boyfriend, looms menacingly over our threshold. 'You can stay at my place until we get you sorted.' With his long black hair loose on his shoulders, his bomber jacket and big knuckle-duster hands, he looks scary and the boys are wide-eyed with nervous excitement.

Ilona stomps up and down the stairs. 'She is angry because she have no sex life,' she sobs, looking daggers at me. 'She jealous of me.'

I say nothing and try to quash a sneaking suspicion that there may be an element of truth in my over-sexed, man-eating au pair's accusation. Her stream of admirers has certainly brought home to me my flagging sex life.

Guy remains oblivious to these attacks on our conjugal life. He is eating his porridge while reading to Maisie. Mercifully, our toddler seems to be listening to *The Little Red Engine* rather than her au pair's sobs. I stand, helpless, humiliated and slightly guilty, by the door, trying not to study the tattoo that snakes its way up Igor's neck. Ilona gives me one last look of contempt, and then they're gone.

Within twenty-four hours I'm a wreck. I've met Ludmila, who speaks two words of English: 'No understand'; Andrea, who is allergic to Rufus; Anya, who won't look me in the eye; and Sacha, who wears a stud in her nose and some strange metal staple in her cheek.

I'm almost tempted to call the whole thing off and promise Ilona and Igor a white wedding if she'll come back.

What's worse, the roof has started leaking in earnest, and the man from the roofing company came down the ladder shaking his head, and asking what 'cowboys' were responsible for 'that lot up there'. We're still waiting for his estimate.

And it's half-term. The boys start off cheerful and buzzing with energy and plans. They spend most of breakfast reading the job ads at the back of the papers.

'Mum, look! You could be Head of Human Resources at the Schools Trust – seventy thousand pounds starting salary.' 'Dad, there's an ad for Development Director of the White Hart Theatre Company – thirty thousand pounds. It says writing skills required. You'd be brilliant!'

I watch my sons vie with one another to come up with the most appealing post and feel guilty that their parents' financial difficulties should be so obvious to them. When I was growing up, I don't remember ever hearing my parents discuss money, and I didn't realize it could be a subject of tension and conflict until my father's death and the question marks over his will.

But here are my boys, trying to find something remunerative for their parents to work in. I feel I have failed to protect their childhood from the harsh realities of our financial straits.

Guy, however, seems to think it normal that our children should take an interest in our income stream. 'It would be brilliant, boys,' he says, looking over their shoulder at the papers. 'But, frankly, I don't think drama is my strong suit. Let's wait and see if that nice television lady rings.'

The job-seekers game soon palls, in any case, and Alex and Tom sink into a sulk. Alex, because Louie, his new best friend at the Griffin, whose invitation to Tuscany we had to turn down, has emailed him boasting about water skiing. Tom is in a foul mood because Alex is bragging about being in the First XV and the excitements of boarding school.

Both are cross, too, because we have to forgo the traditional half-term in Somerset with the Carew grandparents: I have to be here to interview Ilona's would-be successors.

This has not gone down well with the grandparents.

'But the children *need* fresh air! Can't you stay on your own and interview these girls?' Cecily Carew says crossly.

Guy, too, feels cheated of his break at the homestead. He only cheers up when, just before lunch, Archie rings.

'Hmmm, is that Harriet? Archie here. Yes, yes, Cecily and I were just wondering: we're coming up for a funeral next week ... No, no, old friend from army days. We could, of course, stay at the club, but ...'

I gulp. Oh no, not the in-laws! Not here, when we have no au pair, the children are running wild and the roof is leaking. But I look at the boys, spilling cereal on to the tabletop, and at Guy, immersed in the paper. I've cheated them of their grandparents because of the search for Ilona's successor, and I know they're disappointed. So I swallow my reservations and take my cue.

'Of course you must stay with us. Which night did you say?'

'Yippee!! Grandpa and Granny!' The boys reward me with a cheer.

'Darling, you're a star, you really are.' Guy rewards me with a kiss on the cheek and the promise to take the boys to the Laser-Quest in Tooting Bec.

This leaves me with Maisie, who is easy and pliable and as yet unaware of the change in her life. We read after lunch, and then, as soon as she takes her nap, I'm free to think about James Weston.

Is he married – and to whom? Does he really think I looked the same, or at least, not *that* different? Does he live around the corner? The prospect of bumping into my ex at Tesco's gives rise to horrific visions. Me, hair greasy and roots showing, wearing the size-12 jeans that really are a bit too tight, and the T-shirt that has a magic marker squiggly on the left breast, being spotted by a shocked-looking James. Or Guy and me, standing in the frozen meats aisle, arguing over what to buy while James rolls past, his trolley filled with champagne, exotic fruits and an expensive box of chocolates. Or the children and me – Maisie in her buggy, the boys acting up on either side of me – taking up most of the pavement on the High Street, and drawing attention to ourselves as Alex and Tom bicker and demand a gizmo they've spotted in the shop window.

'Oh, are they yours?' James asks me with a raised eyebrow.

* * *

'Hi.' I ring Charlotte. 'Can you talk?'

'Oooooooooooooh, I'd forgotten how awful you feel at the beginning,' Charlotte moans. 'I've been sick every morning and the homeopath I'm seeing can't do a thing for me and we're supposed to fly to Positano tomorrow and …'

I let her go on for a few minutes, then: 'Guess who I saw the other day.'

'Joanna Lumley in her amazing cape again?'

'No.' I pause for effect. 'James.'

'What?!! James Weston? *The* James?' Charlotte's excitement is gratifying.

'Yes. Mary Jane thinks he's a huge potential donor for HAC. Charlotte, can you believe it?!'

'Wow. Well, that *is* something. How bizarre! You didn't feel anything still, did you? I mean, the two of you were so perfect together.'

'I don't know what I feel. I was – am – in shock.'

'Have you told Guy?'

It's my turn to be struck dumb. 'Er … No.'

Why haven't I? It's not some guilty secret – I didn't track down James and invite him to get involved in my work; I don't hold a torch for my ex. Yet I have hugged the fact of James to myself as if he were an exorbitantly expensive dress I don't dare admit to buying.

'It will be *very* interesting. Oh no, it's the door. Harry, I have to run because I've got my Chinese herbs man coming for a consultation!'

I ring my mum.

'James Weston! Oh, Harriet!' Mum sounds like a romantic heroine sighing with longing.

'He's become a big property developer – worth millions, according to Mary Jane Thompson. He's volunteering to help out HAC.'

'How extraordinary.'

'I know, it's such a coincidence.'

'It's like it was meant to be.' Again my mother sounds as if she were sighing with disappointed hopes. I wonder if she had thought James the more suitable husband? She was fond of him, certainly. James was wonderful to her as well as me when Dad died while I was going out with him. Was she cross when I chose Guy over him? She never said so, but allowed me to make my own choice all those years ago. Now, knowing that Guy's career failed to take off after *Lonely Hunter* and that I've had to accommodate his family's very different priorities; now, with hindsight, knowing too that James seems to have made his fortune already – does my mum think I made a mistake?

Do I?

'You're going out with that poncy scribbler? Harriet, you'll never be happy with that bloke.' James looks out of the window, his back to me. I can't bear to look up. We're in my room at home, and it's a warm afternoon in April. Through the open window, I can see my mother squatting by the flower bed, weeding with her big grey gardener's gloves on. She is trying to be discreet – giving James and me the opportunity to confront one another. I didn't want this meeting, but he insisted over the telephone: 'Please, Harriet, you owe me.'

Now I sit, picking at the small roses embroidered on my bed spread, trying not to cry. He's just come back from Nigeria, where he's been working on an oil refinery. I haven't seen him since last September because he couldn't come back for Christmas. He's much bigger than I remember him: he dwarfs my little pink room, and his maleness turns it into a frivolous and feminine boudoir.

I steal a look at my bedside table where a photo stands of Guy and me at a dining society's black-tie drinks party. We're in the midst of a group of bright young things. Some of the girls affect long cigarette holders; they wear heavy eye-shadow and lipstick, plunging dresses, and look far more knowing than mere undergraduates. Most of the boys sport Byronic locks and elegant pouts; they look effete rather than athletic, treasured left-overs from another era. You can tell from their supremely self-confident expressions that these youngsters think the world is theirs to play with. Guy and I stand slightly in the foreground, smiling, carefree – and in love.

'Look at you.' James has turned, and seeing the direction of my gaze, picks up the photograph. 'Silly idiots –' he makes a grimace '– so pleased with themselves. Harriet, you don't belong with them!' He holds up the photo, as if it were proof of my wrong-headedness.

'They're just friends, James …' I begin to defend myself and Guy.

'Friends?' he sneers. 'These people have their heads up their own bottoms.'

'You're being unfair,' I protest.

'I'm not.' He turns his back on me again. 'You've betrayed me – and you.'

'Harriet, it's worse than I thought.' I start, guilty, and find Guy beside me in the kitchen. 'The roof man says the repairs will cost two thousand.' Guy's hand rakes through his hair.

'Can it wait, do you think?' I follow Guy into his study. He falls on the chair by the cluttered desk, looking drained. Above him, a row of Carews in uniform stare stoically ahead.

'Not a chance.' He twirls the small Rajastani dagger he uses as a paper cutter.

'We're lucky that bit of the roof hasn't caved in already.'

I swallow hard, gathering courage. 'What about Oliver's offer?' I try to keep my voice light and casual. 'The brochure-writing – remember? He said it would be really well-paid.'

Guy groans and points to the ancient Filofax in front of him. 'Look –' It's open on the 'M' page, where Oliver Mallard fills the top entry. 'I was just going to ring him.'

'Good luck.' I kiss him on the forehead, and return to the kitchen. I know he doesn't want me to witness his humiliating climb-down.

In the sitting room, Alex is practising the wolf-whistle Grandpa Carew taught him. Tom is feeding Rufus toast. Ilona had never been punctilious in her cleaning, but she had insisted on a minimum of tidying up. Without her frosty looks and menacing silences, my family has succumbed to a lazy mess. A tower of newspapers teeters dangerously on a stool; the stuffing from

Rufus's favourite toy, an ancient mouse of Tom's, covers half the sofa; someone's helped themselves to raisins and a few dozen dot the floor or lie squashed into the carpet.

I sigh. 'Boys, how about a hand?'

'Oh, Mu-um, I'm on holiday!' Alex interrupts his whistle practice to let out a long wail. 'Why am I supposed to clean up after my brother?!'

'It'll only take us a minute, and once Maisie's up I'm taking you on a treat.'

I'm not sure I know what that will be, at this point. After last Monday's visit to Laser-Quest, Guy took the children to the zoo yesterday. At £12 each, this turned out to be far more expensive than he had bargained for, and he came back despondent. 'Almost £50 to see a few mangy, moth-eaten beasties roll about in muck!' Worse, he'd taken the children to the petting zoo, and Maisie had been head-butted by a goat and fled wailing. Today is my turn with the children, as I'm not at HAC, but we did the Imperial War Museum last summer, and the Toy Museum too. The V&A's Children Museum is perfect for Maisie, but the boys get bored. It's too early for ice-skating and too late for rowing in the park.

'Oliver's not back until tomorrow. I've left a message.' Guy slopes in, sinks into one of the armchairs and lovingly pulls one of Rufus's ears. 'Fingers crossed.'

Maisie screams violently upstairs and I rush to her. When I come back, Guy's on his mobile, doing a vigorous thumbs-up sign. 'Well, that sounds great!' he beams. 'Let's definitely meet up.'

'Oliver?' I mouth, relieved.

Guy shakes his head vigorously. 'Perfect, see you then.'

He switches off the mobile and winks at us. 'That was Zoë.'

'Hmmm?' I can't remember any Zoë.

'Zoë Jenning, remember?' I still look puzzled, so he spells it out: 'The TV producer. Says she's got the head of her production company interested in *Lonely Hunter*! They want to meet for a coffee to discuss it.'

'Hurrah!' I cheer. It isn't as concrete as Oliver's brochure, but I can see Guy is relishing the prospect of a new venture. And a TV series, I reckon, will pay quite well.

Safari Park. Jungle Challenge. The Hunt. Hunters in the Wild. Guy and the boys spend about half an hour casting about for names for the forthcoming series. Only then will they be lured by promises of *Sharks in 3-D* on the IMAX screen at the Science Museum. 'Yeah! Do we see them chew humans, Mum?'

We pile into the 137 bus with Maisie in the buggy. Every brat in Britain is at the Science Museum; their mothers lag behind, dazed with half-term fatigue.

Why do private schools torture us with half-term? It's a week that catches out parents like us: the exotic trip, time off work for the duration, an efficient nanny who plans day-trips to places of interest, a comfortable car to ferry the brood around town – if you can't offer your children these 'necessities', half-term is total hell.

The 3-D Sharks prove so popular that the first available tickets, at £6 each, are not until the 4.45 p.m. showing. I look around desperately for a fun, cheap way to kill two hours. Then: 'Harrods!'

'We're going shopping?!' Tom howls his derision.

I will stoop to anything. 'Krispy Kreme doughnuts, anyone?'

In a flash, we're rushing down the Brompton Road.

After the jostling at the Museum, and despite the Krispy Kremes and Christmas decorations everywhere already, Harrods is heavenly. I don't care that Guy's mother says it's vulgar: garlands of fruit and vegetables adorn the ceilings in the food halls, baskets overflow with figs, mangoes, biscuits and jams. Tiny invisible birds chirp on the soundtrack and the scent of baking bread fills the air. In a corner of the bakery a gingerbread house as tall as Maisie stands on a dais covered with sweets. We are in the horn of plenty.

The boys run ahead and I weave my way with the pushchair through Perfumery and Cosmetics. Will James ring me for that catch-up coffee, I wonder as I loiter about the shiny, gaudy counters with their range of sweet-scented, sweet-coloured products. I suddenly realize I haven't bought a lipstick in years; somehow, my life doesn't demand daily make-up sessions. I make an effort when I go to HAC because, the one time I didn't, Mary Jane wouldn't stop talking about the importance of image. But when I bring the children to school or walk Rufus or go grocery shopping, I don't bother. The prospect of bumping into James outside the office, and of seeing him there on a regular basis, makes all the difference. I guiltily buy a 'Whirl' lip-liner for £9 from the MAC counter, which is just the right kind of rose pink. I look in the mirror. If he rings and we do meet, will James make me feel eighteen again?

'The thing about you, Harriet, is that you look your best without any make-up.'

James is leaning over my shoulder, staring at my reflection in the mirror. I am getting ready for Charlotte's eighteenth birthday party. I've bought the prettiest pale blue dress at Monsoon, nearly matching satin slippers, and I've put my hair up with a dozen tiny combs. I, who have never felt confident about my looks, feel suddenly beautiful. James's eyes tell me that he finds me so, as do his hands on my bare shoulders.

'Just a dab of lipstick?' I raise the pale pink stick to my lips.

James shakes his head. 'You don't need it. Come on,' he urges, 'I want to show you off to the gang.' He draws me up, then pulls me close and begins to kiss me.

'Mummyyyyyyyy, come ON!' Alex tugs my hand, impatient. I blink, blush, and follow him and Tom to the lift, pushing Maisie, who has fallen asleep again in the buggy.

The copper-panelled lift rises silently and smoothly to 'Children on Four'. The boys disappear amid a jungle of soft toys while a life-size orang-utan that costs a paltry £3,499 swings his baby from paw to paw and a miniature white rabbit hops, unstoppable, across the floor.

'Whoa!' Tom is at the controls of a rally racing set. An attendant throws a flying saucer made of foil around the room. I duck low over the buggy as I spot Alex at a computer game.

'I'm concentrating!' He waves me away.

As my children take over toys I can't afford, the attendants smile benevolently. I relax – until three burqas file past me, a loud wolf-whistle in their wake. The burqas twitch, the woman at the cash register frowns and I turn to catch Alex grinning.

'What are you doing?' I hiss.

'Grandpa says they're naked underneath.'

I rush my charges to the Sharks.

7

The five best things about my in-laws' visit:

1. Guy has polished the mahogany monstrosities that the Carews regard as prized heirlooms.

2. Cecily found my long-lost silver bangle while checking the invitations on the mantelpiece. 'Oh, the Dermotts – are they the Worcestershire Dermotts or the Hampshire ones?'

3. Alex, Tom and Maisie, mindful of their grandparents' priorities, say 'please' and 'thank you' without being jabbed in the ribs.

4. I have no time to moon over James Weston.

5. I positively look forward to the office tomorrow.

The five worst things about my in-laws' visit:

1. Cecily's constant remonstrations – 'Guy, darling, you are looking terribly thin'; 'Tom, my love, are you all right? You seem very pale …'; 'Am I right in thinking that Maisie's a bit small for her age …'

2. Alcohol. Archie likes a whisky and soda or three at six, Cecily wants sherry, and both have to have 'proper' wine with dinner. Our weekly budget is over-shot by the time I'm serving the pudding.

3. The Guy Appreciation Society. Everything my husband says or does meets with rapturous looks and comments like 'Oh, Guy, you *are* clever, darling,' from his parents. I, on the other hand, could stand on my head and give birth to Carew triplets while singing 'The British Grenadiers' and no one would comment.

4. Food. Cecily is ultra-competitive about cooking, and greets my kedgeree with the expression of a vegan tasting venison: 'Hmm ... very interesting ... not quite the way I make it ...' She approaches my apple cake as if it were some exotic dish based on sheep's testicles: 'Is it saffron that's made it so yellow? I never did get on with these new-fangled spices ...'

5. Conversation. 'How is the undergrowth then?' Archie Carew asks me of his grandsons. Then, turning to them: 'Has your father told you the story of his great-grand-uncle Claude?' Archie Carew pats his mouth with one of the linen napkins I found, crumpled but clean, and grins. He is a big monument of a man, more impressive from a distance than close up, when his tweed jacket shows wear and his hearing aid is visible.

'No, Grandpa, will you tell us?' Alex knows the routine.

'Well, let me tell you about the night he was with his regiment in France ...' Archie clears his throat and booms his anecdote across the table. The Major's treasure trove of family anecdotes features endless battles; a few naval skirmishes, but mainly this is cavalry and infantry stuff, with a great deal about 'Carew forebears' and 'my regiment' thrown in. Archie's own brave exploits, oddly, never seem to get an airing.

The Carews' glory burned brightest in the time of the later Stuarts, when Great-Great-Great-Grandfather Charles and his younger brother William both acquitted themselves with valour. Since the Battle of the Boyne, though, when William III elevated Charles Carew to general, the family's fortunes have suffered, rather. There have been no more generals. The highest rank has been that of colonel, which Guy's great-uncle Reginald attained; and not much mention in the history books that line Major Carew's gloomy dark green study in Somerset.

None of this curbs Archie's enthusiasm for vivid story-telling. He happily holds forth with detailed accounts of battle plans and military campaigns, tortures suffered and hardships endured.

'As for your great-great-uncle Percy, he was the strongest man in the British army,' says Archie. 'He once came into the mess carrying a polo pony under each arm, for a bet. And he could bend a poker round your neck, just like that.'

I sometimes wonder if it is possible for the Major to discuss anyone who is not long dead and buried.

'Have I told you, darling,' Cecily turns to Guy, 'about the Chestertons' daughter Millie? The poor thing has been stepping out with the most appalling young man, Walter Wyndham – not the Wyndhams we know, but a very different lot, from Kent …'

Archie Carew's dead people are rather more interesting than Cecily's live ones, I decide.

Guy, mindful as always of the blow he struck by refusing to follow his Carew ancestors into either army or navy, tries to make amends by unfurling some of his own heroic adventures.

'When it came to writing about Sindipur in *Rajput* I thought I should visit the old kingdom myself ...' Guy looks from mother to father, and is gratified to see them sitting absolutely riveted. 'I found myself there at night, at the old Moon Palace. The scorpions described by the Maharajah of Kalipur in his diary had gone – but there were huge snakes in their place. One approached, whistling as it moved ...'

'Ooooooooh,' Cecily Carew's hand flutters to the old-fashioned brooch pinned to her cream silk shirt.

'Goodness!' The Major's eyes twinkle and he leans forward.

No one lifts a finger to help me remove the dirty dishes or bring in the pudding, and I think, slightly resentfully, that Guy's parents should ask themselves whether their firstborn might not hurry to finish the magnum opus that he has been writing for the last two years now; and whether his family might not be better off if he worked nine to five rather than pursued adventures in exotic lands.

But then Tom, eyes wide and excited, whispers, 'What did you do, Daddy?' And I realize that my children enjoy these tales as much as my in-laws do, Tom especially. I sometimes think he sees his father as the grown-up, real-life version of the fictional heroes of his favourite books, Jennings and Alex Rider and Young Bond.

Alex, by contrast, is already old enough to measure the gap between his father's enthusiastic talk and his achievements. Sometimes, when Guy dreams out loud about how Zoë Jenning, whom he has yet to hear from, will make a six-part series based on his books, or an African chieftain will thank him with a priceless treasure, or Martin Scorsese will ring from Hollywood and ask to base a film on Guy's adventures in Africa, my eldest catches my eye. I watch him now as he smiles – he is still indulgent with, rather than irritated by, his father. Long may it stay that way.

By ten o clock, though, I am cross with everyone and cross-eyed with the effort of keeping up with all the Reggies and Perrys and Berties, not to mention the Udaipurs and Sindipurs and Dungarpurs being batted about the table.

My mother-in-law suddenly insists on 'giving me a hand' and carries a pile of dirty dishes behind me into the kitchen. I cringe at the prospect of her snooping around. Her own kitchen is not only spotless but perfectly organized, with rows of spices in alphabetical order, a few cereal boxes in ranks of descending height, and decorative tins for everything from flour to biscuits. I look helplessly at our mess. Maisie's plate and beaker still sit, dirty, on the table; a cupboard door is open, betraying my higgledy-piggledy collection of spice jars and tins of food. The bag of flour is slightly ripped and a white trail leads from cabinet to counter.

'I'm afraid it's a bit of a mess,' I begin, apologetic. 'We're still looking for an au pair, and minding the children is taking up a lot of my time.'

'And Guy's,' Cecily snaps accusingly. 'He really does have too much on his hands right now.' Then, extracting a greasy oven mitt from the bread basket: 'But don't mind me. I know how difficult most women find it, sitting at the typewriter all day at the office, taking down dictation, being pleasant to the boss – and then rushing home and trying to tidy up. I've been there, you know.'

No matter how often I have tried to explain to my mother-in-law the nature of my work, and the fact that I am not relegated to secretarial duties, she persists in her belief that I work as a secretary at HAC. She herself spent three years as a Wren working as secretary to Admiral (now Lord) Hendrick before settling down with Archie.

'But of course it's so important,' she continues, as she removes one of Maisie's trainers from the fruit-bowl where it sat wedged between the apples and bananas, 'to keep the home quiet and running smoothly for a writer.'

'Yes, of course,' I reply, trying to sound more convinced than I am.

Cecily tilts her head to one side. 'I must say, Harriet …' for a brief moment I think she will follow this with 'that was a delicious supper', or 'you really made an effort, with the candlesticks and the chrysanthemums and the linen napkins'; but my hopes are quickly dashed: 'Isn't it time those boys went to bed?'

'Well, that was very good wine.' The Major looks genuinely pleased as he empties his glass. 'Well done, Guy. I wanted to bring a couple of our bottles up, but couldn't take them to

Bunny's funeral. Poor old Bunny. Pukka chap, really. I remember when …'

Cecily's eyes narrow as they fix on the sideboard in our sitting room. 'Hmmm, perhaps tomorrow I could give you a hand with the furniture, Harriet? This looks as if it could do with a dusting.' She gazes mournfully at yet another Carew treasure I have ruined. The first being her son, of course.

Why is it that my in-laws make me feel such a failure? I have been tested, somehow and at some point, and I have been found deficient in the Carew virtues – army steel, fierce loyalty and respect for Crown, Church and Country.

It was just the same when we first met. Guy had brought me home to their picture-pretty manor house in Somerset for Sunday lunch. From the outset, his parents approached me as if I were a crass, gum-chewing property developer who was eyeing up their precious homestead with a view to turning it into a burger joint. As they ran through their favourite topics of conversation – army life, Oxbridge, schools, Somerset families, bridge – and saw my incomprehension, they swapped worried looks above the lunch-table, and shook my hand so resolutely at the door that I knew they were trying to say 'Goodbye' and not 'See you again soon.'

Tonight, it's the same. It doesn't matter that we're in *my* home and these are *my* children: to the senior Carews, I am an interloper.

'Harry, that was perfect.' Guy stands up. 'I'll load the dishwasher.' He strides forth, bearing a leaning tower of pudding bowls.

'Goodness, you *are* a lucky woman, Harriet!' Cecily looks adoringly at her son. 'I don't think Archie has ever put so much as a glass in our dishwasher.'

'Modern men, Cecily,' Archie says, unconcerned.

'Modern women.' Cecily casts a look in my direction.

'Alex, Tom, say goodnight now – it's way past your bedtime.' I follow my husband into the kitchen.

Once there, I shut the door and breathe a long sigh. 'I'm exhausted.'

'Darling, don't take it to heart. I've told you – after my mum went to meet my father's parents, his mother counted the silver. And look at her now: she's more of a Carew than any of us.'

'Is that what fate has in store for me?' I ask, forlorn.

'It could be worse. You could end up like *your* mother – just kidding!' And Guy dodges the tea towel with which I whip him.

As usual, I feel a pang of guilt at the mention of Mum. She is the least demanding of creatures and, thank God, she is still sprightly and healthy enough for an independent life, and I am not trapped between looking after the children and her. But I feel as if she gets squeezed out of our lives by the Carews, who are constantly on the telephone, in town, or hosting us in Somerset. I resolve to phone her after the in-laws' departure, and to tell her the latest criticisms from 'Her Ladyship', as we call Cecily.

'What about Maisie? Have Granny and Grandpa seen our little bundle?'

'A vague acknowledgment took place,' I tell him, rolling my eyes. For Major Carew and his wife, girls, even their very own granddaughter, are a negligible proposition. Girls didn't forge the Carews' military and naval history, they were not honoured by kings and queens for their valour, and they won't pass on the Carew name to future generations.

Guy looks suitably apologetic. 'Only until tomorrow, Harry.' And he goes back to the sitting room.

Next morning, Archie Carew insists on a cooked breakfast before the journey. 'He's going to Somerset, not Siberia,' I moan to Guy as I fry up eggs, bacon, bread and mushrooms for his father. At the breakfast table, there is grumbling about the temperature in the guests' room, which is in fact Maisie's: all three children had to squash in the boys' room overnight. The energy-saving dim light-bulbs in the reading lamp on the bedside table did not go down very well, nor did the neighbours' meowing cat.

Oh, and Maisie has a runny nose, Alex and Tom bicker, and Guy has a headache because he kept his father company with 'a few wee drams' until one a.m.

Alex is the first to go: he's getting a lift with the McIntyres (parents of Justin and Finn) who live in Battersea and don't seem to mind driving our son to school even though we, without car, cannot repay in kind. He goes round the table, hugging and kissing his grandparents, then us. When I see the love and pride that light the Major's eyes and then Cecily's as they part from their eldest grandchild, I almost forgive them everything. Then I see that I cannot get to the *Telegraph*, as Archie is reading the obituaries, and that Cecily is inspecting the cracked lid on the Spode teapot she gave us a dozen Christmases ago, and I return to anti-Carew mode.

To make up for my trials, I make a second cup of coffee and take it upstairs to my bedroom, to sip on my own. Breathe in deeply, close your eyes: I try to remember the relaxation techniques I picked up from a Paul McKenna tape of Charlotte's. I must take up yoga, I promise myself, or Pilates, which Charlotte swears by. The Holmes Place gym that has just opened round the corner is out of the question, but maybe there are DVDs I could learn from.

I look out of the window down into our neighbour's garden. Lisa, still suntanned from her Barbados holiday, is doing her squats, iPod plugged in, T-shirt tight across her perfect bosom. Lisa would know about any DVD going. In fact, she'd probably have a library's worth, I think with a sigh of envy. My neighbour's figure, her single lifestyle, and her salary make me feel hopelessly inadequate and middle-aged.

All the more so when I see Guy falling over himself to help her replace light-bulbs, carry out heavy rubbish bins, explain the recycling rules. If I had a twenty-four-inch waist and 36-D bust, would my husband remember to take off his muddy shoes in the entrance? Would he finally fix our dripping shower head in the upstairs bathroom?

The grandfather clock in Guy's study sounds and I gulp as I suddenly realize it's eight thirty and Tom will be late if we don't set off immediately.

'Tom!' I call out, and don my trainers and jacket.

I rush down the stairs and see Maisie and Guy, the one sunny and smiley, the other yawning and scowling, setting off for the nursery.

'Hug and a kiss!' Maisie raises her arms, wraps them around my legs and plants a kiss on my right knee. I watch them walk hand in hand down the street and for a moment bask in family love. Then, 'Tom!'

No answer.

'To-o-m!' I call out again as I search the sitting room and the kitchen. Where is he? Then I spot him and his grandfather through the window. I step outside to chivvy him along and see that Major Carew holds a catapult in his hand. Grandfather and grandson are watching a pigeon walk on the wall. They stand stock-still, Archie takes aim and – phwack! – hits the pigeon, which falls to the ground.

'Good shot, Grandpa!' Tom claps his hands furiously.

'Come along, Tom,' I hurry him – worriedly wondering if catapults aren't illegal.

'Did you see, Mum?' my son asks, excited. 'Grandpa and I are practising.'

'Practising for what?'

'We're getting the neighbours' cat when I come home from school.'

'Can you believe it?! My son will get an ASBO and we'll be run out of town if they shoot that cat!' I moan to Charlotte. We're standing at the school gates of St Christopher's – or rather, I stand and Charlotte leans against her Range Rover 4 × 4. The licence plate proclaims CNJ4 EVR, which Charlotte admits is a bit naff, but, 'There's no stopping Jack.' We're waiting for our sons to emerge from the school building – a big, ugly red-brick building from the 1960s, in the shadow of St Christopher's church. But Charlotte won't be fobbed off on Carew Chronicles when what she really wants to know about is the resurfacing of James Weston.

'Come on, what does he look like? Well preserved?'

'Hmmm … the same, really. There's nice laughter lines around the eyes,' I begin dreamily.

Charlotte laughs. 'You sound like a teenager. When are you seeing him again?'

'I don't know.' I try to sound casual, but I've been asking myself that question every day since our shock encounter.

'You watch out, Harriet Tenant!' Charlotte wags her finger at me. 'The ex-factor is very dangerous.'

8

The bursar's letter was short and sharp:

I understand your present difficulties, and as you know I was prepared to make an exception this term. But I'm afraid we cannot make a practice of ignoring deadlines. Next term's fees must be paid on time and in full, otherwise the usual penalties will apply.

I don't get a chance to discuss it properly with Guy until that night in bed.

'Something will turn up, don't you worry.' Beside me, Guy plumps his pillow in a decided manner. 'I'm sure Oliver will come up with another job, since he's let me down on the brochures.'

His sanguine attitude – this, from the man who needs to wear a mouth-guard because he has started grinding his teeth so badly – infuriates me. It's not as though Oliver is in the wrong. Guy was so slow in taking up the offer of writing brochures for *Travel Wise* that Oliver was bound to have found someone else.

'I could talk to Mary Jane.' I roll on to my side to look at him. 'She wants me to do four days a week in any case, and now that Oliver's brochures are not an option, I really think we should consider it. I enjoy HAC.'

'No.' Guy shakes his head. 'I promised you the chance to be Super Mum, and I don't want to take that away from you – or Maisie. She should have you as much as possible, just as the boys did.'

'I could try to bring some of the work home,' I persist. 'A lot of it can be done over the phone and with the computer.'

'You can't work from home. Maisie would never leave you alone, au pair or no au pair. And where would you have a desk? I'm in the study, and there isn't another quiet place in the house.' He sits up. 'We'll sort something. Now sleep: I'm dead.'

He picks up his mouth-guard from its container on the bedside table, and lies down again, his back to me.

I lie against my pillow, visions of Mr Cullen, the Griffin's bursar, looming over me like an unpleasant ghost. I look up at the ceiling. It's not raining tonight, so there's no drip-drip-drip, but the roofers say we must hurry and get the work done before we find ourselves buried in bricks and mortar. I look at the Carew chest of drawers, chipped during one of the children's games of tag, which Guy was so determined to get fixed before it got worse; and beneath it, I know without seeing, stretches a threadbare carpet from Afghanistan. Oh, Guy, I want to shake him, it's not just for the children's education that we need more money!

I draw comfort only from the way Daniela, our new Czech au pair, is shaping up. At breakfast she manages to give Maisie her porridge and Tom and Alex their cornflakes, stops the milk bottle from splashing all over Tom's history notebooks, and corrects Guy's faltering grasp of Slavic languages. 'No, Mr Caroo, *szukam* in Polish means "I look for". But in Czech –' she blushes '– it is very rude word.' Daniela doesn't mind washing pots and pans, is a dab hand with a duster, thinks hoovering is part of her job description, and thus far has shown no eating disorder, or predilection for bull-necked men with tattoos.

I feel pampered, supported, and understood.

I feel as if I have a wife.

But there is something I've been meaning to tell Guy for twenty-four hours now.

'Darling,' I address the *Telegraph* that he holds up at the breakfast table, 'do you remember James Weston?'

'Your ex?' comes from behind the paper.

'He came to the office the other day. The oddest coincidence: he's going to do something with HAC. And –' I keep my voice noncommittal '– he's asked me for a catch-up coffee this morning.'

'That'll be nice, dear.' Guy turns a page. 'Did you see? Chuffer Cowan's died. Friend of Dad's. Hope if they come up for the funeral they can find room at the club.'

* * *

I've cleared my conscience. James rang yesterday to arrange our coffee, 11 a.m., at the Café La Lune on the High Street, and I've been in a state about it ever since. My ex wants to catch up with me. Of course, he may be simply trying to clear the air, as we're about to become colleagues. But I think, I hope, that he's curious about my new life, my work, and maybe my marriage. We may have parted on bad terms, but surely I still mean something to James Weston …

I run upstairs to get dressed. I open my cupboard and wish I had been paying more attention to my wardrobe all these years. Charlotte for one would never allow her suitable clothes to dwindle to a Zara black skirt, which I think too formal for morning coffee; an M&S tweed, which looks horribly boxy suddenly; and a floral patterned skirt, a Caroline Charles I found at Oxfam that is slimming but maybe too 'young'? Trousers? I'm too conscious of my hips in them. A dress? I have lots of summer ones, but nothing autumnal. What I want is something chic and slightly cheeky, something that announces to the ex-boyfriend who has done spectacularly well: I'm not doing so bad myself.

And, no matter what my outfit will be today, it's true. My life may not be the swish of a silk skirt and a cloud of expensive scent, which is how I imagined it when growing up; nor is it the wide-open spaces, ruby sunsets and pungent smells of the wild that I had thought Guy would lead me to experience. Yet there is much that is good. The children, my partnership with Guy, my mum still healthy and active, even the Carews, hovering in the background and propping up a sense of tradition and good old army values.

How different it would have been with James. There would be the money, for a start. And I know that my ex, a grammar school boy who loathed any hint of 'snootiness', would never countenance the obsessive gamesmanship of the private school rigmarole. But also James liked to take care of everything, to shield me, as it were, from life's little bumps. I would be sailing smoothly along, rather than at the helm, hands on the tiller with my co-captain, braving the storms.

'Oh, Mummmmmyyyyyyyy –' Tom's wail calls me back to shore.

'What's wrong, pussy cat?'

Tom comes and drags me out of my room. He stands by his bedroom door where Guy marks, every six months or so, their height. Lines in pencil ladder the white door frame: starting with Alex, five years old, and Tom, three and a half, and Maisie last year, close to the bottom; stretching up through to Alex, last half-term, almost reaching my shoulders.

'I haven't grown at all!' Tom's eyes fill with tears and anxiety as he presses his slim and undeniably small frame against the door.

'Oh, darling.' I hug him to my dressing gown and kiss his furrowed brow. 'You only measured yourself at half-term. You can't expect to have grown since then. Wait until your next growth spurt, then you'll show them.'

'Alex was an inch and a half taller when he was ten.'

I knew this was the real worry. My younger son inevitably compares himself with his older, taller and more athletic brother – and hates the result.

'Alex takes after the Carews, darling. Look at Daddy, Grandpa and Nick – all about six foot two, I'd say. You take after my side: the Tenants are a bit shorter, my dad was about five ten.'

Tom looks utterly despairing. 'Why did I have to take after your side of the family?'

I quickly correct myself: 'Maybe six foot – but you may well grow taller than him … It's all part of evolution.' I'm not quite sure about the science behind this, but I seem to have comforted him. 'Hey!' I suddenly catch sight of my watch. 'You're going to be late for school – Daniela's waiting for you downstairs.'

Here I am, guiltily trying to concentrate on what to wear to a reunion with my one and only ex, and my son is obsessing over my gene pool.

I rush back to my room, where I plump for the Caroline Charles and the cream-coloured twin-set that once elicited an unprecedented appreciative comment from Cecily Carew. I check my tights for runs, draw and fill in my lips with my new MAC Whirl lip-liner and apply two coats of mascara. I haven't been this conscious of my appearance since my wedding day. Why does the First Boyfriend have such a hold on you? You shared so many 'firsts' with him: you embarked on a journey and he was the starting point. With him you first enjoyed the status of a couple – a close-knit unit, treated as such by everyone. Studying side by side in the library, sharing a hotel room, giving him a haircut, grocery shopping – everything began with James.

As I grab my coat in the hall I almost squeal with delight. The sitting room is as neat as my mother's sewing basket, with everything in its proper place and not a raisin or stuffed mouse in sight. The newspapers are out in the street, neatly bagged for recycling, the boys' trainers in a neat row, and Rufus is asleep in his basket. Daniela, bless her, has put my house in order. I can't resist crowing, and seek out Guy. But as I'm about to step into his study, I hear him on the phone:

'Dad? Are you sure? It's just that I can't get this roof fixed otherwise. I'll repay you as soon as I can …'

I tiptoe away.

It threatens to pour all through my bicycle ride. 'Don't, please don't,' I urge Mother Nature as I pedal. I don't want my hair frizzing up, after having carefully blow-dried it. Poor Guy. I know how much he hates going to his parents, cap in hand. The Carew seniors seem so unclear about the state of their finances that I'm never quite confident that they have enough money for a carefree retirement. There is Archie's army pension, and the cottage in Lyme Regis; but there is also a roof that needs retiling in the ancient house in Somerset and a summer rental market that requires far more modern appliances than are to be found in the cottage.

'Best to keep the parents in reserve for when we really feel the crunch,' Guy has always said about seeking financial assistance from his parents.

We must have come to the crunch.

I'm at my desk by ten and it seems as if the next hour is the slowest ever. I read my emails and check my watch, make a phone call and check my watch, answer Mary Jane Thompson's queries and check my watch.

I jump when the phone rings: James cancelling? But it's Charlotte.

'I'm back,' she announces. I remember their minibreak in Positano was this weekend. 'Our hotel had the best spa ever – I had an Ayurvedic facial every day. Cannot tell you how good it is for the complexion.'

'Hmmm,' I mutter grumpily. I do wish my best friend would fight the impulse to share every detail of her five-star holidays with me.

'Anyway, I've suddenly remembered a piece of gossip you might be interested in. Do you recall Ella Bryce-Knight, the one who did Art History with me? I bumped into her about a year ago at the Tate. And guess what she told me? James Weston's married to Jasmine Jerome.'

'Jasmine Jerome?' I know the name but can't quite place it.

'Yes, yes, you know –' Charlotte sounds impatient '– she used to be a model and became famous for those Volkswagen car ads, where she bosses around her boyfriend. Remember?'

Vaguely, I do: a long-legged, dark-haired beauty wearing very little keeps barking orders at her short, fat boyfriend. His only consolation is the VW he drives off in.

My only consolation is that those ads are about ten years old and Jasmine Jerome cannot possibly look as beautifully voluptuous now as then. But legs don't shrink and big green eyes don't change colour, I realize.

'Oh no,' I can't help groaning. 'How awful!'

'He's certainly done well for himself,' Charlotte says – a bit gleefully, I think.

'Yes, well, thank you for sharing that. I'm meeting him for coffee in a minute.'

'Say hi from me! Maybe we could all meet up at some point.'

I'm too preoccupied to even ask her about her holiday, and put the phone down with a rushed goodbye.

Anjie can tell something's up and raises an eyebrow. 'You OK?' she asks.

'Er … yes, yes.'

'You look like Posh Spice waiting for a call from Hollywood.' Anjie shakes her head. 'You're a bundle of nerves and that's not good.'

'I know I know. I'm calmer now,' I say, as we sort through the applications for a place on our holiday camps and make our usual piles. 'Over my dead body': the pile for those youths whom even the GP or the social worker recommending them consider 'challenging', i.e. knife-wielding, glue-sniffing budding criminals who think authority figures should be tested, and so run away a few days into their stay at one of our two homes, but not before conducting a shoplifting spree at the nearby village shops. 'Come again?' is the name we give to the pile for those we've rejected before. These are kids who are determined (or whose parents, social worker, counsellor or GP are determined) to get a holiday with us, and will not accept our thumbs-down. They're convinced that, from one year to the next, the HAC panel, made up of the secretaries of the four London and two Manchester branches, will suddenly overlook

Jim's record for bullying, or decide Molly's drug-taking doesn't matter, and will welcome them with open arms. The third pile is 'Bingo!' for those who sound as if they are in need of precisely what we can offer: a fortnight in a rural idyll under the watchful eye of responsible, kind-hearted adults. These are the ones it thrills me to help: boys and girls who long for a break, even if temporary, from the urban life they lead.

Anjie and I work side by side, in silence. Then my mobile phone bleeps a message. James? I now almost want him to cancel. How can I live up to Ms Jerome? But it's Guy: *Hygiene Queen ruined my filing system. Rajput a mess. God!*

My mobile shows me the time: eleven o'clock.

'Off for a coffee,' I tell Anjie and am out the door before she can ask anything.

'Harriet!' James is sitting at a corner table, an espresso in front of him. He looks relaxed, in leather jacket and open-neck shirt. Folded over the chair beside him are a dozen shirts, each in a dry cleaner's plastic sleeve. Jasmine Jerome obviously doesn't waste her time scrubbing her husband's shirt collars.

'It's great to see you. Here, what can I get you?' He's on his feet and courteously drawing out a chair for me.

'Cappuccino?' I venture. As I watch him approach the counter, my phone bleeps: another text message. I dive into my handbag and look. *Czech has manic compulsive disorder. Note cards in alphabetical order now. Murder certain.*

'You must live nearby.' James is back with my cappuccino. I drop the mobile back in my bag. 'I saw you the other day – but I was in the car and couldn't stop.'

I feel a small tremor of alarm: so James *is* my neighbour. And what was I doing, what did I look like, when he spotted me? Was I with Guy? The children?

'I've just moved to the neighbourhood. You had a pushchair – your one and only?'

'Oh no, I've – we've – got three.'

'Three children and you look just the same!'

I blush idiotically.

'Tell me about HAC.' James leans over, in earnest, intense, and at once I step back fifteen years ago, when he never failed to persuade me to do his bidding. 'Can you see a role for me?'

'I ... I think that's up to Mary Jane. She's probably very keen to get you on board. We do need more support: more money, more time.'

'I can give both.' Again, the sheer intensity of the man has me almost backing away from him. 'I love the whole thinking behind HAC – helping children by expanding their horizons. And I bet it does the volunteers a great deal of good.'

'Yes, many are repeat customers.' I twirl my spoon in the cappuccino. I want to know about him, not about his charitable ambitions. Is Jasmine still stunning? Is their house enormous? Does he still see any of our old crowd?

'I always knew you'd end up doing something with charity.'

'You saw me as a do-gooder.' I am slightly depressed at how boring that sounds.

'No bad thing.' He smiles.

My phone bleeps: yet another text message. I grab it and quickly check it to see: *Divine Daniela found missing footnotes on Mutiny. Xxx*

I switch off the phone. For someone who dismisses mobile phones as 'the devil's gadgets' and hardly ever texts, my husband is unusually forthcoming this morning. I flash an apologetic smile at James.

'What about Jasmine – does she still model?'

'Jasmine? We divorced last year. Didn't have any children, so it wasn't too painful,' he says drily.

I gulp, 'I'm sorry.'

'I've got some things right and some things wrong. On the whole, I can't complain.' The expression on his face is as set as it was that morning when he accused me of betrayal. I squirm despite myself. 'James, I …'

'James!' A beaming Mary Jane Thompson marches up. 'Oh –' my boss's face falls '– Harriet. I hope you're debriefing James? I have great plans for this man.' She flashes us a toothy smile. 'Can I get a coffee and join you?'

As Mary Jane approaches the counter, James draws close to me. The blue eyes make me feel slightly breathless.

'Harriet, before she comes back …' James lowers his voice and I feel at once tense and flattered: is he getting all nostalgic?

He takes a paper napkin and hands it to me. 'You have foam whiskers.'

9

'The vicar is coming, the vicar is coming!' I rush about the house picking up toys, brushing Rufus's hair off the cushions, straightening the pictures, and wishing that Daniela were here rather than getting her passport renewed at the Czech Consulate. She's only been gone since eight, but the house has already sunk back into its pre-Daniela mode with children's clothes and soft toys scattered on the sofa, and Guy's books competing with his notepads for space on the floor. Guy piles a dozen books on India into a precarious pile in the corner, then thinks better of it and takes them to his study, allowing half a manuscript of pages to float to the ground in his wake.

'All I ask for is that it looks tidy,' I implore him. 'Oh, I wish Daniela were here!'

Guy doesn't hear me – and no wonder. Three Polish work-ers from the On the Tiles Roofing Company are upstairs in our bedroom, hammering, sawing, drilling and generally carrying on as if the roof is a demolition rather than a reconstruction job. For three days now, they have arrived at dawn and left at sunset, and although I cannot fault them in terms of dedication to the work in hand – they never seem to take those interminable tea breaks that kept our English builders from ever working more than two hours at a time – the noise level couldn't be worse if we lived on the flight path near Heathrow.

Today they've been quarrelling among themselves in voluble tirades of Polish ever since they trooped in.

I almost welcome the disruption that fixing the roof has brought to our lives. This way, at least, I cannot sit and mull over, day after day, how James Weston's reappearance has shaken my world. I feel like a figurine, an ice-skater in a red skirt, or a snowman with a carrot as a nose, in one of those plastic snow scenes that go from clear to unstoppable flurries of snow with the flick of a wrist.

Mary Jane Thompson is transformed. She skips about the office like a Walt Disney princess, all smiles and soft cooings. Gone are the boxy suits and sensible shoes that made her look older than her years; now she opts for Diane von Furstenberg wrap-arounds and coquettish peep-toe shoes with heels. Her hair is still in the shape of handlebars, but her lipstick is a deep scarlet, with matching nails. She keeps dashing out for what she calls 'a confabulation' with James, leaving me and Anjie to our own devices.

Anjie, to whom I've explained my past with James, has great fun teasing him mercilessly about Mary Jane's obsession. 'Well, if it isn't teacher's pet!' she greets him when he rings. 'The Boss wants you-hoooo!' she calls out when he comes to the office two to three times a week. And she gives him a big wicked grin as she announces his arrival on the intercom: 'Mary Jane, sorry to disturb you, but Mr Weston is here.'

'He looks a bit like a younger version of John Nettles, doesn't he?' she muses as we wait for him and Mary Jane to emerge from Fortress Thompson. 'Or an older Brad Pitt ... Robert Redford with a bit more height ... You know what they say, though: you have to watch the handsome ones. Look at my William: my mama told me that, if I was going to fall for his big brown eyes, I'd have to keep him on a short lead or else.'

I refuse to be drawn. For me, James's return in my life has prompted a great deal of stock-taking. He thinks it splendid that I am working for a charity – but why do I feel so useless here? Should I confront Mary Jane, and argue that I be given some more responsibilities? Is it only since James's arrival that I seem to mind about the way I am pushed, pulled and shoved by children and husband from morning till night, left with only the shreds of the day to call my own?

'For goodness' sake, Harriet, hide Alex's Griffin class photo,' Guy shouts as he moves the sofa back to its usual place. Maisie was doing belly-flops on it this morning, which moved it about a metre from the wall. 'If he finds out we have a son at private school, he'll wonder why on earth we need to put Maisie in a state school.'

I quickly pull the Griffin photo from the mantelpiece.

Bang! Boom! It sounds as if the roof has caved in upstairs.

'Should we go and check?' I ask anxiously.

'Nah – leave them at it.' Guy pushes his papers and a sock and a couple of old magazines into the corner cabinet, and wedges the door shut with an effort. 'We should win a lot of Brownie points with your Christmas bazaar volunteering this year.'

'Don't remind me,' I sigh. It's all Charlotte's fault. She had been the volunteer, but roped me in, in her stead, by pleading morning sickness, fatigue and swollen ankles.

'I've had to get Dr Chang to prepare me a special concoction of ginseng and quo dong to give me energy,' she wailed on the phone. I worry about the baby, who will be called Summer, 'whether it's a boy or a girl'. Charlotte is adamant about complementing Dr Chang's strange potions with Ayurvedic medicines, has ordered a crystal for the nursery, and is insisting on a home birth, complete with birthing pool.

'If you're my friend,' Charlotte moaned, 'you'll take it on.' I am, and do, and have already spent two one-hour sessions listening to Alicia Byam-Shaw explaining the difference between the regular Christmas Pudding at £6 and the deluxe one at £10: more currants but also about an ounce and a half more Brazil nuts and almonds, and two of dried apricots and dates.

The post tumbles on to the floor through the letterbox. 'I'll sort the post if you put on a decent jumper,' I call out as I pick up the letters and catalogues. No bills, Hallelujah! As Guy disappears upstairs I spot an envelope with familiar handwriting. *James Weston requests the pleasure of your company for drinks on 19 December 2007, six thirty onwards.* I check the address – the millionaires' corner of Wandsworth – and that Guy is invited too – he is – and then allow the butterflies free range in my stomach.

The doorbell rings. Quickly I tuck my invitation into my skirt pocket and open the door for the Reverend Michael Thwaites.

'Good morning … er … Father Michael.' Guy, still pulling down his navy-blue jumper, shakes the vicar's hand and leads him in.

'Oh no, not Father.' The vicar stands in our hallway, white head shaking. Guy and I look at one another, petrified: is this a huge faux pas? Has it given away the fact that we are not pious regulars at St Christopher's? How else are we to address the man of the cloth?

The Reverend Michael Thwaites removes his drab and torn Barbour. 'Mike will do. I like to be informal.'

Huge sigh of relief from Guy.

'Some coffee, er, Mike?' I ask as he flops into the flowered embrace of one of our chintz armchairs.

'That would be lovely, Henrietta.' His dog collar hardly shows above the thick jumper he has on.

'Um?'

'Harriet, actually,' Guy says frostily. I fix him with a warning look. I want him on best behaviour with the man who can get our daughter into the parish school.

'It's enough to make me a heathen!' Guy snorted when Eliza Walsh, governor of St Christopher's, told us last Monday that the school continues to be over-subscribed and plans to ask parents of would-be students for proof of regular church attendance. Guy had joined Tom and me on our cycle across the common and we'd bumped into Eliza at the school gates. She explained the new policy while cleaning out the old newspapers, dog hair, sticky sweets from her 4 × 4.

'Once you put your child down for a place –' Eliza jiggled and pawed the floor, looking like a terrier digging up a bone '– you will be issued with little paper squares with your family ID number on them. You drop one into the collection bag every Sunday.' She thought it eminently sensible: 'It's the only way to sort the sheep from the goats.'

'Baah,' bleated Guy, rolling his eyes at me behind Eliza's back as she used her car keys to scrape chewing gum off the back seat.

Because Alex was, and Tom is, at St Christopher's, we always assumed that Maisie was a shoo-in for the school. As a result, our half-hearted church attendance has dwindled to little more than the traditional hatch, match and dispatch. But now, as Guy puts it, 'the Bible bobbies are on to us.'

Not that St Christopher's has proved perfect. Alex did well, but that was despite rather than because of the school. St Christopher's has been slipping over the past few years and SATs results last year were mediocre. Still, it is far better than the other state schools around here: the SATs may not be top notch, but they're well above those of the rest, and the Ofsted report praises its maths and sciences results; and St Christopher's children pay attention when a teacher walks into the room, rather than hiss or jeer at them; they open the door for me on the days I come to deliver or pick up Tom with Maisie in her pushchair; and there's never been an incident of a child carrying a knife, or drugs. And St Christopher's is free.

'There are far too many families who frankly aren't real Christians,' Eliza went on, shaking out a hairy blanket from the back of the car. This is undeniably true. Just as at the Griffin there are plenty of parents who purport to believe in state-funded education but still educate their children privately, so at St Christopher's many parents only look in at church at Christmas and Easter – if then. 'Why should they benefit from our schooling?' Eliza asked, indignant.

'Terrible hypocrites!' Guy agreed, hypocritically.

'Let's have the vicar round for supper,' I suggested to Guy as we cycled back home.

In the event, 'Mike' was fully booked until Twelfth Night. 'This shows,' Guy groaned, 'what we're up against.' But he did think he could fit us in for a coffee before lunch on Wednesday.

'Lovely coffee, thank you, Gus.'

'It's Guy,' snaps Guy.

'Ah yes, of course.' The vicar nods his white head.

From upstairs, we hear what sounds like a mortar attack.

'Sorry, Fath—, I mean Michael,' Guy explains, 'we're having our roof fixed.' The vicar nods wisely, as if to say, *These things are sent to test us.*

'Some chocolates?' I am pole-axed by Guy's furious look. The chocolates are the expensive handmade Belgian ones that Lisa, our neighbour, gave us for looking after her house. I ignore him: we need to win over the vicar for Maisie's sake.

'And you write, I seem to remember, Gus. Books on wildlife, isn't it?'

Guy at this point is indeed doing a very good imitation of wildlife. 'Calm down,' I mouth to him, as I see him ready to roar.

He takes a deep breath: 'Travel, actually – and it is Guy, as in Fawkes.'

The vicar helps himself to another chocolate while Guy drags me by the elbow into the kitchen. 'Look,' he says through gritted teeth, 'all of this is in vain if that God-botherer gets our names wrong!'

'Well,' I hiss back, 'we've got to get Maisie in or it's the comp down the road.'

I follow him back into the sitting room. The vicar, oblivious to our disappearance, is happily smacking his lips.

'Delicious, simply delicious.' He beams at us. 'Now, Guy, tell me – are you a regular at St Christopher's?'

'Er … well, Mike. We try to come most Sundays.'

'Good good.' The vicar settles back comfortably into our armchair, one hand on each knee. 'And tell me, truthfully, what do you think of my sermons? As a writer, I mean. I would value your judgement enormously – any tips you could give me would be immensely appreciated.'

'Well, er …' Guy's face and neck have grown scarlet. 'Er, always good to throw in a joke at the beginning: gets people warmed up, you know.'

'I try.' The vicar nods vigorously. 'I try.'

I try not to laugh as I watch my husband scratch his head for some vestiges of Sunday school memories.

'And … er … an anecdote or two.' Guy is positively sweating. 'A bit of a modern-day parable, if you will … You know, like the Good Samaritan, or the Tower of Babel …'

'Yes, well, I find St Luke's Gospel most helpful.' The Reverend Thwaites slurps his coffee. 'I often analyse the parable about the blind leading the blind – "Let me pull out the mote that is in your eye."'

'Absolutely, yes … Hmm … Bound to get people thinking …' Guy is flailing desperately. He casts a beseeching look in my direction, but I ignore him, instead sitting quite still on the sofa beside him, secretly savouring the prospect of Christmas drinks at James's. I'll see where he lives, and get an idea about his past life with Jasmine Jerome and his present life on his own; I may meet old chums from our Bristol days, I may even see his parents again.

'Helen, I understand we can count on you for the school's Christmas bazaar next month.'

'Yes, of course.' I smile weakly at the vicar.

'Oh, that is so kind. I have found a core group of very dedicated women to help. But another pair of hands –'

He is interrupted in mid-flow by what sounds like an explosion.

'What was that?!' Our vicar looks alarmed.

'I'm gonna keeeell you, you vodka-soaked son of a whore!' One of our builders comes galloping down the stairs. As the vicar stares open-mouthed, the Pole bursts into the sitting room. 'I keeeell him, that bastard sheet-head!' he roars.

'I don't think Mike will be forgetting us in a hurry,' Guy whispers.

10

'I've thought of a title already: *Big Game*. Like it?' On our sofa, Zoë Jenning crosses her long, slim, jean-clad legs.

I'm just back from cycling Tom to St Christopher's. My bike helmet is stuck to my sweaty hair, my jeans are rolled up and I'm wearing a fleece borrowed from Alex. In front of me are a trendily dressed man with a shaven head and Zoë, looking much prettier than I remembered.

'That's great!' Guy beams. 'Harriet, you remember Zoë. And this is Ross Stewart, who heads Rainbow Productions.'

'Hullo.' I try to muster some enthusiasm, but my hair is stuck in the strap of the bicycle helmet.

'Hullo.' The television people turn to me and give me an indifferent look while I yank a few more strands free.

'We see this as a big bold series with a strong, idiosyncratic authorial voice. Yours!' Ross Stewart sits at the edge of our armchair, leaning towards Guy. 'We want you to feel totally free to say whatever you want, no matter how eccentric.'

Guy grins as he looks from Zoë and Ross to me.

'If you don't like something, say it! If you think all the new environmental issues are a waste of time, say so.' Guy nods vigorously. 'If you think there's too much fuss being made about endangered species, tell us.' Guy nods, but with rather less conviction. 'If you find yourself calling the locals savages or …'

'Hold on –' Guy shakes his head, suddenly frowning. 'I don't think of the locals as savages.'

'Of course not,' Zoë quickly interjects, 'Ross just means that you should feel free to be yourself. Because it's Guy Carew's opinion we want, Guy Carew's expertise we're tapping for the viewers.'

'Yes, yes!' Ross is impatient. 'The important thing to get across is that you're not a guilt-ridden, apologetic enemy of the Empire going back to Kenya. You see yourself as knowing Africa better than most Africans do.'

I look at Guy. I don't like Ross's take on *Lonely Hunter*.

'Er, actually, in the book I poke fun at a group of British safari hunters who come out to Kenya and think they know best.'

'Yes, yes, I'm about to read your book, I know from Zoë it's fab.'

I wonder why my husband is not putting up more resistance, but then look up to see his expression. He's eager, wide-eyed, and obviously chomping at the bit to do this television series. If he has to sup with the devil in order to do so, Guy will just bring along a very long spoon.

I'm uncomfortable, though, listening in on their work discussion, and I slip into the kitchen. Through the window I see

Lisa getting into her sporty BMW. It's late for the City, but then last night she held a party. She was careful to invite us, and Guy and I, armed with a bottle of wine, had dutifully popped next door for a drink and a look. Sleek men in jeans and open-necked polo shirts talked to leggy women in LBDs. Everyone drank and the music was outrageously loud. Most depressing of all, as Guy and I bitterly noted when we stole away at nine p.m., everyone was younger and slimmer and, judging by the Rolex watches and stunning jewellery and flash cars parked outside, richer than us.

'Everyone's into travelling these days. I can see you really making it big,' Zoë trills from the sitting room. 'A kind of younger version of Michael Palin.'

'Michael Palin?!' Guy is really beside himself.

'It'll be a lot of work,' Ross's flat voice puts in. 'Three hour-long episodes means, well, about nine months' work. And in Africa, everything is slow.'

'Yes. Well, I'll need to rush to finish my book.' Guy is loving the dilemma posed by his position: finishing that obvious bestseller *Rajput* over telly fame; or becoming a celebrity and postponing the serious literary plaudits he would of course get once his magnum opus was finished.

Don't be so cynical, I chide myself: for once, Guy is right to think big.

This time, it might really happen, I think a few days later as I turn the bicycle, with Maisie fastened in the baby seat, out of our street. Zoë and Ross have already sent Guy a contract, and proposed a schedule: the first trip is set for January.

I pedal hard: I'm late for Maisie's playgroup. The Carews have never been coochy-coo in their child-rearing. Hugs, kisses, caresses are seen as suspect foreign currency, to be thrown at the 'bambinos', but not for our lot. Generations of army and navy fathers, and uncles and grandfathers, have taught the Carew offspring to rely on their own strength, courage and grit, and uphold the code of honour that taught that tears were a sign of weakness and complaints of meanness. Feminine virtues of sympathy and compassion are frowned upon as spineless. 'The firm smack of discipline' is the cure for everything from a temper tantrum to a runny nose. And although Guy is as protective and compassionate as I am when one of our lot is in trouble, any grandchild who approaches Grandpa Carew with a woe is regaled with tales of suffering in Balaclava, Flanders or Korea.

'Your great-great-uncle Reggie nearly bled to death, but he didn't stir, didn't moan, so much so that the nurses took him for dead and were about to cart him off with the corpses ...'
'Your great-grandfather always used to say, "Chin up, chest out, and breathe in deeply. Best way to overcome a little discomfort."'

So Maisie's playgroup, with its pampered toddlers and clucking mummies, is a small act of rebellion, one that my mum heartily endorses. Except this morning I feel more of a wreck than a rebel as I turn the bicycle into the street where the playgroup is meeting today, and encounter a sudden downpour. I want to weep, and not only because of the mixture of rain and sleet that pelts us both. Daniela and Guy quarrelled this morning because he could not find his rolodex with the genealogical trees of the Rajput dynasties and blamed the 'Hygiene Queen'. This had Daniela in tears, which didn't stop even when Guy found the rolodex, of course, under his Afghan blanket in a corner of the daybed in his study, and apologized profusely to her.

Plus, Alex wants to join his rugby team-mates in South Africa and swears he will contribute all of his pocket money to the trip. But at £1 a week, this won't cover the price of his socks. Guy has done all the sums, and we simply can't afford it. I've left Guy sitting at his desk, head in hands, trying to figure out whom he could moonlight for, in order to fulfil his son's Christmas wish.

To cap it all, I'm still cross with Charlotte for inviting me to her new house in Chelsea to attend the feng shui ceremony to 'christen' it. The house boasts four bedrooms, three bathrooms and a pocket handkerchief of grass. It is a skinny, pretty pink thing in a row of pastel-coloured houses off the King's Road. It's the kind of place Charlotte and I used to bike past on our way to waiting on tables at the Chelsea Arts Club. A mulberry tree stands wide and round in the garden, and the street is quiet and quaint and, Charlotte tells me, full of Americans and Russians. The house fills me with envy; the feng shui guru with despair: how *can* my best friend believe in this nonsense? The woman, a mass of black curls, baggy trousers and more beads than the whole of Accessorize, explains to Charlotte where each piece of furniture must be placed, and warns her that she will have to move two internal doors in order to chase away the unhappy spirits of the last owner. She then gives me her card (Faye@FengShui.com) and tells me that Charlotte thinks my home may benefit from the same treatment.

I lock my bicycle to the Moorfields' newly whitewashed fence. Maisie's church playgroup doesn't meet on Fridays, but some mums take turns to host what Allie Moorfield tweely calls a 'babies-together'.

'You're wet!' Allie follows this insight with a flurry of kindness involving white fluffy towels, an offer of mint tea for me and a bottle of warm milk for Maisie.

'Goat or soya?' Allie asks. As she steers us from the elegant ultra-modern sitting room with whitewashed walls, steel sculptures and odd installations, up the deeply carpeted stairs to the cosy yellow nursery, Allie babbles about Tamara's latest allergy tests.

Upstairs three perfect specimens of motherhood, hair glossy and faces uncreased, sip mint tea. They sit, surrounded by toddlers and nannies, talking about a new organic butcher and the latest on MMR research. As I usually have Daniela take Maisie to her playgroup, I feel as if I were the new girl at school, self-conscious and desperate to please – or at least fit in.

'Have you enrolled Maisie in Toddler Yoga?' Rose, one of the model mums asks me. She looks like one of those crisp cotton, apple-cheeked mummies in the Boden catalogue.

'Hmmm, not yet.' I haven't paid this term's playgroup fees yet.

'The Junior Centre does Mandarin at Two as well,' India, another mum, chips in. She looks languid and glamorous. Her son is the one trying to pull Maisie's ear off. 'A foreign language is essential, according to Elsie.'

'Elsie?' I ask, thinking about infanticide.

'You know, Elsie Livingstone's *Happy Baby, Happy You*. I've stuck to her routine with Milo – 14-5-5, that's the formula and it's brilliantly simple. Fourteen hours' rest, five hours feeding, five hours' expansion.'

'Expansion?'

'Learning, drawing, physical training, being read to.'

Milo has Maisie in a headlock.

'Milo, I think you should let go of Maisie's head,' I urge as sweetly as I can.

'You shouldn't get too protective,' his mummy flashes me a cross look. 'It's really important that children be allowed to express themselves. Repressed children are neurotic children.'

Milo frees Maisie to head-butt another, rather larger boy. I wonder if Elsie has written a book called *Neurotic Baby, Neurotic You*.

'Here are the elevenses!' Allie trills happily. Her Filipina nanny bears a huge tray of biscuits and cups and saucers and bottles. The nannies busy themselves with cookies and milk and their small charges. I suddenly realize I feel no more at home with these perfect mums than I did with Lisa's perfect singles last night.

'Lily has no lactose tolerance either,' Rose is telling Allie. She sits cross-legged on the floor beside me, making me feel at once staid and selfish for hogging the piano bench. Rose turns to look up at me. 'You're doing the grotto for St Christopher's, aren't you?'

'I am.' For the umpteenth time I think resentfully of the burden Charlotte has off-loaded on to me.

Rose nods sympathetically. 'It's a lot of work.'

It certainly is. Coffee mornings have taken up an hour a week for a month now. Ten of us meet in Alicia Byam-Shaw's 'conservatory', in reality a poorly insulated annex stuffed with ferns and spindly rattan furniture. Alicia, who once ran a stationery business, now runs her children's lives and increasingly their school and will accept nothing less than total devotion to the task at hand.

'Last year, the Christmas bazaar took in £1,250 – which really is nothing near our target this year.' Alicia taps her fingers on her accountant's notebook. 'I suggest we raise our prices by fifteen per cent and aim to increase the volume of sales by about ten per cent. Careful marketing should help us attain this. The best thing is for all of you to prepare your own pitch and then let me hear them before the end of our next session. Remember, ladies, I want us to earn the school a healthy profit.'

One mum raises a hand. 'But what kind of a pitch do you want?'

Alicia smiles condescendingly. 'Of course, I realize not all of you are familiar with marketing speak. Let me give you an example: "Help build the new auditorium, buy our delicious mince pies!" Or "Help refurbish our labs, buy a gingerbread cake."'

My duties have included everything from taking in Santa's costume, as Guy is thinner than last year's incumbent, to overseeing the construction of the plywood sleigh, which gave

Tom, who was helping his father, a black thumbnail. I was so exhausted from hanging snowflakes and half a mile of fairy lights (in accordance with the Churches' Child Protection Advisory Service recommendation that the grotto be well lit at all times), that I went to Maisie's nativity play last week without our camera.

Which makes me feel terribly guilty – as does the discovery that Ginny Hartwell, whom I scolded for bringing in a broken electric heater, has been left by her husband, a tenor in the St Christopher's choir, for his Russian secretary.

'Is poor Ginny Hartwell managing?' Rose reads my mind.

'As well as can be expected,' India answers before I can. 'She's lost a stone and she says she doesn't dare drink a drop because she gets so down when she does.'

'Milk, anyone? Soya or goat?' Allie asks brightly, holding two little pitchers shaped like Jersey cows.

'We only do soya in our household.' India stretches her long legs in front of her. 'When Lucy came over with Bertie she didn't know what to do, but of course he took to soya milk like a duck to water.'

'Where *is* Lucy?' Rose, still at my feet, asks. Lucy, I seem to remember, is the pretty mother of cherubic twins in the playgroup.

'Don't you know?' Rose shakes her head and so do I. Allie squats between us. 'She and Geoffrey have split up – in fact, I think it's only a separation, but he found out …'

'About Ian?' India asks. The nannies show absolutely no interest in our scandal-mongering.

'Oooooooh!' Rose's eyes widen.

'Yes.' Allie turns to me to explain: 'Lucy's been having an affair with Ian Turner – you know, the rather dishy divorced father with the boy at St Christopher's – for about a year now. She thought no one had noticed, but I think we all knew, didn't we?'

'It was impossible not to.' India has shaken off her languor and is all animation now. 'His BMW was parked outside her house every morning until after lunch time.'

'How *could* she, with the children so young?' Allie shakes her golden head, more in sorrow than in judgement.

'Everyone's doing it. One in two marriages end in divorce. And, to be fair,' Rose whispers, 'they used to date each other before Geoffrey ever came on the scene. I think she never really got him out of her system.' The Toreador song from *Carmen* interrupts her. 'Sorry,' she whispers and answers her mobile. 'Hullo. Yes. Oh, José, she really needs the full hour, thank you, she is soooo tense these days.' Conversation over, she turns to us with a huge smile. 'If anyone wants the number of the best baby masseur in town …'

I consider the revelation of Lucy's affair as I pedal back home: had she and Ian Turner been at uni together? Had they been a couple for long and then split up because of some unimportant quarrel? Had she married Geoffrey on the rebound – or Ian his wife? Will Geoffrey forgive and forget? And what will happen to the children …

'Oi!' another cyclist exclaims angrily as he speeds past me on the cycle lane. I have been zigzagging carelessly, overcome with visions of adultery and divorce and traumatized children.

* * *

'Three pieces of good news!' Guy greets us cheerfully at the door and takes Maisie in his arms.

'A moonlighting job?' I ask as I undo my cycling helmet.

'Better. Simon rang.' Guy grins at my shock. His agent has made himself scarce for months now. 'He's got me a chapter on Lyme Regis in a coffee-table book about the English seaside. Silly money and not much work.' He tosses Maisie into the air.

'Daddeeeeeee!' she squeals, delighted.

'Well done, darling!' I clap.

'And if I keep my head down I can finish it by January, before I set off for Kenya.' Guy gives me a happy smile. 'And, second: the roof is finished!'

'Hurrah!!' I cry; no more explosions, wall-trembling rumbles or dust covers!

'The workers have gone home, leaving, I must say, very little mess if a rather large bill.'

'*More* than the two thousand they quoted?' I ask, disbelieving.

'Two thousand six hundred, I fear.'

The Lyme Regis chapter is £4,000: that means the Griffin fees are still left unpaid, I realize.

'And third: Dad has found some long-lost letters from his great-uncles in the Crimean War – and he's decided to write a family history!' Guy's excitement tells me I should be similarly overjoyed, but all I can muster is 'Wonderful' in an unconvincing voice. I don't want more Carew history, I want less, thank you very much. More intrepid campaigns, more exhortations to be a man, more talk of the stiff upper lip and the patriot's duty. How will I save my children from so much pukka propaganda?

'How was playgroup?'

'Lots of soya and yoga for twos mixed in with a bit of scandal,' I say lightly as I make my way to the kitchen.

'Harry, I've been thinking ...' Guy follows me in. 'We could afford to send Alex. If that's his only Christmas present and if the rest of us tighten our belts a bit. '

I note with a thrill of gratitude that Daniela has washed the floor and the chairs are upturned on the table. 'She's forgiven you, then?'

'I told her she was the best instinctive historian I'd ever encountered.'

'The problem is,' I start peeling the carrots and parsnips for lunch, 'Tom wants a PSP – Argos Direct has it for £120, and I'll never be able to take Maisie to the Early Learning Centre again unless we buy her the Living Doll, which is £55. And I want to get Mum that cardigan I saw at Peter Jones ...' Even as I speak, I wonder if I should forfeit the haircut and colouring session I booked at Mario's; it would save £60, which could go towards the cost of our Christmas presents. But I do so want to look my best for James's drinks party – I was planning on a quick look at the hospice shop as well. 'Glamorous' reads the invitation, under 'dress', and I don't have anything to match that description.

I cook us lunch while Guy reads *The Gruffalo* to Maisie. I love the warmth of his voice when he reads to the children, I love the intake of breath with which our daughter greets the perils facing the mouse. I would never ever do anything to upset our family. Those men and women who do, how *can* they risk all this for a bit of … passion? I feel so virtuous that when Guy proposes we open a bottle of wine to toast his fabulous news, I readily consent. I deserve a treat, bathed in a warm glow of family love.

11

'Three pounds for a chance to tell Santa Claus what you want for Christmas!' After a whole day manning Santa's grotto I am chanting my little spiel like an automaton.

'Ho ho ho!' Guy does his belly laugh for the umpteenth time, allowing himself to be photographed with a little girl in bunches. He has shown remarkable fortitude, despite another little girl tugging off his beard and one tubby older boy who kept singing, 'Jingle bells, Santa smells, the real one's got away!' until Guy got up and chased him off.

Poor Guy. He's been up until three or four every morning for a week now, writing an article on the perils of twenty-first-century travel for *All Aboard* magazine. 'Can't afford to let *Rajput* fall behind,' he mutters when I beg him to be a little less hard on himself.

I wonder if, even with his Herculean efforts, we will make it. We need £5,000 for the Griffin's fees in January, plus more than £1,000 to cover all the Christmas expenditures.

* * *

'Sorry, sorry, sorry!' Ginny Hartwell arrives, carrying a cardboard box. 'I know I'm late, but the traffic was horrid! Bloody Christmas shoppers! I've got the extra books.'

I say nothing because of the husband and the Russian secretary, and then I help her tip the books into Santa's sack. Everything looks just right: the sleigh overflows with soft toy reindeers, snowmen and two sacks of coal. The snow machine which Alicia Byam-Shaw donated whirrs loudly and fills the air with extremely realistic flakes. Fairy lights stretch above the grotto and a queue of children snakes from its entrance to the gingerbread stall.

Daniela and the children have come and gone, and we've taken a whopping £400 – 'That's twenty per cent more than the target I'd set for you!' Alicia Byam-Shaw makes a quick calculation and then beams. 'Well done, Harriet!'

The grotto has kept me so busy, what with sewing Guy's costume and finding a new beard to replace the moth-eaten one from previous years, and organizing for toys light enough to sit in the plywood sleigh, that I'm way behind on the Christmas shopping. A subject already fraught with difficulties, given that Alex wants an iPod that costs £160 and Tom wants a PSP for £120. I hate letting Alex down on the iPod: he is gutted, as the rugby team's trip to South Africa has been cancelled due to injuries incurred during the season. And I know we can't let Tom down because his sense of inferiority could not cope with his bigger brother getting his Christmas wish while he had to renounce his.

When the season starts, in October, I always feel as if I'm about to be caught without candles in a black-out; if I were well organized and forward-thinking I would have the whole trying experience sussed. As it is, I stumble from day to day, happy simply to have survived the crisis.

Christmas puts the children in their most competitive mode: 'Mum, why can't I have the PSP? Ludo's mum says he can!' 'Mum, why can't we go skiing? Everyone else at school is!' And other parents too: 'Oh, we got Marina the doll's house this Christmas, she did *so* want one.' 'Hugo is going to sulk if he doesn't get the PlayStation 3, so we gave in, in the end, and got it for him – £460!'

Every gathering seems to involve you offering expensive food or alcohol at your house, or your bringing the same to someone else's. Keeping up the festive tradition is expensive, with the Advent calendar, the Christmas cards, the decorations and the tree. As for the food, even when plain old turkey is the centrepiece, you have to have plum pudding, dates, marzipan, and Swiss chocolates on hand.

'I want a break,' Santa Claus moans through his fluffy beard. Guy stands up slowly, then groans. 'I *knew* it!' One little visitor has left a wet patch on his red velvet knees. 'A lump of coal for the little bugger! And, darling, what about a cup of tea for me?'

'Of course.' I check my watch: half an hour to go before Charlotte and Jack come to pick us up for James's party. 'I'll be a while – I've got to put my make-up on.' The Ladies' in St Christopher's church hall has one tiny rusted mirror and terrible lighting, but it will have to do: I'm on duty here until the bitter end. As is Guy.

* * *

I put on some powder, mascara, and lip gloss. I brush my hair and smile in the mirror: no lipstick on my teeth and nothing in between them – something to watch when you've eaten a slice of Christmas cake with those tiny raisins.

The Christmas Bazaar couldn't have been timed worse for me. It ends at six thirty, which is precisely when James's drinks start. I had really wanted to indulge in the ritual of Getting Ready for a Party: a hot bath with one of Charlotte's oils from my last birthday present, hair done with the hot brush that was my Christmas present from Guy last year and that I've yet to learn to use properly, a spray from the Allure eau de toilette that Mum bought me and trying on at least five or six outfits before choosing the final one.

On the other hand, the bazaar has allowed me very little time to worry about an event that would otherwise have been my sole preoccupation for weeks. I'm about to see James in context. What will the house be like? Will there be signs of Jasmine still? Is he indulging in total bachelorhood?

Even Charlotte has been talking about little else, and managed to get herself a very elegant blue velvet number from JoJo Maman Bébé. 'Pregnant does not mean drab – and I refuse to have Pamela Holt think that I've let myself go!'

Pamela used to be Jack's girlfriend, but ditched him rather cruelly by letter. Charlotte cannot forgive her for making her feel slightly second choice.

As I go in search of tea, I realize I can't blame Charlotte: we're about to see again, at a distance of almost seventeen years, friends and acquaintances and competitors. Why is it that what friends from school or university think of you matters so much? Proving them wrong or living up to their expectations is a driving force in life. What I really, really want tonight is for Lucy Martin to see me and think, 'Wow, she looks almost the same as when we were reading "Ode to a Nightingale" together!' And I'd like Teresa Bredin to sidle up to me with a few put-downs about my lot as a housewife and mum – and for me to smile sweetly and say, 'Ah, but you do know I run a small urban charity, don't you?' I don't believe in little white lies usually, but a university reunion makes them not only acceptable, but downright compulsory.

'There should be two people at all times manning the grotto!' A big-boned blonde huffs at the entrance of the grotto. She scowls at me as I approach Guy with the two cups of tea, and turns to the mother next in the queue. 'You can't be too careful these days,' she says, sotto voce. Then, loudly, 'I think you've been sitting on Santa's knee quite long enough, Annabel! Come along now!'

'I'm not a perv!' Santa Claus jumps up from his armchair, sending little Annabel tumbling, and stomps off. The woman drags Annabel, now howling, from the grotto.

Santa's tubby nemesis pops up grinning from behind the sleigh: 'Jingle bells, Santa smells, the perv has got away!'

It takes me a good ten minutes to calm the 'perv', and hand over our takings to Alicia Byam-Shaw. By the time I have ushered Guy outside to the freezing car park, Charlotte and Jack sit there waiting in the car.

143

'Just change in the car,' I coax Guy as he stomps about in his red velvet suit and hat. Guy doesn't answer and keeps muttering about 'Horrid little monsters'.

'Hullo, HarrietnSanta!' Jack waves cheerfully from behind the wheel. He is driving Charlotte's car: we wouldn't have fit in his Porsche. In fact, I'm not sure Charlotte could fit in most cars: she is huge, far bigger than in earlier pregnancies. Or maybe she just looks that way to me, as I sit in the back and see her voluptuously swelling blue velvet form, so solid that it doesn't budge even when we go over the speed bumps.

'Thank goodness the morning sickness has stopped – careful, Jack, we don't want to take corners so fast,' Charlotte greets us. 'I had Dr Chang make some special ginseng, or do I mean ginger, potion and it's worked wonders. What do you suppose Ellie Brown will make of me pregnant again? And Sophie Rather – remember her, Harriet, the ferret-looking one? Apparently she's got a brood of six.'

I'm so overwhelmed by my best friend's barrage of words that we're almost halfway to James's house before I realize that Guy's not changing into his charcoal grey suit and the reason is that his suit is not with him.

'Oh, Guyyyyy!' I wail. 'What have you done with it?'

'I don't know, darling.' Beside me, Santa Claus shakes his head, and his beard starts peeling away. 'I just stormed out and didn't remember the bag. I think it's at the grotto.'

'Look, do you want us to turn back?' Jack gives us a cross look over his shoulder.

'Yes,' I cry. I can't bear the thought of making an entrance on Santa Claus's arm. I'm about to see people I really wish to impress and instead, here I am, looking like I've dragged in the evening's panto act.

'No,' Guy over-rules me. 'I'll explain that I've been doing my bit for charity.' Then, with a smile in my direction: 'It doesn't matter what I look like – this is your night.'

'Well, we'll now see what the famous James has managed to do,' Jack says, as an attendant waves, showing him where to park. 'I hear he's got a multi-million-pound house with pool. Interesting that a property developer should choose something here, isn't it? I mean, he can afford Chelsea, Belgravia, Hampstead – and he plonks down here. What's that about?'

Guy is trying to stuff his fur-trimmed Santa gloves carefully into his velvet coat pocket.

'You're very good to go with the wife to her ex's,' Jack carries on. 'If Charlotte asked me along to some drinks party given by Ted Wheeler, I can tell you I wouldn't go and I wouldn't be happy if she insisted on going on her own.'

'Oh, Jack, you do go on!' Charlotte laughs as we troop out of the 4 × 4. 'Guy knows he's got nothing to worry about with Harriet. And anyway, he won her, fair and square.'

'This is rather grand, isn't it?' Guy looks up at the huge house before us as we crunch up the gravel path. Every window of the imposing three-storey building shines bright; a huge wreath decorates the door and long ropes of holly festoon the door frame.

'God knows what the wife walked off with,' Jack whispers; Charlotte digs her elbow into his ribs.

A waitress in black uniform lets us in – and doesn't even blink at the sight of Santa Claus. We stand in an entrance hall that is as big as our entire ground floor, under a chandelier that looks like a spectacular firework.

'We-ell!' Charlotte gives me a worried glance, as if to say, 'Are you filled with regret?'

We join another couple handing in their coats. Guy hands in his hat and beard and then, 'Harriet, here,' he helps me out of my coat.

The woman turns around and peers at me:

'Harriet? Oh, Harriet Tenant! I wouldn't have recognized you in a million years!' she says loudly.

I recognize Hilary March instantly: a good-looking super bitch in my year. 'And with Santa Claus in tow!' She smiles falsely then strides past us, husband in her wake. 'Some people always go OTT with the Christmas thing, don't they?'

'Amy!'

'Charlotte – look at you!' Charlotte and Jack stop to catch up with a friend of Charlotte's I don't recognize.

Guy hands me a champagne flute from the silver tray a waiter holds aloft. 'Do you think that's the ex-model wife?' he asks, staring at a huge orange canvas with a woman's bottom etched in black on it.

'Shshshshsh!' I follow him into a grand room with a few artfully arranged pieces of modern furniture: not a Carew-style mahogany monstrosity in sight. I study the larger-than-life bold canvases that decorate the walls and realize that my ex has an extensive and interesting collection of some big-name contemporary painters. For a moment, I feel a lurch: I would love to have collected canvases like these, would love to have met their creators. I sigh, acutely aware of my charity fund-raiser/housewife/mum persona. Vases with three-foot flowers stand tall on the floor, on the mantelpiece, on a glass-topped sideboard. Waiters and waitresses hand around canapés that smell and look delicious, and the guests mill, voices soft. I look around me and I feel as if I were nearsighted: people look vaguely familiar, yet I cannot make them out clearly. Could that distinctly middle-aged-looking woman with sagging breasts and greying hair be the once sylph-like Elizabeth Mason? Could that corpulent bald fellow be John Lundy, Captain of Rugger? And that willowy woman with a ponytail and sunglasses, could that be Sal Brown, who was considered such a nerd among our English lot?

'Does he have children?' Guy asks me. 'James, I mean?'

'No.'

'That explains things.' He raises his flute to the enormous room and its well-ordered perfection. 'No school fees.'

I want to tell him that James was a strictly state school boy, but then think better of it.

'Hey, Harriet!' Anjie waves at me from beside a huge bronze sculpture of a kissing couple. 'Hullo, Guy – you've been Santa Claus at St Christopher's, haven't you? Bless.' I want to hug my colleague for turning my husband's outlandish outfit into a feather in his cap. She looks stunning in a black velvet dress that shows off her curves. Long dreadlocks with bold-coloured beads are gathered in a soft knot at the nape of her neck.

Beside her, her husband grins. 'Hullo, Harriet-from-HAC,' he copies my telephone voice whenever I've rung their home. William is wearing a black jacket with a Chinese collar and looks handsome and trendy. 'It's some pad, isn't it?' He sips from a glass, then gives Anjie a nudge. 'Let's do like them –' And he kisses her, perfectly replicating the pose of the bronze twosome.

'Well hellooooooo, Harriet!' Peter O'Connor, minus lots of hair and plus lots of chins, bear-hugs me. 'You look even better than you did at uni!' I smile up at one of James's best friends. 'So he's forgiven you, has he, for going off with the posh Cambridge git?'

'Peter,' I interrupt hurriedly, 'let me introduce my husband, Guy Carew.' Guy coolly proffers his hand.

'Oh hullo, thought you were part of the entertainment,' Peter murmurs sheepishly. Just as I begin to wonder how I can navigate the next few minutes, a good-looking blonde in a tuxedo materializes beside us.

'Did you say Guy *Carew*?' She smiles at Guy.

'Yes …?' Guy looks taken aback.

'What a coincidence: my partner is working on your programme! Ross says it's going to be a hit. He says you're a real original.' The woman draws closer to Guy. 'Do you know,' she volunteers conspiratorially, 'how the best presenters get rid of their inhibitions?'

Peter and I exchange a look. 'He'll be rooted to the spot for hours to come,' I whisper.

'Then come on, let's see who else is here.' And Peter takes me firmly by the elbow. 'He's done well for himself, hasn't he?' Peter grins as we pass from one huge room to another. A group of carollers gather around the grand piano to sing 'Away in a Manger'.

I suddenly spot James, standing in the middle of the room, talking to a woman in a revealing red dress.

'Here comes trouble!' Peter whispers. I don't understand, and then realize that James is talking to Jasmine Jerome, ex-*Vogue* model and ex-Mrs James Weston. 'I knew he'd invited her, but I can't believe she came.'

We watch as Jasmine sashays off. 'Come along, he'll need cheering up.' Peter pilots me to our host. 'You all right?' he asks James.

'I'm fine, now that Harriet has arrived.' James's admiring blue eyes make me blush. 'Are you enjoying yourself?'

'Very much. I'm very impressed.' I look around the room.

'Oh,' James shrugs, 'a few lucky deals and you're made.' He follows my gaze to the huge Technicolor canvases that hang above the open fireplace. 'Now *that* I am more proud of. I bought some modern pieces I really liked and they've turned out to be worth quite a lot.' He lowers his voice. 'I seem to remember you were quite good at that yourself. Didn't you ever follow that up?'

'Well … I did try for a while at a small art gallery in London. I enjoyed it. But that was before Alex – before our first child … Anyway,' I continue, a bit defensively, 'I'm really enjoying my work at HAC.'

'I'm sure.' James is smiling. 'But –'

Peter is about to melt away discreetly when we're interrupted:

'James!'

We turn to find Mary Jane Thompson, in a plunging wine-coloured dress. The handlebar hair has been swept up in an elaborate hairdo, and as she advances on us, she is beaming a Hollywood-wattage smile.

'Peter,' James says under his breath, 'I can't have that woman corner me again – will you take care of her while I show Harriet around?' James slips his hand under my elbow and we glide away from Mary Jane, who glares, and Peter, who winks.

We enter yet another huge room, full of milling guests.

'It's funny seeing the old gang, isn't it?' He raises his flute at a middle-aged couple who, as they draw nearer, I recognize from Bristol days. 'This kind of catching-up makes you realize you haven't accomplished nearly as much as you set out to do.'

'But you've done brilliantly, James!'

'Property deals don't exactly stretch you.'

We are about to enter another room when James points to the mistletoe above the door: 'Beware, or we'll have to kiss.'

I freeze. He laughs; whether because I took his little joke seriously or to defuse the situation, I'm not sure.

'Well, if you don't, we will!' Jack has pulled Charlotte beneath the leaves and then, pressing against his wife's bump, he kisses her with a loud smack.

'It's a gorgeous house, James, really gorgeous!' Charlotte comes up for air and grins at our host.

James nods, and – am I imagining this? – looks slightly put out that our tête-à-tête has been interrupted.

'My boss moved to Wandsworth last March. It's such a good investment isn't it?' Jack immediately bounds up to James.

Beside me, Charlotte rolls her eyes and pulls me away from the men. Then, lowering her voice: 'It *is* incredible, isn't it? How much do you think he's worth?'

I shake my head. 'Can't even begin to imagine,' I whisper as I look through the four French windows into a floodlit garden.

'You know, I have this really strong feeling' – Charlotte tugs my hand and looks into my eyes – 'that something *big* is going to happen to you. I don't know what – but I'm sure *he* will have something to do with it.'

'Oh, Charlotte, stop it.' I pull my hand away. 'You're being silly,' I say, only half in jest.

'I'm serious! I've got such a strong instinct. And you know my instincts are always right.'

Before I can inform her that I know no such thing, we are surrounded by a group of former friends and we spend the next hour catching up with, and surreptitiously checking out, men and women we remember in their twenties.

At eleven I set off to find Guy and, just as I turn a corner, I hear my name. 'I knew it was Harriet Carew. But honestly, when I saw her, I couldn't believe this was the woman James had been going on about. I mean, did you see her hips?'

Jasmine and I stand, face to face, and she draws herself up to her full, near-six-foot height. The green eyes are still striking, the legs still impossibly long, and she exudes voluptuousness, glamour and femininity all rolled into one.

'Er, hello …' I feebly stretch out my hand for an automatic greeting when suddenly I hear Guy.

'There you are!' I have never been so glad to see my husband. 'Just thanked James for a splendid party. Come on, old thing.'

Guy escorts me out of the room.

'I thought Mrs Weston might belt you at any moment.' Guy wraps his arm around me. 'Recognized her by her bottom –' he points to the naked figure in black ink hanging above us.

12

'Now, peel the sprouts in the sink, Harriet, and cross the stems with that little sharp knife I gave you. You know how, don't you?'

I am standing in the Carews' large and spotless kitchen, beneath shiny copper pots and bouquets of dry herbs. It's a country kitchen worthy of a magazine cover. Delft-style plates line the old-fashioned wooden dresser; labelled white tins hide away such unsightly objects as 'bread' and 'flour' and a white-and-blue gingham tablecloth matches the six plump little chair cushions.

But the crafts-and-cosy look cannot conceal that this is my mother-in-law's domain and, as such, more forbidding than inviting – at least in my eyes. Here, for instance, is a bag of green sprouts by the sink, ready to test my culinary skills. I have already been tested by the potatoes, the sweet potatoes, and the carrots – all of which I have failed to scrub, peel or chop to Cecily's satisfaction. I proved so incompetent at stirring the white sauce for yesterday's cauliflower cheese that I was taken off kitchen duty for the rest of the day. But apart from that brief taste of freedom, I've been at my mother-in-law's beck and call for the past forty-eight hours.

This has not prompted a warm and womanly complicity. Cecily clearly regards me much as a grand cook might have regarded a scullery maid: a wench too heavy-handed to be trusted with anything but the dirty work.

Cecily cooks and cleans to Classic FM, and will sometimes mutter things to herself such as 'Too salty, maybe a pinch of sugar?' or 'That recipe *must* have the wrong amount'. With me, though, she limits her exchanges to: 'Have the boys lost weight since we came to London, Harriet? They do seem terribly thin …' and 'Does Maisie really not read yet? How peculiar, for a Carew: all of them started by the age of five.' I am too humbled by this stage to explain that the boys have both grown since she last inspected them, and that Maisie is three and a half, not five.

I am also feeling blue because last night, after my bath when I indulged in a rare fifteen whole minutes of what Charlotte calls 'me-time', I studied myself in the mirror. Jasmine Jerome was right about my hips: they are the kind they used to call child-bearing but now call fat. They curve out on either side of a stomach that is no longer flat, above thighs that can make no claim to being lean and toned. I probably should never wear trousers, or tight dresses. I sigh. The gym? Not at £40 a month for the Council's high-tech leisure centre – and God alone knows how much for one of those chi-chi places that have space-age machines and Molton Brown liquid soap and body lotion in the Ladies' changing rooms.

I was so sure that those bicycle rides to St Christopher's with Tom were keeping me trim – but I suppose I slow down to talk, and I day-dream on the way back. It's a wonder James so much as looked at me, let alone seemed to like doing so.

Christmas Day at the Carews' always follows a rigid schedule. Despite Midnight Mass, by ten breakfast things must be whisked away from the dining room. 'Can't have people wandering down for breakfast when it suits them,' Cecily snorts. By ten thirty children and grandchildren must set off for an hour's walk. 'Those poor children look so pale –' Cecily shakes her head '– some fresh air will do them good.' From eleven thirty children and grandchildren must entertain themselves while the cook sweats by the Aga barking orders at her 'helper'. 'The thing is, Harriet, I like everything "just so".' Cecily intimidates me from the start. 'I could use a hand, but really, we must do things my way.'

Guy, instead, is allowed to read by the fire, a mug of tea beside him, Rufus snoring at his feet. He is poring through the Carew letters that Archie has unearthed during his trawl through the attic, and every now and then I hear him snort with amusement at some dead Carew's wit, or whistle with appreciation at yet another daring feat by some admirable ancestor. With his worn Tattersall shirt and cords, my husband looks the archetypal county gent, lazing away the hours while the women carry out their duties.

'You need to take it easy, darling.' Cecily has been fussing over her eldest son since the moment we arrived, two days ago. 'You look like a ghost – all that hard work.'

Well, some of the hard work has been down to her. Guy had to spend about two hours scraping Cecily's mince pies off the windows of the sitting room and study yesterday. Armed with a brush and pail, my husband swept away the sticky evidence of his error of judgement – an error due in part to his filial devotion. Yesterday's visit by a group of young carollers had seemed a pleasant interlude, despite Rufus's barking and Grandpa Carew's audible groans when, all too frequently, the youths hit a flat note. The boys had listened silently, perched on the stairs, but Maisie had been unstoppable, belting out 'Away in a Manger' and 'Silent Night' as if she were auditioning for the King's College Choir. When the last carol was sung the carollers, who'd been stomping their feet, as the wind had picked up and it was getting chilly, shut their music books and looked at us expectantly. Guy proffered a plate of his mother's home-made mince pies. Some of the youths stared at him open-mouthed, but others muttered, 'What about a few quid, gov?'

'What a cheek!' Guy thundered. 'These are delicious! Honestly, whatever happened to the Christmas spirit?!' He banged the door shut. Whereupon we heard hissing and whistling outside the door and then thump, thump as the house was pelted with Cecily's lovingly baked pies.

'Hullo. Any chance of a Coke around here?' Nick, Guy's younger brother, rubs the sleep from his eyes. Nick often exasperates with his head-in-the-clouds air, which belies a capacity to make an awful lot of money on the stock market. But at times like this, when I'm stranded in a Carew outpost, surrounded by the clan, I look to him as a soul mate. He is the one ally I have in my battle against Cecily's organizing mania, the one person who doesn't take the Carew Legacy seriously. How his uniformed, mustachioed ancestors must despair of this thirty-three-year-old Carew as he slopes about barefoot, in jeans and V-necked jumper, and flicks open his breakfast can of Coca-Cola.

'Darling, don't you have a proper shirt?' Cecily cries, as she notices his get-up. 'Do make an effort – it's Christmas Day!'

Nick merely shrugs. A man less likely to enlist in the army or navy cannot be found. Nick's idea of a campaign is posters of a half-naked babe advertising beer, while a march would mean inching forth as he sways slightly to the music coming from the iPod stuck in his ears, and his idea of boot camp is … Christmas at home.

'Oh, darling, *must* you drink that foul stuff?' Cecily pulls the turkey out of the Aga and slowly, lovingly bastes it. 'I could rustle up some bacon and eggs …?'

'Nah, thanks, I'll be all right with this –' Nick holds up the tin of Coke. 'Best hair of the dog there is. Where's everyone?' he asks.

'Guy's in the sitting room, reading your father's treasure trove.'

'Is he, now?' Nick and I exchange a look at this proof that for Cecily her firstborn is her idea of 'everyone'. 'General Charles's letters home, or Colonel Hector's?'

'Oh, he has stacks of both. And more.'

Cecily turns to me, accusingly. 'How are those sprouts coming along, Harriet?'

To my shame, I realize I have managed to clean and cross only a fraction. 'Just coming …' I tug frantically at the tight little leaves and wish for the umpteenth time that our holiday calendar could shift so that we did Easter with the Carews but Christmas with my mum. There is less of an emotional investment in Easter, somehow. And yet, I have to admit, the children look forward to Christmas with their Carew grandparents all year. They love the space and the garden, which, although it has not been a white Christmas this year, still looks properly frosted and wintry-bare. They love the great roaring fires that they can help light in the rooms downstairs and the treasure trove of ancient toy soldiers, dolls, tea sets, train sets, Meccano, marbles and even a puppet theatre that fill the nursery upstairs. They love the bedrooms with their low-beamed ceilings and the living rooms with the great windows. They love the field beyond the garden where Farmer Gundy's sheep graze, and the orchard with its plump apple and pear trees. I recognize that, for my three, the Carews' home will be cherished as a favourite childhood memory – and I try to relax.

Bang! A shot resounds, followed by a huge crash. Rufus runs, whimpering, past us. Nick covers his ears and grimaces.

'Oh, I *do* wish the boys would stop that racket!' Cecily shakes her head as she takes over the Brussels sprouts in the sink.

I look out of the kitchen window. I don't dare inform Cecily that her husband is to blame for that big 'bang!' Archie has been letting the boys use his .22 rifle all morning, and set up a pyramid of tin cans as target practice. Mrs Wynn Jones, the neighbour, has already rung once in protest.

'Die, scum!' Alex's voice rings out.

'Nick, will you tell the boys –' But Nick has vanished. Cecily sighs. 'Oh, where has he gone off to now?' She purses her lips. 'Sometimes I wonder if Daisy doesn't deserve our sympathy.'

This is an extraordinary admission from a Carew. It shows just how much Cecily's second son has worried her, from when he was expelled from Wolsingham for smoking dope, through his failing to get into Oxbridge and ultimately having to make do with Sussex, to last summer's acrimonious divorce from wife Daisy, a brassy blonde who claimed to be 'in property' when she was in fact a Foxtons estate agent.

'Perhaps I could lay the table?' I offer as consolation.

'No, don't worry, Harriet, I'll do that.'

'Shall I lay the table, Mother?' Guy comes in, Maisie trailing him.

'Thank you, darling.' Cecily beams at her son. I want to yelp in protest – does she think I don't know which knife goes where? I swallow my indignation and follow my husband into the dining room.

Portraits of four generations of Carews look down on us. The table is tastefully covered with a white linen tablecloth, the furniture is glossy, the silver shines; in a corner the Christmas tree twinkles – white lights only, as the multi-coloured ones are 'common', and only a bit of discreet tinsel. The rest of the decorations are all ancient, hand-made ones, that, as Cecily never tires of explaining, 'have been in the family for decades'.

'You all right, darling?' This is Guy's unspoken admission that staying at his parents' may prove a bit of a strain for me.

'Just about.' I follow him around the table, setting down the silver cutlery.

'The boys are having a whale of a time.' Guy smiles to himself.

'Yes,' I admit. 'Even Tom, who's been out of sorts lately, has perked up.'

'I've been thinking ...' Guy carries a tray of crystal wine glasses, kept locked away for all but the most sacred family occasions '... about poor old James.'

I start guiltily, as I have spent a great deal of time thinking about the same thing myself.

'It's an easy mistake to make, I suppose,' Guy goes on, 'marrying someone glamorous on the outside but nasty on the inside.' He grins at me across the table. 'I'm so glad I married you.'

'Well!' I slap down the beautifully ironed linen napkins. 'I am so glad my dumpy dowdy charm did the trick.'

'Harry, I love you the way you are and ...'

'Guy, will you come and uncork the wine!'

Guy's fumbling defence of his unpardonable slight is interrupted by his mother's call.

I am left fuming – and remembering Charlotte's excitement over her mug of Manic Organic tea the other day:

'Harriet Tenant Carew, you cannot pretend to me that it's all over between you and James!' She is leaning against the counter in her sun-lit, recently completed Chelsea kitchen. It has been carefully set out in accordance with Feng Shui Faye's instructions for better energy. 'It was electric!' Charlotte is stroking her voluminous stomach. 'When the two of you stood together, Jack said he could practically *see* the vibes between you.'

'Oh, Charlotte, don't be silly!' I shake my head, but in spite of myself I smile. 'He is my ex, it would be very odd if there was nothing left between us.'

'He was eating you with his eyes. It's the first time I actually understood that expression.' Charlotte's own eyes are wide with excitement.

'You're romanticizing the whole thing,' I protest, but not too vehemently.

'You just be careful.' Charlotte wags her finger at me. 'Or poor old Guy will get very jealous.'

'He won't – he has his own admirer. The redhead who wants to make a film out of *Lonely Hunter*. She's about ten years younger and two sizes smaller than me.'

'Ah, but there's nothing like an ex suddenly reappearing, unattached and doing extremely well for himself.'

'Lunch is ready!' Cecily calls out as she comes in with two covered tureens. Feet come pounding from every direction – the boys and Archie, Nick and Guy and Maisie and Rufus.

'Wash hands!' Cecily calls out before I can open my mouth, and then we all take our seats.

Lunch takes the best part of three hours. It is delicious, and Cecily, regal between her sons, basks in our repeated compliments. The children behave beautifully – though Alex surreptitiously slips some turkey to Rufus and Maisie at one point lays her head on the table as she's tired after Midnight Mass last night. A look from Granny soon puts a stop to that.

As usual, I don't need to worry about making conversation.

'Nick, I do wish you'd ask Laura Forrester for a drink while you're down, darling.' Cecily looks beseechingly at her younger son. 'She's a pretty girl, and the Forresters have been friends of ours for years … You remember how much you and Guy used to like climbing in their orchard at the Manor House? Such a nice family …'

And: 'Guy, whatever happened to Guppy Leighton? Wasn't his family the Leightons from Wiltshire? I think I saw something about their estate in the Torygraph last week.'

We also have to listen to Grandpa Carew and Guy take turns in regaling us with tales from the great Carew stash of letters. We learn from Archie about Major Reggie Carew, who dreamed of 'coming back to Somerset to tend my apple orchard', whilst in the trenches at the Battle of the Somme. Then Guy tells us about Lieutenant Commander Charles Robert Carew (Chukka), a giant of a man, who complained bitterly of his diet of dry rusks aboard the fleet sent through the Dardanelles at the outbreak of the Crimean War: 'My dear Mother, facing salvo after salvo from the guns of the Tsarist fleet will be, believe me, a trifle compared to masticating these wretched bricks of sawdust.' At which point Archie interrupts to tell us how, a few months later, Chukka's younger brother, Captain Percy Carew, was wounded at the Battle of Sebastopol – and fell in love with 'Lillian', one of Florence Nightingale's nurses, who cured him back at the camp in Balaclava.

'Jolly interesting, Dad!' Nick has downed his first glass and is now pouring himself a second: 'But none of these are half as much fun as the stories about *you*.' Nick pauses for a moment and winks at me. 'What about the one of you assuring Widow Land that you'd converted to Islam when you were out in the Trucial States and could therefore marry three more wives?'

'Er, well, yes. I told her that Cecily wouldn't mind!' Archie chortles. His wife turns puce.

'And what about old Tigger at Wolsingham?' Nick fills his father's glass. 'The one who let his class off detention if they each wrote a poem describing the sound of a cane whacking a naked bottom?'

'Yes, yes, that's right!' Archie beams at the memory, and turns to his grandsons, who sit open-mouthed before him. 'So, boys, I wrote that …'

'Er, I think that's enough tripping down memory lane, Dad,' Guy interrupts anxiously. 'Let's help Granny light the pudding, shall we?'

13

Christmas lunch sets the tone for the rest of our stay: tales of yesteryear from Archie and Guy, Nick stirring trouble when he's not half-asleep, and Cecily steering the conversation to people 'one knows', and her husband away from dangerous topics.

Despite my mother-in-law's best efforts to orchestrate every move we make, after a few days in anything-but-solitary confinement we all mercifully begin to disperse within the house.

Cecily herself seems anchored to the kitchen. In her blue-and-white gingham apron, she chops, dices, kneads, fries, poaches, boils, roasts non-stop. The result is a steady stream of ever more elaborate dishes – we've progressed through shepherd's pie to Beef Wellington over the course of forty-eight hours – and ever greater disappointment if so much as a crumb of her offerings is left. 'What, Tom, you're leaving all that? I thought Granny's shepherd's pie was your favourite dish? I made it specially.' 'Oh, Alex, can't you finish that little bit of Pavlova that's left? Granny's been working all day at the stove.'

She has imposed, as usual, a strict rota on our dishwasher duties (though somehow, Guy's turn never seems to come), which means that after every meal she puts on her spectacles and checks her 'kitchen notebook' to see which grown-up and child have to fill the dishwasher 'just so'. We also have to put up with her 'star' system – 'Oh, Alex, you win a star from Granny for having cleaned your plate. Well done, darling,' and 'Maisie, put away your toys, there, dear. Now Granny will give you a star.'

Archie is either in his study or in the garden. He is delighted with his discovery of three generations of Carew letters: 'Can you believe it, they were sitting right under my nose in that old tea chest – and I never bothered to open it!' he tells us for the hundredth time. Archie begins each day with a magnifying glass in hand, poring over the thin and yellowing papers. He has decided he will publish the letters through a tiny publisher in the neighbouring village of Wainscoat who, for a small sum, will turn the Carew correspondence into a proper book. He is now, as he explains incessantly, at the editing stage and daily facing such decisions as whether to keep the letter about the runny tummy from the Somme, or just the less gruesome parts of it. To preserve the letter about a less-than-noble quarrel between brothers over a saucy little nurse, or to choose instead a lyrical description of the Dardanelles. And so forth.

After two to three hours of communing with Carews past, Archie emerges to play with Carews present – his grandsons. Target practice with his .22, darts in the barn, fencing with swords from Guy's and Nick's fencing days, and jumping over a wide stream notorious for its fast-running currents. If it can't harm you, or get you knee-deep in mud, Grandpa Carew is not interested in it. The boys, naturally, love it, and shadow their grandfather's every step. They'll put up with a few stories about battles in places with unpronounceable names when they get to load a rifle and play with real darts as opposed to the magnetic ones at home.

Guy, happy to play dutiful son, moves from his father's study, where he sifts through the Carew correspondence, to the kitchen, where he listens to Cecily's gossip and complaints. He is at his most relaxed these days, and I don't grudge him this brief parenthesis of serenity. Here, at home with his adoring parents, the grinding, daily pressure of scraping together money for the school fees or the council tax lets up – even if only momentarily. Food is eaten and wine drunk without his having to worry about the cost; his children run around having fun, without his having to pay through the nose for scuba-diving lessons or skiing equipment; none of his peers – and the odious comparisons they inevitably prompt – are around; and his parents heartily approve of every priority he sets. Being in his parents' home is like retreating to our downstairs loo for him, as every photo, every memento, every book speaks of that happy time before a three-bedroom house somewhere decent cost near a million, and school fees were higher than a teacher's salary.

Nick, instead, is literally all over the place. He paces the house, ear to his mobile; he searches the rooms for now the business section of the newspaper, now the pack of Camels which Cecily insists he smokes outside the kitchen door; and he darts in and out of the kitchen to help himself to 'a little something' (usually in liquid form).

I find myself alternating between kitchen duty, which places me under Cecily's strict tutelage, and monitoring Rufus and the children, which does the same.

'You really must teach them not to leave wet glasses on nice furniture!' my mother-in-law huffs as she rubs furiously at a wet ring on her sideboard. 'This is Chippendale, you know.' And, 'Do you allow the children to leave their rooms in London in such a mess, Harriet?'

My worst offence is when Anjie calls me about a grant application deadline we've missed for HAC. 'I do think,' Cecily huffs, 'that Christmas holidays should be respected – even these days!'

I ignore her: it's the twenty-eighth, for heaven's sake – most people are back at the office by now! I strain to hear Anjie's voice as she describes the grant of £25,000 and its form, which required an attachment of 'up to fifteen pages' detailing why HAC merits a grant.

'Oh hell!' I panic. 'It's my fault entirely – has Mary Jane found out yet?'

'Hush, children, follow me, your mother is working,' Cecily admonishes the children as, with a disapproving look, she makes a great show of leading them away from me into the garden.

Anjie acknowledges that the boss herself discovered my oversight. 'She's going to try to pull strings, she says, to get us an extension. But meanwhile your name is mud.' Anjie sounds mournful, though I suspect it is because she has to bear the brunt of Mary Jane's fury as well as concern for my welfare.

That night, as I immerse Maisie in her bath, my daughter looks up at me, eyes big and searching. 'Mummy, did you want to have me?'

I am horrified at the possibility of Maisie somehow having guessed or overheard that she was an accident – and one that provoked, initially, despair rather than delight (well, at least in Guy's case). 'Oh, pussy cat, what a question! Of course Mummy wanted you. I thought you would be the most wonderful little baby – and you were!' I soap her slowly, waiting with beating heart for her to explain the question.

'My duck!' She finds the rubber duck she leaves here, in the Carews' guest bathroom, from one stay to the next. Then, as it floats away from her. 'I don't know why mummies who work have babies.'

I recognize my mother-in-law's sentiments, and words, and am ready to rush downstairs to commit matricide or whatever the murder of one's mother-in-law would be called, except that of course I can't leave my toddler in the bath on her own. By the time I have Maisie dry and in her pyjamas and cosily snuggled against me as I read from Guy's childhood copy of *The Happy Lion,* I couldn't care less what Cecily Carew thinks about working mothers, and just breathe in the lovely talcum-y scent of my little girl.

But rebellion has set in. After a week's captivity, I'm ready to break with the Carews' 'family ways', ignore Cecily's barking and reject her schedule. On New Year's Day I refuse to eat yet another breakfast of eggs, bacon and fried bread. 'Just juice and toast for me, thank you, Cecily,' I say firmly – which prompts my mother-in-law to wheel round from the Aga, looking as shocked as if I had asked for minced bone-marrow topped with duck's blood. I do not offer Cecily my assistance when she cooks the ham or, that evening, the ham-and-pea soup. Instead I plump myself down for a nice long session with *Bergdorf Blondes* in the sitting room. Maisie has ripped the paperback cover, which allows me to pass it off as an improving book on Ingmar Bergman, should any Carew inquire. And, in the ultimate act of sabotage, when Maisie runs up to me, stricken because Granny won't give her a star as she has left her ducks on the bathroom floor, I shrug: 'Don't worry, darling, I'll give you lots of nice little stars at home.'

I slip out for a covert mobile phone call to my mother, feeling like a naughty schoolgirl sneaking out for a secret cigarette during break. I cross the frozen garden and the field beyond for a private chat. 'Mum? How are you? Is Auntie Bess still there?' I suddenly feel a tremendous nostalgia for my mother and *her* kind of Christmas, with the big lunch and the presents and games of Monopoly, Pass the Parcel and Risk on the day, followed by a long stretch of lie-ins and left-over meals and nothing more arduous than a late night in front of the telly.

'She runs the family like an army camp,' I moan, 'and wants everything just so. I'm trying so hard, I really am, but I still feel like the bag lady who stumbled in off the street.'

'It can't be much fun for the children.' My mum sounds at once concerned and satisfied that all her predictions have come to pass.

'They don't seem to mind – but then she doesn't practise her put-downs on them.'

'It's probably the army background that makes them so rigid and ...'

'Demanding and insensitive,' I chip in.

'Poor darling,' Mum sighs. 'They come from a different world and they're convinced it's the only way to be.'

It's true, I think as, refusing to end my brief spell of solitude, I walk on. The Carews believe that theirs is the real and proper way to live, and that their vision of England, family, church and army is the only possible one.

I wander to the end of the field. Hills, some crowned by clumps of trees, some bare, roll against the grey sky. I look back to the large, red-brick house, half-hidden by a wide-spreading chestnut tree. I should feel so close to Guy here in his childhood home, but instead I feel as if the differences between us, normally so workable, grow tenfold here. This is the place of family traditions and preoccupations. It is the heart of Carewdom, not Guy.

We have yet another three-course lunch. Afterwards, Archie comes into the sitting room to chivvy us all out 'to get some fresh air'. I refuse to join them. I feel like Heidi without the goats, I've had so much fresh air. In any case, I have Maisie, asleep beside Rufus on the sofa, as my excuse. When the front door shuts behind the troops, Nick, who has been sprawled in the armchair in front of me, opens first one eye and then the other. 'Coast is clear?'

'Yes. They've gone.'

'Phew! Peace and quiet at last. Mum too?'

'In the kitchen, washing up. I await my summons.' I must have sounded more bitter than I meant, because Nick laughs.

'Oh dear, poor Mum, bless her, she can be a bit of a dragon, can't she?' Then, looking at my blush, 'Don't answer that. I know daughters-in-law can't afford to be too honest. Daisy found Mum demanding, overbearing, insensitive … oh, and a snob.'

'Did she?' I ask guiltily, listening to a list of adjectives I have used myself. I stretch my legs out to the fire.

'Well, by the time she admitted it' – for a moment Nick looks grim – 'things between us were so bad that she hated anything to do with me.'

I sit still, unsure how to respond. This sudden intimacy with my brother-in-law is at odds with his habitual shoulder-shrugging indifference to everything around him.

'What gets me is there was no need to turn nasty.' Nick pats his trousers for the packet of Camel, finds it, draws out a cigarette, then puts it down on the coffee table in front of him. 'There was no third party involved. We just' – he shrugs – 'stopped having fun. No laughs left, no spark.' I suddenly worry: how would his brother describe his marriage to me? There are laughs, I think – but sparks?

'And money played into it. Daisy never thought we had enough.'

'But you earn masses!' I can't help objecting. Nick's stockbroker's salary is several times Guy's. 'She should try making do on a travel writer's income – and a part-time charity worker's.'

'I feel like a fag.' Nick jumps up and strides over to the window. 'Let's be wicked!' He gives me a wink as he opens the window, then raises the cigarette and a lighter to his lips. 'Ahhhhh,' he sighs with satisfaction as he inhales deeply. 'Daisy was right about one thing: marriage isn't for me – it's the same old thing with the same "Old Thing".'

'What about security and stability and respect and shared interests?' I try to counter.

'Aw, come on, Harriet, that's muzak. You want the proper stuff, don't you? Big, passionate, spine-tingling, hair-grabbing stuff.'

I look away: is Nick right? Does Guy think of me as Mantovani when he longs for Mozart? I can't claim that my husband and I are clinched in a spine-tingling, passionate embrace. I can't even remember the last time we had dinner *à deux*, let alone grabbed one another's hair … in fact we've *never* grabbed each other's hair.

And then, unbidden and unexpected, a memory steals into my thoughts: James and I, slightly tipsy after a friend's birthday dinner, stumbling into our room in the shabby house we shared with two others. I am still in my coat, and giggling, when he comes towards me, a bit unsteady. His face is suddenly serious. 'I want you. Now.' With one hand he peels the coat off me and with the other he grabs hold of my hair, coils it round his hand and pulls me towards him. His mouth searches mine and we begin breathlessly tearing at each other's clothes.

Bang! Rufus wakes up with a start. 'Hey, what *are* they doing?' Nick leans out of the window.

Then a second Bang! splits the air, followed by a hair-raising dog's yowl.

'Bella!' Mrs Wynn-Jones's scream echoes in the garden and the house.

'Oh my God, they've done it now! They've hit Mrs Wynn-Jones's Pekinese!' Nick shakes with laughter. Quickly he throws his cigarette into the bushes outside, and shuts the window just as Grandpa Carew, Guy and the boys troop in. Archie is carrying the .22. They look defiant.

'The dog chased a squirrel right across the line of fire,' says Alex firmly. 'It was on our land and it wasn't Grandpa's fault.'

Guy comes to stand by the fire. He looks sheepish rather than cross. 'Oh dear, this could be serious.' He shakes his head at Maisie, who is blinking herself awake. 'Naughty Grandpa, naughty brothers.'

The doorbell rings.

'Let Cecily sort her out,' Grandpa Carew calls out as he slinks upstairs with our sons.

The doorbell goes once more.

'Do get it – someone!' Cecily cries from the kitchen. She has no idea about the carnage her menfolk have wrought.

Beside me, Guy's mobile suddenly bleeps. 'How sweet!' He smiles down at it. I look over his shoulder and see *This will be your best year yet* and a row of happy faces. And then *Zoë*.

'Is that TV Zoë?' I ask.

'Yes. What a sweet thing to do.'

My husband is grinning from ear to ear. As I open the front door, I ask myself if Zoë is going to accompany him and the crew on their fortnight in Kenya later this month.

'You're disgusting!' A trembling ball of fur is thrust in my face. 'Look at Bella's tail! Monsters! I'm going to call the police right now!'

14

It's 1.30 a.m., and Guy and I strike up the usual conversation.

'Greenford is actually quite nice, you know.' Guy is sitting up, arms crossed. Neither one of us can sleep because the prospect of the £5,000 payment to the Griffin looms. John Merritt, the headmaster, has over-ruled the bursar and granted us a month's extension on this term's fees.

'Denmark Hill has fabulous green spaces. And there are bits of Deptford that are supposed to be really nice.'

'Well ...' I lie back against the pillows, ticking off the draw-backs on my fingers, 'we would have to get a car. I'd have to commute to HAC. The state schools there aren't really all that good – for that, we'd have to go to ...'

'Kent, I know, I know.' Guy rakes a hand through his hair. 'And your mother could live in a granny flat.'

'We couldn't afford a house with a granny flat, Guy: house prices in Kent have gone through the roof over the past two years. They're not that much lower than around here.' I turn away from him, on my side, and slip my hands under the pillow. 'It comes down to the children's schooling. One at the Griffin is hard enough. Wolsingham for two is beyond our reach – no matter where we live.'

'But we want the best for them.'

'We can't keep racking our brains and losing sleep every time the school fees are due. What kind of life is that?'

'The kind that people who didn't go into the City have to lead. Look at anyone who has a job that needs a brain – they're struggling to survive.'

'But this is not about survival. This is about saying that our children should only be in the most exclusive schools.' I sigh, feeling defeated.

'Come on, darling, you can't honestly say that you'd be prepared to send the children to a state school? I mean, St Christopher's, yes, but …'

'There are private schools out there that cost half as much as the Griffin and Wolsingham.'

'No Wolsingham? Help! Help!' Guy's hands close around his throat as he cries out in mock alarm. 'The Carew ancestors are coming down to throttle me for defiling their sacred memory.' He places a hand on my shoulder and tries to turn me back to him.

'Tell them to pay up or shut up.' I shake him off crossly.

It's always the same. The bills loom, we worry, we discuss the prospects before us, and then Guy tries to lighten the mood with some sally or comic turn. But I feel incapable of laughing at our penury now. I am worn out. There are other ways of leading our life and raising our children. No school is worth this heart-ache. I play dead as under the duvet my husband tries to stroke my shoulder, arm and then hip. After a while, I hear a gentle purring besides me. Guy is snoring. I roll over and study my sleeping husband's form. Poor Guy, he has lost that pink-cheeked contentment he wore at his parents'. He looks drawn even in sleep, and a slight frown hovers over his brow. Percy's payment for the two extra manuscripts Guy edited before Christmas won't be here until the end of February. This means we'll have a problem with the second-term fees which, with the extension, are due halfway through February. My husband is spending hours on the phone nego-tiating with everyone from his agent, to find a contract that pays instantly, to Oliver Mallard, to scrounge some extra work.

But I'm exasperated, too. Why won't Guy discuss seriously other options for our children's schooling? This afternoon, the boys came home from school and woke him up. Because he sleeps so badly at night, my husband sometimes falls asleep at his desk or, like today, in one of the armchairs in the sitting room. Instead of being cranky or fuming about the distur-bance, Guy transformed the incident into a joyous tickling-session that had Alex and Tom screaming for mercy. Yet he does the opposite when it comes to their schooling. What could be such an easy part of all our lives has become a lengthy, arduous obstacle-course that leaves us weary and depleted rather than on a high.

Grrr ... Guy is now grinding his teeth; he's forgotten to put on his mouth-guard. I try to gently move his head from side to side, but he rolls over and away from me in crescent-shaped rejection. I remember months, years even, when waking up at one thirty in the morning meant we were ready to make love all over again. These nights, it simply means we haven't paid the mortgage, the gas bill or the Griffin. The romance between us is as frayed as Guy's shirt-collars and as scuffed as our children's shoes.

Guy stops grinding his teeth, stirs restlessly. I wonder how much he notices – and minds – that passion's spent. I think of today when Lisa, our neighbour, came over to ask if she could borrow our ladder to change the bathroom light-bulbs. Guy was in the kitchen having a cup of tea. 'Builder's tea, please, none of that stuff Manic Organic gave you,' he ordered before listening to Lisa's account of her wild party the night before. A private equities friend had hired Saville House and treated two hundred guests to non-stop champagne, a floor show with belly dancers, and a suckling pig. By the end, the pig's apple ended up in the host's mouth and half the guests disappeared into a room where they were doing God knows what.

'Sex, sex, sex – what fun you young people have!' Guy laughs, obviously enjoying the glimpse of how the other half lives – not to mention Lisa's extremely slim legs in her short tartan skirt. 'I'm going to introduce you to my brother Nick – I'm sure you'll hit it off.'

'Guy!' I cry. 'Your brother's getting over a bitter divorce, says he hates the idea of marriage, smokes like a Turk and drinks like a fish!'

'Give me his mobile number and I'll ask him out,' Lisa says immediately. Then, noticing my shocked expression: 'Just for a drink. I mean, I'm getting to the stage where I'll try anyone who's single and solvent. I've tried my dentist, I've tried my trainer, I've tried my decorator. Why not try my neighbour – or his brother?' Then, shrugging, 'It's dog-eat-dog out there and if you don't move fast you can be left with nothing. The odds are in the guys' favour.'

'They were never in this Guy's favour,' mopes Guy.

'Hey, you didn't do too badly.' Lisa smiles in my direction. Guy nods but without conviction, I feel, and slopes out. Lisa and I hear him sing, Maisie and Daniela trying to keep up with him, '*Everybody hates me, nobody loves me, think I'll go and eat worms. Long thin skinny ones, short fat juicy ones, watch them wriggle and squirm ...*'

Again I look at his sleeping form beside me. Does he know that I am nursing a guilty secret? That, for the past week, I have been seeing James day in, day out?

It's Mary Jane's fault. She has insisted that James sit in on her meetings with John Radler, 'the man who turned waste plastic into gold', as the tabloids dub the manufacturer of everything from milk crates to park benches. HAC is trying to get Radler to sponsor our Open Day – the one chance we have to show potential donors, the local authorities and the lottery people how appealing and well run our charity is. The idea is to choose an attractive venue, show video footage from a couple of idyllic holidays at our houses in Devon and Suffolk, and hold a brief Q and A session with satisfied children and their families. This, plus a speech from Radler, something to drink and nibble on, and a local celeb doing the final tear-jerking cap-in-hand speech, is bound to win us huge goodwill and raise loads of funds. Or so Mary Jane keeps telling us.

Whether James subscribes to this plan or not, he is good-naturedly going along with it, and has shown up at the HAC offices every morning at ten, ready for the first meeting. He has come up with a draft of a pitch for Mary Jane to use with Radler, a profile of Radler's interests, professional and personal, and brochures from a dozen high-profile but small charities that have struck gold with the plastics magnate.

James manages to bridge the gulf that separates Fortress Thompson from the rest of the office. He continually entertains Anjie and me with stories of the preposterous behaviour of millionaires and CEOs he has encountered; with his gift for mimicry, he reproduces some of the meetings he attends with Mary Jane; he makes us giggle with his outrageous plans to get money out of potential donors: 'Blackmail him over his toupee – he'd pay through the nose rather than be exposed as a baldy'; or 'Get a pretty young man to do all the talking and she's yours – she's got a thing about toy boys.'

James is suntanned from his Christmas travels: 'Jamaica. We ... I had a property out there that I wanted to sell,' he tells us. He's full of energy and ideas while the rest of the world mopes about, sluggish and sulky with post-holiday blues. Actually, I must confess to not feeling too sulky myself. Not any more. Bicycling to work has become a whole new challenge: how can I pedal and chat with Tom without getting my skirt mud-splattered, or working up a sweat which would wreck my make-up and hair? The water-cooler and the kettle have become magnets. Every time I approach either, I know James could walk up and innocently ask for a cup. Lunch breaks are pregnant with possibilities: could James opt to grab a sandwich with me and Anjie, or will he escort Mary Jane to a restaurant with some would-be donor? Even Mary Jane scolding me because she has had to obtain an extension for a grant application has exciting potential. While she snorts that 'I seem to spend half my life mopping up other people's messes!' I think that I may have to stay late in the office to fill in the form, and Anjie will have gone home and Mary Jane might leave early, and James and I will be alone.

Not a chance, of course. Mary Jane cannot be prised out of the office with a crowbar these days, she is so delighted with James's presence. 'Oh, James, wasn't that man brilliant?' she twitters at my ex as she sits behind her desk, her red-rimmed spectacles crowning her dark hair. 'James what do you think – was I on the money, so to speak?' she asks, looking up adoringly.

From behind her *Grazia*, Anjie can't stop giggling. 'Just you wait until Mary Jane realizes you're the competition.'

'I don't know what you mean,' I say, looking over my shoulder to make sure no one can hear us.

'Don't you try that line on me!' Anjie wags her finger. 'His nibs says James was making eyes at you at his Christmas party,' she whispers. 'And when it comes to that kind of thing, my William is nobody's fool.'

Anjie's words swirl round and round my head, and I can't help feeling excitement stir. It's not just in my imagination that James was looking at me in – *that* way … Is this why I do not mind that my husband's passion seems half-asleep – because I know someone else's has re-awakened? Guy's expressions of desire have dwindled to a rare occurrence: a wolf-whistle when

I came out of the bath Sunday morning, his hand on my bottom as I bend to empty the dishwasher, a sudden pressing against me when he found me trying on an ancient black dress that Daniela had discovered when she was clearing the airing cupboard. But maybe I can put up with this because I know someone else is fighting not to express *his* passion? Have I become one of those women who, without slipping into outright duplicity or infidelity, allows her marriage to dry up while mooning about a potential lover?

The very next day, though, I realize that I'm not quite ready to yield to the inevitability of marital indifference. I come back from shopping at Tesco's, feeling as if my arms, dragged down by carrier bags filled with potatoes, bottles of milk and apples, have grown an inch, and hear a tinkling girlish laughter.

'Oh, that is the *best*!' More laughter.

Now Guy's voice: 'Hands, faces, smeared with Marmite! I asked what they were up to: they were spreading Marmite on the legs of the camp-beds to keep the bugs away.'

'Guy, this is priceless! You must tell that story! Oh, hullo!' The pretty redhead turns and beams me an innocent smile as I step in, followed by Tom.

'Hullo, darling. Zoë's here!' Guy sounds like a child announcing Santa Claus's arrival.

'Hello, Zoë.' I wish I could defrost my voice, but the sight of the unlined milky complexion and the size-10, possibly -8, body curled up beside Guy on the sofa sets me on edge.

'Zoë's just told me we've got the green light from BBC2, and we set off at the end of the month!'

'Wow! That's wonderful!' I cry and then wince as two kilos of potatoes fall through the bottom of the carrier bag on to my foot.

'She's giving me tips on how to prepare for pieces to camera.' Guy looks over at Zoë with undisguised admiration.

'First,' Zoë joins her hands as if in prayer, 'I get myself into that mental space that allows you to real-ly re-lax.'

Zoë is a true no-com, I think. 'First' in my book always precedes 'Maisie must be bathed' or 'Tom must do his maths homework' or 'Alex needs to get a T-shirt from Primark' or 'I must get Guy's tea.' As for 'mental spaces', there's no room for them.

'Tea, anyone?' I ask, but am ignored.

I go to the kitchen thoroughly disgruntled. My husband is going to become a television star, surrounded by admiring, fawning, size-10 twenty-somethings, while I keep his house and bring up his children.

I boil the kettle and rummage in the cupboard for biscuits.

'Please, Harriet, can I have tea too?' Daniela stands suddenly behind me. She's wearing her glasses, a sure sign that she's been at the computer again.

'As bad as Ilona,' Guy keeps saying, head shaking in sorrow. 'She's going to come a cropper one of these days. Some big brute will promise her a life free of Carews and Clapham and she'll fall for it.'

'I don't understand it,' I defend my au pair. 'She's so quiet and sensible. I'd never have guessed she'd be one for Internet dating.'

'Still waters run deep.' Guy shrugs. 'She's probably been speed-dating since she was thirteen and her FriendScout codename is Miss Whiplash.'

'Except she never seems to go out.' I'm dismayed at the prospect of yet another au pair enjoying an over-active nightlife.

'Ha! You never saw Igor either, and he was slinking in and out of our house as he pleased!'

I look at Daniela now, so meek and innocent-looking in her spectacles and round-neck jumper. I feel protective about her, and wish I could find a way to alert her to the dangers of her Internet activities without offending her. If Maisie were abroad au pairing, I'd certainly want her host mother to look after her, rather than throw her to the wolves in skin-tight rubber and leather.

'Today is a special day.' Daniela interrupts my train of thoughts. She smiles beatifically, and beyond the spectacles her blue eyes shine with tears.

'Really? Your birthday?' I ask, suddenly worried that I should be baking a two-tiered chocolate cake.

'No. Our Lady has sent message.' Again the innocent smile lights up the young face before me.

'Hmmm?' I ask, confused.

'Come, I show you.' And Daniela slips her hand in mine and pulls me upstairs to her tiny, immaculate bedroom. 'Look –' she motions me to the computer on her desk. The image on the screen is dark, almost pitch-black, though there is a soft glow in a corner. Suddenly the glow grows wider and wider, brighter and brighter. At its centre a white statue of the Madonna smiles softly and mysteriously.

'I don't understand?' I ask Daniela.

'Lourdes. We have webcam in shrine. So we can look at what happens. Miracles, signs, we can see them.'

'So *that's* what you do when you sit up here at the computer!' In the space of a few minutes, my au pair has gone from being Miss Whiplash to Mother Teresa.

'Yes, yes, it is wonderful, isn't it?'

Back down in the kitchen, my mobile rings. I'm almost relieved at the interruption.

'Sorry, Daniela, you must show me more later!' I run down. My mobile is on the table, I check it – Private Number – and answer.

'Hi – it's James. Can we talk?'

15

I feel guilty even talking to James on the telephone. I know perfectly well that I could repeat every word of our exchange to Guy without my husband so much as raising an eyebrow. Yet I persist in lowering my voice and shutting the door, I feel a rush of excitement course through me, and I act as if my ex and I are planning a clandestine meeting. I chide myself for my overactive imagination. I'm getting like those women who see an admirer in every man, and a passionate courtship in every occasional encounter. And yet ... Surely James is interested in me as Harriet, rather than me as his colleague?

'This isn't working,' James says, voice firm.

I gulp: what is he telling me?

'She's driving me bonkers with all these meetings and questions and plans. She's eating up all my free time. I told myself I'd give HAC two weeks – and it's now a month.'

'I know.' I try to keep my voice light, and hide my disappointment. 'You've been patient well beyond the call of duty.'

'I'm going to cut down on my time in the office.'

'Oh?' I think with a pang how much I'll miss seeing him.

'I'm not back-pedalling,' James continues. 'I mean, I've enjoyed it.'

'Enjoyed it?' I'm stung. This is not about his attitude to HAC, this is about his attitude to me. Am I some bit of fun on the side, a bit of fluff he toys with between nine and five a few days a week?

'Yes, enjoyed working a bit, getting to know everyone.'

'HAC is not some social club.' I hate myself for sounding like a brown-sandalled do-gooder, but I can't stop myself. 'It's about helping people. Or perhaps you hadn't noticed.'

'Yes, of course.' James sounds surprised by my outburst. 'I'm still committed. It's just that I'm not a full-time volunteer.'

'Of course not. You're a full-time property developer who wanted to do something to make himself look good.'

'That's unfair, Harriet.' James speaks gently, as if to rein in my fury. 'I wanted to do something different, that had nothing to do with earning huge profits or dealing with greedy moneymen.'

'So you picked up a little local charity,' I say bitterly. 'And now that you're bored, you're going to set it down again.'

'What I can bring to the party is not about sitting in the office holding Mary Jane's hand while she talks to a potential donor.'

'I don't know what you can bring to the party, James. It sounds to me like you've made up your mind not to give HAC any more of your precious time. But don't worry,' I say wildly, 'we'll survive without you.' I hang up the receiver and burst into tears.

James's absence weighs heavily on HAC. Mary Jane has returned to her old forbidding, scratchy, and generally difficult ways. Her meetings with potential donors are once again conducted behind closed doors in Fortress Thompson, without James offering us an entertaining autopsy afterwards. Her power suits have been restored, her handlebar hairstyle has reappeared, and the slightest hint of me and Anjie straying from the business at hand elicits a furious 'I do hope you're hard at work, you two!'

Anjie misses teasing James, and keeps her head low. She keeps wondering if James will ever resurface. 'Do you think the Dragon has scared him off, good and proper?' she asks me in a whisper. 'If I had known then what I know now, I would have warned him not to let her take advantage of him. She's worn him out and I just hope he hasn't fled the country.'

I sink into feeling blue. I'm listless, tired, slightly out of tune with everyone around me. No sooner have I found James again than I'm pushing him away. It's not that I suspect him of harbouring an illicit passion for me; I'm scared he sees me as part of his professional life – and a rather dissatisfying part, at that.

Again and again I replay the awful telephone conversation: why did I sound so shrill and so spiteful? Why did I mock his desire to help the charity?

I feel as if suddenly I'm not only part-time at HAC, but I've gone part-time in the rest of my life. I only half participate in the conversation at supper, only half enjoy listening to *What's My Line?*, only half register Daniela's diligent cleaning and tidying.

Only the children, with their daily routines and absorbing questions, engage me fully. I can't brood about James when Alex asks me to help him practise his French conversation, Tom needs me to move the buttons on his second-hand uniform shirt, and both seek my attention with regard to notebooks misplaced and snacks needed. I can't muse about what I should have said, or what James meant, when Maisie asks me questions like 'When can I wear lipstick?' and 'Will Granny die soon?'

It's in those mid-morning hours when I am not needed by my offspring that I find myself settling into an uneasy longing I am unfamiliar with. I indulge it – and that too is unfamiliar. I, who will not take time away from my home duties to go for a walk or see a film, suddenly take time off everything in order to think about my ex-boyfriend. Will he return? What does he make of me? How much does he relive our past when we are together now? I sit and watch snow melt into sludge as the rain pelts our window panes, the bare trees sway, and the red tops of double-decker buses cross beneath the HAC windows. *I miss him, I miss him*: the words go round and round in my head.

My blues are in marked contrast with Guy's elation these days. Zoë's flattering attentions, and the imminent filming in Kenya, have transformed my husband. 'One, two …' He has started doing sit-ups on our bedroom floor. 'I must be in shape if I'm an action-man performer … one, three – don't interrupt me, Tom – one, four …'

Although he always preferred a book to the telly, Guy now sits every night in front of the box, offering a running commentary that annoys me and the boys: 'Gosh, he really loses it in the pieces to camera!' 'Have you seen how this woman blinks – hopeless!' 'He doesn't convey any authority, does he?' Never one to preen before, he has started to rake his hair in front of the mirror and try out a range of expressions: enthusiastic, pensive, quiet, dismissive.

Unfortunately this new self finds it very difficult to focus on such mundane matters as the bills that pile up, and the income stream that, while he disappears to work with his production team, dries up. Reminders about the Visa bill and the council tax are brushed off with a 'Darling I *must* focus, you do realize that, don't you?'

What I do realize is that Guy risks alienating his work contacts. Percy's phone calls don't get returned, Simon's reminders of the deadline for the chapter on Lyme Regis are ignored. At one point, while I am cooking our lunch, Guy answers the phone: 'Hullo, hullo. Yes, it is. Well, Oscar, that's a great idea and I normally would be really up for that kind of thing. But as I said, this new project is really, really demanding. No, no – writing *and* presenting. Apparently a long lead time. Rather pleased, yes. Sorry about that, bye bye.' He hangs up.

I finish dressing the salad in silence. Then, as we sit down to eat, I ask Guy what 'Oscar' had wanted.

'It was Oscar Wurtzel from *No Boundaries*,' Guy tells me between mouthfuls of bread and cheese. 'Wanted to get me on board for a big piece on Seville.'

'*No Boundaries*? But, Guy, that's great! They were always so snooty before.'

'They were, they were, but I think they've heard on the grapevine about the film.'

'And they pay so well, don't they?'

'Yeah, he was talking about two grand for the special.' Guy waves this colossal sum off as if it were one of those annoying fliers that slip through the letter box. 'There's no way I can take anything on at this point.'

'Bbbbbut, Guy!' I hear my voice grow shrill. 'It's so much money! We can't afford to pass up that opportunity!' I calm down, and lower my voice. 'Guy, we have so many bills to pay still, and the TV people haven't paid anything yet. It doesn't make sense to turn down Oscar's piece.'

'My wife, ever the optimist!' Guy laughs. 'Don't worry, Harriet, we're on a roll.' He gets up and puts his plate in the dishwasher, stretches to his full height, and beats his chest, Tarzan style: 'Owwahwahwahwah … Me Tarzan, you Jane, me worry about finances, you relax.' And with that he's off.

I'm left behind to consider our income stream: there is the chapter on Lyme Regis still outstanding. When the coffee-table book is published, not until early next year, it should bring in about £4,000. Guy's regular bread and butter, or sweat and slog, as he calls it, editing the manuscripts that Percy sends him, brings in £1,200 every six weeks if he's really focused. There's *Rajput* too: the first part of the advance was £7,500, but we've already eaten through that. Guy, Guy, I want to scream, can't you see we're not on a roll – we're on our way to bankruptcy!

* * *

My money worries may not touch Guy, but they have transmitted themselves to the children. One night, as I climb wearily to our bedroom, I overhear the boys talking in Alex's room:

'We could hold a car boot sale,' Tom sounds excited. 'Zac Mackie's family made over a thousand pounds from theirs.'

'We don't have a car,' Alex reminds him.

'What about …' Tom persists, 'a garage sale …'

'No garage either. Besides, you have to sell stuff to make some money, and what is there around the house that's valuable?'

'Well, Daddy says that the Carew sideboard is a Ship-and-Dale and that that is really valuable,' Tom says.

'But if it's a Carew thing, Daddy won't ever agree to sell it, will he? And anyway I don't think furniture fetches a good price.'

'Mummy's jewels?'

'She doesn't have any, Tom,' Alex sighs. 'I mean, she's got the ruby ring, but she never takes that off because it's her engagement ring.'

Silence. I tiptoe away, and feel like laughing and crying all at the same time: my darling boys, trying to step in where they see a deficit – literally. Has it come to this? How could Guy and I fail our children so badly? Here they are, ten and thirteen, worrying about giving their parents a hand-out rather than how to spell 'awkward' or find the square root of 10. In our determination to get them into the best schools, at no matter what sacrifice to ourselves, we have ignored their ability to see our struggle close-up, and their concern over it.

I resolve to allay their fears. And my own.

* * *

Money trouble, though, is as nothing in comparison to a child's unhappiness. 'Harriet, is Tom all right?' my mother asks me over the phone.

I feel stung: in my stupid, self-centred haze of longing for James to resurface, have I missed clues to my younger son's well-being?

'We-ell …'

'I'm only asking,' Mum goes on, 'because twice now when I've asked him about school, he has put on that voice from the dead that tells you something's not quite right.'

With a pang I realize that a niggling worry about Tom *has* been at the back of my thoughts for some time now. Our morning cycle ride to school used to always offer me a chatty catch-up session with my younger son. Lately, though, it has grown silent and, instead of trying to keep up with me, Tom hangs back, constantly forcing me to chivvy him along.

'No one from school has said anything about a problem,' I say weakly.

'Oh, school!' my mother sniffs. 'They're always the last to know. I hope it's nothing, but you know my instincts are never wrong on this kind of thing.'

It's true. When I had a rotten time at my primary school, teased for being 'a fatty' by Alice 'Skinny' Trowbridge and her sidekick Susie Spanner, my mum sensed it immediately, and drew me out, slowly and patiently, until I had told her about every slight I had endured. And later, when Mel had a hard time keeping up because the school was very academic and my sister not a bit, it was Mum who insisted that Mel change school halfway through the year rather than sit through extra daily tutorials, as the school suggested.

The telephone call shakes me and fills me with guilt. I try to seek out Tom. But my younger son, usually so articulate and talkative, has turned monosyllabic. My every question elicits a grunt in reply, and when I probe about school friends he flinches.

That night, Alex and I watch *Big Cat Diary*, hoping to get through it before Guy returns from a meeting with Zoë and starts criticizing Saba Douglas-Hamilton for her presenting style. Tom is upstairs trying to explain in 150 words why he loved his visit to the V&A, Maisie is asleep, probably dreaming of Makka Pakka in *The Night Garden*, and Daniela is monitoring the apparitions at Lourdes on the webcam.

'Darling,' I ask as Saba pursues her prey in the Masai Mara, 'do you think something's up with Tom?' I keep my voice casual.

'Hmmm …' Alex shrugs and keeps his eyes on the screen. 'I dunno …'

'Is he being bullied?'

Again, Alex shrugs.

I can't make my eldest confide in me, I couldn't work out that my younger son was unhappy: I don't think I'll be in the running for mother of the year, somehow.

By the time I'm sitting at my desk at HAC the next day, after another silent ride across the common with Tom, I feel like I should hand myself in to Social Services.

'I just don't know whether I should push him, get him to open up,' I confide in Anjie over our sandwich as Mary Jane is being lunched by someone from the Mayor's office, 'or leave it up to him. He's such a private little person.'

'You know what we say in the Jones family?' Anjie takes the onion rings out of the cheese-and-pickle sandwich. 'A child that's gone all quiet is a child that's festering. And it's up to Mum to lance the boil.'

'Oh, Anjie, what kind of a mum am I that I didn't notice all this before?' I sigh.

'A busy mum.' Anjie smiles. 'Don't beat yourself up, girl. It's hard enough doing everything when the kids are happy and healthy. When one of them needs extra attention, it just tips the whole apple cart.'

I nod, forlorn. I approach the kettle and start rustling about, in search of our tin of instant coffee. 'Coffee?' I call out over my shoulder.

'Yes, please,' answers Anjie.

'Make that two,' adds a man's voice.

I wheel around: it's James. 'Hi!' I cry out inanely, and realize I am grinning like Upsy Daisy in one of Maisie's beloved television shows.

'Hullo. Thought I'd drop by to see how my favourite do-gooders were doing.' James's smile takes us both in, but his eyes stop on me.

'She's not too good —' Anjie points at me with her thumb.

'Mary Jane?' James asks immediately. 'I'll sort her.'

'Nah. Mary Jane's in a filthy mood.' Anjie winks at him. 'No guesses why … but we're used to that. It's kid trouble.'

And money, and Guy, and the future and … *you*, I want to say. Instead I bring them both a mug of coffee and sit back at my desk. James is perched on Anjie's and he swivels so as to look at me properly.

'What's happened? Someone ill?'

His warm voice betrays no resentment for my outburst over the phone, and his eyes are full of genuine concern. I feel as if he's unpicked every stitch with which I had sewn up my fears, so that they lie exposed. Still, I hesitate.

Anjie looks at her watch. 'William's working around the corner. I'm going to see if he has time for a break with the wife.' She disappears.

James follows my eyes and shakes his head. 'That woman,' he laughs, 'has an uncanny ability to make herself scarce at the most opportune of times.'

I blush: is it so obvious that I long to see James on my own?

'Are we still friends?' James asks, wary.

'I'm sorry I had a go at you.' I don't dare meet his eyes.

'I deserved a bit of a ticking off. Maybe I wasn't taking my role here seriously enough.'

'I had no business saying any of it.' I study my keyboard.

'I had no business waltzing off just because I felt like a break from Mrs Thompson.' Here James laughs: 'But you know something?'

'What?' I look up.

'I missed it.' He lowers his voice. 'And you.' He pauses, as if to let those words sink in. Then he approaches my desk. 'But what's been happening while my back was turned? You look a bit down.'

'Tom is so quiet these days. He's just a little boy, I know. I mean, it's not only that he is young, but he's also slight and not that tall. You remember Dad?' I look up to see James nod. 'Tom's the spitting image of him. I don't know what to do because he's obviously unhappy, but he's not telling me anything and I think he's being bullied. He just looks at me and refuses to speak.' My voice shakes so I take a deep breath to calm myself. I don't want to be disloyal to Guy, I tell myself. I really want only to talk to James about Tom.

'Don't worry: it's in the school's interest to sort it to you and your husband's satisfaction.'

'Guy?!' I forget all my resolutions to be discreet. 'Guy's too busy with some TV company to notice! They keep telling him that he's going to present a three-part documentary based on *Lonely Hunter*, but meanwhile it just means he doesn't even think about the bills – gas, council tax … and that's without Alex's school fees, which come to five thousand a term.'

James whistles. 'Five grand?! What is this – Junior Harvard?'

'The Griffin. Which is supposed to feed into Wolsingham, which is where every Carew since God created the world went.' By this time I'm unstoppable, the words rushing out of me without pause: 'We can't afford it, James, we really can't, but Guy keeps saying we'd be robbing our children of the right start in life.' Here James snorts derision. 'And I …' I burst into tears. I hold my head low, and feel myself shake with sobs. Suddenly James is beside me, taking my hands in his. He squats so I am forced to look down on him. 'Harriet,' he whispers, his fingers gently squeezing mine, 'you need some proper looking after.'

16

I look at James through my tears: he couldn't have been more seductive if he had danced with me cheek to cheek on a terrace in the summer moonlight. 'You need some proper looking after': when was the last time anyone said that to me? In our household, Guy stands at the centre and I am his satellite, spinning round him to satisfy his need for a cup of tea, his house keys, a jumper from upstairs, a warm meal, and above all, an audience. There's no room in our home life for 'proper looking after'. In our daily battle to survive bills, deadlines, children's demands, competition stoked by school and envy stoked by other people's advantages, Guy and I are lucky if we exchange a few words when we fall into bed; anything that requires more emotional effort is out of the question.

'Do you really believe all that toff nonsense about public schools?' James is asking. He is now standing beside me, holding out a tissue from the box on Anjie's desk. 'I mean, it may make sense for millionaires, but for you ... How much ...?' he checks himself. 'You can't earn very much and I don't suppose Guy's travel writing brings in a lot more.'

'No, not really.' I wipe away my tears and shake my head. Once again I don't want to be disloyal to my husband, but I can't resist letting James glimpse just how difficult things are.

'I can't believe you even consider sending the children to private schools on your income.'

'Sometimes I can't believe it either,' I tell him. 'And it seems to get more difficult with every term. I could build a tower with the stacks of unpaid bills on my desk.' I feel my eyes filling with tears again. 'Every time the phone rings I jump, because I'm scared it's someone warning us they're cutting off the phone or the heating or sending in the bailiffs.'

'Maybe,' James offers me the tissue again, 'a brush with the bailiffs would give the Carews a reality check. Sounds like they need it.'

'They'd die of shame.' I smile weakly, balling up the tissue. 'All those army ancestors would turn over in their graves.'

'They deserve it: think of the misery they've inflicted on you and Guy.'

'It's not so miserable, really.' I try to keep my voice steady. 'It's just that … things won't get any better,' I sniffle. 'More years of scrimping and saving to put the children through "proper" schools, or a move to Denmark Hill or one of the other suburbs.'

'Hey, what's wrong with the suburbs,' James laughs. 'I was brought up in Surbiton.'

'Well, look who's here!' Mary Jane Thompson's voice is like an explosion ricocheting around the office. I'm so startled

I drop my ball of tissue, and James takes an involuntary step away from me.

'Where have you been, stranger?' My boss is smiling but her voice is clipped and sharp. 'We haven't seen you in weeks!' I haven't come into Mary Jane's line of vision yet. Her eyes are fixed on James.

'I had to get a few things sorted out.' James turns to me. 'I was explaining to Harriet that I was in danger of getting sucked into HAC.'

Mary Jane takes me in. 'Oh, Harriet, I didn't see you there.' She turns back to James. 'Well, if you've got a few minutes, I have an interesting development to ask you about.'

James doesn't try to hide his sigh, but he slips off Anjie's desk and follows her into Fortress Thompson. Mary Jane shuts the door firmly behind him.

That evening, while Guy is locked in his study, finally taking time to edit Percy's manuscript, and Maisie's asleep, the boys and I make popcorn and watch *Harry Potter and the Sorcerer's Stone* on television. I wallow in this happy moment. My sons press against me on the sofa, Rufus slumbers at our feet and the microwaved popcorn smells artificial but cosy. Right now, I don't mind that our home is fraying at the edges, that Guy is preoccupied with his telly series and that our bills collect on my desk. I only half-watch Daniel Radcliffe, and delight instead in the feel of Alex and Tom, their after-bath smell, their chatting, munching presences. During the interminable commercial breaks, Alex channel-hops.

'Look at that!' Tom cries, excited.

A hugely obese woman is stuffing her face in a pastry shop. 'Luella cannot stop herself from cheating on her doctor's diet,' the voice-over informs us. 'Here, our hidden camera reveals our eighteen-stone friend raiding the fridge.' The cool, class-less, female voice-over drips sarcasm. The camera focuses unblinkingly on every mouthful, every gulp, and then slowly slides down the obscene folds of flesh. Every excess ounce, every cellulite dimple is carefully recorded. It's cruel, but hyp-notizing, and I feel a pang of guilt. I'm no better than one of those Romans cheering on the lions in the Colosseum.

'That's *Cheats*. Our teacher said it was a great series,' Tom explains.

Alex switches us back to Harry Potter's more inviting world, but at the next break, I ask to see another glimpse of *Cheats*. We come in at the end, though, and the credits roll slowly on to lively pop music. Suddenly I sit up: *A Rainbow Production*. Rainbow? That's Ross and Zoë and co. The people behind *Cheats* do not strike me as the kind of colleagues my husband should trust blindly. I pick up the TV guide and read the blurb: *Cruel, darkly comic documentary in which dieters are lured into cheating. The use of hidden cameras seems vaguely unethical when applied to these sad over-eaters, but the results make for addictive viewing.* I must warn Guy, put him on his guard. 'Back in a minute,' I whisper and get up, ignored by the boys.

'Darling?' I knock on the study door and look in. My hus-band sets down his pen, the fat manuscript from Percy, and gives me a tired smile. 'I think you should know – they've just shown a very nasty comic documentary about fat people falling off a diet. It's made by Rainbow Productions.'

'*Cheats*? Oh yes, I meant to watch it. Ross told me about it. He knows it is going for the jugular, but he said there were moments of pure fun.'

'I hope they won't go for the jugular with you?'

'Me? No, darling. I'm the one making fun of the hunters on the safari. Just like in the book. I'm on the side of the angels.' He grins.

'OK. Just as long as you know what they're capable of doing …' I draw closer to the desk and stroke the back of his head protectively. 'Don't stay up too late.'

'Something's up with Tom at school.' Guy greets me at the door when I return home on Wednesday. 'Mr Sandlane rang just now. Says he needs to talk to us about some "issues".'

I'm worried about the letter from Thames Water threatening to cut off our water supply, and I had Mary Jane rapping me over the knuckles because it's almost April and I have yet to finish a written assessment on a potential volunteer. Yet nothing has hit my solar plexus as this news has.

'What's happening, Guy?' I sound agonized enough to stop my husband in his tracks. Guy puts a finger to his lips. 'Upstairs,' he whispers, pointing up to the children's room. He helps me out of my dripping jacket. 'I don't know, but we'll find out tomorrow – he's asked us for a meeting at ten.'

I walk into the kitchen and fall on to a chair. 'Mummy!!!!!' Maisie throws herself into my lap. Daniela is scrubbing potatoes at the sink. I feel too worn out to make a cup of tea, and too worried about Tom to play with Maisie. I bury my face in my daughter's blonde curls. I must go upstairs and talk to Tom.

But my son refuses to talk. He lies on his bunk-bed, reading *Young Bond*. Rufus lies asleep on the bunk below; he stirs when I climb on to the third rung of the ladder in order to see Tom properly. My heart fills with pity and guilt: how could I let it get to this? His face looks pinched, and his spectacles sit slightly lopsided on his nose.

'Darling, Mr Sandlane wants to see us tomorrow. Do you have any idea what it's about?'

Silence. *Young Bond* goes up to cover the little face.

'Is everything all right, Tom?' I wish I could stroke him, ruffle his hair, hold him in my arms, but I hold on to the ladder lest I slip.

'It's OK,' answers a muffled voice. 'Really, Mum.' Tom turns his head to the wall and I see his shoulders shake.

'Oh, Tom,' I cry, and I reach out as if to comfort him. My stockinged foot slips, and I come crashing down.

'They're hiding something, I can tell.' Guy cracks his knuckles. We are sitting outside the headmaster's office at St Christopher's. Mr Sandlane is seeing us at ten, but we've been here, stiff with foreboding, since quarter to.

'Something's up, and they don't dare tell us,' Guy goes on.

'Stop it, you're getting me even more worried.'

'Ah, come in, come in, Mr and Mrs Carew!' The door opens and Sandlane, smiling cheerfully in his capable tweeds, ushers us into his office. 'Now, I suspect you have understood what's up with young, er, Tom?' The headmaster of St Christopher's sits across from us and looks expectantly from one to the other.

'Not really, no.' Guy frowns. He is on the edge of his seat.

'We think …' Sandlane crosses his hands on his desk '… that Tom needs a few sessions with our counsellor here at the school. He is a lovely man, excellent pastoral skills … He's the school trouble-shooter.'

'Counsellor? But what's Tom *done*?' Guy asks sharply. I squirm in my chair.

'Well, he seems to be under-performing this term. He's a bright boy and should be constantly getting high marks. Instead, all the teachers are complaining that his attitude leaves a lot to be desired.'

'He does seem rather in a slump,' I begin.

Guy bursts in: 'Have any of the teachers had a guess at what's bothering him?'

'Well …' Sandlane starts rustling some papers on his desk. 'There is some talk of …' he begins hesitantly. 'There is a boy called Ben who seems to have taken exception to Tom.'

'Exception to Tom?!' Guy is indignant. 'What does that mean?'

Sandlane brings his fingertips together and talks as slowly as if we were some of his more obtuse students. 'Ben has difficulty articulating his emotions. He sometimes lashes out. He is very large – in fact, the other boys call him Big Ben. But we take the attitude, Guy …' (my husband visibly bristles at the first-name terms) 'that the boy who has been targeted should *also* be assisted. It seems that Tom is having difficulty socializing. He seems detached from class activities and, well, he sits in the play-ground reading during break-time. Other boys don't like it …'

'Mr Sandlane …' Guy looks as if he will erupt.

'Guy –' I try to intervene. But my husband takes no notice.

'My son's being bullied. Don't you think this is obviously at the root of Tom's difficulty at school?'

'Not all children react in the same way.'

'What precisely are you going to do about Big Ben?'

'Well …' Sandlane looks taken aback. 'Our anti-bullying strategy is holistic – we deal with both participants and encourage them to talk through their differences.'

'*Holistic*!! This is not a spa, this is a school! I think you need to tell this child to stop bullying my son.' Guy stands up, takes my elbow. 'Please let me know when you have dealt with him and we will be glad to bring Tom back to school.'

'Guy,' I whisper as we rush through the school corridor, 'I wish you hadn't alienated him – Tom needs the school on side.'

'I want that bully carpeted,' Guy says through gritted teeth.

At home, Tom is locked in his room and Alex, who shares it, is knocking indignantly on the door. Rufus, also keen to gain admission, barks intermittently. Alex doesn't look surprised when we tell him about the bullying – Big Ben had been guilty of roughing up a couple of boys even when Alex was still at St Christopher's.

'Poor Tom.' He shakes his head. Then, in a whisper: 'It doesn't help that he's such a weakling.'

'You'll never guess what Zoë's insisting I get for Kenya!' Guy's undressing in our bedroom. 'A floppy khaki bush hat. I told her that those went out with the Bronze Age, but she's adamant.'

'I do hope' – I look up from brushing my teeth – 'that they won't make you look …' I stop. I don't dare use the word ridiculous. I plump for 'old-fashioned' instead.

'I know. They want me to wear a safari suit with shorts rather than trousers ...' Guy sighs, balls up shirt, pants and socks in one bundle and throws it into the dirty clothes basket.

'Well, as long as they don't put words in your mouth.' I follow him to bed. I heave a sigh when I lie there. 'My poor, poor Tom.' Guy searches his chaotic bedside table for his copy of Bruce Chatwin's *Songlines*.

'Downstairs, behind a pillow on the sofa,' I remind him. 'I feel so guilty that he was miserable for so long before I recognized any signs.' I feel so guilty, I tell myself, that his mother's energy was going into thinking about her ex-boyfriend rather than her bullied son.

'I'm not going down to fetch it. I'm bushed anyway.' Guy lies back, crossing his arms behind his head. 'He needs to toughen up. He's too fragile for his own good.'

'He's a little boy, Guy!' I slap the duvet down with my hands. 'And he's physically quite small: he's probably intimidated by these big thugs.'

'That's the problem. I don't want him growing up a coward. He's got to remember that he *can* fight; it doesn't matter if he's a bit smaller than the others. He can pit his brains against their brawn. Uncle Fred was small at that age and had a rough time at Pangbourne. I think he took up ju-jitsu eventually. Anyway, Tom's my son, and he's just got to hack it. He's a –'

'A Carew?' I finish his sentence. 'Oh, I do wish you wouldn't go on about the blasted Carews! I don't care what they would do in his shoes, I care about *him*.'

205

'And I don't?' Guy's voice throbs with anger. 'I'm working my socks off, as you *may* have noticed.' My husband sits up, punches the pillow, places it under his head, and turns his back on me.

Our quarrel has not faded by the next day. This is unusual. On those rare occasions when Guy and I row, some small domestic crisis arises within a couple of hours to bind us in a joint effort to remember the date, find the cheque book, unearth the manuscript. But Guy is finished with breakfast and out of the kitchen before I've even had time to pour my cup of coffee. It's Saturday, and for once I'd like to take it easy. 'Tom!' he calls up from the bottom of the stairs. 'Hurry up! We're going for our ride!'

Alex gives me a look. Maisie asks me to cut up a banana into her cornflakes.

'Harriet –' Guy, bicycle helmet on, looks in briefly '– I won't be here for lunch. Going to White City.'

'What's in the white city?' Maisie asks, curious.

'The BBC,' Alex answers importantly.

We hear Tom's footsteps coming slowly down the stairs and then the door bangs shut. I rush out to wave goodbye but catch only their retreating figures as Guy wraps his arm round Tom's shoulders. 'Please, please let my little boy be all right,' I whisper into the cold.

'I feel terrible, Charlotte: it was going on right under my nose and I did nothing about it.'

We sit in Charlotte's sun-drenched kitchen, sipping some horrendous new tea her Chinese quack has recommended her. I deserve to suffer, I tell myself bitterly as I savour the full horror of the orange liquid, I'm a second-rate mum. And I'm not doing too well as a wife either, these days.

'That kind of thing happens all the time.' Charlotte pats my hand in sympathy. I can't help noticing the new watch on her right wrist. 'Pretty, isn't it?' Charlotte twists it round her wrist. 'Jack's bonus was huge this year.'

I stifle a sigh. I look around at the big gleaming room and marvel, as usual, at how quiet Charlotte's home is. Even on a weekend, with three children and a nanny (Charlotte hasn't ever done au pairs) somewhere in the house, all is calm and tidy.

'We're doing it properly this time,' Charlotte is saying. 'Cotton nappies. I can't bear the thought of a mountain of disposable nappies.'

'Oh? Isn't it a lot of work?' Then I remember: Charlotte's nanny will be doing the dirty work.

'It's worth it. Ouch!' Charlotte winces, and both hands go to her belly. 'Little Summer is kicking a lot these days! I bet it's a he. Kicks just like Marcus did.'

'I think it's a girl,' I begin, and then I wince, even though no one is kicking *my* stomach. Wouldn't it have been lovely, to have another little girl? Two of each, a perfect foursome.

'What about Guy in all this?' Charlotte raises an eyebrow.

'Guy's being brilliant with him,' I immediately defend my husband, 'talking to Tom all the time. Took him out for a bicycle ride today and they're off to the cinema tomorrow. But he's away a lot of the time, working on this telly thing. I hardly see him these days.'

'Is this documentary really going to see the light of day?' Charlotte, as ever when it comes to Guy, sounds sceptical.

'Looks like it. The people from the production company say he's great. He knows his stuff, he looks good in front of the camera.'

'Hmmm ...' Charlotte pats her large bump pensively. 'I didn't like the sound of that girl producer, I must say.'

'Zoë? She's awful, Charlotte.' It is only as I say it that I realize how much I resent Zoë's intrusion in our lives. 'She really, really plays up to Guy, goes on and on about how clever and amusing he is. Do you know, she calls him "Lonely Hunter"? Which really gets me: as if Guy were lonely!'

'Oh-oh!' Charlotte raises an eyebrow. 'I wouldn't like my husband having a luscious, twenty-something acolyte.'

'I *don't* like it, not one little bit.' I lean forward across the table. 'You don't think ...' I lower my voice and blush '... he's wondering what on earth he's doing with an old bag like me when he's clearly still attractive to a pretty young thing like her?'

'What?!' Charlotte explodes. 'Harriet Carew, your husband is damn lucky to have someone as supportive as you. Any other woman would have lost patience by now with all his nonsense.'

I remain unconvinced. 'I just don't feel up to the mark somehow.'

'Well, let me tell you, James Weston certainly thinks you're up to the mark. And more!' Charlotte winks. 'Harriet, he bombarded me the other day with questions about you, your family, even Guy. That man has *not* got you out of his system!'

17

'He's going to embarrass me in front of everyone, Daddy,' Tom
pleads. 'Tell Grandpa not to come. Please.'

Tom has only been back at school for two weeks. Guy
insisted on allowing him back only once Mr Sandlane had
given his assurance that Big Ben was being dealt with. My
younger son is still wary, and when I drop him off I see him
holding back from the other children and looking over his
shoulder, as if frightened of being attacked again.

'Mr Whitam organized it ages ago, Tom.' Guy continues
packing. Rufus arrives, looking despondently from Guy's
open case to Guy: our dog suffers from separation anxiety,
and whines miserably whenever Guy prepares to go off somewhere. 'And Grandpa is so looking forward to it. Darling,
where is my bush hat? Maisie, give me those socks, please.
Anyway, Tom, we can't stop him, he's already on the train.'

Guy's off to Kenya to start filming just as Archie is coming –
happily, staying at his club – to teach Tom's history class about

'old-fashioned warfare'. My heart goes out to my son. I'm not sure Archie will win him many friends, with his interminable memories of Carew exploits and heroes long dead.

But it's no use telling his father that. Guy is cock-a-hoop because Ross Stewart told him the controller of BBC 2 loves the sound of *Big Game*. Now, as he packs, he can't stop whistling tunelessly, grinning inanely as he throws atlases, travel guides, and countless khaki garments into the bag.

'Are you going to need all these?' I ask, dubious.

'Well, Zoë says they really want me to look the part, with twill shirt, cargo shorts, bush hat, the lot.'

'Sounds like a fancy-dress-party version of safari gear rather than what you used to wear,' I worry, and flash back to the cruel comedy of *Cheats*. 'You do want to make it look authentic.'

'Authenticity is the name of the game, darling.'

I haven't seen him this busy and excited since the days of *Lonely Hunter*, and I notice how youthful he suddenly looks as he plans the expedition down to the last detail. The hunch of the shoulders that betrayed the travel writer down on his luck has gone, replaced by a Masai warrior's confident posture. The eyes shine as bright as an explorer's on spotting his goal, and his steps bounce with the energy of a man who sees marvellous possibilities just around the corner. I still my concerns with an effort. I refuse to pour cold water on his excitement.

'Malaria tablets – don't want to forget them. And Daniela has given me a little St Christopher medal.'

Daniela is at her computer as we speak, monitoring the shrine at Lourdes. She claims there have been two miracles over the past week. I wonder if we could ask her to pray for a third: enough money for us to pay the school fees up front, and a bigger house with a long lease and no mortgage.

'I'd better warn the crew about bringing proper clothes for our dinner at Muthaiga,' Guy says as he folds an ancient navy-blue blazer. 'They probably don't know the Country Club rules.'

'I doubt the crew will need any tips, Guy.' I fold three rather frayed twill shirts. 'I mean, they'll have hired locals who know the lie of the land. Maisie!' I try to pull her off as she starts jumping on the bed.

'Yes, they probably have a fixer.' Rufus is whining and Guy bends to scratch his ears. 'But I doubt they can get anyone with my knowledge of that area round the Mara River.' Guy lifts Maisie clear off the bed. She squeals, and Alex pops his head round the door.

'You're really going, Daddy?'

'Yes, we're off tonight at nine.' Guy beams: everyone has congregated to see him prepare for the fortnight away. 'I'll send you postcards.'

That evening, when I have forced Alex into a bath, I tiptoe into the boys' room. Tom is reading.

'It'll be fine tomorrow, you know.' I take hold of his hand. I don't dare brave the ladder again. 'Grandpa is so good with children.'

Tom claps his book shut, sits up and takes off his spectacles. 'I'm going to sleep, Mummy,' he says wearily, handing me book and spectacles. 'I wish Daddy could have stopped him from coming.'

'How are things? Better since Mr Sandlane had his talk with Ben?'

'Better. But some of the others still pick on me. They call me square eyes. And say I'm skinny.' Tom lies back and squeezes his eyes shut. 'Why do I have to look different?'

'Plenty of boys are skinny and wear glasses, darling.' I stroke his hand. 'In any case, being different can be very rewarding later on. Think of your daddy – I noticed him and fell in love with him precisely because he was different from everyone else.'

'Daddy is big and tall, though.'

'You'll be a lot bigger and taller by the time you grow up.'

'They'll make fun of me if Grandpa goes on and on –'

'He won't. He can be very entertaining.' I try to convince myself.

'They'll tease me,' Tom murmurs, but he sounds less nervous than tired, and when I switch off the reading light clamped on to the bed-post, he seems already half asleep.

In the event, to my delight and surprise, Archie proved perfect. Mr Whitam, Year 5's popular history teacher, barely had time to introduce 'our distinguished guest, Major Archibald Carew, Tom's grandfather' before Archie took over. As Tom explained to me jubilantly that evening, after he and Archie had come back on the bus from Archie's club, Grandpa Carew had brought an entire armoury of World War II weapons ('You do have a gun licence, Major?' Mr Whitam had asked, looking worried). In loving detail Archie had described a Sten gun, a Browning .50, a Lee Enfield .303, allowing the children to examine every inch. He had also passed around a stick grenade.

'Is that safe?' asked Mr Whitam, blanching.

'Safe? Was war ever safe?' Archie snorted. He then painted a vivid, gory portrait of the Allies' beating back the Germans in Tobruk, the sinking of the *Bismarck*, the Battle of Monte Cassino and Operation Overlord. 'Mummy,' Tom tells me, eyes shiny, 'everyone just sat still and didn't say a word the whole way through!'

His audience, 'a bit confused about the dates', Archie winks at me, was convinced the Major had participated in the battles described. Archie didn't disabuse them, and by the time he showed off his collection of medals (all, it must be admitted, awarded to various ancestors rather than himself), he held the Year 5 history class in the palm of his hand.

'They clapped and clapped at the end, and Big Ben wolf-whistled!'

Even more promising, after school, Big Ben had asked his former victim if he could come over to photograph Grandpa Carew's medals. 'But I insisted,' Archie gives me a knowing look, 'on inviting Tom's friends, as well as Big Ben and his dad, back to the club. I told them some of my more lurid memories – the ones I thought some of their classmates might not have the stomach for – and Ben took photographs of my medals. I think his dad knows more about guns than I do. We had ginger beer and sandwiches.'

I'm so grateful to Archie I almost ask him over for supper – but then remember that we have nothing but fish-fingers to offer. In any case, he pre-empts me. He's off with an old chum from the regiment.

'Oh and I've brought these for Guy: he'd asked particularly for them.' He hands over a stash of yellowing envelopes. 'From his great-grandfather Hector to his fiancé – she was a Harriet, too. A pretty nurse Grandpa met on the Somme.'

'Darling, everything all right?' Guy sounds cheerful and surprisingly clear when he calls from Nairobi the following day.

'Yes. Major Carew was a huge success at school. I think actually he may have saved the day with regard to Big Ben.'

'Super! It's been fabulous here. We're travelling along with two safaris full of horrific White Man's Burden types. You couldn't make them up. Ross had the brilliant idea of having a drinking competition round the campfire last night. I hate to say it, but I got blotto. So did the others. The crew have promised to edit everything. Children all OK? You?'

'Children are fine. Poor you, bad hang-over?'

'Filthy. Anything coming up I should know about?'

'I'm nervous about Mary Jane's auction next week. I do wish you could come.'

'I know, I know. Get Nick instead, he's great at that sort of thing.'

'OK.'

'Ah, Zoë's come to fetch me for supper. So long, darling.'

I hang up the phone, feeling slightly uneasy. Uneasy because I was lying to Guy, which I hate doing, about wishing that he were coming to Mary Jane's auction. In fact, James is coming as one of HAC's patrons, and I'm excited at the prospect of seeing my ex without Guy on hand to protect me from I know not what.

I feel uneasy too because of Zoë's constant presence in Guy's professional life. I don't like the way she hangs on to his every word, I don't like the way she builds him into a super hero, I don't like – I stop myself, and reason that, in fact, if the telly programme really is a success, and Guy's career takes off, Zoë may well turn out to be this family's saviour. And Guy deserves what Charlotte calls an acolyte. I have been too taken up with trying to decipher my feelings about James, and James's feelings about me, to pay him enough attention.

I must be a better wife, I resolve as I phone my brother-in-law.

Mary Jane's annual auction is always held at the Langdon Hotel in Mayfair. The same two celebrities will be on hand – Matt Slicker, the game-show host, who lives next door to Mary Jane, and Selina Slade, a patron of HAC's since its launch twenty years ago. Mary Jane manages to invite about three hundred guests every time and, at £150 a ticket, that's not bad. Anjie and William, Guy and I are allowed to come for free; but usually we are not invited on to Mary Jane's table. This year, though, she rather sulkily asked us to sit with her and her 'special guests'.

'I think your James shamed her into getting us at top table,' Anjie giggles. 'She was none too pleased, but since he's going with Mary Jane she didn't want to cut up rough.'

Mary Jane has been organizing the event since well before Christmas. The band, the auctioneer, the caterers, the flower arrangements – my boss has been fussing over this auction as if it were her wedding. Anjie and I have had to do very little, except sell tickets. Anjie is really good at this. I hear her over the phone, shaming everyone from her bank manager to a local councillor into parting with £150, or £300. Although I'm the one who is always cap in hand as I approach potential donors and sponsors, I'm uncomfortable with the cold calling and arm-twisting that Anjie manages without a second thought. Still, I've managed to raise almost £5,000 myself, including four tickets to Nick's banker friends, and a pair to Jack and Charlotte, who now don't think they can come, but 'We don't mind losing the money, it's for a good cause,' Charlotte tells me, sounding as pious as if she'd sacrificed her coat for the Samaritan.

I've also sold one ticket to Lisa, our American neighbour. 'Great!' she laughed as she wrote out her cheque. 'Charity dos are perfect pick-up places: you can meet the kind-hearted and loaded.'

I spend hours trying on dresses in front of the mirror. I feel too fat to wear any of them, and invest in a pair of Donna Karan control-top tights that at £14 cost as much as the hospice shop dress in my wardrobe that I eventually settle for. I needn't have bothered. When I climb out of Lisa's Porsche, I catch my skirt on my heel, and hear a sinister tear. Half my skirt at the back has dropped three inches. I suddenly find myself wishing that Guy were here, after all: he would make me laugh about the accident, and then steer me through the crowded room safely to our table.

But there's no Guy, only Lisa, who has not noticed my predicament, but has definitely noticed Nick. 'Hey, he's not bad!' Her step quickens as she approaches my brother-in-law. 'Bulkier than Guy, isn't he? Reminds me of my college boyfriend.' Lisa strides right up to our table, ignores William and Anjie, and gives Nick an enormous smile. 'Hi, I'm Lisa Lynche, your brother's neighbour.'

I'm left to watch, awe-struck, as my brother-in-law comes under assault: questions, exclamations, smiles, looks, orders. Lisa is unstoppable. I see her changing the placement so that he sits beside her, and catch Nick's eye. For someone being targeted by a lethal operator, he looks tremendously pleased.

I read the place-card on my right and feel a flutter of excitement: James Weston.

'Where's the boss?' Anjie asks me, from her seat across the table. She looks soft and feminine in a pretty pink dress.

'And James?' William pipes up beside her. He gives me a wicked grin as he adjusts his tie. 'It'll be interesting to see how he will handle himself tonight.'

I shake my head, but can't hide a smile. 'You are wicked.'

William takes Anjie's hand in his. 'I'm not, am I, sweetpea?' Anjie doesn't answer but leans over and kisses her husband. Beside me, Nick gives me his back so he can concentrate on Lisa. I feel a little stab of jealousy. These days, do Guy and I ever give the appearance of such closeness, or sexual interest?

Two couples, friends of Mary Jane, come, introduce themselves, and take their seat around the table. And then, with a flourish of her red silk shawl, Mary Jane arrives on James's arm. I immediately forget my jealousy, my worry about the torn dress or my plump hips as James sits beside me and gives me an accomplice's wink. 'Well, here goes,' he whispers.

During the first and second courses of crab pâté followed by lamb, Mary Jane (hair up, dress plunging) monopolizes James. As Nick continues to give Lisa his full attention, I have time to survey the enormous dining room. Mary Jane has pulled it off, once again: everyone has been praising the décor of huge bouquets of white and yellow roses, which match the gold and white interiors of the Langdon; and the wine, a gift from Bold Brothers, the posh wine merchants in the City. The blue-and-white eagle that is the emblem of the Corral Bank, sponsors of the event, is prominently displayed on a large screen that hangs from the ceiling and replicated on small flags that adorn each table. The promotional pamphlet, which I edited last spring, sits neatly inside the auction guide. And everyone has made an effort: there are some splendid floor-length dresses, and complicated hairstyles with flowers and combs, and every man is either in a suit or black tie. There is a contented buzz over the white-clothed tables. Everyone has contributed to a good cause, and now feels entitled to a good time.

As the waiters clear our plates, the band strike up. They're playing quietly, because we still have the pudding to get through and then a short film that Mary Jane forced Matt Slicker into presenting about HAC's achievements and future projects. Suddenly, I feel goose-bumps: the band is playing 'Need You Tonight'. It was a song by Tinnitus, a band I can barely remember; but that song was everywhere in the winter when James and I first started going out. I wonder if James remembers.

'What does this remind you of?' He turns to me.

I don't answer. I am at Bristol, a terrified eighteen-year-old agonizing over whether I should sleep with my first boyfriend. James is patient, kind, and protective: 'I don't want to do anything you're not ready for,' he keeps telling me. We are sitting in a popular pub, with a group of his rugby friends. One – I can't remember his name, only that he was slightly drunk – makes some crass comment about my looking like I'd give a bloke a good time. James explodes, springing up from the table, and makes as if to throttle the friend. I try to calm him down, but I'm upset too, and by the time his team mates have ushered their rude friend out of the pub, I have slipped outside to cry in privacy. I feel overwhelmed by my feelings for James, the intimacy we share after only four months together, the love I can see in his eyes when he looks at me. Could this be *it*? I wonder. Mum, after all, met Dad when she was eighteen, and they've been blissfully happy together since. Is James really the man of my life? I cry and cry, standing under a tree outside the pub, in the freezing night air. Through the windows I can hear laughter. I hug my coat more tightly to myself, and wish I could run away. Suddenly, James stands before me. 'Harriet, come on, let's go.' He wraps me in his arms. From the pub I can hear the strains of 'Need You Tonight' and wonder whether this is a sign. I cling to James silently as we walk home. When we get there, our flat-mates are downstairs waiting for us. They look frightened as they greet me, and then explain. Mum's called, and when she heard I was out, she broke down over the phone. Dad's died. A massive stroke. James holds me while I make the telephone call home, holds me when I slowly walk upstairs to my room, holds me all night as I weep. I beg him to make love to me, and he does.

'It still gives me goose-bumps ...' James leans over to tell me. I nod, but daren't say anything. 'That night, Harriet ...' He doesn't go on. I feel a thrill of alarm go through me. I see Mary Jane put her hand on James's arm, and he turns to her.

Around us, the auction has begun. Buffy Lyle, the legendary Sotheby's auctioneer, is doing his patter, pushing now this, now that diner to outbid the others. I can't concentrate, conscious as I am of James's arm on my chair, his eyes on me, his leg beside mine.

'Dinner for two at the Caprice,' Buffy doesn't draw breath, 'one of London's most exclusive restaurants. Superb French food and, yes, since you ask, I would be available as guest any night from now on!' The audience laughs. 'Do I have £400? Good – £400, £450 ... Do I see £450? Yes, you, sir – excellent, the man over there in the spectacular tie.' Buffy is on a roll. 'Let's have £600 – remember, ladies, the way to a man's heart is through the stomach!' More laughter. 'Ah, yes, perfect, sir – and if that's your wife beside you, I can see why she's worth a £600 dinner. So £600 – do I hear £650 ... £650 for a night to remember in one of the capital's best restaurants ...'

James sticks his hand up. On his other side, Mary Jane gasps with happiness.

'Bravo – £650 from the gentleman at table one – very fitting, as I can see our organizer Mary Jane Thompson is right beside you, sir. Do I hear £700 ... £700 for an exquisite dinner at the Caprice?' Buffy squints as he surveys the room. 'There!'

he beams at a jowly elderly man a few tables from ours. 'Yes, £700 from our friend in the corner … Excellent! Shall we try for £750, though?' James's hand shoots up again. 'That's the spirit. The gentleman at table one is determined, let's see whether he will get his dinner. Do I hear £800 … £800 … No?' Buffy asks the jowly man. He shakes his head. 'No takers at £800?' Buffy pauses for a few seconds. 'Then, gone to the man at table one.'

'James, you're marvellous!' Mary Jane claps her hands and beams at him.

But James pays her no attention. He leans instead to me, and whispers, 'I'm taking you.'

18

'Look, Mummy: it's Uncle Nick!' Maisie presses her nose against our kitchen window. I look through the glass above her head: Nick is slipping out of Lisa's door, looking tousled if happy. He picks his way carefully across her garden, trying to avoid ours, but Maisie knocks furiously on the window pane until he turns and spots her. He looks panic-stricken at the sight of the little figure (and mine behind it). Then, sheepishly, he waves, and moves on.

Poor Nick, he's tried to conceal his visits by leaving his red Aston Martin around the corner in Wales Street. But to keep his secret he probably shouldn't leave Lisa's when we're all having breakfast.

'Well, well, how nice to see Uncle Nick.' Guy grins over the box of cornflakes. 'But we can't ask him over for a coffee or you'll be late for school.'

I'm amazed at the speed with which Lisa has struck: she completely forgot me (or pretended to) on the night of the auction, and offered Nick a ride home instead. And since then, Nick has been sneaking out of her front door every morning.

And popping up with Lisa everywhere. The other day I was pushing the buggy with Maisie and three Tesco carrier bags when I saw, through Lisa's sitting-room window, the couple embracing. The room was well lit, and they were completely unaware of passers-by, or indeed neighbours, as they clung to one another as if they were about to be forced apart for ever. Yesterday when I was cycling to school with Tom we pedalled past them as they were snogging in Nick's Aston Martin. Tom, who'd recognized his uncle's car, was all excited and wanted to stop and greet the two. But I, a few yards in front of my son, had spotted that Lisa's shirt was unbuttoned to her navel and promptly warned Tom not to look because the two were quarrelling. He dutifully pedalled quickly on, and only looked back over his shoulder once we were a safe distance from the car.

'What are they rowing about, Mummy? They're both rich!'

'Quick work, eh?' Guy is excited about the development in his brother's life. 'Singles these days don't have hang-ups the way we did …'

'Hmmm,' I murmur. It's spring and everyone seems buzzing with life. Not just Nick and Lisa: Mary Jane keeps inviting James to 'strategy lunches'. Our saintly Daniela has a secret happy smile when she answers her mobile these days. And at the school gates Charlotte keeps singing 'Love is in the Air'. Surely they don't do it when she's about to pop any second?!

As for Guy, he's been perky for days; ever since his return, in fact. He is memorizing more pieces to camera for the bits of the documentary that are Britain-based. He'll be interviewing two of the safari hunters at home, in their huge piles in the Home Counties; and doing a few scenes here, as Ross insists the audience must get a feel for Guy's background. He needs to come up with some leading questions before setting off with the crew (and Zoë, I think bitterly). My husband is spending hours on end repeating his lines in the study, sometimes pacing, sometimes standing at the window. He hasn't had a chance, yet, to read the letters that Archie left for him.

'I must – there are about twenty letters between Great-Grandfather Hector and his sweetheart. She's the original Harriet Carew, darling. A really impressive woman … As soon as I've wrapped this up, I want to have a proper read.'

'You have quite a lot on your plate already. There's *Rajput* and the chapter on Lyme Regis …' I try not to sound like a nag. 'And have you been able to do anything for Percy lately?'

Guy looks up from the mobile he is always clutching these days ('It could be Zoë or the crew trying to get hold of me urgently') and utters a bored-sounding 'Huh?'

I give up and call upstairs to Daniela that I'm off to school with Tom. It's Tuesday, one of my days off, and I'm eager to get to Charlotte's. I need to talk over James's invitation to the Caprice.

As I arrive, Charlotte's organic farm box is being delivered – I spot broccoli, lettuce, carrots, watercress, tomatoes and apples.

'I've started on my juicing again – Dr Guong says I need more iron,' my best friend explains as she leads me into the kitchen. 'Mint tea? Green? Or a fresh juice with ginger?'

'How about a fresh juice and hold the ginger?' I sit down and then jump back up. 'But I feel as if I should be doing this for you – it's getting awfully near.'

'I know.' Charlotte beams, holding on to her enormous stomach with both hands. 'If Summer is like the first three, he/she will be early.'

As usual, I feel a broody wave wash over me – then I will it away. Charlotte whizzes a few carrots, lemon halves and celery sticks in her juicer, then hands over the glass with a dreamy look. 'Nanny says it's a girl, just as you thought.'

I don't answer and take up my foaming glass instead: 'Yum, delicious!'

Charlotte sips her glass then turns to me. 'I'm sorry we couldn't make it the other night. Jack's been working all hours at the bank. How was it?'

'Charlotte, it was great, but then they played "Need You Tonight". Do you remember, it was James's and my song. James was sitting there beside me, telling me how he still got goose-bumps when he thinks about that night we first made love.'

'Goodness, that's a dangerous thing to say!'

I look at Charlotte: does she disapprove of me? Does she think I'm taking this whole thing too far? Her expression tells me nothing.

'And then' – I'm sounding as breathless as a teen boasting about her hot date – 'he outbid everyone to win a dinner for two at the Caprice and he asked me!'

'Hmmm …' Charlotte downs the remaining juice. 'Are you going to go?'

'I don't think I should,' I say, gaze sunk into my orange glass. 'I mean, it doesn't seem right, somehow. A lunch, a coffee, yes, but …'

'So you've had those, then?' Charlotte looks curious.

'He comes into HAC a lot, Charlotte.' I try to defend myself.

'Why might that be?' Charlotte gives me a wicked little smile.

'Nothing's happened between us.' I shake my head resolutely. 'I would never lie to Guy or cheat him in any way. It's just that I know James so well; being with him feels absolutely natural. So I sometimes find it difficult to remember that he's a divorced man and I am a married woman. Does that sound amoral?'

'How does Guy feel about this?' Charlotte presses me.

'Guy?' I ask, blank. Then I answer, rather crossly, 'Guy doesn't know any of this is happening. Quite frankly, Charlotte, I could elope with James and leave them all behind and Guy wouldn't notice, he's so taken up with his telly work.'

'You mean the Zoë programme?'

'Exactly. He's off with her, discussing the film, every other night, and they're having endless lunches and coffees and dinners.'

'Oh, Harriet, you are the limit!' Charlotte laughs. 'Here you are, worrying about *one* dinner invitation from James Weston, while your husband is merrily enjoying countless coffees, lunches and dinners with a girl half his age who thinks he's the cat's whiskers!'

I allow Charlotte's words to sink in. Slowly I ask, 'You think …?'

'I don't think anything.' Charlotte adopts her most matter-of-fact voice and manner. 'All I know is that we're all approaching middle age' – Ha! I think, looking at Charlotte blooming and pregnant, *you* are not; the rest of us are – 'and a mid-life crisis is not uncommon – especially among men. Two years ago, do you remember when Sally came to work for Jack?' I vaguely remember talk of Jack's pert new secretary. 'I had a real wake-up call. Jack works long hours. Sally is pretty, fun and very young. She thought her colleagues were *gods,* which was extremely flattering for someone who thought he was getting over the hill. Jack started mentioning her whenever he talked about his day at the office ...' I shut my eyes: doesn't Guy do the same with Zoë? 'Then he started bringing her up when we were discussing which restaurant to go to, and what film to see. The worst was when we went clothes shopping and he kept saying that some dress would look stunning on Sally. I had a real scare, I can tell you.' Charlotte's eyes narrow at the memory. 'So I whipped into action. I knew I'd slightly let myself go – I'd put on a stone since Lily, my hair-cut was a bit old-fashioned, wrinkles were popping up. Trophy wife, I wasn't. So I started going to the gym and got on a diet and I decided I'd have regular maintenance sessions with the hairdresser and the manicurist, and I even started with botox.'

'But, Charlotte!' I cry in dismay. 'I don't have the time or the money for all that!'

'You *make* the time,' Charlotte goes on, relentless. 'And OK, you may not be able to go to Mario's every six weeks, but you can certainly keep yourself groomed on your own. It's *really* important.'

I suddenly remember Leo's mum at the hair dresser's and her comment about my roots. And I think of Jasmine Jerome carping about my hips. Now my best friend is raising the alarm about my husband's mid-life crisis. I want to cry. Last time I came to this kitchen, I was beating myself up because I'd managed to ignore the warning signs of Tom being bullied; should I now be panicking because I've failed to see the warn-ing signs that my husband is wearying of me? I think back to how proud Guy was of Zoë's admiration at Waterstone's; how much time he has carved out of every day to spend with her 'discussing things'; how itchy he gets when the phone doesn't ring and Zoë doesn't call him urgently to some meeting. Have I been blind? Suddenly I don't want Charlotte's advice, I just want to run away from this perfect gleaming kitchen and her dreadful insinuations.

'I … I forgot that I'm the one who's supposed to pick Maisie up today from playgroup.' I stand up, bringing my glass to the shiny bathtub-sized sink. 'Let me know the moment anything happens.' I make a vague gesture towards Charlotte's belly in its stretchy, JoJo Maman Bébé top.

But Charlotte knows me too well: with difficulty she stands up, and gives me a hug. 'I didn't mean to upset you, Harry. I just think you shouldn't worry about James. He's devoted to you still, and that's clear. It's your marriage that needs your attention.' I breathe in the almond-and-coconut aro-matherapy oils she massages on to herself daily – 'but no laven-der, because that could harm Summer' – and feel slightly calmer as a result. 'Just be firm with James and say coffee is one thing, but you know Guy would be a bit surprised if you had dinner with your ex.'

I get another hug and then I'm allowed to go.

I feel so rattled, I walk the bicycle down the street rather than get on it and risk falling off. I love Guy, I love our children, and if sometimes our life together seems stressful and too domesticated, I also know that I don't want to upset any of them, ever. The thought that I might have alienated Guy, or ignored his needs, haunts me and I find myself playing short films in my mind of recent times together: the day when Guy came home exulting about his meeting with Zoë and Ross at the BBC – was I suitably supportive and proud? Or was I mooning over some incident with James at the office? What about all those phone calls from Nairobi: did I ask enough about his filming, or did I always moan about an unpaid bill or some difficulty at school? And just this morning, when he was so excited about the letters of the first Harriet Carew: did I show any interest whatever? Wasn't I bursting to rush off and ask Charlotte about the Caprice instead?

I feel my stomach sink with foreboding. Charlotte's right: I should stop thinking about my relationship with James deepening, and think instead of how my marriage is fraying into a few wisps of could-have-been and should-have-been.

By the time I'm home, I've worked myself into such a state of fear that I'm ready to throw myself at Guy's feet and offer to toast his slippers, bring him a pipe and a cuppa, and ask him what he would like for supper. And then I suddenly think that this is precisely what is wrong with Harriet the wife. I should be thinking of slipping into some sexy little number, throwing myself at Guy's feet, and asking him what he would like in bed.

I push open the door and call out tentatively, 'Guy?' Silence. I throw off my bicycle helmet and jacket and walk into the study: no one. I look in the kitchen, then in our room: he's not there. For an instant I think wildly that he's left me, run off with Zoë, and that if I look, I'll find a note listing all my faults. My lower lip trembles, then my eyes fill, then I'm bawling, and looking so fish-like when I catch sight of my face in the mirror that I throw myself face down on our bed to avoid the reflection.

I cry and cry, for I don't know how long. When I finish, and the sobs have given way to sniffles, I sit up and ring Mum. She's the only person who can console me, the only one who I know to be one hundred per cent unquestioningly behind me.

'Have you been crying?' she asks immediately.

'No ... er ... yes. Oh, Mum, I think Guy's unhappy with the way things are ... I mean, I think he's unhappy with *me* ... He may even be thinking of leaving ...'

I hear my mother's sharp intake of breath at the other end. 'Why do you say that?' she asks.

'He's so preoccupied with his TV thing, and I've been so preoccupied with James, and I don't think we're on the same wave-length at all these days. And there's a young, pretty producer who seems to be spending an awful lot of time with him.' I choke back another sob. 'Mum?' I try to break my mother's silence at the other end of the phone. 'Are you still there?'

'Of course. You're at that dangerous age.' My mother speaks slowly and softly, as if she were imparting an important lesson to a child. 'Middle age. Or mid-life crisis, as they call it now. Men are particularly susceptible. It takes a little flirtation, some young colleague who thinks they're wonderful, or an old flame from the past …' It's my turn for a sharp intake of breath. 'And twenty years' marriage goes up in smoke.' I stifle a sob. 'Look, don't panic. Guy is a good person. Just don't ignore him because of anyone else.'

I hang up the phone and guilt fills me: I've been so obvious in my preoccupation with James that my mother is having to warn me against it. Oh, Guy, what have I been risking?

And then I hear keys in our front door, and Guy's footsteps downstairs. 'Guy!' I call out, and almost warily descend our stairs.

'Harriet …' My husband stands at the foot of the stairs, his face serious, his eyes on me. 'Shall we talk?'

19

I look down at Guy's serious expression, and hold my breath.

'Zoë says we're down to one hour,' Guy is saying as I tune back in. 'We're over-budget and the BBC says there's too many travel programmes in the schedule to allow for three parts. I can't believe it: all the work we've put into it, and now this.'

Relief swamps me: he's not leaving me after all. Or at least, not yet.

'Guy!' I cry joyfully, and then check myself when I see his quizzical look. 'I mean, darling, I'm so sorry. But one hour at the right time is better than a three-hour series shown at ten past midnight. Do you remember how Crispin Kerr's last series was shunted to some ungodly hour and no one even saw it?'

The cloud over Guy lifts slightly. 'Yes …' He nods, remembering his glee at his rival's set-back. 'Yes, I know you're right. But you should *see* how many fabulous scenes we managed to get: Harry Phillips makes a complete ass of himself when he gets drunk as a skunk and starts chasing a monkey and begs it to kiss him. We've got Bobo Langham-Dole coming out with incredibly insulting remarks about his fellow safari hunters ... Loads of really revealing stuff. How will we compress it all into one hour?'

'Don't worry, darling: they're experts, this is their job.' I move into the kitchen, offering my usual panacea: 'What about some tea?'

Guy happily accepts, and sets down a folder full of papers, then helps himself to chocolate-chip biscuits. He looks pensively through the window. 'This Lisa-Nick thing seems to be getting serious. And Lisa wouldn't be bad, you know. As a sister-in-law, I mean. Hard as nails, like all those City people, but she's fun – and the two of them would have plenty of dosh.'

'Yes.' I'm filling the teapot. 'From the glimpses I've caught of him sneaking out of her house, he looks happy.'

I splash a bit of tea on to the table, and realize my hands are trembling. I've had a scare. I will never, ever, ever jeopardize our relationship again, I tell myself forcefully.

'It's odd, seeing them go through all the stages that we went through back in our twenties.' Guy smiles avuncularly.

'Hmmm, yes,' I murmur, and then remember the first time we met. It was Rory Williams's birthday party. He was at Cambridge with Guy, his sister Louise at Bristol with me. Louise and I were invited to Rory's party, and I had been terribly nervous about meeting his glamorous friends. They were posh, at Cambridge and artsy: some were stars in the 'Footlights', others led grown-up social lives in London and popped up in *Tatler* and *Vogue* like celebrities. For half the evening I despaired of ever being asked to dance; I knew no one and caught no one's eye. Then suddenly I noticed a dark-haired, attractive boy beckoning me. 'Sorry, but could you come here?'

I looked surprised, took a step towards him then pointed to my chest. 'Me?' I mouthed. 'Yes, you,' the youth hissed. When I reached him, he beamed with relief. 'Thanks. It's just that I can't move.'

'What's happened?' I asked, fearing an accident or a terrible sports injury.

'I teased the Hound of the Baskervilles over there –' he pointed to Louise's 'naughty little Tintin', a four-foot mastiff with nasty eyes and long fangs '– and he took revenge on me by tearing my pants into strips. Take a look – hey, not too closely …' I bent down and looked: a gash gaped down the back of his trousers.

'What are you going to do?'

'Avoid humiliation by staying quite still right here, monopolizing you. I hope you won't mind.' He flashed me a smile that promised such fun and adventure that I completely forgot Louise, who was looking everywhere for me; and, soon, James, out in Nigeria.

'Thanks.' Guy takes a sip of his tea then waves at me. 'Back to the grindstone. I've got to get those lines word-perfect.' Mug in hand, he goes off.

I sigh happily, and sit back in the chair. All is well, all is as before. I shall park my fantasy about James in a safe corner, and allow it to gather dust and rust, because it will never be taken out again.

My eyes alight on the folder Guy left behind. *Lyme Regis*, the fat red letters spell. I feel a small tremor of alarm: surely the chapter on Lyme Regis for that coffee-table book was due weeks ago? I take a peek inside the folder: page after page of notes in Guy's handwriting, page after page of photocopied articles and photographs about the topography, history, and tourist attractions of Lyme. But not a paragraph of what might constitute a chapter of a book. I breathe in deeply: gone are all my worries about not being able to keep my husband's interest. All I can think about is how we cannot afford to lose this contract. Or offend Simon, who secured it for Guy.

I pick up the folder, wondering if I should say anything. Then, suddenly determined, follow Guy to the study. I stop in my tracks as I hear him on the phone: 'It's no problem, really. I know how tight budgets are these days.' Who is he talking to? 'I won't hear of it, Zoë: I'm happy to postpone payment until we finish.' Guy chuckles at something Zoë is telling him. 'It's been such fun.'

Fun? Fun! I want to scream. 'Fun' to worry about how to pay our bills? 'Fun' to darn for the third time Alex's uniform shirt at the elbow or Tom's uniform trousers at the knee? 'Fun' to know that Maisie won't be doing ballet with her friends because it costs £100 a term? 'Fun' to have nightmares about the bursar at the Griffin, or the woman from an Asian call-centre telling you quietly but firmly that she *must* have the minimum payment for the credit card *now*.

If this is fun, Guy Carew, you have a seriously warped sense of humour. I breathe in deeply and knock on the door.

'Darling, what about the chapter on Lyme Regis?' I try to sound cheerful and unbothered.

'Oh, I'm going to have to deliver it late, I'm afraid.' Guy sounds completely unfazed. 'Too much on with the telly stuff.'

'What does Simon say?' I ask, and realize that my despairing tone has betrayed my concern.

'Oh, Simon always fusses.' Guy shrugs. 'But he knows that, if this series is a hit, my value goes up tenfold.'

'Guy,' I try to control my voice but I'm livid, 'what if the programme isn't this huge, earth-shaking success? What if it's good, but no one notices? We can't afford to let everything else fall by the wayside!' My voice is shaking and I can feel the sting of tears on their way. 'Have you seen our bills? They're huge, and I haven't been able to pay them yet. What are we going to do?'

'Harriet, let's approach this logically, shall we?' Guy snaps. 'There's no problem with pushing the deadline back a little. Publishers make allowance for small changes to their schedule. As for Simon, he's accepted it, and in fact he's even more excited about this series than I am. Now' – he turns back to his desk – 'I need to practise my lines.'

I stomp off, out of the study and into the sitting room. I sit there, fuming. Where will this end?

I take out the calculator and start adding up our bills. Gas – £130. Visa – £370. This includes two weekly Tesco shops; three children's birthday presents – you can't show up empty-handed when the parents have rented a clown and a fire-eater; a little adjustable bed for Maisie from Lotts' Road auction house – all the money we saved on the price was spent on hiring a minivan to ferry it across the river; and new spectacles for Tom. Plus £180 for the quarterly Thames Water bill. That's …

I stop and hear Daniela and Maisie chatting cheerfully outside our front door. I must pull myself together. I don't want Daniela to worry about our finances any more than she already does – I had to postpone her last month's salary once again. And I won't have my little girl find her mother in a state. I cock my head to listen to Daniela and her charge. I almost smile, despite my worries, at how grown-up Maisie sounds already. It is only when I make out two tall figures through the frosted panes of the door that I realize that's not my daughter Daniela is talking to, but Allie Moorfield: I'd forgotten that she and Tamara were coming over for a play session this afternoon. Omigod: I haven't got the soya milk for Tamara (she's lactose intolerant), I doubt I've got the peppermint tea for Allie ('I'm no good with caffeine'), I haven't baked cookies (which Allie does every time we visit her home) and I haven't tidied either Maisie's bedroom or the sitting room or … the bills! I almost scream, and push the pile of red-letter reminders and bills into my little desk drawer only just in time before Allie glides in.

'Hello, hello,' she cries out as she smiles brightly like a posh Pollyanna, all feel-good and look-good. Her concern at the sight of our untidy sitting room becomes naked alarm when Rufus comes bounding in, barking furiously, from his bed in the kitchen. Before I can say or do anything to protect her, Allie is tottering backwards as Rufus's tongue and paws smear her white corduroys. She lets out a little yelp, while Tamara, in her wake, starts wailing.

It's a nightmare two hours. Allie takes a long time to recover from Rufus's 'attack', as she calls it; as does Tamara, who unfortunately consoles herself with the tin of chocolate-chip biscuits Guy had left open. She has helped herself to three before her mother realizes the crime being committed and sends her off to the 'quiet corner', practically in sobs about 'the poison in those ready-made biscuits ... how *could* you, Tamara?'

The quiet corner turns out to be the one corner where Daniela, usually so scrupulous, must not have swept this morning, for Tamara lets out a loud 'ugh!' as she holds up a ball of hair and dust. I want to die – or at least call down Daniela for a helping hand; but our au pair has retreated upstairs to her room, and I know she will be deaf to all entreaties for hours now, as she sits staring wide-eyed at the dark grotto in Lourdes. As I turn my attention to the peppermint tea (hurrah! I've located one ancient bag) Maisie extracts a red reminder from British Gas out of an envelope I'd overlooked on the window sill, and presents it grandly to Allie, who blushes and then casts a long pitying look in my direction.

'That is the worst catalogue of disasters I've ever heard!' James laughs. He sets down his cappuccino. 'Do you think Allie will ever darken your doorway again?'

'Doubt it,' I sigh. We're sitting in the café on the High Street, and I feel as if all the horror was a long, long time ago. 'I'm sure she'll be telling all the other mums in Maisie's playgroup about the chaos and squalor we live in. I shouldn't be surprised if they raised a collection for Maisie and her family.'

I can't help a giggle, but then turn serious. 'James …' I don't dare look him in the eye. 'That was very generous of you the other night.'

'Let me know what night suits you best and I'll book it.'

'Well, I don't have a very busy social life, so really, whenever fits in with you.'

'And Guy?' James's eyes search me as he brings the cappuccino to his lips.

'Oh, he's fine about it,' I say breezily. 'He knows we're working together.'

In fact, I have yet to bring up the dinner with Guy. But after overhearing him talk to Zoë, and seeing him take our financial crisis so lightly, I feel the urge to punish him: dinner with an old pal in an exorbitantly priced West End restaurant sounds just the ticket.

'No jealousy?' James lowers his voice.

'Hmmm?' I ask – then blush.

'He's a cool customer.' James shakes his head as if in wonderment at Guy's indifference. 'I'd be watching you with a beady eye.'

'James, we're old friends. And now we're colleagues,' I persist, though my voice lacks conviction.

'I suppose he's guessed why I decided to work for HAC in the first place.'

'What?' I frown, puzzled.

'I mean that Guy's probably guessed that it's no accident that I should end up working for the same charity as you.' I am burning under his intense blue gaze. 'I saw your name on the HAC brochure when it came through the post. My marriage with Jasmine was breaking up, and I wanted to do something to pull me out of the rut. Then I saw your name on that brochure and I knew that I wanted to see you again.'

I bring the skinny latte to my lips, but cannot take so much as a sip. I'm so stunned by James's confession that I don't know what to say. He joined HAC because of me. It was no extraordinary coincidence, our ending up working side by side.

'I'm sorry if I've shocked you.' James half smiles. 'I didn't want to stalk you, I just wanted to see you again. I wanted to see whether you'd changed with your – new circumstances.'

Now he's at a loss for words and we sit there, at the corner table, in complete silence.

Suddenly someone taps the glass beside me: there's Anjie, making a face, her hand in William's. William is in his 'work clothes' – baseball cap, low-slung jeans and, despite the chilly April wind, a T-shirt that shows off his bulging arm muscles. The two try to meet up during the day whenever 'his nibs' is on a job near the office.

I'm so grateful to Anjie for breaking the tension between James and me that I start waving furiously back at her. 'I think she's trying to warn us that Mary Jane's back at the office and on the look-out.' I smile at James.

'Let's go, then.' James obeys my need to defuse the situation. We walk back to the office about a yard apart, self-consciously avoiding any point of contact between us.

'Why's Granny not here with us for Easter?' Tom asks, cross. He hates any change to our family traditions.

240

'Auntie Mel's offered to take her on a cruise around the Mediterranean,' I explain, sounding almost as cross.

Of course I am delighted for my mum, who hasn't been abroad for years now. But I will miss her, as will the children, and it annoys me that of all the times to make her grand generous offer, my sister should have chosen Easter, which she knows full well Mum always spends here with us. And if I'm honest, I resent the way my sister can always do the big gesture, out-flanking me in my mother's eyes in terms of money spent, distance travelled and effort made.

'It won't be the same without Granny.' Tom shakes his head gravely. 'But Daddy *will* be back, won't he?' The children are no longer amused by Daddy's film trips, and they want him home at their beck and call. With a sigh, I cut the fifth fairy out of Maisie's *Princess Fairies* magazine. The phone rings.

'Mum!' Alex calls from upstairs. 'It's Simon Calder!'

Guy's agent – what does he want? I wonder, with a stab of fear. I pick up the kitchen extension. 'Hullo, Simon.' I try to ooze charm.

'Just wondering where Guy's got to.' I'm not important enough (nor is my husband) for Simon to try to conceal his annoyance. 'That chapter on Lyme Regis was due on the fourteenth and he promised if I wrangled an extension for him he'd have it in my hands on the thirtieth. Today's the fourth, Hilda.'

'Harriet,' I counter mildly. We really have plummeted to bottom of his list. There was a time when Simon knew not only my name but our children's too.

'Sorry – of course, Harriet. Well, Harriet, I wish you could use your powers of persuasion to convince that husband of yours that this is serious stuff.' Simon's voice is agitated, and slightly blurred. I check my watch: 3 p.m., perhaps he's just had a boozy lunch. 'I can't be doing with clients who don't take their commitments seriously.'

'Of course not.'

'Well, get it into his head – whenever he does resurface. Sorry to throw this C-R-A-P at you, but I never seem to get a hold of him these days. Goodbye, Harriet.'

I hang up the phone and bury my face in my hands. 'Mummy, Mummy, what's wrong?' Maisie wraps her arms around me.

'Oh, darling, it's … it's just … that I've cut off your little blue fairy's arm.' Which I have.

'It's a girl!' Charlotte sounds ecstatic over the phone. 'Harriet, she's the most beautiful thing you've ever seen!'

'Oh, Charlotte!!!' I'm moved, and happy, and in the end not jealous, after all.

'Will you come and see her?'

'At home?' Charlotte had been proposing to have the baby in a birthing pool Jack and the boys would build in their capacious kitchen: 'So good for baby, to be welcomed into this world by warm water,' Charlotte had explained.

'No-no-no-no, we're at the Portland …' Then, slightly sheepishly, 'I started getting a bit worried about the pain … And Jack had booked a room here as a precaution.'

Jack, I think, knows his Manic Organic better than she does herself.

I rush off by bus to the Portland, leaving Daniela in charge of the household. Guy is filming in Wiltshire with his crew.

There are more flowers at the Portland than in Kew Gardens, and the staff, quiet-spoken and in white tunics, are as solicitous as at some country spa. They look like they're ready for your lymphatic massage session rather than delivering your baby. A number of the names on the private rooms are famous – and I recognize one or two of the visitors from Anjie's readings of *Hello!*

'Hello,' Charlotte looks white as a sheet, with huge dark circles round her eyes. But as she beams at the little pink thing asleep in her arms, she looks soft and radiant, a Renaissance Madonna cradling the Holy Infant. Jack sits beside her, looking washed out but proud.

'She's beautiful,' I whisper.

'Her mother's looks.' Jack grins at his youngest. 'It was a hell of a night, but look at her … Worth every minute …'

'Can I?'

Charlotte nods and lifts Summer into my arms. She is unbelievably light, and the scent of her, that very distinct, new-born baby smell, brings memories of my children's births flooding back. 'Summer,' I whisper and the name doesn't seem so silly after all. The sleeping baby doesn't stir but half smiles in her slumber. I could weep with tenderness, and hold her close to my bosom.

'What a blessing,' Charlotte whispers.

'How long will you stay here?' I whisper back, thinking that the place looks so inviting, I may check in myself.

'We've got the maternity nurse scheduled for Thursday.' Jack munches on a few of the grapes left on Charlotte's tray. 'We've got her for a month, and then, since Mary Rose can't cope with four, we'll be getting her some help – someone who can do a bit of household stuff as well.'

I nod, as if I could understand such arrangements.

'The children are over the moon.' Jack has now moved on to the chocolates that sit in a huge deluxe assortment. 'You should have seen them this morning, Theo held her like a pro.' I suddenly realize why Jack looks so odd – he's not reaching for his BlackBerry every second. But no sooner have I formulated the thought, than Jack's hand goes to his chest. 'Sorry, love, let me check on this.' And he moves into a corner of the room. 'Charlie, what's up? … Yeah, keep pushing up the price till we squeeze them all out. No, no, you won't see me later – I've just had a baby.'

20

'Darling ...' I choose my moment carefully: Guy's brushing his teeth in our bathroom and I'm retrieving two bras and my tummy-control tights (if you wash them carefully they last and last and last) from the provisional washing line I've set up across our bathtub. 'James Weston's invited me to dinner on Thursday night. It's part of the package he got at the HAC auction. I've asked Daniela, and she's happy to stay in and help you with the children.'

There. I've said it. I don't turn to look at my husband, but open the top drawer of our dresser and rustle through my bras and knickers with the greatest concentration.

'That's fine, darling.' Guy speaks through a mouthful of Colgate. 'Just make sure you leave something for us to eat. Czech food is absolutely foul.'

'Of course.' Crossly I bang the drawer shut: jealousy is a bore in one's spouse, I'm sure; but this total indifference is off-putting too. And to punish my husband I feign sleep when, having checked on the doors downstairs, given Rufus a fresh bowl of water, and told Alex to switch off his light, Guy gets into bed.

I climb the stairs at HAC two at a time. I'm late and I really, really don't want Mary Jane Thompson to see me. Last week she made a point of looking at her watch as I ran in, late and sweaty and exhausted after having chased Rufus round the common in pursuit of a pretty little Yorkshire terrier bitch.

'Harriet, could we have a word?' I freeze: Mary Jane Thompson stands directly behind me.

'Of course.' I turn, hoping that Anjie is there to give me a sign of encouragement. But Anjie hasn't come in yet, and it's just me and our boss.

'Let's go down for a coffee, shall we?' Mary Jane's voice gives nothing away and I feel the shivers run down my spine: has she discovered that I'm late in applying for the Ford grant? But surely even she doesn't think we are an 'international charity promoting dialogue between East and West'. Has she cottoned on to my having fun at her expense with Anjie? But surely no one could accuse Mary Jane of being thin-skinned. Is she going to fire me? I admit I'm not on the same wave-length, and yes, I know that I've taken some liberties with our schedule when the children have been ill and maybe not been one hundred per cent concentrated when James has been around. But …

And then, as I follow Mary Jane in her high heels down the stairs and on to the High Street, I suddenly fear the worst: she's going to ask me whom James is inviting to the Caprice for his dinner à deux.

Silently, she leads me to the café down the street. My stomach churns nervously: maybe I should throw myself at her feet and explain that I won't accept the dinner invitation after all, that I'm not interested in rekindling an old friendship and that, if she wants, I could suggest that she go in my place.

'Espresso? Cappuccino?' Mary Jane barks.

'Cappuccino, thanks,' I say, and only too late remember the danger of whiskers. Oh well, I don't mind giving her a good laugh.

'Harriet, I've been meaning to talk to you …' Mary Jane slips into the chair beside me. We sit in a corner of the café, and I'm grateful for the dim lighting: I feel I've gone white as a sheet, I'm so frightened. 'But it's all a bit difficult …' Mary Jane pauses, and I could swear she looks uncomfortable. Omigod, she's going to do it: she's going to fire me. 'I know you're closer to Anjie than I am, and this is why I think I should tell you.'

'What's happened?' Any fear for my future dissipates, replaced by concern about my colleague.

'Nnnnothing …' Mary Jane turns to look over her shoulder. 'Or at least nothing that I know of. But … oh, I might as well tell you: I saw William with another woman.'

'What do you mean another woman?'

'I mean William had his hand on another woman's thigh, and his tongue down her throat.' Mary Jane winces with distaste at the memory. 'I had left the car at the garage for an MOT. I got on the bus and I saw William at once. No mistaking him. He didn't see me, he was so engrossed in this woman.' She looks at my open-mouthed shock. 'Then he started kissing her. Dreadful. She was half his age, blonde and tarty.' Mary Jane sighs, takes the first sip of her espresso. 'I simply don't know whether to tell Anjie. It's been a week now, and I just don't know what I should do.'

I've never seen Mary Jane unsure of her position, and for a moment I forget Anjie and study my boss in this new light. But then the misery, the horror, that Anjie will suffer strikes me like a blow.

'I can't bear it! She adores him. And they're so close: she's always stealing out for a coffee with him when he works any-where near HAC.' I gulp, suddenly feeling awkward: I wouldn't want Mary Jane to think Anjie was skiving.

Mary Jane merely nods. 'I know, I know.'

'But as to what you should do ...' I shake my head. 'I just can't think.'

'Maybe best to leave it. It's just that ...' Mary Jane sighs. 'It's exactly what happened to me ten years ago, and I wish to God someone had given me a warning, because when he told me, it came out of nowhere. I sometimes wonder whether – had I been prepared – I could have salvaged the situation.'

I open my mouth to say something, then shut it again. My boss is confiding in me, and I must do nothing to stop this.

'Then again, was there anything worth salvaging? My mother used to say that a marriage can be as brittle as one of those high-maintenance older women with gold chains and gold highlights, risking a broken hip wearing sky-high heels.' Mary Jane finishes her espresso and casts me a soft look. 'I wouldn't want Anjie to hang on to something worthless.'

'Don't say anything, Mary Jane,' I tell her resolutely. 'It's important that we're there for her when he tells her, or is caught red-handed. But I don't think you can be the whistle-blower.'

'Phew!' Mary Jane looks relieved. 'All right, if you say so. You know them better.'

I leave half my cappuccino, and feel terribly empty as we make our way back. But I also experience a small warm glow. My boss is a human being after all.

It's been a case of 'don't mention the war'. Ever since I've told Guy that I'm having dinner with James on Thursday, I have done nothing but make slips of the tongue. As I step out the door to go to Tesco's, I say, 'Just going for a brief affair'; when Maisie shows me a collage of tinsel scraps, I praise her, 'That's great, my lover.' Worst of all was when I called Guy up to bed: 'Jam – Guy, darling, come to bed, you're exhausted!'

I have James on my mind. James and the dinner at the Caprice next Thursday. Guy seems impervious to my agitation, but I've caught Alex twirling his finger by his temple when, for the umpteenth time, I call him 'Ja-lex'. And even Daniela's serene composure buckles under the strain of my losing my train of thought three times in the space of our five-minute conversation: 'Mrs Caroo, everything OK?'

No, I want to shout, nothing is OK. How can it be, when I'm off for dinner with my first lover, who happens to be working with me, and happens to make me feel sexy and young and absolutely the focus of his attention? How can everything be OK when what I want to look like is my eighteen-year-old self, slim and pink-cheeked in pale blue, while my reflection shows me a faded thirty-five-plus in a size-14 second-hand dress from Hobbs?

* * *

By Thursday evening I'm in a frenzy. I can't find the right dress, I can't find the right shoes, I don't know whether to put my hair up or leave it down, I don't know whether to wear a necklace, and I can't think where I've put my mascara.

It's as if my tension has infected my entire family: Guy shouts at the boys when they start quarrelling over whose turn it is to update their Facebook profile, Maisie refuses to eat her baked beans on toast, and Daniela worries about the way the miracle-count at Lourdes has halved this month.

'Tonight is James Weston, isn't it?' For a second, Guy raises his eyes from the William Dalrymple book he is reading. I'm putting on my tummy-control tights.

'Ummmm, yes, tonight.' I try to sound casual: has he noticed the elaborate preparations?

'What are you wearing?' In fourteen years of marriage, I don't believe Guy has ever asked me that before.

'Oh, just this thing –' I say from inside the little black dress I'm slipping on. It's my second-best dress, a winter sales find from Whistles last year. I wore my best dress to James's Christmas drinks, and I don't dare wear it again. 'The shepherd's pie is in the oven, so you won't have to suffer some Czech horror,' I reassure him as I slip on my shoes. 'Just make sure Tom rings Miles to see if he can come to his birthday party. And' – I pretend to check the contents of my evening bag – 'don't bother to wait up, darling.'

Then I'm off to the station to take the tube to Mayfair. As I get out at Green Park, I do two things I normally never do: I extract a small pocket mirror in which I check my hair, which needs brushing, and my lips, which are fine;

and then I switch off my mobile. Guy is with the children, after all.

I walk past the doorman in a bowler hat, through the revolving doors, and find myself in a softly lit room. The maître-d' is welcoming rather than intimidating, but I still feel self-conscious as I'm led past the diners in this intimate space. When we reach the table where James sits waiting, though, he gives me a look of such admiration that my embarrassment melts.

'You look fabulous,' he smiles as I settle down beside him.

'I've never been here,' I confess as I study the chrome and monochrome interior, the black-and-white photos on the walls. How could I, when dinner for two probably costs as much as my weekly wage from HAC?

'David Bailey –' James points out the photograph close to us.

As we read the menu, the piano player tinkles 'As Time Goes By' and I thrill at the guilty thought that nothing could be more romantic.

When we've ordered, James entertains me with a few anecdotes from his business deals in France.

'I sometimes think –' he tells me as the waiter fills my glass with red wine '– that it wouldn't be a bad idea to settle there. Great food, great wine and better weather.'

He casts me a sideways look as if he's testing my reaction to this threat.

'You wouldn't really move there, would you?' I ask, trying to control the disappointment in my voice.

'Well, there's not much to keep me here, is there?' Again he shoots me an appraising look. I study my bouillabaisse as if a jewel were sunk in its delicious broth. 'It's the great advantage of not having a family,' James persists. 'You're responsible only for yourself.'

'It's not the only one,' I smile as I attempt to lighten the mood. 'Mary Jane is always telling me that my family responsibilities are an obstacle to my work.'

'Oh, Mary Jane –' James shrugs his shoulders '– there's a woman who's played her cards wrong. She's so angry with the world because her husband left her, she risks missing out on life altogether.'

'She has a soft spot for you.'

'Not any more.' He laughs. 'I took her out, you know.'

'You took her out?' I ask, unsure of what he means: I know that they've been out to endless lunches and probably dinners because of HAC, or with HAC donors and potential donors.

'"Out" as in I took her for a candle-lit dinner in a restaurant, me picking her up and escorting her home. The works.'

'Oh.' I cannot trust myself to say more: I feel as if I've been taken up by a gale-force wind in which jealousy and anger and sheer disbelief swirl around me.

'I think she was pleased by the attention. But then I started asking her so many questions about you, she got annoyed.' He pauses. I don't say anything. 'To give her credit, she didn't tell me to buzz off. She just told me she didn't know you well enough to give me any of the information I was asking for.'

'What – what did you want to know?' I ask softly, and I feel as if, with these words, I'm betraying Guy. I'm allowing James to ask me about my married life, an existence spent hovering over children, trying to support my husband, making ends meet. I'm giving him the opportunity to probe the threadbare bits, the frayed corners, the humdrum minutes. What marriage could withstand such scrutiny?

'Oh, I wanted to know if you were happy, if he was good enough for you, if you needed my help in any way.' James speaks lightly, as if making fun of his over-protective self. 'You know, all the stuff an ex-boyfriend would be thinking about.'

'We-ell,' I begin, carefully tiptoeing into this dangerous territory, 'I *am* happy. Not always, not unconditionally. No fireworks, more a kind of pleasant hum.'

'A pleasant hum sounds pretty good,' James says shortly. I wonder if he's disappointed by my answer, or whether it's forced him to probe his own relationship with Jasmine.

'What I mean is …'

'What you mean is that you don't need help from busybodies.' He issues a short bark of a laugh.

'That's not what I mean at all. I'm not some smug married with three children and a luxurious lifestyle. I don't have it all.' James doesn't say anything, and I fear I've lost this chance for openness. 'In fact, it's your coming along that has made me look at my life. If you're a wife and mother and also trying to do a job, even if only part time, it's such a rush … I don't think I've ever been able to stop and actually take stock. And you forcing me to is no bad thing.'

No bad thing. What I really want to say is that I've grown so used to his presence somewhere in the background that, in the midst of the overly familiar routines of day-in day-out, I draw pleasure from the knowledge that out there not too far away is a man who wants me. My husband's love feels safe and domesticated, but being wanted by James makes me feel vibrant and exciting, and – I feel silly at the importance I attach to this – young. Without him, I'm scared I'll slide gently into a middle age of elasticated waistbands, bunions, corns, and three-times-a-night visits to the loo.

We finish dinner and I feel wonderfully warm and slightly tipsy and it seems only natural when James wraps his arm around my shoulders as he leads me to his car. It's a Mercedes S320L and I'm on the brink of telling him that I once drove this very car, though it was only hired, when I bite back the admission as disloyal to Guy. I look around at the perfect, brown leather interior: you can't imagine a baby seat strapped into these soft seats. As for the sticky wrappers, half-chewed sweets and dog hair that fill any car we hire, that kind of familiar debris would have no place here.

We both grow silent once we're in the car. There are no other diners, no maître-d', no waiters. Only us. We drive down Park Lane, still busy though it's past eleven, and then through the dark, quiet streets of Belgravia, Chelsea, and across Chelsea Bridge.

'Do you want to come back for coffee?' James asks as we approach Clapham Common.

'Nnnnno, thanks, it's late already.'

'I guess so.' James stares straight ahead at the road.

'Sorry,' I whisper.

'Don't worry. It probably wouldn't be a good idea.' We're turning into Elton Road, and then James parks the car: we're not directly in front of our home, but a few yards down. Just enough, I catch myself thinking, for us to be invisible.

My left hand is already on the door handle, as if I'm about to bolt. 'Thank you, that was lovely.' It's so staccato and formal, James laughs.

'Don't! You sound so proper!' He leans towards me, and I grow tense. 'Good night, Mrs Carew.' He makes as if to kiss me on the cheek and then, as he draws near, he takes my face in his hands and kisses me full on the lips. It's a long, fierce kiss. I'm so shocked I stop breathing. I sense his urgency and desire – and something else too: Anger? Need? Impatience with my brief attempt at pulling back?

I hesitate for a second only, then kiss him back. James's lips move from my mouth to my nose, cheeks, temple, throat. 'Harriet,' he whispers. 'Harriet.'

I can't say a thing as his hands, which know me so well, caress my body beneath the coat. They feel as warm and sure, as tender and hungry as they did when we were eighteen. Why didn't I expect this to happen? What was I thinking of, as I prepared myself for dinner, switched off the mobile and smiled coyly at my ex across the table?

James coils my hair around his hand and pulls my head away from him. 'I've been waiting for this moment for fifteen years.' We kiss again, and I nestle against him, and wish away the gear stick that separates our seats. 'Do you know something? I always knew it would happen.'

'Oh, James,' I sigh.

James has slipped my coat off, and now he runs his lips down my throat. 'Let's go home. To my house.'

I'm so tempted: I feel as if we've started sliding down a steep incline, and have worked up an impetus we can't stop. But then through the window I see a light going on in Lisa's house, and suddenly I think of Lisa, which makes me think of Nick, and in turn of Guy, and then the children, asleep in their beds, waiting for morning – and Mummy.

'We can't,' I tell him. 'We can't.'

'Why not?' James caresses my legs, and his hands push up my dress. 'We made a mistake, we shouldn't let it ruin our lives.'

'You can't call my family a mistake.' I push his hands away in protest.

'I didn't mean that.' James's lips find my mouth again. Then, as he pulls away, 'But you can't tell me *this* doesn't feel right.'

It does. It feels so right that I can't believe I ever doubted it; so right that I'm scared everything else will feel wrong. Even my family.

'I can't stand this,' James is whispering. 'I see you practically every day, but I know I can't say anything, I can't get too close, I can't take you away. I'm frustrated on every front.'

'Please be patient,' I plead.

'Patient?' James grabs my hands, pulls me towards him so I'm forced to look at him. 'I've wasted fifteen years of my life already, looking for you. I won't waste any more time.'

His urgency terrifies me: how long can I resist him before he'll leave me, angry that I've wasted more of his time? But, if I give in, how quickly will I lose everything else?

'Harriet,' James brings my hand to his lips, 'I know you're scared.'

'I'm terrified.'

'I promise, I'll give you more time.' Then, after he has placed a kiss on every finger: 'I'm not going to lose you again.'

21

'Pow! You're dead!' Miles Collins screams as he rushes into the maze.

I shake myself out of my reverie. 'No need to shout, Miles,' I address Charlotte's son, mild reproof in my voice. It's been forty-eight hours since my dinner with James, and he hasn't contacted me, and I don't know what this means.

'I'm sure there'll be a study out soon saying that Laser-Quest makes children violent.' Charlotte shakes her head as the loud techno music bounces off the walls. 'Like those video nasties.'

We're sitting in the viewing room outside the Laser-Quest, sipping elderflower cordial and trying to hear ourselves above the noise. A television screen reveals the goings-on within the maze, where strobe lights pierce the fog and light upon luminescent graffiti. Two teams of four boys each (plus Guy and Alex) crawl through the derelict urban scene, laser guns at the ready. It's Tom's birthday, and we've organized eight of his best friends to come and kill each other in Tooting Bec.

'I sometimes wonder what it would have been like to have girls.' Alicia Byam-Shaw, mother of Sam, Tom's best friend, sighs. 'I mean, Barbie doesn't pierce your eardrums.'

I nod, approving the wisdom of her remark, but in fact, all I can think of is whether James is regretting our kiss. Does he feel a fool for having told me about not wanting to lose me again, or about taking Mary Jane out, or …

'But then my sister's got two girls and she says they become a nightmare in their teens!' Alicia Byam-Shaw goes on. 'From princess to pole dancer in the blink of an eye.'

'God help me!' Charlotte shakes her head.

James. I relive the warmth of his mouth, his hands, and that delicious sensation I felt in their wake. I feel suddenly awake, like the Tin Man in Maisie's favourite DVD, *The Wizard of Oz*, who'd grown rusty and useless. Except that it wasn't Dorothy who came along to set me on my feet again.

I spot Guy on the television screen above our heads: he's sweating in the compulsory heavy rubber vest, and waves a huge plastic gun as he blasts away at three eleven-year-olds. We woke up at six to do Marmite and butter, egg and cress, and sausage sandwiches. Between us we have blown up one hundred balloons, baked one birthday cake shaped in a giant T and twenty-four chocolate cupcakes dotted with hundreds and thousands, stuffed ten goody bags with notepad, stickers, Terminator figurine and chocolate buttons from my trip to Woolworth's last Saturday, and packed three bottles of ginger beer in an ice box.

I experience a hint of that sweet camaraderie that steals over us whenever we've done something special for the children. Except that, this time, I'm conscious of how paltry our birthday effort must seem to some of the guests and their parents. The last birthday party we were invited to with Tom, at the Byam-Shaws', was aboard the SS *Allegro*, hired for the day to fit in with the Pirates of the Caribbean theme. The crew wore eye-patches, daggers and *Happy Birthday Sam* T-shirts, and there was also a face painter, a girl who did hair extensions, and a clown called Long John Silver. It must have cost £5,000, and in the best-birthday-party stakes it ranks just below Sandy Lowe's, a boy in Alex's class, whose parents hired a hot-air balloon for the day.

But the real reason for my being subdued is last Thursday's dinner. I feel guilty, but I'm used to guilt. Every day I experience a guilty pang about a child's lunch coming out of a tin, or a pillar of the Carews' army code being ignored or the au pair's payday being delayed. What I cannot believe is that everything is the same as before. How can Guy still have that ready laugh, or the boys be so full of energy; how can Charlotte look the way she always does, or Laser-Quest be exactly as it always is? My encounter with James has made me feel so different from the Harriet that hovers over Guy and children, puts in three days a week at HAC, and jumps every time a letter is delivered, for fear it is yet another bill. I've been shaken out of my world: so why is everything as before?

'I'm so glad you don't let Tom play Grand Theft Auto San Andreas,' Alicia Byam-Shaw tells me. 'Sam's addicted, and I can't get him to budge from the PlayStation.'

In a way, this birthday party, like yesterday's shopping for Tom's presents, is a God-send, stopping me from *my* addiction: thinking of James.

Guy organized the Laser-Quest even though each session lasts only twenty minutes at £4.50 per child, rather than the full hour at £10 provided by the climbing wall (our other favourite birthday party venue). He remembered that we had vouchers from Alex's birthday party here last year, and the deciding factor was when the sports centre issued us with a three-page form for the climbing wall, requiring our guests' parents to describe their sons' physical condition and accept all responsibility if they were to break a limb or cut their heads.

I was in charge of the décor, which in this case meant finding a Simpsons tablecloth and matching napkins. I was also supposed to send out invitations, with maps enclosed of how to get to the Greenearth shopping mall. We'd categorically refused to allow Tom more than seven guests, but then had to relax the limit because he decided he liked Will Hartwell, after all, and wanted to invite him.

'Do you mind if I sneak one early?' Charlotte points to the sandwiches on the table across the room. 'I always get ravenous about now: it's quite a job keeping up the milk flow.'

Charlotte is breastfeeding – and won't allow anyone to forget it. She keeps asking other mums how many months they breastfed their children, and almost shrieked her disapproval when Alicia admitted Sam only got formula. 'Formula! But don't you know that every month of breastfeeding adds one and a half points to his IQ?!'

In fact, this is the first time I've seen Charlotte without baby Summer clamped to her breast: even Supermum realized that bringing a month-old baby to this den would be too much. Usually, though, you can't find mother without daughter: proximity, Charlotte keeps telling me, facilitates the bonding. 'They need to feel your heartbeat. The more they do, the calmer and more secure they'll be. I don't know *how* women who go back to work after three months manage. I mean, what happens to Baby when you've deprived her of all that!'

I bite my lip in order not to snap that not every new mum has a husband who earns £200 grand plus bonus. My best friend's determination to cover all traces of her impecunious past has divorced her from too many people's reality. Like mine.

Charlotte makes for the tower of sandwiches that teeter on the table. 'You all right? You seem a bit under the weather.'

'No, everything's fine,' I reply hurriedly. But how could it be? I feel a traitor, sitting here among my family and my son's friends and their mums. What would they think, if they knew what I'd been up to? The kiss was the final betrayal, but the conversation, the looks, the whole mood of my encounter with James were so highly charged that I couldn't be guiltier if his Merc had been a barn and we'd been rolling in the hay. For more than four hours I forgot anything in my life that wasn't James. Now, I'm filled with a desperate need to know if that was it: will he now back off and disappear?

'Surely they could afford to make it soundproof?' Ginny Hartwell's hands cover her ears as the techno music resounds.

Charlotte and Alicia nod in unison. Whatever Ginny says is taken into serious consideration: she has earned everyone's sympathy after the humiliation of her husband ditching her for his Russian secretary.

I can barely look at Ginny. If Guy were ever to discover my lapse and kick me out, or if I were to leave him, would he be reduced to this – a thin peaky creature surviving on the crumbs of other people's pity? I picture Guy crying on Charlotte's shoulder, asking if she's heard anything from his wayward wife. I see him settling into a domesticated relationship with Zoë, who casts pitying looks at my children while planning her own with their father. I imagine him attending all the St Christopher's fêtes and Christmas parties on his own, attracting sympathy and the single mums. 'Poor Guy,' everyone will say, 'that' – and here they'll look at their children and spell out loud – 'b-i-t-c-h has ruined his life and the children's … ran off with some property millionaire. Dis-gusting.' I feel my stomach tighten: I've gone too far.

'Die, scum, die!' Alex points a laser gun at my stomach. 'Mum, can I drop out? I'm dying of thirst and I don't think Tom needs me on his team.' My eldest is dripping with sweat and wipes his face on the back of his sleeve.

'The session's almost finished, darling.' I pour him a plastic glass of ginger beer. 'Have a drink and then go back in.'

'He's in the scholarship set at the Griffin, isn't he?' Alicia Byam-Shaw watches Alex retreat.

'Yes.' I try not to sound proud. 'Down for Wolsingham. Guy's worried that he's not working hard enough. He doesn't seem to have taken on board what a difference a scholarship would make.'

'Those scholarships are not easy.' Alicia Byam-Shaw can't stop a smug little smile: her eldest, Adam, won one to Harrow last year.

'They certainly aren't.' Charlotte brushes a little crumb from her lips. 'We've got Phil Warren from Extra-Tutorials practically living at our house to get Benjie ready for the Hampton House exams: and we're not even thinking of having him try for the scholarship exams.'

'Goodness,' I'm impressed. 'Extra-Tutorials! How much do they charge?'

'Thirty-five pounds an hour if you are doing more than an hour a day, five days a week – which is very much our case.' Charlotte rolls her eyes. 'I promise you, this is all Jack's doing. He was hopeless at school and he just can't bear to see his children follow suit. I hate the idea of private tutors at age thirteen.'

'I hate the idea of their prices,' I murmur.

'And let me tell you, Extra-Tutorials have so many people queuing up to use their tutors, they're thinking of setting up a sister outfit in North London.' Charlotte lowers her voice: 'You know, it might not be such a bad idea if Guy were to look into it.'

'Look into it? But we could never afford it!' I exclaim.

'I mean he could look into becoming one of their tutors – he'd make a packet.'

'Loser, loser!' The boys come rushing out of the maze. Everyone is suitably red-faced and sweaty and Tom beams, even if his glasses seem to have taken a bashing and now sit slightly askew on his nose.

'Food!' The hungry hordes charge the table with its offerings.

'Yummmmm … Marmite!' Charlotte's Miles wolfs down a sandwich.

'Marmite sandwiches, how sweet,' Alicia Byam-Shaw says in her slightly superior way: aboard the SS *Allegro* there were chocolate fountains and ice-cream sundaes and crêpes. For the umpteenth time I wish that Tom and Alex could have been as considerate as Maisie was, by being born in August when school's out and no one but a neighbour or a friend met over the summer is available to attend her birthday party, strain our budget and tax our imagination and patience.

'Miles, you've already had two cupcakes!' Charlotte reproves her second son, who has his father's solid build.

'Harriet, can't I have one more? Everyone else has had one!' Miles, thinking that his mother's concern is for the rest of the guests, holds up a cupcake and casts me a beseeching look.

'Of course you may,' I smile. It's my revenge on Charlotte: she knows I had dinner with James but hasn't even asked me how it went.

Bleep! bleep! My phone announces a text message. Quickly, heart pounding, I grab it out of my handbag. Does he dare?

But it's Daniela: *Can M sing happy b-day to T?*

'Tom!' I wave my son over. 'Maisie wants to sing "Happy Birthday" again'. The whole family had already sung at breakfast and Guy made pancakes to celebrate.

'All right.' With an eye on his friends and a cupcake in his hand, Tom stops long enough to ring his little sister.

He's no sooner off the phone than it bleeps another message: 'Mum,' he calls out, 'are you OK?' Tom peers at me through glasses that are still slightly askew.

'Of course, darling. Why?'

'That's what the message asks: *Are you OK?*'

I snatch my mobile from Tom's hand: I don't recognize the number, but I know who sent the message.

I wait for the birthday boy to resume his place among his friends and then study the message again, as if a second reading will yield some mysterious subtext. That James is writing to me after our dinner means he doesn't see it as a one-off moment of folly. He may even think of it as a prelude to …

But I look at the boys chasing one another around the table with its Simpsons tablecloth. I look at Guy, in a huddle with Alex and Charlotte, sticking birthday candles into the cake. Yes, I often feel as if I've pulled out a drawer full of odd socks and am now forced to sort through bills and school fees and birthday parties and second-hand school shops for the rest of my life. Yes, I'm exasperated by Guy postponing good work in order to concentrate on a documentary that so far has yielded very little. But in the fourteen years of my marriage, I've never wondered what life was about, or asked myself where I belonged, or yearned for 'home'. My family is the answer to the big questions I'm asked.

But then I remember being wrapped in James's arms, and that embrace feeling so familiar yet exciting, and I tell myself that there *are* questions that my family cannot answer. I remember James looking at me – really looking at me. Guy hasn't done that in years. I am no more the object of his desire than I'm the archivist of his *Rajput* notes. I think my husband loves me, but he thrills at the prospect of starring in a one-hour telly programme, or getting his magnum opus published next spring. He wants me to be happy, so long as it does not mean renouncing family traditions like Wolsingham or Lyme Regis.

Again I look down at the phone: I'll answer him. I must.

'He's being so difficult about child maintenance that I may have to put the boys in state schools when they finish at St Christopher's.' Ginny Hartwell's shoulders are hunched, and her expression speaks of lonely misery.

'Oh no,' Charlotte whistles her commiseration. 'Surely there's something you can *do* – I mean, legally speaking?'

'You can't send them to the local comp, Ginny, even *he* must see that!' Alicia Byam-Shaw cries. 'There was a knifing there last year. And what about that poor teacher who told off her pupil for breaking into her car? Did you see in the papers – his father threatened to bury her six feet deep.'

'Not to mention the Ofsted report,' moans Ginny. 'The students' Average Point Score was so poor. But what can I do?'

'Move?' Alicia Byam-Shaw keeps her voice low because Will Hartwell, unaware of the dreadful fate that awaits him, is happily pulling party poppers a few yards from us.

'Where to?' Ginny shakes her head. 'Any area in London that has good state schools is too expensive. But he says he doesn't want me to move to the suburbs because it would make it tricky for him to come and see the children … I'm stuck.'

'Happy birthday to you! Happy birthday to you!' Guy bears the T-shaped cake with its eleven black candles alight. He approaches the table and everyone joins in the singing. I put away my mobile and do the same.

'Happy Birthday, dear To-om!'

Guy takes out the digital camera my mother gave us two years ago at Christmas and starts snapping the table. Suddenly he points the lens at me. 'Give me a smile, darling!'

I start, and smile guiltily. But I am so unconvincing that Guy bursts out laughing. 'Come on, Harry, a proper smile! Alex, Tom, give your mum a hug!'

I'm suddenly surrounded, squeezed tight by my sons. I feel them against me, and Alex's head on my shoulder, and I want to weep, not smile.

'Pre-sents! Pre-sents!' the boys start chanting.

I won't allow myself to take another false step, I tell myself firmly. I won't risk losing all this.

All under control thanks. I text from the Ladies', five minutes later. And, message sent, I resolutely switch off my mobile and join once again my son's party.

Rat-at-at-at! A sharp series of stuttering bangs ring through Laser Quest.

'Oh no, Dad's sent Tom an automatic BB gun.' Guy shakes his head.

22

It's cold, it's wet, it's grey. Lyme Regis at Easter is definitely worse than Lyme Regis in August, when it turns hot, wet and grey. But Guy spent every childhood holiday here, and can't think of vacationing anywhere else. His parents always lend us Crabbe Cottage for a fortnight in August – and, as happened this year, at Easter if we want to get out of London.

The best thing about Lyme, I decide as I climb the South West Coast path, is that I can take off on my own, Rufus at my heels, without anyone minding. I've left the children collecting seashells and fossils with Guy; there's talk of maybe taking a mackerel boat out to sea – though Guy huffs and puffs at the £8 per person price tag.

I want to walk because I want to think. James keeps texting me, despite my attempt at a brush-off. 'We need to talk.' 'We can't pretend nothing happened.' 'Please ring.' I feel besieged, but the sensation is not altogether unpleasant. If he'd ignored me and ditched me after our kiss, I'd be miserable. If he'd written an off-hand message that basically shrugged its shoulders at our encounter, I'd feel slightly soiled and full of regret. As it is, James's pleas confirm that this was not a one-off casual incident that meant nothing to him. Part of me is reassured and flattered; yet I'm also conscious that now even our professional exchanges are potentially dangerous. James is a millionaire with a conscience; but he may also be my wealthy ex-boyfriend with a plan.

If I engage with him, by ringing or texting, I'm tacitly admitting my interest. But what am I interested in? Sex? Every touch made me realize that I'm hungry for this: Guy and I are brother and sister, in comparison. And if James and I do have mad, passionate sex: then what? A secret life that runs parallel to my marriage? A divorce? A confession to Guy, followed by a promise to give up James? A reconciliation with James, or Guy?

I reach the undercliff, and leave the South Coast for South America: lush and tropical plants surround me and Rufus; through their branches, the sea blinks.

No matter what I decide, I know that ultimately it will be James's call. I feel a twinge of unease: once again, James is in control. It was the same at Bristol. He was there, always, for me: protective, encouraging, inspirational. But sometimes he gave me the sense that he hovered and worried and fussed out of a sense of proprietorship as well as genuine concern. I was *his* girl, and he would look after me. It was a lovely feeling after Dad's sudden death. But I also remember wondering whether I was penned in by James's affection and attention.

'He's so in love with you,' Charlotte would say to me, 'I always see him looking around for you, to make sure you're all right. You're so lucky!'

And yet sometimes, when I would stay later than expected at a party, or decide to pursue some other course of action than the one James suggested; sometimes I had the feeling that I was guilty of breaking the rules. In the same way that in Guy's world I'm conscious of a host of unwritten laws, covering everything from duty and loyalty to Christmas decorations and my clothes, so too the world I was about to enter, with James, upheld an unwritten law: James Weston is in charge.

The path grows steeper and I'm walking more slowly now. Rufus rushes ahead, but then stops every now and then to let me catch up with him.

If James is a potential control freak, then Guy is a dreamer: the news that *Big Game* has been shorn of two-thirds of its length does not seem to have dented my husband's awesome self-confidence. He's come back from Gloucestershire, where he filmed Harry Phillips, one of his safari hunters, acting as crassly and repulsively at home as in the wild, and is now even more optimistic about his chances of success.

When I told him about Simon's call, he immediately rang his agent. But I could tell from the tenor of the phone call that Guy regards Simon's contract for the coffee-table book as an incidental, rather than crucial income. 'I'll hand it in at the end of the break, don't worry,' Guy promised Simon. 'Oh, come on, Simon,' I heard him protest. 'Of course you can rely on me.' I don't think Simon believes him. I'm not sure I do, either.

It's only because my salary came in last Monday that I've been able to settle (most of) the bills that have practically grown roots on my desk. But Daniela will not be getting her salary until next month, and as for the Visa bill, I've sent only the minimum payment of £14.

Furious barking interrupts my thoughts and I look up to see Rufus wandering off: he's sniffed something among a clump of leaves. I attempt to whistle, fail miserably and call him. He stops in his tracks, sniffs some more and then, with a heavy heart, trots back to me. 'Come along!' I pat him. Together we make our way back.

Crabbe Cottage is minutes from the seafront and it's been in the family since Guy's great-grandfather bought it in the nineteenth century, when Lyme was a hotspot and the Carews could afford to keep up with the fashionable set.

The cottage was never grand, but these days it is bordering on the shabby. The floorboards are so uneven they creak at every footstep, the water in the upstairs bathroom is a trickle and there's an ominous musty smell in the downstairs loo. Cecily still manages to organize a fresh coat of paint, and every now and then does the garden herself, and gets round to waxing the handful of antiques twice a year, but even she cannot quite keep the property spick and span.

This, despite her daily phone calls to me. She delivers a long list of instructions and a couple of sermons about how it's no good for the boys to be allowed to be so untidy, and no good for Guy to be so trusting and leave the front door always on the latch. Cecily's phone calls last for at least half an hour. 'Are you there, Harriet?' she barks whenever she can sense I'm trying to multi-task, like wiping the kitchen table or pouring water into a thermos while cradling the receiver on my shoulder.

None of this matters to Guy, whose idea of heaven is bustling about on the West Beach in an ancient fleece, ripped shorts and an Australian sheep-farmer's hat. He looks for seashells with Maisie, organizes barbecues, and above all retreats into a Boys' Own existence where he spends hours scouring the rock pools with Alex and Tom (Tom in a T-shirt because even at Easter he burns easily, just as my father used to), mending their fishing nets, exploring every rock for fossils. They spring about, the three of them, sometimes with Rufus making up the fourth, the air full of excited shouts. 'Look, Dad! I think it's an ammonite!' 'Tom, Alex, this is probably the fin of a giant Jurassic fish!' They're oblivious to the passage of time or my pleas for them to come and eat lunch.

Lyme Regis is as much about ritual as fun. Every year, we have the walk up Golden Cap: 'Come along, think of Uncle Alfie leading his men up the Khyber Pass!' The boys run ahead with Guy and Rufus, while I alternately coax and drag Maisie, but inevitably, halfway up the Cap, rain cuts our expedition short. Every year, we have one mackerel fishing expedition, though half the time we come back empty-handed. And also every year we have the sand-castle competition, with Guy determined to outdo not only the boys but anyone else on the beach.

Not for him those dinky plastic shovels others wield: he keeps a workman's shovel in the cottage for this purpose, and a bucket filled with used cocktail parasols. This morning, he spotted a young man building a sand castle, his two toddlers cheering him on. Within minutes, Guy sloped off to get his prized workman's shovel and began digging in the sand. Maisie stood by, bucket and spade dangling from her plump little hands, watching her father's construction. The other toddlers cheered when their father produced a twin-turreted castle. Without so much as a look in Guy's direction, their father led away his fans.

Guy was left digging, and he didn't stop until he'd built a gigantic castle with a moat and a four-turreted keep. 'There, Maisie, look at that ...' he beamed.

Maisie looked up from sieving sand. 'That daddy finished first,' she pointed out, before returning to work.

By midday, the children are ravenous. Chants of 'Bar-be-cue! Bar-be-cue!' resound within the whitewashed walls. The cottage kitchen has room only for a tiny sink and a Baby Belling and it's filled to the limit with the twelve bags of shopping we brought down ('Only tourists would pay their prices!' grumbles Guy of the local grocers).

Guy piles up driftwood and regales our sons with tales of encampments in the Sahara and the Hindu Kush, increasingly punctuated with admonishments: 'No, no, Alex, don't press down those twigs, the fire needs oxygen.'

Inside the cottage, I check my mobile: nothing. Will James desist if I don't keep up a dialogue? Then I chide myself: I hate the furtive way I'm sneaking out for walks, checking my phone, texting from the Ladies'. I'm acting like a middle-aged woman squeezing into Top Shop clothes; this kind of carry on is fine in a teenager, but undignified in a woman who is the wrong side of 35.

I get the salad things out and a box of Ritz crackers and some cheddar. I look out of the open window and watch our neighbours, the elderly Fairweathers, share their al fresco lunch with a guest under their umbrella.

As we huddle round the fire, stomachs full of sausages and chops (part burned, part raw), a bar of chocolate doing the rounds, I feel a warm glow of family love. Maisie, cheeks red and curls full of salt, lies against me, her cheek on my thigh; the boys are wrestling in the sand; and Guy whistles 'Clementine' softly beside me.

'The thing about this place,' Guy says as we sip our beers, 'is that it's so romantic … Do you know that this is where Great-Grandfather Hector proposed to Harriet?'

'Hector was the colonel, wasn't he?' I try to sift through my Carew family index.

'Yes. Dad's done a list of the letters by date, which should make it much easier for me to trawl through them. Who knows, Harry, those letters might form the basis of the next book.' Guy lies back, satisfied, and lifts his face up to the grey sky.

'I suppose there is a lot of interest in World War I romantic sagas.' I feel guilty and slightly tarnished in comparison to those long-ago lovers.

'Ahhhhh,' Guy breathes in deeply. 'I know this area like the back of my hand. I'm the world's expert on Lyme Regis.'

'That's why,' I venture cautiously, 'Simon got you the contract to do the chapter.'

'Yes, of course.' Guy nods energetically.

'Hey, look, a television crew!' Alex is off, Tom at his heels. In the distance, I make out a television crew and an oddly familiar figure standing barefoot in the shallows. 'That's not ...?' I begin.

'Crispin Kerr!' Guy's anguished cry prompts Maisie to stir against me, and the perfectly bronzed windswept figure to wave.

'It's him,' Guy mutters through gritted teeth. Crispin jogs towards us. He looks more like a soap opera star than an over-rated travel writer who, according to my (unbiased) husband, makes Viranasi and Vilnius sound equally boring.

'Hey, you two! I didn't know you were here!' Kerr flashes his perfect teeth. 'I'm doing this place for my new series.' He laughs at our blank looks. 'Don't worry, it's not out yet, you haven't missed it.' His left hand rakes through thick, sunkissed locks. 'We're calling it *Crispin Cruises* and I mainly get to travel wherever I want. Frankly,' Kerr winks and continues in a stage whisper, 'I haven't come here that often, but they think I'm some kind of expert on Lyme. It's a great wheeze: my agent says it gets the books flying off the shelf.' He turns to look at the crew. 'I'd better go, we're in the middle of a shoot. Why don't you come and meet the guys?!'

Guy is struck dumb. Maisie starts bawling on cue.

'Oh, Crispin, we'd love to,' I smile apologetically, 'but Maisie's not terribly well.'

Crispin immediately recoils, cupping his nose and mouth. 'Gosh, don't want to catch that! Well, see ya!' He dashes back to his crew and the small audience that has gathered. It includes our sons.

'I don't believe it!' Guy hisses. He sets aside his tin of beer in disgust. 'How can *anyone* take that man seriously? A television series, when he shouldn't even be allowed five minutes of air time.'

I'm stroking Maisie back to sleep, and try to comfort my husband. 'Darling, he's yesterday's news. You're the one who's just starting out and may be on your way to becoming a huge hit.' I hate myself for feeding Guy's optimistic fantasy, but he looks so downcast as he sits beside me, hunched over and silent.

'Look, Mummy, we got an autograph from the television man!' Tom runs up, waving his arm: there, as if tattooed, I read *Crispin Kerr*.

'He's giving autographs,' Alex points excitedly, 'but we didn't have any paper so he signed our arms instead. Isn't that cool?!'

'Oh, Guy!!!!!' I wail. 'Do we have to?'

My husband shrugs his shoulders, looking sheepish. 'What could I do? We're right on their way to the Barrett-Blows in Colliton. Mum will be dying to break the journey, you know how she hates Dad's driving ... And they'd think it odd if we didn't invite them for a cup of tea ...'

I shake my head in despair: the Carews' arrival this afternoon means a major clean-up operation. After almost a week here, we've managed to turn Crabbe Cottage into a smaller version of our Clapham home: the boys' books and socks litter the floor of the sitting room and their bedroom, Maisie's toys punctuate the kitchen and the sitting room, and Guy's laptop and a couple of guide books to Lyme Regis occupy half the sofa. We have yet to find the missing hotels in Cecily's Monopoly set and, worse, though Guy has glued the top of the teapot, it is by no means an invisible mend. I can feel sand under my feet, and see Rufus's hair all over the rugs and armchairs. Cecily will go mental.

The tidying-up effort is not without its pluses: the Monopoly hotels resurface; as does my ancient Boots concealer stick, which has found its way to the children's bathroom ('Well, what *am* I supposed to do about these?' moans Alex, revealing three pimples on either side of his nostrils). But it takes me so long to tidy up that I don't have the time to bake anything for tea.

'Shop-bought?' Cecily's disdain over the ginger snaps is plain. 'Not that I mind,' she papers hastily over the fault line she's created. 'I'm watching my weight these days.' She checks her slim wrist-watch. 'Archie, don't settle in too comfortably. You know that the Barrett-Blows are expecting us for supper.'

'Yes, yes, dear. Looks like it's cleared up.' Archie chomps happily through the biscuits and even the shop-bought teacake. He turns to his eldest grandson: 'I hope you're prepping for the Wolsingham exams. The new head there seems a very sound man. Not as good as old Colonel Banner, of course.' Archie begins to wander down memory lane. 'Known as One-Armed Bandit, because he lost an arm in Normandy ...'

The history lesson that follows saves Alex from lying: he hasn't brought down so much as one textbook for revision. His marks have been good, as always, but I do wish his attitude was a bit more serious. According to family lore, Guy, too, sailed through schoolwork and exams. But look where it's got him: a maddening optimism about the future, and an unswerving faith in his own ability that will not be dented by critics or crises.

'Must say, I have a whole new appreciation for the writer's craft since starting on my little family chronicle.' Archie beams at Guy.

'Well, Dad, maybe we should consider a collaboration.' Guy generously chooses to forget the terrible rows that his decision to forego the army gave rise to. 'The Carew Chronicles as retold by two descendants.'

'With your name on it, we might not need to opt for a vanity publisher.' Archie empties his cup.

'Of course not. We might even get a documentary out of it. I've been enjoying the shooting very much.' Guy beams at his parents.

'How's that going?' Archie holds out a cup for more tea. 'Has Hollywood come knocking yet?'

'Not yet, not yet.' Guy leans back in his chair grinning. 'But the production team seem pretty pleased. In fact, I'd go so far as to say I think a whole new career beckons.'

I try not to show my frustration. Will my husband ever learn to be cautious or even simply realistic? Guy has already conveniently forgotten that his seminal series has been cut down to a one-hour-long episode: not, I suspect, the sign of his production team's overwhelming confidence in the film. I half-listen as he launches into a long description of various new possible series, all starring himself. His enthusiasm is so infectious, I've been bitten time and time again. But nowadays

I've developed an immunity, and I cannot follow Guy in his grand visions.

'Is that a new mend?' Cecily's index finger traces the grey crack that Guy's glueing has left on the teapot.

'Afraid so, Mother,' Guy admits, then ably turns her attention to the neighbours. 'The Fairweathers are here, but no sign of the Stricklands. I wonder if they've sold up?'

'Annabel and Hugo? Never!' Cecily shakes her head. 'They've had Hawthorn Cottage even longer than the Carews have had Crabbe. Used to be very grand; there was a Strickland Hall in Warwickshire, I seem to remember ...'

I feign interest in Cecily's social register. But I'm thinking about Charlotte's phone call this morning: 'Summer's absolutely adorable, of course, but she's not sleeping through the night and I'm exhausted. I'm too old for this, you know.'

I feel old too: my son's coming up to full-blown puberty, my husband's biggest fan is half my age and, unlike Charlotte, I'm no fertility goddess. It is precisely because of my age, *our* age, that I find James so troubling. Yes, it was technically only a kiss, but everything we say or do sets off deep, long echoes. Our every encounter threatens to peel away three or four layers of memories. That kiss took me back to my youth, to Bristol, to the dreams I shared with James of setting up house together. And I remember more: what it felt like to have James inside me, what it was like to stretch out beside him through the night, what he looked like, naked in the morning light. Some memories are dangerous.

James, James ... What would James make of this place? A run-down cottage stuffed with ancient memories and furniture, conversation that sounds like someone reading Debrett's, Cecily finding it impossible to relax, Archie sinking ever further into his armchair and the past.

'Harriet? Harriet?' Archie's hand is on my arm.

I blink, and try to smile, but realize that I've not been listening to anything that has been said. 'Sor-sorry,' I stammer. Cecily looks at Guy with a raised eyebrow.

'Don't worry, Harriet, just asking how you'd found the new fishmonger?' Archie smiles benevolently.

'Well,' Cecily doesn't wait for my answer but wipes the cotton folds of her skirt, as if she's about to get up, 'I do think we should be thinking of making a move, Archie. It's nearly six.'

'Yes, yes, darling.' Archie nods, but holds out his plate for another slice of teacake. 'Doctor's orders.' He winks at me naughtily. 'Now, as I was saying, your great-grandfather knew that Harriet Murray was from a different background …'

Cecily looks black but bites her lip. The moment Archie sets down his cup, she fills the tray with our dirty cups and saucers and leads me into the kitchen. I wish I could dissuade her from helping with the washing up, as I'm sure she'll find me wanting on the cleanliness front as much as on every other level, but she rolls up her sleeves and starts filling the plastic basin with warm water.

'Honestly, that man would try the patience of a saint,' she snorts.

My mobile, which I've left somewhere in the kitchen, suddenly bleeps. I uncover it (it is nestling under Maisie's Angelina Ballerina T-shirt, which I'd left on the stool so that I'd remember to soak away the cocoa stain on it), and read:

You don't know how much I miss you. I blush, shake my head, and then look up to see Cecily's curious and appraising gaze. 'That's a … a colleague …' I find myself offering an explanation before she even asks for one. 'From work … er … funniest coincidence: someone I had known at Bristol and he suddenly turned up …'

'Ah. James Weston.' Cecily half-smiles at me as I stare, too stunned to say anything: 'Guy told me about the amazing coincidence.' Something in her tone tells me that Cecily does not believe in coincidences, amazing or otherwise, and suspects James of orchestrating our reunion. 'Guy seems very taken with this television programme.' Cecily brushes a cup vigorously. 'Is he ever home these days?'

'Oh, not much,' I answer lightly. 'I mean, I can understand it's an important professional breakthrough and everything.'

'Men never *think*, do they?' Cecily bursts out. I'm shocked: given the adoration she bestows upon the men in her life, I didn't have Cecily down as a feminist sister brimming with sympathy for her sex. She continues, 'Can't they see that if you leave a young woman on her own for months on end she might look for comfort somewhere else?'

23

I gawp at Cecily.

We can hear the men and children outside, shouting at Rufus and trying to restrain him from another swim.

'Is there someone ...? No!' Cecily interrupts herself, sets down the kitchen brush. 'It's none of my business, Harriet. I just want you to know that I've been in your shoes. And it's awful, because we're damned if we do, and damned if we don't.' Cecily rinses plate after plate under the tap.

'Yes?' I manage, dazed.

Cecily takes up the tea towel and starts rubbing hard, while I lean against the counter.

'I know what it's like when your husband is thrilled to bits with what he does, and automatically expects you to feel the same. Archie was away for months at a time, first in one post then another. I was desperately lonely, with two small boys to bring up virtually on my own. I didn't dare follow him to Ceylon, or India, or Kenya, because of the children.' Cecily pauses here as if she expects me to say something.

'Of course not,' I murmur. What is my mother-in-law trying to tell me?

'We were living in London, at the time, near Regent's Park.' She doesn't look up as she rubs and rubs the porcelain in her hands. 'Guy had started school, and I used to bring him every day, pushing Nick in the pram. And every day his teacher, David, would be there, greeting the pupils and us parents. He was a really, really nice man, very idealistic, very young.' Cecily's voice has grown soft, and she wears a far-away expression. 'It turned out David lived around the corner, and sometimes he would walk home with us when I picked Guy up. He was interested in everything, but especially poetry. He could recite dozens of poems off by heart, and it was marvellous for me and Guy. We'd be there, walking on some busy street, and we'd be listening to "The Raven" or to "Jabberwocky" or "My Love is Like a Red, Red Rose". Because Archie was away, he thought it improper to come into our house. Not even for a glass of water.' Cecily breathes in, then releases a huge sigh. 'So we stood outside our front door, even in winter, though I'd let Guy and Nick go into the sitting room to keep warm, and just talk and talk. And then, one day, at the end of the school year, he told me that he'd decided he had to move. Take a job somewhere else. He didn't say why.' Cecily holds up the cup to the light and blinks several times. 'I knew, though.'

I want to simultaneously wrap my arm around Cecily's shoulders, hang my head in shame, and ask her why she is unburdening herself to me *now*. But I only whisper, 'How sad.'

'Time to go, old girl!' Archie's head pops in through the kitchen window. 'Can't keep the Barrett-Blows waiting!' He looks flushed and slightly sweaty, but tremendously pleased with life.

Cecily smiles weakly. 'Yes, darling.'

The sun's come out, and suddenly the sea is almost blue. The children stand in a row waving their grandparents' car away, and Rufus chases it for a few yards before returning home for supper.

'Goodness, did you *see* how cross Mum was about the crack in her teapot?!' Guy is laughing as he stamps his feet on the doorstep to get rid of (most of) the sand. 'I thought she was going to bite me!'

'Oh, I don't know ...' I fold the little cotton tablecloth I'd laid out for tea. 'She's not so bad.'

'We're moving to Kent!' Anjie greets me on my first day back at the office.

'What?!' I take off my cycle helmet, damp jacket and trainers, and don my work pumps. 'Why?'

'The schools are excellent and his nibs' – I flinch here at the mention of the *bastard* – 'is going to be working on a big new office building in Tunbridge Wells.' Anjie grins. 'We're looking at a nice flat that's a lot less than the mousetrap we've got here; there's a nice church round the corner. But ...' she lowers her voice and leans towards me with a conspiratorial air, 'I'm not sure that I can continue to work here. I haven't decided yet. Can't think of many jobs going for a forty-three-year-old Jamaican woman in Tunbridge Wells, can you?'

'You're not just *any* forty-three-year-old Jamaican,' I reply enthusiastically. 'You're a great asset to any office!'

'Oh yeah?' Anjie laughs. 'I can do very good Hollywood gossip and am not too bad at office goss either. But I don't think I'm irreplaceable as a receptionist or have got fab secretarial skills.'

'Mary Jane Thompson is irreplaceable,' I wink, as our boss comes through the door, 'we are recyclable.'

'Recycling? Are we on top of our recycling?' Mary Jane shakes her umbrella and places it by the waste-paper bin. 'Wouldn't do HAC's reputation any good if we aren't punctilious about recycling.'

'Don't worry, don't worry,' Anjie murmurs quickly as she starts sorting the post. Then, as soon as the drawbridge to Fortress Thompson has been raised and the door shut: 'Anyway, I haven't told you the best: the husband wants me to give up work and become a lady of leisure.'

'Can you afford it?' I raise an eyebrow. Is William Jones trying to pen in his wife so that she doesn't risk coming into contact with the tart? Or rather, so that Anjie won't cramp his style? Tunbridge Wells is not big enough for William to carry on as he has been doing here without risking discovery.

'Don't forget, we're downsizing – and getting free schools into the bargain.' Anjie is the kind to do her sums carefully, I figure.

I stop thinking of the Joneses' set-up, and how much longer Anjie's blissful ignorance will last. I find myself wondering, once again, if this is precisely what Guy and I should be doing. Kent would mean great grammar schools, cheaper housing, my mum nearby. We'd have a garden, the children could get some fresh air. How they hated coming back to London after Lyme! Crime rates are better too. I would agree to send the boys to Wolsingham – but we could skip the Griffin altogether for Tom – a saving of £60,000.

Guy can work anywhere. So what's tying us to London? Only HAC – and James.

I could give up HAC. I look around the office, at the ancient kettle, the limp potted plants by the water-cooler, the window through which I can glimpse the High Street below, the annoying Worker Bee poster. Would it be so very difficult to wave farewell to all this? I like what I do, and I get a sense of satisfaction when one of our children thanks me for a holiday they could never have dreamt of without us. But this is not curating an exhibition, or discovering a visionary new artist; this is a job I have adapted to, rather than a career I have chosen. We could never afford for me to stay at home, but I'm sure I could find a new part-time job that would engage me just as much.

But then I echo Anjie's words: are there really many part-time jobs out there for a thirty-seven-year-old mum? I feel a little shiver of fear: it's not going to be easy to persuade some would-be employer that I'm an ambitious, dedicated worker who has ably compartmentalized her life and deals with three children, a husband and an au pair only in out-of-work hours. One look at me, and they'll know.

The bad news is that the kind of work where I can rush off when Daniela calls me and says Maisie has flu, or where I come in late because I had to make a detour past the Griffin when Alex forgets his English homework, or coast for a few weeks because Guy is away filming, that kind of work exists only here, at HAC, where Anjie shields me from Mary Jane, and Mary Jane is so consumed with her networking that she cannot be bothered to check on me too thoroughly.

As for James ... could I give him up? Never, I want to scream. I'm addicted to the frisson he's brought to my life. I love the trepidation I felt cycling here, wondering if he'd show up, if I'd see him. I love the way I can hardly focus on anything when he's around, as if James has cleared the floor so that he can be centre-stage in my life. How could I go back to a life where my excitement is purely vicarious – my friend's child being born, my husband starring in a documentary, my son getting into (we hope) the scholarship set at Wolsingham?

I try to force myself to stop thinking about James, but every time the phone rings or the door opens, I think it's him. The morning passes slowly and, by lunch time I can hardly mask my disappointment. 'What about James, is he coming in?' I finally ask Anjie.

'Dunno,' Anjie shrugs. 'He hasn't been heard from in days.'

I set off downstairs to grab a sandwich. Usually I make my own, but this morning there was nothing in the fridge apart from milk, a few tomatoes and two tins of beer. A big shop is overdue, I tell myself, and sigh at the prospect of cycling down to Tesco's and then laboriously wheeling the bike back, laden with carrier bags.

'What's that sigh for?' I wheel around to find James on the pavement beside me. I stop dead. 'Hullo you.' He looks at me as he did that night during our dinner: as if no one should dare approach us. He tilts his head to one side. 'Catch any mackerel?' His voice is light, but his expression serious.

'The children did.' My voice sounds strangled.

James puts a hand on my elbow and pilots me gently through the passers-by. 'Why didn't you ring me?' I look straight ahead as I try to walk naturally. 'Do you have any idea what I've been through?' James's voice is low and urgent in my ear. 'I was going mad, not knowing when I'd see you again.'

We're walking down the High Street, past the NatWest Bank and the Italian café, and the hospice shop, past men and women and children who rush or dawdle or push buggies. But I hardly register any of this, or the fine rain that suddenly starts, as James tightens his hold on my elbow. 'Don't push me away, Harriet. Not again.'

'I'm not pushing you away.' I try to choose the right words, to make sense of what I feel. 'I'm scared.' I'm grateful that I needn't face him.

'I know you are.' James suddenly pulls me into a doorway. It's pouring, and I realize my hair, face, and jacket are wet. We're standing in front of a disused bakery and a *retail space to let* sign stretches above us. 'Look, we've got to talk.' James looks down at me. 'We can't ignore what happened.'

'If I don't ignore it, I risk losing everything.'

'Everything? It doesn't cover much. You are leading a half-life, Harriet, where you're pathetically grateful for any attention, ground down by bills and school fees, and scared of being alone with an ex-boyfriend.'

'We can't talk like this now.' I'm looking up at him, at once terrified and eager.

'I know. We can't talk here, because someone might see us; we can't meet at my place, because you'd be compromised.' He talks fast, impatient. 'I've got a plan. Just say yes.'

I search his expression: he is absolutely unstoppable, determined to get what he wants. And what he wants is me.

'I've got an old friend – no, not Bristol days; later, in Nigeria. Sam's been selected as a Tory candidate. His dad's left him a huge place in Wiltshire. Sam doesn't know what to do with it. He doesn't want the expense of running it himself, can't afford it. And he thought a charity link might help him in politics. You and I could go down there.' I look at him blankly. 'A third holiday house for HAC.' I still look confused. 'You and I go down and have a look, then report back.' He leans forward so he's almost against me. 'Don't you see? It's all above board: a professional trip you have to make. And we buy ourselves a day together.'

'All right,' I say slowly. 'Yes, I'll come.'

'It's perfect. You study the place to see whether, with disabled access, central heating, and proper security, it will do. I'll study you.' He grins and points at the HAC office down the street. 'I'll persuade her in there. You can tell your husband it's a professional outing.' He shuts his eyes for a moment. Then he whispers: 'I said I'm not going to lose you again, and I meant it.'

We stand silently, completely still, watching the passers-by run under the rain in front of us. Then James pulls his jacket over his head and shoulders to shield him from the rain. 'Stay here until it stops. I'll go now, so we can make separate entrances.'

We're not moving to Kent, I've decided.

'Supine, please!' I hear Guy shouting in the study. He has been closeted in there with Alex all morning: the Wolsingham scholarship exams are about twenty days away, and my husband has decided that our eldest needs his full attention. Alex is less sure. 'Dad, we've been going over it for an hour now, and I've memorized all the endings. Do you think I could have a break?'

'Alex, I have better things to do than to sit here all day conjugating Latin verbs with you. This scholarship will determine the rest of your life. And it's a matter of family honour. Your great-grandfather, your great-uncle Alfie, Grandpa *and* I all won scholarships in our time.'

'What about Uncle Nick?' Alex asks mischievously.

'We-ell ... no ... Nick didn't, but as a result he's always been slightly ...'

'But Uncle Nick is making lots of money, isn't he, Daddy?'

'Money isn't everything,' Guy snaps. 'Don't they teach you anything at the Griffin? In any case, how does *quaero* go? Infinitive like *amo,* but what happens in the perfect?'

On Sunday, Guy goes filming in Gloucestershire. As Daniela and I give the children supper, I find myself, for the first time since my dinner with James, relaxed. I'm no closer to knowing what it is I want from James, but I now am certain that he wants me. He's received Mary Jane's go-ahead for our recce next weekend. He comes to the office every day and finds any pretext to come up to my desk, sit beside me, talk, gaze and generally make me feel as if I'm the only important thing in his life.

'No begging, Rufus, please.' I push his paws down. 'Maisie, keep your bib on when you're eating spag bol.'

I've just taken out our treat of Tesco's soft vanilla ice cream, a bargain at seventy-four pence for two litres, to great cheers, when there's a ring at the door.

It's Lisa, looking, for the first time ever, a fright: her eyes are small and swollen, her hair is lanky, her scarlet T-shirt is crumpled and clashes horribly with her wine-red jeans. Only illness or heartbreak could explain any of this.

'Oh, Harriet!' Her wail has Daniela and the children look up expectantly; mealtimes are a bit quiet when Guy's not here, and our visitor looks sure to introduce some drama. 'He's ended it. This morning. I haven't been able to go to the office.' 'He', it is clear, means Nick. 'Harriet what should I *do*?' Lisa's lower lip quivers and her eyes fill with tears.

'Come and sit down. Ice cream?' I hold up the tub.

'No-no-no-no, I'm miserable as it is, I don't want to be *fat* and miserable.' Lisa shakes her head mournfully. 'It just felt so great, we were so natural together …' She shows no compunction about discussing her love-life in front of the three children, who stare at her round-eyed, or Daniela, with whom she has barely exchanged a word in all the time she's been working with us. 'He says he needs his "space". Well, fine, I can give him "space". I just don't think we should stop seeing each other. I mean, doesn't this guy know how difficult it is out there?' Her mobile rings. 'Yes, yes, oh, Bill, will you stop!' Lisa says sharply. 'I can't talk about hedge funds right now.' She absent-mindedly picks up a spoon and digs into the white mound on Maisie's plate. My daughter lets out a squeal of protest, but quiets down when Daniela scoops her another ball. Lisa snaps her phone shut.

'Why don't you talk to him?' Lisa turns to me, pleading. 'He really likes you.'

'Why doesn't Lisa want to talk about the hedgehogs?' Maisie wants to know.

'You want me to talk to Nick?' I somehow doubt my brother-in-law will look to me for tips on his emotional life.

'Please.' Lisa digs herself another spoonful of ice cream, this time from Alex's bowl. 'I can't seem to get through to him.' She sighs, casting an unseeing glance around the table. 'You're so lucky, you have it all: husband, children, dog, nanny.' Daniela doesn't blink at ranking somewhere below Rufus on Lisa's must-have list. 'That's all I want, honestly. I'd give up the job and the parties and the shopping.'

'You wouldn't have to give up any of that with Nick,' I point out.

'Uncle Nick *loves* parties,' Alex pipes up helpfully. 'He said that's where he can pick up his bed bunnies.'

'What's a bed bunny?' Tom and Maisie ask in chorus.

'I'm afraid, madam, Major Carew has had a bad fall …' the man's voice is calm, posh and anonymous. He is the nameless steward of the Delphi, Archie's club. 'He's broken his hip. Slipped down the staircase. Marble, you see … He gave us your home number – he has been admitted to hospital. The operation is scheduled for tomorrow morning.'

'Of course.' I say. Poor, poor Archie, I think. And immediately try ringing, then texting, Guy.

I leave Daniela in charge of Maisie, and round up the boys. I play down the fall, and tomorrow's operation, and they stumble over themselves in their rush to go with me to the bus stop, and then on to the Chelsea and Westminster Hospital. They prattle and laugh and are in high spirits when we troop into the ward. But the sight of their grandfather shocks them into silence. Fragile, grey, and hollow-eyed, Archie lies half-asleep against the pillow. His lips keep working, as if he's trying to stop himself from crying out in pain.

'Hullo, Archie …' I reach out to hold his hand. 'I've brought you the boys.'

Alex and Tom, who've been standing at the foot of the hospital bed, move closer. Alex slips his hand into his grandfather's.

Archie manages a smile. 'Look what Grandpa will do, just to see you.'

'He looks awful.' Guy, soaking in his bath. 'God, Harriet, you realize that in the over-sixties, there's a twenty per cent chance that they die within a year of breaking their hip?'

'Don't. He'll be fine, he's strong, and we just have to make sure he gets on his feet again as soon as possible …' I study Guy's body beneath the water: every inch of him is familiar. The white chest with only a few tufts of black hair, the arms and legs still tanned from Kenya. He stands up and I hand him the towel, looking with wonder at the round muscular bottom that is still so boyish. We haven't seen each other for a week, yet I'm not burning with longing, or melting with lust. Is this James's doing, or simply time?

Guy steps into his pyjamas. I want to hug him and reassure him about his father – and confess everything to him.

'I couldn't bear it if something happened to Dad. To either one of them.' Guy buttons his pyjama top. 'And he is starting to really get into his history of the Carews. Did you hear, he came up to London to meet with Harriet Murray's nieces?'

'Really?' I follow Guy back into our bedroom.

'Yes. They know a lot about the family pressure Great Grandfather Hector encountered. But you can see why he stuck by Harriet: she was gor-geous.' Guy wraps me in his arms and pecks my nose. 'Though not a patch on you.'

I swallow my guilt and smile back.

24

'Good God! Zoë, I hate to turn a tragedy into a trump card, but that is amazing!' I watch Guy pace our bedroom, clutching his mobile.

I'm half-asleep, exhausted from an argument with Alex over his refusal to work harder for the Wolsingham entrance exams next month; and listening to Mary Jane, who wanted to explain which forms I'd need to take down to Wiltshire next weekend. It's almost eleven, but Zoë's phone call obviously brings good news, so I don't mind.

'OK, OK, that's great. Good night. Oh, and thanks for telling me immediately.'

Guy practically bounces back on to our bed. 'Guess what? A lion has killed some obese chav Brit on safari in Tanzania. Zoë says that's just the kind of news that will make the BBC bosses want to get us on air immediately. Harriet!'

'Shshshshsh.' I put my finger to my lips: everyone's asleep.

'Harriet, this is it! Thank God we've got the voice-overs done and dusted. Zoë says the Beeb will re-arrange the schedule and we can look to be on air by the weekend.' Guy's hand strays to the telephone. 'Should I ring Mum and Dad? They could do with some good news.'

Archie was released from hospital last week. 'Strong constitution, he should be fit as a fiddle in no time,' the operating consultant opined cheerfully. Since then he has been in Somerset recuperating under Cecily's tender ministrations.

'Don't ring them now, Guy: they'll think it's bad news, at this time of night. Tell them tomorrow morning. Better still, why don't you wait until you have a date and a time when they should tune in?' I know this advice will be ignored. Guy's enthusiasm cannot be contained, and by tomorrow morning he will be on the phone to the Carews.

Now he lifts the duvet and gets into his side of the bed. He switches off the light on his bedside table. 'Darling, we've made it!' And he peels off my nightgown and starts covering me with increasingly lusty kisses. I feel safe and tender, and smile as he comes inside me. 'Oh, I love you!' he cries out, as always, and as always he falls back on the bed, curls around me and is almost instantly asleep. But as I lie on my side and stroke my husband's dark head, I can't help wonder what it would be like to make love with James again.

'Phew! What a mess!' Nick rakes his hands through his hair – rather too long and thoroughly wet – and then pats his trousers for his packet of cigarettes. I'm not sure whether by mess he means Archie, who has come down with a nasty chest infection and coughs non-stop whenever we try to talk to him, or Lisa. It is because of Lisa that Nick arrived completely soaked half an hour ago; soaked, because he thought it best not to park his red Aston Martin in front of our house, thereby blatantly announcing his visit, and only found a parking spot at the bottom of the next road. 'I could do with a drink, dear Bro.'

Guy nods, and hands over a beer. He's still in overdrive from last night. 'Dad will pull through, I'm sure of it. But we should take this as a warning and get a few things sorted.'

'What?' Nick looks puzzled.

'Well, do *you* know what he's been up to in terms of his finances?'

'No. I've given him a bit of advice, but ...' Nick drinks his beer straight out of the tin. 'I have no idea what he's got.'

'Has he repaid the mortgage on the house?' Guy asks. 'Has he had the house and the cottage valued?'

'I don't know.'

'We should.'

'There's some lawyer who knows everything.' Nick sounds defensive. 'And in any case, don't you have power of attorney?' He reaches for his cigarettes; then, with a look at me, pushes the pack away.

'Guy, you should sort that out,' I urge my husband.

Guy issues a deep sigh. 'That army discipline has not exactly extended to his financial affairs, has it?'

'Dad thinks he's immortal.' Nick shrugs. 'And we want him to be.'

The two brothers sit at the kitchen table in silence. Nick looks so miserable, I yield and hand him an ashtray.

'What's going on with you and Lisa?' Guy asks.

'She's a typical City girl.' Nick lights up a Camel. 'She's got loads of dosh, but suddenly woke up one morning to the fact that she's thirty-five. Now she wants someone in her bed who can discuss the nursery walls.'

'Sounds reasonable,' Guy puts in mildly. 'It's high time you had children. You realize your nephew's about to sit the Wolsingham entrance exams?' Guy cannot keep the note of pride from his voice.

'Poor thing! Couldn't you spare Alex the indignities we were subjected to?' Nick winks at me as he utters his words of betrayal.

'Don't be silly.'

'Anyway, Lisa's not the one.' Nick shakes his head. 'She's always in City mode. Even after work, she's unstoppable. What I'm looking for is someone who wants to go to the country for a long walk, not suss out whether a weekend cottage is a good investment. Someone who cries at the end of *Casablanca* rather than because she lost out to a colleague on some mega-deal.' Nick takes a long drag of his Camel. 'I'm not sure Lisa fits that description.'

'You, my dear Nick, are looking for Harriet!' Guy grins. Then, when Nick gives me a look and I blush, embarrassed: 'Nononono!' he laughs. 'Harriet Murray. Great-Grandfather Hector's girl. Hold on, just wait here, I'll show you.' He rushes to the study then emerges with a thin yellowish page: the handwriting is faint and close together, but Guy is clearly familiar with it. 'Listen to this: "My dearest Harriet, they tell me that I am to be transported back to Somerset within the week, so I hurry to write this to you. The leg is not much better than it was at the Fourteenth Casualty Clearing Station."' Here Guy looks at us. 'He loses his leg – they have to amputate it when he gets back to England. "But despite the pain, I feel almost grateful that I was shot: how else would I have met you? I look down at this sorry limb and smell the garlic juice you used to disinfect our wounds. I see you in your apron, bending over me as you try to remain expressionless when tending to me. I see you in your cape, wandering among the stretchers and the ambulances, the mist swirling round you. Harriet, I long to be with you, away from the fighting. To follow the lovely walks you described to me in the New Forest. I long to walk hand in hand beneath the ancient trees, catching glimpses of ponies dancing in the moonlight. Dear, dear Harriet, promise that we shall see one another again soon."' Guy looks from me to Nick. 'It's marvellous, isn't it? Written in August 1918. He moved heaven and earth to see her again after the war. The Carews were dead set against it: Harriet was the daughter of a foreman and seamstress from Southampton. Still, love prevailed.'

His mobile rings. Guy jumps: 'Yes? Hi, I *thought* it was you. Oh, that's fab!' He turns to us. 'It's on Sunday: nine p.m. Prime-time slot!' And he wraps me in a tight hug and swings me round the kitchen.

'Alex, a lot rides on this!' I urge my eldest, who blinks at me with screen-weary eyes. He's been on his PSP since mid-morning and is totally immersed in Virtual Tennis: World Tour. But on Monday he has the first of his Wolsingham entrance exams and that leaves us less than forty-eight hours in which to cram everything a thirteen-year-old needs to know about the subjunctive, trigonometry and the Spanish Armada.

Part of me would quite like Alex to sabotage his chances of getting into Wolsingham. I don't want to lose my eldest to boarding school. He keeps telling me how exciting it will be; I can only envisage harrowing incidents of bullying, and unbearable pressure, on a diet of Brussels sprouts and rice pudding.

But, 'The scholarship means a lot to your father,' I persist. 'And think of how happy you'd make Grandpa.' Both of us turn serious at the mention of Archie. His cough is worrying.

'Yes, Mum,' Alex insists. 'Mr Lourie says I'm on track, so I don't think we need to panic.'

'Fine, but some last-minute revision never hurt anyone.' I lower my voice. 'A cut in your school fees would be very welcome at this point.'

Again, Alex nods. Then he suddenly wraps an arm around my waist.

'Mum, I know that I keep saying that I'd love Wolsingham. But I'll miss you.' He lays his head on my shoulder. 'And Dad.' Here he whispers, 'I can't wait to watch it tomorrow night! I hope Dad becomes a real star.'

Everyone clusters in the sitting room to watch *Big Game* on Sunday night. The boys sit on either side of their father, looking as nervous as if they were about to hear their school report for the year. Maisie sits beside Rufus on the floor, eyes wide and shiny with expectation.

Daniela has wet hair and is in her bathrobe, but is so excited she practically squeaks. 'Oh, Mr Caroo! You are on television!'

Nick has come over, taken the last drags of a cigarette on our front steps, and now slouches in the armchair.

I've rung Charlotte and Jack, Cecily and Archie to make sure they won't miss the programme.

Guy opens a bottle of Chablis and pours four glasses with great ceremony.

'I tried to persuade Percy to come over and watch with us, but he couldn't. You know, I do believe he's slightly jealous about it.' Guy raises his glass, 'Still, here's to our big break!' We clink glasses just as a sultry woman's voice announces: 'Next, *Big Game*, the diary of a safari hunter.'

With hindsight, I think I guessed everything the moment I saw the opening sequence, where Guy appears in the distance, a small khaki dot that blends perfectly against the grassy plains, then draws ever closer, until we see a floppy khaki bush hat, twill shirt and cargo shorts. A close-up reveals the pearls of perspiration on his forehead and upper lip. Not a good look.

'*This* is Keen-yah, and I know this land like the back of my hand. My name is Guy Carew, and my family have served the British Empire from Delhi to Nairobi.' Cut to: a camp-fire scene, at night, with Guy mixing what I take to be Marmite into a tin cup of boiled water. He clinks his spoon inside the cup, takes a sip, then turns to the camera: 'Safari is Swahili for journey. And I'm going to take you on an extraordinary journey, among lions, cheetahs, buffaloes, flamingos – and hunters, British and African.'

Cut to: zebras and giraffes elegantly galloping across a grassy plain. A jeep bearing white and black men comes into view. The camera zooms in on Guy, sitting beside the driver. 'A big part of the problems today in Keen-yah are the new Keen-yahns. They blame the West for robbing them of their resources.'

'Guy believes things were better under British rule.' A woman's voice, cool and classless, speaks off-screen. I recognize Zoë's voice and I shoot Guy a look: he stiffens visibly, but says nothing.

'It's fashionable to blame the British for every problem Kenya faces,' television Guy is saying with a shrug, 'but I don't think we should buy this PC attitude. It's what aid-workers hand out with their food packages. But God save us from the kind of do-gooders who hire "diversity trainers" for "conflict-resolution workers" and then are surprised tribal conflicts go on. These are the people who will not admit that Kenya was better off before.'

'In what way?' the invisible Zoë asks quickly.

'Under the British there was rule of law, limited corruption, no crime to speak of and actually quite a flourishing economy. Nowadays, Nairobi is Nairobbery. It's a lawless place with a soaring crime rate. Its corrupt elite siphons off money to line their pockets.'

'Surely you're not saying that anyone who's made money in Africa is corrupt?'

'There are some exceptions, but corruption is rife. What's the point of our doubling aid to the continent, erasing its debts, when all we're doing is re-routing money into a few men's pockets at the top?'

And so *Big Game* rolls on. We get stunning wide-angle shots of savannahs and roaming wild animals; the white hunters whom Guy accompanies on safari put in an appearance, and are comically crass and ignorant. But mostly we have Guy the presenter sharing his views of colonialism (not altogether a bad thing), African democracy (not altogether a good thing), and aid (downright awful) with his audience. Whenever Guy speaks, Zoë, like some invisible Jiminy Cricket, pops up and chides him: she's the liberal conscience of this unrepentantly un-PC, white, middle-aged, middle-class man.

I shrink into my chair and see Nick doing the same.

We're in the jeep, accompanying the two British white hunters. Guy: 'This will be a great shoot. Everything's allowed here, except elephants.'

'I thought cheetahs were an endangered species?' Jiminy Cricket asks.

Guy: 'Oh, come on, if you listened to some people, no one would go hunting any more. And where's the fun in that? It's like the environment: Westerners get all Puritanical and go overboard. Remember DDT? The West decided to ban it from Africa because of their green concerns. As a result, millions of African children have died.'

We go to a remote village, with children running out of their huts to greet the jeep.

'Why do you regard Western technical assistance as "hopeless"?' Zoë asks.

Guy: 'Because it's like trying to teach a man to fish when he lives in a land-locked, drought-ridden country. All the angling lessons in the world, even if they're given by Angelina, Bono and the World Bank, won't solve a thing.'

Thanks to the editing and Zoë's insinuating tone and sarcastic voice-overs, by the time the credits roll, we are left with the distinct impression that Guy is an apologist for colonialism, a privileged white man brought up with a crudely nationalistic army ethos, who thinks nothing of shooting everything that moves.

No one dares say anything. Then Daniela stands up, clutching the towel turban on her head: 'Good night. That was interesting.' She tiptoes out and up the stairs.

I steal a look at Guy: my husband's face is pale, his shoulders are hunched, and his voice trembles. 'God! I sounded like an idiot,' he moans. 'It was a set-up!'

I place my hand on his arm, concerned, and the boys huddle closer.

Maisie climbs on to his lap and hugs him. 'Daddy, don't be sad.' Even Nick, slouched in his armchair, looks worried.

'I can't believe it. Why would anyone do that?' Guy shakes his head miserably. 'Oh gawd!' He buries his head in his hands. 'I've been made to look like a fool. And about four million people saw that. I'll never be able to work again. I won't be able to set foot outside this house. Arghhhhhhh!'

I wrap my arms around him. 'Darling one,' I murmur, my head against his.

'Daddy!' the children cry in chorus.

Nick pours his brother the last few drops of Chablis. 'Here, you need this.'

'That's it, you know. That's it.' Guy takes a gulp of the wine, then turns to me. 'Harriet, I'm a failure. You only get one crack at television, and I've failed with mine.'

'Stop it, Guy. Everything will be all right. You just pass it off as a send-up. Tell everyone it was a post-modern ironic personal statement.' My words sound hollow even to my ears.

The boys wrap their arms around their father and hold him tight.

'No, no, it's over.' Guy shakes his head over theirs, disconsolate.

'You've got quite a few strings to your bow,' Nick says firmly. 'There's *Rajput*, the stuff from the publishing house … and weren't you doing something about Lyme Regis?'

'Don't, don't!' Guy moans in agony. 'I put everything on the back-burner because I wanted to concentrate on this telly thing.' Guy looks down at the floor. 'What an idiot I've been.'

'Daddy, you're not an idiot!' Alex counters with feeling.

'You're the best daddy in the world!' Tom follows suit.

'Nick's right, Guy.' I smile encouragingly. 'You've got plenty of other work to rely on. Percy's still keen on you working for him, and the manuscripts do bring in quite a bit.' But even as I'm saying it, I'm wondering if Percy really is well disposed towards Guy after he kept missing his editing deadlines. And Simon is certainly unhappy with the way Guy has put Lyme Regis 'on the back-burner'.

'In any case,' Nick downs his last gulp of beer, 'should you ever be in need, I've got no liquidity problem, and no school fees to worry about, so just give us a shout.'

* * *

'As if I'd borrow money from my little brother!' Guy is put out by Nick's offer. We're lying in bed, side by side in the dark. I don't say anything, but stare up at the ceiling and wonder how we'll ever tackle the mounting bills now that Guy's great success has gone up in smoke. Nick's offer offends him, but Guy may not be in a position to be so sensitive. I review our options: Making up with Simon? Last time I spoke to him, he didn't sound malleable. Going full time at HAC? Perhaps, but I'm not sure it is wise for me to court more opportunities to be with James. Kent? It suddenly makes a lot more sense. Even if it means I'll miss *him* so.

'You know,' Guy addresses me in the dark, 'when *Lonely Hunter* came out, and I was only twenty, I thought my life was settled. I'd travel, I'd write, and I'd make a great living from it. I thought I might be lucky enough to have a nice wife, a sweet little family; but what I was one hundred per cent convinced about was my work. I was going to make it.' Guy issues an immense sigh. 'Now look at me: I haven't done anything. A few books that don't sell, a chapter in a coffee table, a one-hour film that shows me to be a buffoon with antiquated ideas. Doesn't amount to much, does it?'

'Guy, don't be so hard on yourself.' I take his hand on the sheet. He stares up at the ceiling, unmoving. 'You do what you love – how many people can say that? You've had more fun and more adventures than anyone I can think of.'

'I've failed you. You should have never got mixed up with me. You should never have left James Weston.' I start, but say nothing. 'He would have made you happy, provided for you.'

Guy pulls his hand from mine, turns away from me and lies there, still and silent.

I can't move, either. If I could start over again, would I exchange my husband – the failed television presenter and only moderately successful travel writer – for the millionaire property developer? Would I swap the charming man with his head in the clouds for the attractive man with eyes only for me? Almost fifteen years ago, I rejected James Weston and threw my lot in with Guy Carew, the funny and eccentric literary sensation. But right now, I'm obsessed with James. He makes me feel giddy and sexy, but is that because he's the *one* – or is he simply an attractive man who pays me flattering attention in the midst of my messy, tiring, penny-pinching domesticity?

Do I see James as the man who can save me from jam spread on Winnie the Pooh pyjamas, pedalling to and from school in the rain, bathroom taps that come off in my hand and raisins stamped into the carpet? I know that with James I would inhabit a spacious, minimalist house and have a solicitous daily, a luxury car, and no notion of what anything costs. Is that what I want?

I fall asleep at last with images of James's huge entrance hall floating in my head – the white walls, chandelier, three-foot flowers in vases … and mysteriously no trace of the large nude portrait of his ex-wife.

25

For the next few days, everyone tiptoes around the house. Daniela says nothing about her Pilgrimcam visions, Rufus slopes about with his ears back in fright, Maisie looks warily from Guy to me and back again. As for the boys, they try to keep out of Guy's way, but every now and then one of them will come up to their father, and whisper: 'You all right, Dad?' And come away with a half-hearted pat on their head or shoulder.

Guy mopes as I've never seen him mope. He sleeps late, doesn't shave, refuses to talk to anyone on the phone and keeps his mobile permanently switched off. He only makes an effort to sound cheerful when Cecily and Archie ring.

'You were jolly good,' Cecily says loyally. 'And I thought it was wonderful how you sent up everyone, including yourself.'

'Oh my God, how's he taking it?' Charlotte whispers over the phone. 'I can't believe they stitched him up! That bitch!'

'Don't, it's awful,' I whisper back. 'He's so upset he can hardly speak. I'm so worried there may be some nasty reviews in the papers. I rushed down to check the *Telegraph* this morning just in case I needed to confiscate the TV page, but it wasn't mentioned.'

'Poor Guy!' Charlotte sighs.

My mother is less indulgent.

'Well, it might have been cunningly edited and it might have been a set-up, but it was very *like* Guy. In any case, I bet it sold thousands of copies of *Lonely Hunter*. And it's put his name on the map again.'

'His name on the map?! He worries it's brought his name into disrepute. He says his honour is at stake.'

'Honour? A very nice Carew word, but it doesn't pay the bills. Tell him to buck up. He should stop the public school nonsense and move out here.'

'Mum, Alex has just sat his Wolsingham scholarship exams. There's no way Guy will rethink this.'

'Then Alex can go to boarding school and be miserable, but the other two can go to state schools here.' My mother sounds brisk and in charge. 'And I've seen some lovely homes in the estate agents' windows. I'd be more than happy to have a first look at them.' She presses on: 'You can't let Guy vegetate like this. He needs a good kick, and a change of scenery would do him a power of good.' She turns her attention to where I am vulnerable: 'And with all the savings you'll be making, you can afford to work *less* not *more*. The children will love that.'

After the long spell of ignoring every bill and every notice, Guy is now obsessing about our finances even more than I do. As we don't have a car, or go out, or have expensive taste in clothes or grooming, Guy can't decree that we cut down on that; and he still resists any talk of reviewing the children's schooling. But he has decided that other areas of our lives, and budget, could be trimmed.

'We won't need any heating until the winter,' he informs me. 'But I really think we have to have a word with the Hygiene Queen about her showers. She's in there for hours, and it's costing us a fortune. Tell her only shallow baths in future.'

'Guy!' I protest. 'Leave Daniela alone! If she goes, I'll die.' Daniela is the only smooth-running element in our household: the machines are as temperamental as the rest of us, everything creaks, has cracks, or has cracked up. Our Czech au pair is an oasis of sanity in this turmoil. Let her stand under a hot shower for three hours if she wants, she's worth every drop.

'I'm wondering whether we shouldn't convert my study into another bedroom and get a lodger?' Guy won't stop. 'But of course the lodger would want an en suite bathroom and that would cost a fortune to install.'

'There are plenty of people in this house as it is,' I answer patiently. 'There's not enough oxygen for more.'

My husband has also decided that we should give up drinking wine and eating meat because it's too expensive.

'Lentils and rice are the healthy alternative,' he tells me at breakfast. 'Just ask Manic Organic.'

'But what about a glass to unwind with when you come home from work?' I protest feebly.

'I work from home, remember?' Guy snaps. 'In any case, they say meditation is perfect for unwinding. And it doesn't cost £6.99 a bottle.'

'Oh Guy,' I sigh, 'are you going to ban every little pleasure?' I stop short: my husband gives me a look that makes me blush scarlet. What does he think I am referring to? Or rather, whom? Guilt fills me. Next weekend James and I are driving down to Wiltshire to his friend's house. It means several hours on my own with him, in close proximity. I haven't told Guy yet because last night's admission of failure has worried me. I don't want him doubting my love when he's doubting himself. Sins of omission are often necessary in a good marriage. Aren't they?

When Guy is not moping about his career he is being nervous about his son's academic one. 'If he doesn't get the scholarship, we're finished. All the more so now.' He has asked Alex a hundred times about his exams: were the questions the ones he'd prepared, did he read the questions all the way through, did he have a chance to finish all his answers, did he feel he pulled through or sailed through?

'It was fine, Dad, really,' Alex keeps repeating, looking more worn by paternal inquisition than by the exams.

Every afternoon my eldest asks me whether the letter from Wolsingham has come with the post. 'It won't come yet, Alex,' I repeat endlessly, exasperated. 'They've warned us it takes at least a week.'

I'm anxious for both father and son – as well as for Archie, who has been diagnosed with pneumonia and re-admitted to hospital in Yeovil.

'He'll pull through, he's as tough as old boots,' Guy reassures Cecily. 'And he's got a project to look forward to: the book of Carew letters.'

Guy has holed himself up in the study. When I tiptoe by the door, I can hear excruciating snatches of conversation: 'Er, yes, but, Simon, I did have lots of positive feedback from them at the time. I thought I was justified in putting all my efforts into it.' 'Hullo, Percy. What? Oh, I see. Right. I thought I had kept up the editing through it all.'

I feel a pit in my stomach open up. For the first time in years, I'm really scared of what the future may bring. Forget Wolsingham and the Griffin, I'm beginning to wonder if we can afford to stay in our home.

I resolve not to bring up the subject of schooling with Guy until we know the outcome of Alex's scholarship exams.

But I must sound out Mary Jane Thompson about the possibility of full-time work. Anjie has announced her departure and I need to get in quick, before Mary Jane starts thinking about restructuring our little operation.

It's a challenge I would have been loath to tackle only a few days back, but now I'm desperate enough to be assertive; and, too, I feel as if our conversation in the café has built a bond between Mary Jane and me. So it is with a bold step that I leave Anjie and our conversation about which kitchen outfitters she should opt for when it comes to re-doing the kitchen in Tunbridge Wells, and approach Mary Jane's door.

'Yes?' Mary Jane looks particularly scary when she peers over her red-rimmed spectacles.

'I wonder if I could have a word?' I step into Fortress Thompson.

'Hmmm?'

'You've often told me, Mary Jane, that I might contribute more to HAC if I were to go full time. I've been thinking this over and I recently came to the conclusion that you're right. I probably would get a lot more work done if I were working here five days a week rather than three.'

Mary Jane's eyebrow shoots up over the red-rimmed spectacles. 'I'm delighted you see the wisdom of my words, Harriet. But frankly our budget cannot stretch to a full-time secretary, fund-raiser and receptionist.'

'Oh … but when you were talking about it a few months ago, I thought it was all right?'

'A few months ago, yes. But things change. We have yet to attain our target for next year. Our usual donors have not been as generous as in the past.' She gives me a long look: this is obviously a failing on my part. 'Perhaps we could increase you to five days a week and throw in some light receptionist duties as well? There's very little manning of the telephones, the sorting of the post is done in a few minutes.'

I gulp. I have been demoted to receptionist. Three years at university, two years helping to run a small art gallery, and two as HAC's fund-raiser – all leading to 'manning the phones and sorting the post'? I'm indignant and I want to rage at the woman before me. But my desk at home, with its tower of bills, suddenly looms; and Zoë's horrible insinuating voice on *Big Game* echoes in my ears: 'What do you mean, Guy?'

'What would I be paid?' I ask Mary Jane.

'Let me see what we can afford. I'll let you know.'

I'm so dispirited by the time I get home, I hardly notice that Lisa is in our kitchen. This is not Lisa as I know her: she is drinking a cup of mint tea with Daniela, and allowing Maisie to show her *This Rabbit Belongs to Emily Brown*. No sign of a BlackBerry or mobile. No hint of boredom or need to talk about me, me and me again. I'm wondering whether this domestic goddess is the work of a life coach, an analyst, or the break-up with Nick, when Lisa cuddles Maisie on her lap, which is a first, and fires me a question: 'How did you find each other?'

I assume she's asking about Guy and me and am about to launch into a sentimental recollection of our first encounter when Daniela speaks up:

'Harriet found my number on Mumsnet. Then she interview me, then I move in.'

'Mumsnet?' Lisa looks confused.

'Mumsnet,' Maisie repeats as she takes her book from Lisa's lap to Rufus's basket: she is determined that she and Rufus will learn to read before she turns four.

'Website for mums: offers everything from tips on how to deal with colic to want ads for au pairs, nannies, and leg waxers.' I stare at Lisa in wonder: her interest in Mumsnet is almost as peculiar as her interest in Daniela. I'm not even sure she knows Daniela's name.

'Ooooh …' Lisa breathes in and her blue eyes look as alert as they do at the tip of a hot stock, or the mention of a fab new personal trainer. 'How useful.' Useful? Mumsnet is about as useful to a single City high-flier as a BlackBerry would be to Maisie. 'And have you ever considered … I mean,' Lisa blushes and smiles uncertainly, 'a friend who lives nearby asked me, would you ever consider sharing an au pair?'

'No, you couldn't share au pairs, they usually don't work enough hours. And you're not meant to leave them on their own for too long anyway. I suppose one could do a nanny share.' I suddenly spot a money-saving proposition. 'Where does your friend live? Maybe she and I could have a discussion about Daniela – obviously, only if you're willing, Daniela, to work a bit more for more money?'

'Oh yes.' Daniela nods, beams at us kindly, and then: 'I go upstairs.' She's wearing the serene expression she always has when she's about to experience her Pilgrimcam. Maybe I should warn Lisa's friend about that. I'm about to explain the Pilgrimcam when I see Lisa gently stroking her stomach. She looks down, with that secretive, pleased air I know so well.

'You're pregnant!' I cry.

Lisa's hand freezes, she blushes scarlet, opens her mouth as if to deny it, and then gives up. 'Yes.' She hangs her head. 'Nick. Can you believe it?' She looks up and smiles sheepishly at me: 'Are you shocked?'

'Not at all,' I lie. 'I think, I think you'll make a great mummy, and a fabulous sister-in-law!'

Lisa's face falls. 'No, that's not on the cards.'

'Why ever not? Have you told Nick?'

'Yes, but he said he'll be happy to pay for anything I need but he's not going to commit to a baby he never wanted. He's not looking for more responsibilities.' Lisa's eyes fill – but then she sets her jaw and flicks her golden hair. 'I don't care. I've seen so many women at the bank who've lost out on having a child because they kept postponing it. I was thinking about doing it now, and yes, I'd prefer to be married and have 2.1 children with a devoted husband, but, hey, if this is the way it's going to be, I'm ready. I've got the money, the house, and if I organize myself carefully I figure I can work full time *and* have a munchkin.'

'I'm sure you'll manage brilliantly. And we'll help you. Not just with Daniela, who, by the way, is absolutely brilliant with "munchkins", but I can baby-sit, and my best friend's just had a baby and can hand down all kinds of furniture and clothes and – oh, it will be amazing!' I believe it, too, despite my misgivings about a lone mum who needs to work City hours at City pace. 'The most important thing is to get plenty of rest and …'

'Folic acid, support tights …' Lisa ticks off each item on her fingers '… pregnancy bras, cocoa butter for stretch marks, loads of greens, sensible shoes. Don't worry, I've been looking into it. It's three months now, I've just had my first scan. I've been on the internet looking up everything from breastfeeding to private schools.' She gives a mirthless little laugh. 'If it's a boy, I'll send him to Wolsingham, to follow in his ancestors' footsteps.'

'I'm disappointed in Nick.' I purse my lips.

Lisa shrugs. 'You can't force love.'

'I'm disappointed in Nick,' I repeat that night to Guy when I crawl into our bed.

'He's acting like a cad,' Guy sighs as he pulls off his socks, leaning against the dresser. 'I'd like to give him a talking to, but I don't feel I have any right to preach to anybody at the minute.' He steps out of his corduroys and boxers and into his pyjamas. 'I hope Mum and Dad never find out. What would they think?'

Ever since *Big Game* was broadcast, Guy has been retreating more and more into the familiar and comforting world of Carew lore. He's immersed in the correspondence between Hector and Harriet, but has also found some interesting letters in which his great-uncle Reggie describes D-Day, and a cache of letters from the young Captain Alfie Carew describing climbing in Tibet. He emerges from communion with these missives full of nostalgia: for more heroic times, an old honour code, and better Carew specimens than his brother – and himself.

'I don't believe it! What a bastard!' Charlotte splutters with indignation the next day at the school gates. 'Well, she'll need a lot of healing, and I know just the person she should see to channel the anger. She mustn't store it inside, or it will harm Baby.' We are sitting inside her 4 × 4, sheltering from the rain. I notice a tower of small white boxes in the back, beside the new baby-seat.

'What are you carting about?'

'My new project,' Charlotte whispers, excited. 'Promise you'll keep it secret – I don't want to jinx it.'

'Cross my heart and hope to die, stick a needle in my eye,' I chant childishly.

'I'm going to open a shop.'

'What?!' My mouth falls open in shock.

'Yes, with Feng Shui Faye, remember her? She had this brilliant idea of a New Age boutique on the King's Road, but she didn't know how to come up with the money, and I persuaded Jack this is a growth industry, which it is, and – maybe just to humour me but maybe because he really does see we're on to something – Jack's come up with the money for a lease. Oh, Harriet –' Charlotte claps her hands, excited '– it will be amazing: crystals, hot stones, scented candles and essential oils, and loads of books to help people like you and me, and maybe we can even have a little meditation corner and a reflexologist on hand.' Charlotte turns back and picks up two of the white boxes behind us. 'This is a range of the most expensive essential oils. Here – smell.' She holds one box under my nose. 'And this one –' she shakes another one '– is the best healing crystal *ever*: any cut, bruise or sting miraculously disappears within minutes. I swear by it.'

I listen to Charlotte and feel a wave of dismay wash over me: my best friend is fitting into the Manic Organic mould my husband made for her, and I can't laugh it off. How can I follow Charlotte down this path? I feel I'm losing her in a thicket of reflexology, essential oils, aromatherapy, reiki and tai chi. 'I want you to come and see the shop before we go to Aix with the children,' Charlotte goes on, heedless. 'We leave on the seventeenth.'

Through the rain we don't hear the children coming out of school, but suddenly the playground fills with running, skipping, hopping uniforms. I spot Tom, who, shielding his head with his rucksack, runs towards the gates. I open the car door and stand outside and wave so that he can see me. He rushes towards me, and for a moment my heart jumps with happiness at the look of delighted recognition that lights his face. Then I see Miles Collins. He also runs towards us and is within a yard of his mother's car when he skids on the wet tarmac and falls hard on to his knees. Not even the crashing rain can drown out his scream.

Charlotte jumps out from behind the wheel. 'Miles!'

Her son hobbles to his feet, one knee bleeding profusely.

'Oh, babyyyyyyyyyy!' Charlotte cries out. She rushes to him and wraps her arms around him. 'Quick, Harriet, we've got a first-aid kit in the glove compartment.'

I hold out a box doubtfully: 'What about the healing crystal?'

'Don't be daft!' Charlotte shrieks. 'Hurry!'

Our friendship may survive after all.

26

Anjie is in before me, as usual, but does not greet me with her cheerful, 'Hey, girl!' She's sitting at her desk, but is not opening the post, or surreptitiously flicking through *Grazia* or *Heat*. She has yet to switch on her computer and looks vacantly through the window.

'Hiya,' I call out as I remove my helmet. When my colleague does not turn around, I fear the worst: she knows about William. I don't say a thing as I get to my desk. I sit down, and try to work out what to do. If Anjie confides in me, do I admit that I know? Mary Jane and I agreed she shouldn't break the news – but, after the event, do we admit she saw William and the other woman?

I don't dare look in Anjie's direction but, whether in a good or bad mood, Anjie is impossible to ignore, and I find my eyes drawn to her. She sits there, black and voluptuous, with bright beads punctuating her shoulder-length dreadlocks, and tears streaming down her cheeks.

'Anjie?' I whisper. Mary Jane's door is shut, but I can hear our boss on the phone. Anjie doesn't respond. I approach her desk. 'Anjie, what is it?' I keep my voice low.

'I'm sitting in the kitchen last night,' Anjie begins, her voice heavy and weary. 'William's in the bath. He's tired and I put some nice bath stuff in the water to relax his muscles. And then the buzzer goes and it's some boy downstairs who wants a word with William. He says it's urgent, he can't wait, and he gets real angry. So I ask who it is, and I go to William and tell him who's looking for him. And William goes *white* and tells me to say he's not here. So I feel a pit in my stomach and I think: Drugs? Debts? What's he been up to? And I don't know what makes me do it, but I press the door and I let the boy in. Skinny, ugly, white-van man. The kind who calls me nigger when I'm in his way in the street. I tell him William's not in, but I want to know what it's all about. And he starts f-ing and blinding at me and says if my husband doesn't stop messing around with his girl-friend, he's gonna kill him. And he says it's been going on three months now and he's fed up to the back teeth of my man hav-ing it off with his Ashley. William doesn't come out of the bath-room, he's so scared. And it takes me half an hour to get the boy out of the flat.' Anjie's monotone now changes pitch and becomes shrill: 'I hate him! I hate him! He told me not to believe it, that it was a big fat lie, and then he admitted it was true but it would never happen again, and said she was just a tart he'd had sex with and there was no feeling and ... All those lies men tell you when they've broken your heart.'

I wrap my arm around her shoulders, feeling guilty that I've known about this tragedy-waiting-to-happen before

Anjie did. My colleague sobs openly, and wipes her cheeks with the back of her hand. I take out a ball of tissue that I used this morning to wipe away Maisie's Marmite splodges. 'Here, don't cry.'

Anjie takes the tissue and shakes her head. 'I don't want to kick him out because of the children, but I don't want him in my bed because he makes me feel dirty.' She looks at me, eyes bright with tears and anger. 'I know I'll never trust him again. Never!' She shakes her dreadlocks disconsolately, and their bright beads swing prettily. 'Once that trust is broken, there's no mending it.'

I swallow hard: she is telling me this and I, on Sunday, am driving two hours with James to do a recce at his friend's house in Wiltshire. It's all above board, all professional. But then why is it that I have very consciously allowed Guy to think that I'm going down in the car with Mary Jane and James, rather than admit that it's just me and my ex-boyfriend? Why do I feel so deliciously tense at the mere prospect of the drive? And why have I been choosing what to wear for the past five days? I'm trifling with Guy's trust, just as William has done with Anjie.

'Even if he swears he will stop seeing her, how can I believe him?' Anjie blows her nose. 'Harriet, he's lied once, he can lie again.' She throws the tissue into the bin. 'And pretending every Sunday at church that he's a God-fearing man!'

'What about Kent? Will you go ahead with the move?' I ask, as Anjie finally switches on her computer.

'I don't know! I think he was trying to get closer to that bitch, because she lives there. And me thinking he was trying to do the best for his family. And why do you think he wanted me to give up work and stay home and be a lady of leisure?' Anjie's eyes flash indignantly. 'Because then he could have me out of the way! I was to stay nice and quiet inside so I wouldn't be able to see him and his carryings on.' Anjie breathes in deeply. 'I better do the post: she'll be off the phone any second now.'

'Cup of tea?' I ask feebly, feeling as if I were offering to hold in a flood of emotions with a little white picket fence.

'Yeah.' Anjie flashes me a grateful smile, but as I approach the kettle, she stops me in my tracks. 'You're off with James on Sunday isn't it to see the house? You be careful, girl: one bad marriage between us is enough.'

Anjie's words chase one another round my head as I wait outside the HAC offices for James. I've pretended to him that I forgot the relevant files from Social Services in the office. 'They've got all the specifications we need to see if a venue is suitable,' I explained over the mobile last night, voice low. I'd locked myself in the bathroom for this surreptitious call, and had to send away Tom, who came knocking on the door, looking for our nail scissors. 'Honestly, I can't leave the files behind. Why don't I pick them up from the offices tomorrow morning, and we meet there.' *Honestly*, my foot. I simply don't want James to pick me up from home with Guy there.

So at 10 a.m. on Sunday morning I'm standing on the front steps of my office, waiting for James to pick me up. I feel as guilty and exposed as if I had a huge letter *A* sewn in scarlet thread on to my summer dress. Passers-by, cyclists, cars, minivans, buses: they come and go, buzz and roar, along the High Street. Do they realize what I'm about to do? Can they see the secret I'm nursing within a sleeveless, low-cut dress that is far too summery for this chilly morning? I feel as if everyone can see through me and passes me with a disapproving look. What do I think I'm doing? I have as good as lied to my dearest and nearest about this fateful drive. 'Oh, darling,' I told Guy, 'it's one of those tedious HAC meetings about holiday homes I always seem to get roped into.' But it's too late now to cancel. I stand here on the pavement, on the look-out for a silver Merc that belongs to a man I've had carnal knowledge of and – what's worse – could pleasurably imagine having more of the same. And this on a Sunday, for God's sake.

Guy's wife, mother of three, HAC fund-raiser – I don't so much multi-task as multi-exist, pulled into so many different directions I've been left as shapeless as the jumpers surly Ilona ruined in the washing machine. But do I really want to step into yet another role as James Weston's lover?

When my phone rings (Chopin, chosen by Guy as my signature tune, and programmed by Alex), I practically jump out of my skin. James is cancelling. Or he's forgotten that we were meeting here and is ringing the door at home. Or Guy has spotted me. Or one of the children is registering 101 temperature. But it's Charlotte: 'Have you seen L.L. Munro's review of Guy's programme?'

'No!' I moan: Guy doesn't deserve this further public humiliation – and at the hands of that acerbic critic. Fate cannot be so cruel.

'Listen to this: "Guy Carew does for the British colonial expat what Borat does for Kazakhstan. This is a brilliant black comedy, where the antihero blows the whistle on the emperor with no clothes: the aid circus, with its glitzy ditzy celebrity supporters like Brangelina and Bono; the rewriting of history that decrees the white man ruined the lot of happy Africans; the guilt about the spoiled First World wreaking environmental damage on the poor Third World. Guy Carew doesn't put up with any of this nonsense, and tells us we don't need to either." Wait, it gets better!' Charlotte chortles. '"This is unmissable TV. I don't know if his worthy lefty BBC documentary makers are in collusion with Guy Carew, or whether he is having fun at their expense, but he punctures every PC platitude with reckless wit and energy."'

'Oh my God!'

'It's a two-page spread, with a huge photo of Guy. Makes him look really dishy, by the way, and the caption reads "Guy Carew: the BBC unleashes its secret weapon".'

'Charlotte!' I gasp.

'He is *made!*' Charlotte chuckles. 'I've tried your home number and it's engaged. Will you tell him? And, congratulations!'

'Yes!' I almost laugh out loud at my best friend's U-turn. No more asides about Guy finding a job with Extra-Tutorials, no more questions about his life's ambitions. Goodness, if Charlotte has changed her tune, then L.L. Munro really has changed Guy's fortunes.

I dial our home number: engaged. I dial Guy's mobile: voicemail. 'Darling, ring me ASAP,' I tell him, trying to contain my excitement.

And then I see James waving at me from his Merc. 'Harriet – ready then?'

* * *

I'm sitting a foot away from James, and I feel as tense as if we were naked. One lurch to the right and I'll brush against his thigh; one sudden stop and I'll reach for him beside me. I steal a glance at his profile: he's concentrating on the road ahead. We've been driving for more than an hour, engaged in an easy, friendly chitchat about everything from the merits of Richmond Park to the trouble with wind farms. James describes at some length his newest project, an exclusive resort complex in Marbella. I tell him about my fear that my three days a week at HAC will soon become five. He avoids any mention of *Big Game* and I avoid telling him about L.L. Munro's rave review. We could be two old friends, driving down the M3 in perfect harmony. Except we aren't.

'You may have to map-read' – James points to the AA map in the pocket of my door – 'when we leave the M3 behind.' And then, looking straight ahead: 'I seem to remember you were very good at it.'

I remember too. How many car journeys we made together, as undergraduates, sitting just like this, him at the wheel, me beside him, looking from the map on my lap to James and then back again. Parties, home to meet his parents, home to meet my mum and Mel, a holiday in Cornwall, a weekend with friends in Yorkshire. Each and every excursion featured James in the driver's seat, eyes steely blue as they focused on the road ahead, lips half smiling as he listened to me, or the music, or held my hand. 'No, James!' I'd plead, half serious, half joking. 'Keep both hands on the wheel!'

'How can you expect me to keep my hands off you when you're so gorgeous?' he'd counter. And his hand, large and warm, would keep mine captive, regardless of my protestations. As he ferried me from A to B, I was supposed to map-read and guide us through the maze of country roads, but there was no doubt that the one in control was James. And as I sat there beside him, I had an inkling of what life would be like as Mrs Weston. I'd be taken care of, and looked after, and I'd never want for anything. I'd be the cherished possession, the lucky passenger ferried around by the capable driver.

'I think it will be perfect, with a few changes to comply with regulations. Sam says it's a huge house with at least four reception rooms that could do for meeting rooms. Grounds are lovely too.' James is talking and I realize I haven't been paying attention.

'Sorry, what?'

He takes my hand and squeezes it. 'A penny for your thoughts.'

'Nothing. It's so beautiful.' I don't take my hand away and feel it grow warm in his hold.

'I'll tell you mine for free ...' James looks at the road. 'I will do whatever you want. See you every day, leave you alone, go away from London.'

'No!' the word comes out before I can stop it.

'You don't want me to go away?' James lowers his voice to a whisper. 'Even knowing how I feel about you?'

'I couldn't bear it if you went.'

We drive on in silence. The day has grown hot and James opens the windows. I feel intoxicated by the warm air that rushes in the car and by the thoughts chasing round my head. I love him, I love him not, I love him, I love him not.

We come off the M3 and I start giving directions: left out of Little Bowen from the A303, then five miles and, when we're just past Colby, look out for a lane marked Mallay Manor.

It's a gorgeous shadow-filled drive, lined by lime trees and oak trees. The house itself is huge, a sprawling eighteenth-century edifice with dozens of chimneys and annexes.

'How grand,' I whisper. As we walk up the ancient stone steps, I feel as if we're about to embark on another journey.

Mr Nelson the caretaker, a squat, bald man with a friendly expression, shows us round the house. 'The conservatory, the morning room, the sitting room, the drawing room – good enough for any meeting, Mr Weston.' He's right. The rooms are large, high-ceilinged and speak of a grand family's past. The Mallays have lived here since the days of George III, he explains; important land-owners who over the past two generations went into the financial markets.

'They were wealthy enough not to open the house to the public,' James explains. 'But now Sam can't afford the upkeep, let alone the taxes.'

James and I wander about the rooms: they are pastel-coloured, with huge, heavily corniced fireplaces and the same dark parquet flooring; they could be the backdrop of a Gainsborough painting. Some are fully furnished, others have only a few enormous sofas and tables. Mr Nelson leads us up the grand wooden stairs and to the eighteen bedrooms, some with en suite bathrooms.

'It would be perfect for HAC.' James sounds excited. 'In fact, it would probably force the charity to expand. With three holiday homes instead of two at your disposal, you could increase the number of children you help by a third.' He talks, plans, projects into the future, while Mr Nelson and I stand beside him in the wood-panelled library. I watch his excitement, his eyes bright with a vision, and think how absolutely unnecessary I am on this recce. I don't resent James taking over the exercise: it's just that I see how he runs his life – and would run mine.

'You realize that, if it works out, Mary Jane will win loads of brownie points? She'll take all the credit, no doubt, and we'll be rubbed out of the picture.'

'I don't care, so long as she agrees to give me a good salary.' I refrain from telling him the humiliating demotion I may have to accept in order to secure that increase in salary.

'You shouldn't have to work full time.' James shoots me a look and then draws near. I see Mr Nelson diplomatically exit through the French doors into the garden. 'Do you know what I wish?' James takes both my hands in his. 'I wish I could just wipe these away –' with his finger he traces gently the lines across my forehead, and then the two parentheses on either side of my lips. 'Please, won't you let me try?'

27

James stands so close I can feel his breath on my face. As I shut my eyes, we're back at Bristol and that first kiss when he walked me down to the river. It was a glorious day, autumnal but sunny, and we had been talking intensely about our expectations of life: we would both make our parents tremendously proud, and make a bit of money, and above all see through our dreams. James did not want to end up like his father, a disaffected policeman, and I didn't want my father's staid life of an NHS dentist. We were drawing up to the boathouse, where some of James's rowing friends were waiting, when suddenly he stopped in his tracks. 'Do you know something, Harriet Tenant? I think you're fantastic. Absolutely fantastic.' James gripped my shoulders, and forced me to look at him. 'I think I've fallen in love with you.' And then, as I shut my eyes, he leant down so that I could feel his warm breath sweep my face, and kissed me.

* * *

He is kissing me now. I open my eyes as he wraps me in his arms.

'James,' I whisper into his chest, 'don't let go.'

'I'm never letting you go again.' He kisses my eyes shut, then my nose, my lips again, and starts working his way down my throat and my collarbone. He pushes the flimsy dress strap off my right shoulder and, as he plants a kiss there, my breath comes quick and sharp. This is not me, I tell myself, this is not like me at all. But another voice, mine, asks: 'What have I been doing all these years?'

'You've been working too hard and worrying too much.'

'Show me a mum who doesn't.'

'But life isn't only about motherhood!' James snaps impatiently, releasing me. 'I mean,' he corrects himself quickly, as I take a step back, 'you need some time for yourself.'

'I would love that,' I reply crossly. 'But it's a bit difficult to arrange when you have three squealing, wailing, over-active creatures in your care.' And that's without speaking of Guy, I think.

'Children grow up,' James insists. 'Then what?'

'We grow old, then what?' I shrug.

'I'd love to grow old with you.' My ex reaches out again, and takes both my hands. With me but without my children, I want to say: how will you manage that? But he goes on, 'Can I tempt you with something?'

'What?' I feel like Eve taking that apple.

'Marbella. I'll have to work there for the next year and a half. They've given me a villa by the site, it's gorgeous, two balconies and a swimming pool.' He talks, animated, as the sun comes in from behind him to gild his figure. 'I'd love to have you there beside me. You wouldn't have to lift a finger, I'd take care of everything. You can relax, sit at the villa, lounge by the pool, and I'll get my work done in the morning and then join you for lunch.'

I look into his eyes and know it could be just as he describes it. I'd be a lady who lounges, who has to keep her lover's Bollinger cold, his bed warm, the wrinkles at bay, her décolleté on display. It sounds a bit superficial, but a lot less stressful than chasing homework, doing nine-to-five at HAC three (soon to be five) days a week, and staying one step ahead of the bailiffs. James would plan meticulously our easy, elegant life, and I would float in his wake.

Somewhere my mobile rings. And rings. I open my eyes, see James's annoyance at the insistent Chopin. Oh no, what can it be? Guy calling me because he's got my message? Or because he's read the L.L. Munro review? Or, I change gear, envisioning more dramatic scenarios: one of the boys has slipped and chipped his tooth, Maisie has broken a plate and cut her hand so badly she needs stitches, Guy has allowed the boys to try their hand at cooking lunch and they've burnt down the house.

My first love is proposing to map out my future, but my maternal instinct won't allow me to ignore the mobile call. I feel caught between the youthful, desirable Harriet I see in James's eyes, and the slightly worn, thoroughly dependable Harriet I appear to everyone else. If I don't answer, I may open a whole new chapter in my life: passionate love-making, secret rendezvous, heart-beating rushes to grab my mobile whenever I think *he* is ringing, slips of the tongue that betray my preoccupation with one James Weston. If I do answer, Harriet will have resisted temptation and returned to her routine of wife, mum and part-time charity worker.

I hesitate only a second more. Then I draw away from James, fumble in my handbag and reach for the mobile.

'Mum,' Alex bleats, 'I really don't want to go to church and Dad is making me and I know it's for Maisie's place at St Christopher's but why should I?'

'Alex,' I hiss furiously, looking at James, who's withdrawn to stare out of the French windows, his back to me, 'deal with your father, please.'

'Where are you, Mum? The reception's really fuzzy – are you in the tube?'

'Can't talk now, will ring you later,' I spit crossly down the phone.

I walk up to my ex-boyfriend. 'I'm sorry. A little difficulty at home.'

James turns to me. 'Do you think you could ever suspend all this –' he waves towards the handbag I've just laid on the table, mobile phone safely tucked away in it. 'Get away altogether?'

'Sometimes,' I hold his gaze. 'Sometimes I dream of just getting away.'

James grips my shoulders and slowly he smiles. 'If you really think so, I could take you to the most amazing places. I've been to some pretty spectacular spots for my work, and I've always thought they were wasted on me because I was on my own.' His grip is tight and warm. 'Even when I was with Jasmine, it just didn't feel right. And I remember lying on beaches, or sitting on terraces, thinking, "I would love to bring someone special here."'

I look at him. Does James want me to steal away for the odd secret tryst with him in a luxurious hotel while staying married to Guy? Or does he want me to taste the life of luxury with him in order to have the strength to leave my family behind? Whatever the scenario, there's room only for me and him. I don't think James's idea of a perfect day is Sunday lunch with a noisy brood.

'What's the point of making a pretty sizeable packet and having no one to share it with?'

True. And adultery on a sun-bleached island sounds as floaty as mosquito netting covering a double bed. It's here at home that it feels as heavy as those carrier bags that weigh me down when I make my way home from the supermarket.

My mobile goes again.

James frowns. 'The children again?'

I nod: it's bound to be Alex, unable to accept that he's not getting his way. 'I'm going to ignore it.' Let Chopin play on – I'm not going to break the spell.

My refusal to take the phone call convinces James that I'm seriously contemplating a change. Again he draws me to him. 'I'll make it worth your while,' he whispers in my ear. 'I'll make you happy as you've never been before.' When he kisses me, it is a gentle, soft 'thank you' which then grows urgent and greedy, an 'I want you' that cannot be ignored. But why would I want to ignore this, I ask myself, as James's hands caress my hips, my thighs, moving up my back, then down again. How could I do without it?

We are standing by the door that Mr Nelson left open, and a breeze blows through my hair. I am vaguely aware of the giant trees in the sunlit garden beyond, of birds chirping and a summer warmth: but only vaguely, as I cannot concentrate on anything that is not part of James's body. His mouth has moved down to my throat. I shiver, and then the lips move on, drawing close to my breasts. I want this, I think; I want this now.

'We can't wait any more,' James whispers.

A discreet cough makes me pull away instantly. 'Lunch, Mr Weston.' Mr Nelson stands in the door, looking somewhere into the middle distance. 'Mr Mallay asked me to provide a light lunch.'

'Er, thank you.' James combs a hand through his hair. 'What the butler saw!' he whispers as we follow Mr Nelson out of the library.

'He's a caretaker, not a butler,' I whisper back.

'All too grand for me.' James is laughing, and as he gently pilots me to the dining room, our complicity feels delicious. My body is still humming with desire.

'I'm starving!' James grins at me across the white tablecloth. Mr Nelson is fussing around us, trying to serve warm chicken salad and bread. 'Here's to us –' James raises his glass of wine.

Our eyes meet. I take a sip – but I'm already light-headed. I feel as if I have shed years, obligations, responsibilities.

'And here's to Marbella, and the South of France, and Tuscany … And about a hundred other places I'm going to take you to.'

James refuses another glass from Mr Nelson ('I have to drive this gorgeous lady back in one piece'). I can't stop smiling: his desire for me fills me with an intoxicating energy. I feel as if I could do anything right now, anything at all.

After lunch, while James waits for a coffee, I go to check my phone. Mr Nelson finds me in the great oak corridor, looking for the guests' loo, and leads me to a room about the size of our sitting room in Clapham. Here, among the rose-scented soaps and the crested towels, I switch my mobile back on and press 121 to hear my message.

'Harry!' It's Guy, voice cracked with emotion. 'Darling, Dad's very ill … they're not …they're not sure he's going to make it …' Guy tries to choke back a sob. 'He's in hospital. I'm getting on the first train to Yeovil with the children. Hurry, darling. We need you.'

I rush back to the dining room and James.

He looks up at me. 'What's happened?'

'Guy's father –' My voice sounds high-pitched. 'He's in hospital in Yeovil and Guy and the children have gone down.'

'I'll drive you,' James offers. His voice is flat, and I can't tell whether he's resigned or resentful.

'Thanks.' I realize I'm shaking, shocked by the way I've been propelled from James's arms to my father-in-law's bedside in the space of a minute. Dear Archie, please pull through. Your son needs you, he's at a turning point in his life – the television, the great review – who knows what the future could bring.

But I realize I'm not talking to Archie, I'm talking to Harriet.

James makes his, our, excuses to Mr Nelson, who nods sympathetically. Then we're back in the car.

'The father was in the army, wasn't he?' James asks as he drives us past the picturesque villages we'd seen on the way down.

'Yes. Has an anecdote for every battle you've ever had to learn.' I add quickly, 'He's very good with the children. And Guy adores him.'

I try to calculate how long ago Guy left the message: an hour and a half? Two? It will take them at least three and a half to get to the hospital.

I sit back and watch the road disappear. I feel as if we're speeding away not only from Mallay Manor but from Marbella, the South of France, sun-baked terraces and al fresco dinners. From life as it might have been.

'When you finished with me when I got back from Nigeria, I was so angry.' James shoots me a look. 'I didn't know how to handle rejection. But I was sure that you'd realize you'd made a mistake. I knew we would get together again. You just needed some time to sort things out for yourself.'

'Ye-es …' I nod, but I wish he would hurry; hurry, because I want to be there if Archie dies, for Guy and the children. I want to comfort them in their loss. My whole being is focused on them once more.

'I think the same now.' James's voice is calm and low. 'I know you have commitments. But your most important commitment is to Harriet. Harriet Tenant.'

Is it? I wonder. *We need you* … I hear the plea in Guy's voice. Yes I know they do. My family need me to be there, at the school gates and the school play, at the kettle and on the phone, at the stove and at their bedside. They need me as wailing wall and homework supervisor, as critic and provider. As for Guy, I need to be all this and more: his confidante and his interpreter and his partner in adventure. Even though I have not been able to join him on his recent travels to Kenya, Guy still sees us as braving the journey together. He does not promise to keep me in style, but to keep me at his side.

My existential crisis will have to wait. Even James must see that.

James is playing a jazz CD I don't recognize: this way, we needn't talk. We hurtle in silence towards Somerset. It is only when we reach the hospital that he looks at me. 'Will you be all right?'

'Yes. Thank you.' He makes as if to take my hands in his, but I'm fumbling already with the door handle.

'I'll see you tomorrow.' He releases the lock.

'Yes.' I jump out and run towards the revolving doors.

Inside I get a whiff of antiseptic struggling to overcome more unpleasant odours. Men and women in green aprons stride purposefully down the ward. Cheery posters adorn the walls and an important-looking woman in a white coat leads a clutch of earnest and weary-looking youths with notepads down the corridor. Outside Ward 6, Respiratory Diseases, I wash my hands with the anti-bacterial soap dispensed by a box fixed to the wall and am admitted. I ask for Major Carew's bed – but I needn't have: I can hear the children trying to cajole Archie into a good mood.

'Grandpa, I'm going to take your trunk, the one Daddy had too, to Wolsingham in September,' Alex is saying. 'There are some brilliant stamps on it still … it's been halfway round the world, hasn't it!'

'Big Ben keeps asking after you, Grandpa!' Tom adds. 'He says he'd like to take a photo of you in your uniform for his history assignment.'

'What's that tube in Grandpa's arm?' Maisie asks, worried.

'It's for Grandpa's medicine to get to him quickly,' Guy explains as I arrive: he looks almost as ashen as his father, who is lying, vacant-eyed, in his bed.

'What a racket!' an ancient man in the bed beside Archie's complains loudly. He looks like a multi-armed squid, there are so many tubes coming out of him.

Cecily stands, head bowed, her hand in her husband's. Behind her is Nick, eyes wide and frightened, hair tousled, looking suddenly like a little boy in T-shirt and jeans.

'Darling!' My husband spots me and the expression on his face is transformed. He rushes to hug me and hides his face in my hair. 'Thank you for coming so quickly,' he whispers.

'Mummy!' a chorus rings out in the ward. I'm hugged and kissed and Maisie presses herself against my leg.

Cecily looks up through tear-filled eyes and mouths, 'Hullo.'

'Archie …' I approach the bed and hold my father-in-law's hand. The fingers hardly move to grasp mine, and his expression shows no recognition. He looks as if Life has had enough of Major Carew and decided to drop him from her ranks.

'Visiting hours over, I'm afraid.' A nurse sweeps down the corridor to us. 'Your grandfather's very tired.' She hushes the children with an index finger to her lips. I read her name tag– *Diane Stuckey* – before she moves down the ward to warn the other visitors.

'Well, Dad, we should make a move …' Guy makes as if to round up his troops.

'Wait!' I cry. 'Did you see the papers today?'

'Nnnno …?'

'Then wait a minute.' I take Guy's hand and make him hold Archie's and I run to the receptionist's desk. 'Do you have any of the Sundays?' It takes me five minutes to locate the visitors' room, another five to locate the one copy of the *Sunday Tribune* left. I leaf through it furiously, until there, grinning at me is a stunning photo of Guy Carew, the BBC's 'secret weapon'. I clutch it tightly and return to Ward 6, where I press on the door for admission.

'I'm sorry, visiting time's over.' Nurse Stuckey plants herself in front of the door to the ward.

'Please, I have something that will make one of your patients very happy,' I plead.

'Rules are rules.' She shakes her head.

'Look –' I show her the double-page spread and Guy's photo. 'It's his son!'

'Oh?' Nurse Stuckey beams approval. 'All right, in you go – only for a few minutes, mind!'

I run to Archie's bedside, brandishing the newspaper. 'Look!' I cry, holding up Guy's photo for all to see. 'L.L. Munro thinks Guy Carew is the BBC's secret weapon!'

Archie stirs and gestures at the paper with his hand. Beside him, Cecily smiles for the first time. The children cluster round their father as Nick looks over Tom's shoulder.

'Wha-at?!' Guy grabs the paper from me. He reads it, the expression on his face at first stunned, then ecstatic. 'Dad! It's fabulous! Shall I read it?'

Archie tries to smile: 'Yes,' he says, with difficulty.

I watch Guy read: here is his reward for all those years spent living in hope, here is a vindication for those days spent nursing the humiliation of betrayal by Rainbow Productions. Guy Carew has finally made it. My husband stands as proud as one of his ancestors might have done after leading his men into battle, or heading an exploratory party into dangerous terrain.

'Darling, it's marvellous!' Cecily clasps her hands to her bosom.

'Well done, Bro.' Nick gives a thumbs-up sign. 'This will make *Rajput* sell like hotcakes!'

'Visiting hour's over!' Nurse Stuckey is back and she scowls at us, hands on hips. 'Do I need to call for assistance?'

'Stop hollering out there!' Archie's neighbour huffs. He is sitting up now, trying to watch the television that dangles above him.

Against his pillow, Archie smiles, tears in his eyes. 'Guy … well done,' he whispers. Then he shuts his eyes and winces in pain again.

'Out!' Nurse Stuckey stomps her foot. 'Out!'

'No,' Cecily says quietly. She sticks out her jaw, and for a moment looks like one of those Carew memsahibs who withstood malaria, yellow fever and massacres to stand by their men as they carried out their patriot's duty. This is the look of determination and bloody-mindedness that has defeated foes, set up missions and painted a quarter of the globe pink; and now it is turned on Nurse Stuckey at Yeovil Hospital. 'I shall stay with my husband. He needs me.' Cecily settles down in the visitors' armchair and draws it closer to Archie's bedside. Something in the way she moves discourages Nurse Stuckey from shooing her out.

We instead troop silently through the doors and down the ward until Maisie, ahead with Guy, turns to her father. 'Grandpa is all right, isn't he?' She is close to tears and I hug her to me.

Grandpa wasn't all right. Major Archibald Carew died that evening, his wife's hand in his.

At the news of his father's death, Guy weeps silently, holding me tight. We're in his parents' dining room. It's midnight and we're the only ones up. Cecily was exhausted and slipped upstairs at ten; Nick crashed out half an hour ago.

Guy and I had been relishing Simon's message on his voicemail: 'Guy! Everyone wants a piece of you! When you catch your breath, what about lunch at the Wolseley?' Simon's message had been, as I had guessed, the first; but there were many others. A long rambling one from Star Productions, an independent production company, seeking a meeting to discuss a possible series; a short burst of praise from Percy, reminding

Guy 'who's been your friend all along'; and a sheepish greeting from Zoë, saying, 'Well done.'

Amidst these congratulations, Cecily's arrival with its sad tidings seems all the more bitter.

'Why now?' Guy's voice breaks. He has kept calm and wept no tears while comforting his mother. But now that she has retired, he slumps forward in his chair, head in hands. 'Why now? We're finally going to enjoy some success. He would have loved it.' Tears fill his eyes and his voice shakes. 'I've been trying to prepare myself for this ever since he had that nasty fall at the club, but I'm as winded as if it were a car crash.' Guy breathes in deeply. 'Poor Dad. I wish I'd never disappointed him. I still remember how awful it was when I refused to go into the army. He went on and on about duty and patriotism, and I kept telling him these were empty words. I wish I hadn't made fun.'

'You made it up to him, Guy. He was immensely proud of you.' I stroke my husband's shoulder.

'Even after *Lonely Hunter* he kept warning me that a writer's lot was a hard one. He said I risked a lifetime of penury, and he was right.'

'But he so enjoyed writing those Carew chronicles.' I get out the whisky from the drinks cabinet. 'I think he really came to understand your love of writing.' I pour us two shots. 'And he did get a sense of your being on the brink of success: did you see how he smiled when you read out the rave review? He died a happy man.'

'I feel so old suddenly.' Guy shakes his head disconsolately over the table. 'There's so much to worry about – and what about Mum?'

28

Cecily is determined not to cry. She bears her husband's passing with fortitude and insists on cooking us a three-course lunch before we set off for London. She refuses to panic and holds her head high. 'I shall be fine, boys, don't worry,' she keeps repeating. 'The important thing is that we have a proper funeral. I don't think Archie is …' she corrects herself with a slight falter '… was, entitled to an army funeral. Majors usually aren't. They were fond of him, though; they might make an exception. He would have loved the army buglers to sound the "Last Post". They did it for old Chip Rogers's funeral. But Chip *was* a colonel.' She takes a sip of her tea and frowns slightly. 'And the headstone, too. We must decide. Guy, will you write a draft of the inscription?'

'Will we bury him with his medals?' Guy asks as he waves away my offer of a second slice of cake.

'Yes.' Cecily nods vigorously. 'I think that's what he would have wanted.' Then, briskly, 'Tonight I'll draw up a list of

344

friends. St Michael's can fit two hundred easily. I'll get Rosie and her son and daughter to give me a hand with the catering.' She takes up pen and pad. 'Let me see, definitely the Gorson-Browns and the Wilsons from his regiment. And the Callums who used to live near us in Wells, and …'

I lead the children upstairs for their bath and sigh with relief: here among the yellow rubber ducks and Bart Simpson bath towels, there is no need to remember whether the Gorson-Browns are related to the Gorson-Browns in Wiltshire, or whether the Wilsons are *the* Wilsons whose great-grandfather had the big pile in Somerset next to the Carews' old family home.

Nick is inconsolable: he sobs and smokes, and hugs the children tight. They are subdued, and Maisie cranky because she can sense a big change.

Nick wants to postpone any talk of financial matters 'until we're over the worst'. Which means the drive back home is signposted by different possibilities. 'Mum won't want to stay in the house now. There was a house in the window at Ball Brothers Estate Agents that was only four bedrooms going for £650,000.' Guy tells me, full of hope. 'That would mean she'd have plenty for a smaller house, plus there might even be a little left over for us. It could mean an end to our school-fee worries.' 'Dad's solicitor, John Finch, is the executor. I've been in touch and he said everything's in order and the sorting out won't be difficult.' 'I've a feeling Dad was investing in some American stocks – we'll have to see if Nick knows anything about them.'

* * *

More bad news awaits us at home. Alex has done spectacularly well in the Wolsingham scholarship exams, but the letter from the school informs us that Wolsingham has decided that its scholarships as of the next academic year will be cut back from covering fifty per cent of the school fees to fifteen per cent. This, in order for the school to give more substantial bursaries.

'I can't believe it – why didn't they give us advance notice ?' Guy explodes. 'Of course I believe in bursaries. But what about *us*? We're too poor to pay the fees without some assistance and are probably too well-off' (and too proud, I think) 'to be eligible for the bursaries.'

'Dad, can we still afford for me to go?' Alex asks, worried. I feel for him: his moment of glory has been spoiled.

Guy forgets to praise his eldest and instead storms about the house, despairing of the 'short-sighted academics' and their 'contempt for the middle classes'. He vows to give the headmaster a piece of his mind, and to contact his father's old friend Lionel Wyman, on the governing body.

'Mum, I wish I hadn't worked so hard, you know.' Alex is sitting in the boys' bedroom, staring into his Facebook profile on the computer. 'I mean, am I going to Wolsingham or not?' He looks ready to burst into tears.

'Darling, don't worry. Dad believes in Wolsingham, and he'll do everything to get you there.' I stroke my son's dark hair, follow it to the curls on his T-shirt. For once, instead of brushing me off, my eldest snuggles up against me.

'I want to go.'

'You've kept your side of the bargain; we'll keep ours,' I whisper as I kiss his forehead.

And I mean it: if Guy's new success is not enough to ensure that we can afford Wolsingham's fees, I'm ready to go full time. Part time is for those who can organize a job-share, or have made themselves so indispensable in their job that their downsizing doesn't raise eyebrows.

None of which applies to me. I wonder what kind of a salary Mary Jane can afford – she still hasn't got back to me. We need me to bring in about £25,000, I figure, to keep the worst-case scenarios at bay. That £25,000, however, would come at a steep price. Not because of the humiliation of taking on receptionist duties. But because of the children.

I relive the afternoon two years ago when I was at HAC and, from the window above Clapham High Street, I saw a rainbow stretch across the sky. Immediately, I rang home and asked our then au pair, Ewa: 'Please, Ewa, will you show Maisie the rainbow? She hasn't seen one before, I know she'll love it!' And then I hung on to the telephone, listening to Maisie's squeal of delight, and felt tears sting my eyes: here was my daughter, experiencing a 'first' in the arms of an au pair. I was at work when Tom came home from school with a broken collarbone which no one had spotted; I was at work when Alex announced he had been admitted into the scholarship set at the Griffin; I was at work when Tom brought his unsuitable friend Joey for a playdate that ended with two windows broken and the beginning of a bonfire in Guy's study; at work when ...

* * *

Needs must, I tell myself firmly. Too true. When John Finch rings Guy the next morning, it is with bad news: unbeknownst to his sons, or indeed, his wife, Archie Carew had released substantial equity in the house in Somerset. Guy and Nick are in shock: the sale of their family home will bring in next to nothing.

Guy and Nick retire to the kitchen to thrash out the family's dismal fortunes, and their mother's future. From the sitting room I overhear them rumbling about 'naïve', 'foolish advisors', 'terrible choices'. Their tone alternates from angry and frustrated to loving and resigned, and it is not until tea time that they are calm enough to join us for a slice of apple upside-down cake.

'The army pension is decent ...' Guy rakes his hand through his hair. 'But we may need to sell Lyme Regis to buy a decent bungalow.'

'But she loves Lyme!' Nick protests.

'Can you see any way around this? It's a mess!'

The family finances may be in chaos, but Cecily is determined that the funeral will be a splendid occasion. She rings us incessantly with new tasks, requirements, schedules. Every detail, from the flowers to the extra chairs, is carefully pored over. Even the children's clothes for the day are discussed: 'No, Harriet, a grey shirt will not do. I want them both in white shirts and dark suits.'

Which is why on Tuesday morning the children and I are walking down the High Street in search of a white shirt for Tom to wear to the funeral. I'm pushing the buggy in which

Maisie lies half asleep, and trying to keep the peace between the boys, who're arguing over who wiped the messages on our answering machine this morning. My sons are out of sorts because of their grandfather's death, and their every little quarrel escalates into a full-blown row. Their shoves and shouts take over the pavement, which forces passers-by on to the street as they try to avoid being elbowed or kicked.

'Can't you keep those boys in check?!' A woman shoots me a murderous look.

'Alex! Tom!' I try in vain to calm my offspring.

'There's no such thing as bad children, only bad parents,' a know-it-all tells her polite little girl as they skirt our rowdy group.

'Are they yours?' a man asks.

'Oh, for heaven's sake, they're just boys!' I wheel around to confront him. It's James, sitting at an outdoor table at Café La Lune. I blush crimson, and then almost cry out in dismay as I realize I'm wearing my size-12 jeans, the ones that really are too tight, and a white T-shirt with a pink magic marker squiggly on the left breast.

'Oh, hi … my sons … I'm sorry …' I've been caught out: a bad mum and a public nuisance. Not to mention, as James knows only too well, a bad wife and, once upon a time, a bad girlfriend.

'Hullo.' James grins at the boys from his table. He wears sunglasses and looks impossibly glamorous in his open jacket and shirt. The boys stop their tussling and shoot me a look.

'Alex, Tom, this is James, he works at HAC.' The boys wave 'hi' then resume their quarrel.

'How's your father in law?' James pulls out the chair beside him, but I shake my head, pointing down to Maisie, only half-asleep.

'He died. Sunday evening.'

'I'm sorry.' James looks concerned.

'It's been a bit of a shock. The funeral is on Friday.'

'I didn't think it would be appropriate to ring,' James tells me as he watches the boys staring into a shop window.

'No.'

'Will you be in next week?'

'I don't think so.' I shake my head and half smile. 'Even Mary Jane allows compassionate leave.'

'You'll let me know if there's something I can do?'

'No. I mean, thank you, but I don't think there *is* anything. It's a bit chaotic, all those family things, like making sure all his friends are invited, and sorting through correspondence, and the accounts.' I look down at him, at the sunglasses and the casual shirt and the late-morning cappuccino beside him, and I feel suddenly as if he belongs to a completely different universe. 'I'm so sorry …'

'No, I'm the one who is sorry.' He speaks softly. 'You're the one who knows where she belongs. I've no business being here.'

'James …' I start, but then I realize I have no idea what I would go on to say.

'Mu-um!' Tom brings hands to mouth, tannoy-style.

'Mu-um!' Alex calls out. 'There's a brilliant mobile phone in there; can we go take a look?'

I shake my head, shrug, give James an apologetic smile and start pushing the buggy towards the boys.

'Goodbye,' I hear him call out. I turn around. 'Goodbye, Harriet Carew.'

St Michael's church in Woodfern stands at one end of the village green, a small, Victorian edifice surrounded by buddleia and holly bushes. The Reverend Lawrence Mullin, much abused by Archie Carew as 'that nancy boy in a dog collar', is not in a good mood. His recollection of Archie is far from fond, he feels uncomfortable among army people, and he has three baptisms to perform on Saturday morning, which means his weekend trip to Bath is off. As we file out of his church, he practically trips over Maisie in his rush to leave.

'Sorry, sorry!' He gallops away, surplice and cassock billowing. The children, sombre and silent throughout the ceremony, look after him in wonder.

'I don't think the padre understood old Archie,' Colonel Smythe, from Archie's old regiment, huffs as we file out of the funeral.

'Unimpressive, really,' Thomasina Bailey tut-tuts. 'They don't write sermons the way they used to. Still, I can't hear "I Vow to Thee My Country" without weeping.' And she dabs at her eyes with a monogrammed pocket handkerchief.

The funeral boasted more hats than Royal Ascot, and enough titles to please Cecily. It is a noisy procession that makes its way from St Michael's to the Carews' home. Two plump elderly ladies hand out the delicate sandwiches Cecily has prepared, and a young man helps Guy and Nick pour the sherry. Condolences and the scent of lilies fill the air as we troop past Cecily over the threshold.

Almost immediately, a handful of mourners have clustered round John Finch, the executor. He's a thin, pale little man who looks overwhelmed by all the bids for his attention being made today.

'My daughter Mary was always meant to get that piano, you know,' one agitated old dragon in lilac booms at him. 'Archie was very partial to her playing.'

'I was with Archie in 1958 in Cairo, and I know that he always meant me to have that barograph,' a bearded octogenarian announces. 'He'd be very upset if it didn't come to me.'

Muttering and demanding, they have Finch with his back against a wall, and the poor executor throws beseeching looks in our direction.

In vain, as I am being subjected to a Grand Inquisition by an aggressive French woman who claims to be married to a Carew cousin. 'Ah, *le pauvre*,' Marie Louise sighs dramatically. 'Was it liver?'

'No, no, pneumonia, and he was so frail.'

'But the house must be worth a lot. Cecily will be well provided for,' she continues, peering at me sharply through her tiny rectangular spectacles. I mumble something indistinct, which is ignored. 'But not much left of the valuable furniture, is there?' And Marie Louise appraises the crowded dining room. 'Or perhaps Guy' – she pronounces it 'Ghee' – 'and Nicholas already have taken their share?'

'Ghee' is being mobbed by friends and relatives, all of whom claim to have found *Big Game* brilliant, wonderful, and just the thing to restore their faith in 'the box'. Guy smiles proudly, though these are the same Carew connections who once sniffed at his choice of profession, and constantly needled Archie about his firstborn refusing to follow in the family's glorious footsteps in either the army or the navy.

By five the children are running about in the garden and most people have started leaving. A small group of ex-army types somehow have found a bottle of Teacher's whisky, and stand about trading anecdotes. I'm surprised to notice, among the leave-takers, Sonny Ward, the famous former boxer who now runs a trendy art gallery in Hoxton.

'Turns out he used to go shooting with Dad, and was very fond of him.' Nick comes to stand beside me, taking one of the last salmon-and-cucumber sandwiches. 'But the rest, they really are gargoyles, aren't they?' Then, as he spots his mother looking anxiously around the room. 'Still, she's pulled it off. Dad would have approved.'

'Yes. But he would have snuck off into the garden with the children and started shooting one of his guns.'

Crack! Crack! – the sound of gunshots makes everyone jump.

'What's that?!' someone from the whisky-drinking circle huffs. 'Someone with a rifle?'

'Sounds like a .22,' another voice pitches in.

Through the window I see the boys cheering and jumping up and down as Guy gets ready to fire another round on his father's ancient rifle.

'A proper send-off!' Nick smiles as he raises his glass.

When I go to HAC on Wednesday, Anjie tells me that Mary Jane has taken the day off. When I ask what could have brought on this unheard-of behaviour, Anjie gives me a knowing look. 'I think someone has told her he won't be around so much these days.'

I nod, but say nothing.

My colleague also reveals that she has decided that she and the family will stay in London – William included. 'I need my work now, and I need my friends and my church. If he really has a good job in Tunbridge Wells, he can commute. I'm not upping sticks.' She looks determined, calm, strong: the Anjie I've always known.

With Anjie staying in her post, will Mary Jane let me increase to five days a week? I doubt that HAC has the money for three full-time employees. I say nothing to Anjie about what her change of mind means for me, but resolve to speak to Mary Jane as soon as she is back.

After the funeral, Cecily comes to stay. But she acts most unlike the mother-in-law I've grown used to. She moves from Maisie's room, which doubles as the guest bedroom, to the armchair in the sitting room without so much as a word about Alex's sports socks and Maisie's *Peter Rabbit* puzzle and Tom's *Harry Potter* littering carpet and sofa. She manages to eat my cooking without querying the recipe and to see me off to work without making any comments about the wrongs of working mothers. Instead she plays Scrabble or Racing Demon with the boys, helps Daniela sort out socks, and I even find her drawing with Maisie in her lap.

* * *

While this new, crestfallen Cecily stays meekly in her place, her future is being planned by her eldest.

'Lyme Regis, that's where Mum will live. Nick and I have figured it out and talked to her: we sell the house and invest what's left – it's not very much – in doing up the cottage. She can move there. She knows the house and she'll be near people she likes. I think she'll be happy.'

Guy and I are in bed. His arms are crossed behind his head, and I lie on my side, studying the Carews' new pater familias in profile. 'I raised the possibility of her living with us …' I freeze beneath our sheet, waiting for the answer. 'But she immediately turned down the suggestion.' He smiles at my loud sigh of relief. 'She doesn't want to be a burden. God, Dad didn't think things through at all. All that army training, but if this had been a military campaign it would have ended in a very bloody defeat!'

Having avoided the danger of a live-in mother-in-law, I breathe more easily. 'He would be appalled if he thought his legacy was causing you problems.'

'I know, I know. He loved his family.' Guy wraps his arm around me, drawing me closer. I nestle against him, head on his shoulder. 'He always let us know how much we meant to him.' Guy's voice breaks. He falls silent. Then, 'Dad loved those foreign posts. But he gave them up because of us; he took the boring job managing Lord Winter's estate because Nick and I were at Wolsingham. It was a huge sacrifice.' Guy draws a deep breath: 'God, I'll miss him.'

'The boys too.'

'Has Nick been heard from?' Guy asks.

'His car's been parked outside Lisa's house three days in a row now.'

'I think he's come to his senses.' Guy gives my hair a playful tug. 'He understands the importance of a good woman in his life.'

'I hope so – it would be fun if they stayed here and the children could have a little cousin next door.' My husband's fingers twirl a lock of my hair round and round.

'And did you get the message from Ross? Left it on the answer-phone.'

'I can't believe he's got the nerve to ring me after the stitch-up he'd planned,' Guy snorts, but he sounds amused rather than bitter.

'He wants to see you urgently. The controller of BBC2 has put you at the top of his dream list of new presenters.' I touch his cheek. 'You're hot property.'

'For now. TV is fine as the icing on the cake, but I think I'd rather invest in something more solid and regular.'

I try not to betray my surprise. 'You mean the book? *Rajput*?'

'I mean that Ollie Mallard has approached me to edit his new *Travel Wise* mag. It's had lots of teething problems and the launch editor has proved a bit hopeless, so Ollie wants some fresh blood.'

'Guy,' I gasp. 'That's great!'

'It's nothing to brag about. But it's quite a good salary, and I can finish *Rajput* and maybe start on the *Carew Chronicles* after that.' He draws a deep breath. 'I want a regular income.

The other stuff is great when it comes – but it's too risky.' I listen silently, marvelling at my husband's new-found wisdom. 'School-fees will still be a grind, but at least we won't have to sell the house. And you won't have to go full time.'

'That's good.' I steal a look at his profile. 'I hated the thought of that.'

'Not even if it meant seeing more of James Weston?' Guy runs his fingers gently over my shoulder.

'No. And I have a feeling James won't be visiting the offices so regularly any more.'

Even as I say it, I know it's true: James is too proud and too conscious of what happened between us to hang about the HAC offices now. He'll continue to be our benefactor, he'll persuade Mary Jane to take on the work on Sam's house in Wiltshire, and eventually to expand HAC's operations. But he won't want to come into the office on Clapham High Street.

'Won't you mind that?' Guy asks softly. On my shoulder, his fingers come to a stand-still.

'No.' I turn my face towards his. 'I made my choice a long time ago.'

'Good.' Guy's happy expression is touching. 'Then I hope you won't mind my having given your name to Sonny Ward.'

'What?' I'm puzzled.

'He called me. Some portrait painter he knows has a few very good sketches of Dad. And then he mentioned that he's looking for someone who could help him in the gallery. It would only be part time to start off with, because he says it's his lifeline.' Here I sit up and gawp at Guy, who keeps smiling. 'But he *is* getting on and he claims he's looking for someone he could trust to become a full-time collaborator in the long term, and perhaps ...'

'Oh, Guy! The Ward Gallery is huge!' I laugh at the sheer outrageousness of the suggestion.

'Well, he liked the sound of you, and I told him you'd go for an interview if I could persuade you to give it a try.'

'I will, of course I will!'

'That's that, then.' Guy pulls me back down against him. 'I'll give you his number tomorrow.'

'That's that.' I breathe out a sigh of satisfaction. Archie's death and James's disappearance make me feel as if I've come to the end of something. And perhaps to the beginning of a whole new chapter – leaving HAC to work part time at an art gallery, having Guy earn a regular income, having Alex at boarding school ...

'Guy and Harriet,' Guy intones, as if reading a script, 'managed to overcome a series of hardships. They found that, with a bit of patience and perseverance, not to mention industry, thrift and a sense of humour, they, like so many others before them and since, could just about keep their family in a style they were not ashamed of.'

'Not ashamed of?' I stop stroking my husband's head. 'That's a bit grim, isn't it?'

'All right then,' Guy corrects himself. 'They kept their family well fed, entertained and brilliantly educated.' He turns to me with a grin. 'There – will that do?'

'And they lived happily ever after.' I kiss him. 'We hope.'

ACKNOWLEDGEMENTS

This novel was conceived in the middle of the night, when my husband, sleepless because of mounting school fees, bills and general worries, shook me awake to share his brilliant idea for a television documentary. It would be called 'Posh but Poor' and would feature those downwardly mobile couples who suddenly realise that life isn't turning out quite as they had dreamed.

I was taken with the idea, and wrote it up, but it took Liz Hunt, Assistant Editor at the *Daily Telegraph,* to see its potential as a weekly column; and Clare Smith, a star editor at HarperCollins, to spot that it might work as a novel. Without these two women, I would never have had the courage to let Harriet come alive.

My husband Edward continued to provide me with some of the best lines and funniest incidents in *The Dilemmas of Harriet Carew.* David Cox's comments on the first few chapters were indispensable.

ACKNOWLEDGEMENTS

Thanks also to Xan Smiley for casting his expert eye over Guy's trips to Kenya; and to John McDonald for allowing me to see the workings of the Family Holidays Association up close.

Johnny and Hugo Lucas gave me an invaluable insight into a boy's world, while Isabella, their sister, brought Maisie to life. Lina Singh kept our home from becoming too much like the Carews'. Matt Portal explained the idiosyncrasies of army families. Catharine Eaton and Margaret Mulholland gave spot-on advice for the column and then the novel, while Patsy Baker, Becky Pugh and Jill Chisholm were always on hand as sympathetic sounding boards.

Georgina Capel, my agent, was an indefatigable and much-needed cheerleader. The team at HarperCollins managed to convince me that writing a novel can be fun as well as all-consuming.

Throughout, my father, mother and brother, as well as John and Morar Lucas, my wonderful in-laws, never stopped supporting and encouraging me.

To all these and my long-suffering friends, who put up with my distracted state for the past year, many thanks.

CHAMPNEYS
Win a mid-week Champneys Spa Break

Champneys Health Resorts are offering a reader and their guest the chance to win a luxury one-night break at the glamorous Forest Mere in Hampshire, the modern Springs in Leicestershire or the cosy Henlow in Bedfordshire, all set in sweeping countryside. If you want to escape for a peaceful couple of days away, a Champneys health resort spa offers an idyllic country haven where you can relax and unwind.

Enjoy an indulgent body massage and a relaxing facial each, unlimited use of all facilities and all meals. If you can't wait to win call 08703 300 300 or visit www.champneys.com to book your own spa break.

To enter, or to view the terms and conditions, visit the competition page on **www.mumsnet.com** or follow the links from **www.fifthestate.co.uk**

Feeling desperate, baby waking every two hours at night? Any recommendations for ballet-themed novels for an eight year old? **Single and pregnant – tips needed** Any IVFers out there? **Separating – how do you explain it to a three year old?** Are school secretaries all jobsworths? **Alexander McCall Smith: is he pure genius?** My four-month-old doesn't like Grandma **Need a saucy read …** I am rubbish at expressing – tips please? **What does a contraction actually feel like (kinda urgent)?!** Feeling broody – should I try for baby number three? **Best treatment for nits?** Personal trainers – do they work? …

… Another day on **mumsnet.com** by parents, for parents